On the Power Play

CANADIAN PLAYED
BOOK FOUR

CYNTHIA GUNDERSON

With Gratitude

Editing and Critique
Scott Gunderson, Jordan Truex, and Amy Walker

Cover Design
Mitxeren

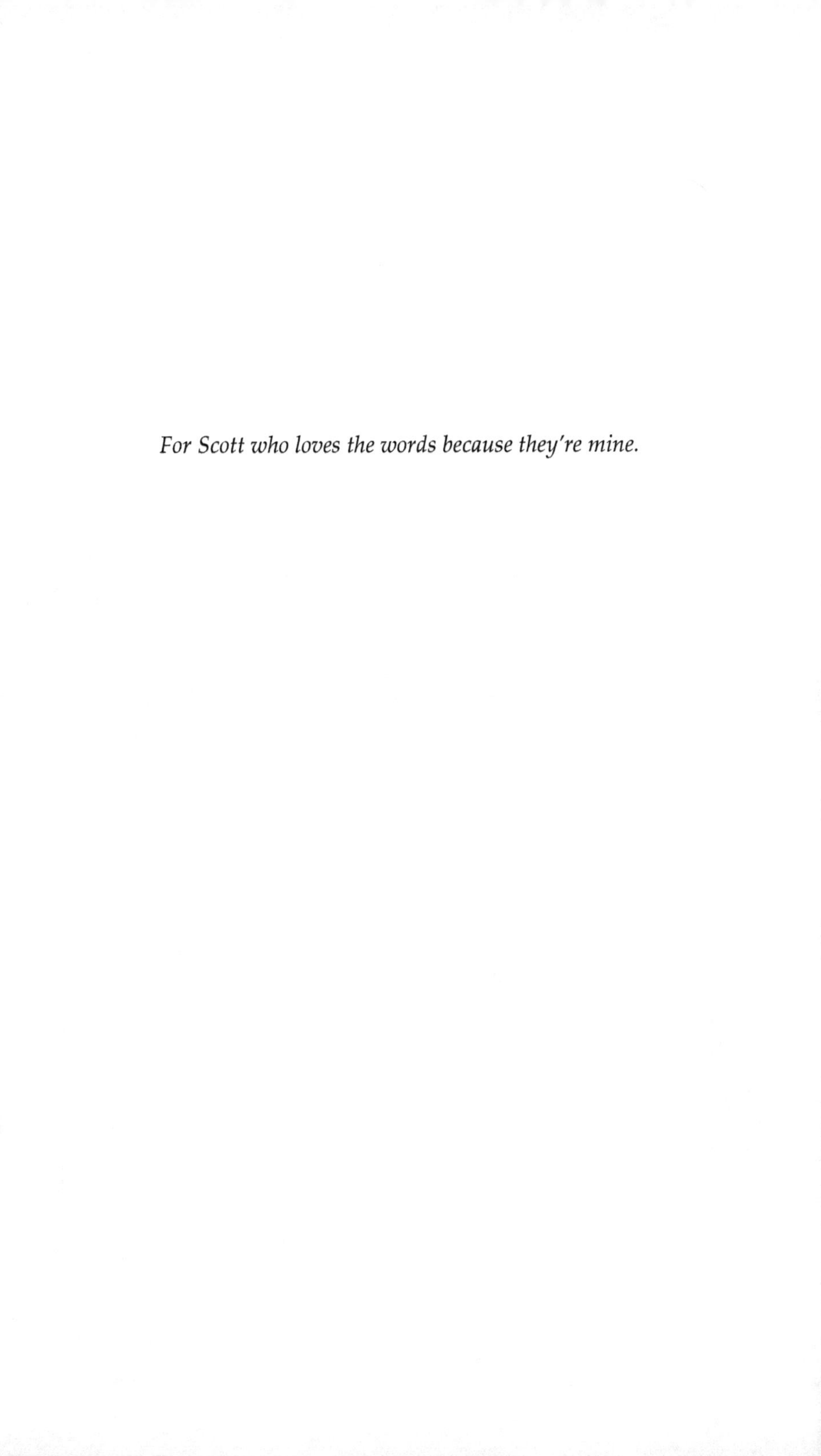

For Scott who loves the words because they're mine.

In previous books of this series, I used real NHL teams during broadcasts and banter. This was for world-building purposes only, any players mentioned were fictional, and the teams were not in any way a focus of the story.

That all changed with this book, *On the Power Play*. Initially, I wasn't expecting to venture into the world of the NHL. Otherwise, I would've planned ahead and used a fictional name for the team based in Calgary. So, I'm making that adjustment now!

In the fictional world you're about to enter, the NHL team in Calgary is called the Blizzard. This will also be changed in previous books in the series for consistency when you get your hands on this one. The versions you own are now special editions! Ha! Audio listeners, just imagine the Flames got bought out and have undergone a rebrand. Lol. Maybe someday I'll get around to changing the previous audio files, but today is not that day.

Sometimes the characters who want their stories told refuse to make adjustments, and I'm left holding the bag. Thank you for going on this journey with me and loving the books even though they are a delightful work in progress!

xo Cindy G

Prologue

JACK HAD NEVER FELT MORE like an impotent old man than when sitting on the bench in the Blizzard dressing room. He was surrounded by younger players he'd seen on TV and a couple of guys who'd been drafted instead of him. Noticeably absent were eight key Blizzard wingers and defencemen laid out by illness, including Monahan and Lindholm.

Hardship claim. He'd been pulled up from the dregs of old AHL prospects to play for one night only because of a hardship claim. How he'd been lucky enough to get that phone call, he'd never know, and he'd never ask. He didn't want to find out how many people they'd phoned before him.

The weight of the moment sat heavy in his stomach. There wasn't anything expected of him. That was abundantly clear by the way the other players barely glanced in his direction. He was a filler. A body to give guys like Gaudreau and Johannsen a break. Fortunately, it didn't matter what anyone else in that dressing room thought of him. He knew what he was capable of. Or would've been. Had his coaches in Toronto not cut him off at the knees because he dared disagree with their line calls and player management.

Live and learn.

He'd keep his skates laced, his mind focused, and his damn mouth zipped shut.

"Alright, listen up," one of the coaches began. Jack couldn't remember his name, but he thought it started with a *K*. "Tonight, we're not just a team. We're a testament to what this sport is all about. We've been decimated this season. Injuries, sickness, it's been one blow after another. But it's not about the hits we take but how we drag our asses up off the ice after the fact."

He waited for the nods and grunts of agreement, then made eye contact with each of the call-ups. "Tonight, we're calling in reinforcements because nobody here is expected to be a solo act. These guys next to you have stepped into the breach without a second thought. That's the kind of spirit that defines the Blizzard. So tonight, let's play for each other, for the jersey, for the fans. Tonight, we fight, we bleed, we play Blizzard hockey."

Tkachuk, a killer defenceman next to Jack, leaned in as the rest of the players applauded the speech. "You going to throw up?"

Jack forced a grin. "Probably. But I'll wait till I'm standing next to Timm."

Manning laughed out loud. "I want a front-row seat."

Jack strapped on his helmet, pulled on his gloves, and followed the guys onto the ice for warm-ups. His heart bucked against his ribs as he worked to stay on his feet.

He'd played for full arenas before, but not like this. The Saddledome was a sea of white and ice-blue, and the energy was electric. He felt like he was trying to ride an escalator for the first time as he pushed his stick across the ice. *He could do this.*

Jack dropped into his warm-up and didn't worry about the names on the backs of the jerseys swirling around him. By the time he hustled back to the bench for puck drop, he'd almost convinced himself he was skating at the ice arena in the Northwest with Country, Tyler, and Brett wearing Snowballs' baby blue.

The first shift was a blur. The bench felt both like a sanctuary and a prison as he awaited his ice time. Flashbacks of team tryouts and a particularly heinous school talent show in grade seven made his stomach churn. *Don't choke. Don't choke. Don't choke.*

When Coach barked his name, his pulse hammered a frantic Morse code, but he forced himself over the lip of the boards and onto the ice. Then everythin—the shouts from the crowd, the horns and music—blurred as he jumped into the play.

The air was crisp. His equipment snug. Jack settled into himself, and muscle memory took over.

He'd played with a cracked sternum once and scored while pain sliced through his left arm. He'd played with multiple muscle and ligament tears, with no sleep for thirty-six hours, and so hungover it felt like a construction crew had taken up residence in his cerebellum. What was the roar of fifteen thousand people?

Jack moved with the puck, feeling its weight and that hair of resistance through the stick that had become an extension of his own body. The game narrowed to pinpoints of focus—his teammates in red, two opponents narrowing in, and the net. He calculated his next move like he was playing chess, analyzing his likelihood of success in a nanosecond.

He passed. He caught. He deked. He checked. Then a few minutes later, he dropped back on the bench, sweating and heaving for breath.

The exertion focused him like sunshine through a magnifying glass, and during shift number two, Jack found a deeper rhythm. He forgot all about the lights and the cacophony from the crowd and jumbotron. *He was playing in an NHL game.* He was on the ice with the best of the best, and he was damn well going to enjoy it.

Jack sensed the play before it happened.

He charged up the ice, and as he approached the blue line, a pass to another call-up, Obelensky, was the obvious choice. But then his defender budged. He bit right on a small shift of Jack's hips, and in that split second, Jack knew he had an opening straight to the net.

He took it, tearing forward, holding the puck just out of reach with those extra few centimetres he'd gained with the deke. He didn't plan to make a spectacle of it, but with his defender hugging his flank and the goalie cheating left, he didn't have the guaranteed shot he'd hoped for.

It hadn't been a decision, his left leg just dragged, pulling him into a tight spiral. He coiled, scooping the puck from the ice and cradling it on his stick like a raw egg, then backhanded it as soon as he pulled out of his pirouette.

The goalie's mitt shot up a second too late. The puck disappeared top shelf.

The lights went off.

The buzzer sounded.

All of it felt like it was happening on the other side of a soundproof wall. Even as his one-night-only teammates swarmed around him, Jack couldn't convince himself any of it had happened.

Reality had set in later that night when he lay alone in his bed watching his name splashed across every sports news headline in the country. Jack's only goal had been not to make a fool of himself, but in less than an hour, hockey fans were chanting his name in the streets.

Jack was numb as he swiped out of his internet browser and checked his text messages. *Eighty-seven.* He hadn't had that many text messages since . . . well, since the accident.

He ran a hand over his face as his gut clenched, then started at the bottom.

Thanks, Mom. Love you

It was electric

Talk more at practice

The more replies he sent, the faster his heart raced. The excitement that came with playing hockey on the big stage had lifted him into the clouds, but when he woke up the next morning, he'd be standing on the ground. Specifically, laminate hardwood floors.

Tomorrow, he'd wake up and eat eggs with his sister Clara and her husband Oscar.

Tomorrow, he'd turn on his computer and work from home, playing the middleman between designers and the executive team and hunting down new retail channels.

Tomorrow, he'd go back to being Jack Harrison, twenty-nine, with a +10 in his last AHL season. Which nobody would care about because tomorrow he wouldn't be a player in the NHL.

Jack exhaled and moved on to the next text message.

Maybe he didn't need to go to bed just yet.

CHAPTER

One

DELIA EXHALED in relief as the final chords of her guitar quivered in the air. The crowd in front of her—directly in front of her, since the stage was only six inches off the main floor of the makeshift theatre—erupted as the strings still buzzed against her fingertips. Not with the fervour you'd see at a Mother Mother or Drake concert or something, but with more energy than she'd ever anticipated after an acoustic set.

She'd spent the past three years playing dive bars, open mic nights, and house parties before signing last summer with Indie-Lake Records. Since then, her professional life had gotten a full-on glow-up. She'd played shows across the country with full bands, larger venues and stadiums, and yet these simple evenings with just her and her guitar were still her favourite.

Delia closed her eyes and let the applause wash over her, then slipped the strap over her head and gripped her guitar as she gave one final wave, blew a kiss, and made her way backstage.

"Great set, babe." Her best friend and manager, Mary, gave her a side hug. Delia collapsed against her. Every time she walked from the spotlight into the darkness between the curtains, it was like a switch inside her body flipped. She was done. She could throw on a sweatshirt, flop onto a couch in the green room, and introvert for as long as she wanted.

Mary knew the drill. She wiped Delia's shoulder sweat from her palm onto her pants as they walked to the stairs.

Delia plucked out her earpieces. "Enthusiastic crowd tonight."

Mary grinned, and it looked almost sinister in the shadows as they descended to the green room. "I knew this was a good idea. Tony wanted to book the Guilded Ballroom again, but I told him we needed a break from turn-of-the-century soundboards."

Delia nodded, her head still thrumming from the lights and the music pumping into her ears. It was quiet as they entered the room. Which was the cue for her internal thoughts to swell to the surface like sirens from the sea.

You missed this lyric on C'est un Fait.

Your voice cracked on the bridge for Shiny People.

Was that guy on the front row licking his lips purposefully whenever you looked at him?

Playing live was an existential trip. She lost track of time. Felt disconnected from her body, or sometimes slammed into it so fully, she couldn't process anything outside of her breath. Her lips brushing the microphone. Her fingers on the guitar strings. Then, that reality warp was followed by an intense and almost debilitating deep dive into an anxious abyss.

Not that she was a stranger to that sensation. Her mind spun a thousand times a second on a regular Tuesday.

Delia had discovered in preschool that music was the trick to pulling all the wheels onto the tracks, and she'd played everything she could get her tiny hands on. Cutlery on pots. Her dad's old harmonica in its leather sleeve. A plastic toy piano her mom had spotted at a garage sale. She'd gotten her first guitar at age ten and had never looked back.

Signing with IndieLake was supposed to be the end of that journey. The tippy-top of her climb. *She'd made it.*

If only someone would've told her that getting a record deal meant you were automatically enrolled in a battle-to-the-death, king-of-the-hill competition. If death were the top of the music charts and the battle was misting her vocal cords and sitting in front of a microphone pop filter.

Still. The pressure to produce songs and shows that people loved seemed to gradually leech that old magic. Homeostasis required a regular supply of caffeine and a daily dose of ADHD medication.

Except when she wanted to create. Then she took neither.

"Dels?"

Delia's head snapped up. "Hmm?"

Mary exhaled and held out the two tea packets. "Throat Coat or Echinacea?"

Delia pointed at the Throat Coat, then slumped onto the stool in front of the row of mirrors and exposed bulbs. "Thanks, Mary. Sorry, I'm out of it."

"When are you going to stop apologizing? You're always dead inside after a show."

"I wish I wasn't." Delia grabbed a makeup wipe and started scrubbing her face, pushing her auburn waves behind her ears. Shouldn't she be one of those singers who got amped after all the cheers? Who wanted to party, French kiss men she barely knew, and make headlines with her antics until the wee hours of the morning?

"It's just who you are." Mary ripped open the packet of tea.

"But wouldn't I be easier to work with if I was extroverted? Or, I don't know, able to remember where I put my phone?"

"Did you lose it again?"

Delia gave her a guilty look as she swiped the wipe over her lips. "I thought it was down here on the counter, but now I'm wondering if I took it up and set it on that little table on stage right."

Mary laughed and poured hot water from the collapsible kettle she always brought to shows. She handed Delia the disposable coffee cup with the tea bag already steeping. "I'll go check."

"I can—"

"I'll go."

Delia smiled weakly as Mary exited the room, then pulled on the string and watched the bag of herbs bob up and down in the steaming water, inhaling the scent of warm spice. Heels scraped on the wooden floor above them, and post-show music wafted through the vents.

If she had to guess, there had probably been five hundred people there, and ticket prices were fifty-five a piece. She wasn't exactly sure what they'd contracted to pay the venue, but the last time they'd played there, it had been ten percent. Then they had to take out the production costs, advertising, and the contracted amount for IndieLake, which meant—if she'd done the math in her head right—she'd be left with around twelve grand personally. That she'd never see.

Not *never*. It only *seemed* like never since she was still hundreds of thousands of dollars away from earning out her advance. All of it had been her choice. When she'd met with IndieLake, she could've asked for a lower advance and higher royalty rates, but at the end of last summer, she'd been paying seven hundred a month for a shared room in a shitty apartment, and her mom didn't have hot water.

Delia tossed the makeup wipe in the trash, then stood and wet her microfiber face cloth in the sink. She held the cloth over her eyes and let the hot water seep into her skin. That windfall of three hundred grand had given her the ability to buy a house and keep money in the bank so she could work full-time as an artist. No more working as an administrative assistant. All of that was beyond her wildest dreams, but the real win was having her mom move in with her. She didn't think she'd ever forget the look on her mom's face when she beheld her very own master bath.

Delia dropped the cloth just as Mary walked back into the room, holding out her phone. "Where was it?"

"On the floor next to the rat's nest of electrical cords."

Delia's memory snapped into focus. "I had to tie my shoe, I must have set it there." She reached out and took it, then swiped up to find two messages from Tony. Her brow furrowed.

"What does he want?" Mary asked.

"Emergency strategy session?"

"Like, tonight?"

Delia started texting. "I don't know, he just . . ." she trailed off, not able to type and verbalize at the same time.

> Finished. Show went well. When did you want to talk?

Within thirty seconds, a call came through from Tony's number. She waved the screen at Mary, who nodded and motioned for her to answer.

Delia hit the green button, then immediately put her publicist on speakerphone. "Hey, Tony."

"Delia! Is Mary there?"

"Yep, right here. You're on speaker."

"Good show?"

Delia nodded. "Excellent. Crowd was great, and no dead mics, so win-win."

Tony chuckled. "Well, you're probably halfway to sweatpants and donuts right now—"

Delia frowned and gave Mary a look. Was that what Tony thought they did after shows? Donut shops weren't open at this time of night. Mary rolled her eyes.

"—but I was talking with the guys at IndieLake. I know you're concerned about promotion for the new album."

That was the understatement of 2024. Her music had gone viral on social media twice since the fall, each time catapulting her singles into the top ten in the Canadian charts, but then . . . nothing. No added media tours. No public appearances besides the previously scheduled shows. No contests or meet-and-greets.

It was like IndieLake had made the unilateral decision to collect regular checks from their various represented artists instead of trying to maximize any one of them. Her TikTok channel was the reason for the success of those singles, and that was *her* baby.

She could've done all of that without them.

It was not a thought that served her. Especially since it wasn't true. She couldn't have bought her house without the advance, and that was what she'd needed at the time. A price had to be paid.

"What did they say?" Delia asked.

"Not much, besides the fact that they loved my new idea and were fully onboard as long as you were."

Delia shifted on the stool and flicked her eyes to Mary. *What idea was he talking about?* "I'm getting nervous, Tony."

He laughed. "No, it's a good thing, I promise. Better than good, actually. Probably one of the best ideas I've ever had."

Delia's stomach dropped. He was talking this up too much for it to be net positive. The last time he'd had one of his "best ideas," he'd convinced Mary to schedule her for a three-night stint at a casino outside of Orillia, Ontario that still allowed indoor smoking. She'd sounded like Marge Simpson for a week.

"Just spit it out." Delia set the phone on the counter and pulled her hair back with a clip.

"So, you know how certain pop stars and athletes have been making huge waves south of the border?"

"You can just say Taylor Swift."

"Right, I didn't want to get political."

Mary threw out her hands with a *What the hell is he talking about?* look. Delia stifled a laugh.

"But it's a fantastic strategy for garnering insane press," Tony said.

Delia sighed. "Perfect, I'll hit up one of those hot professional athletes lining up outside my venues that keep pestering me with friendship bracelets."

Mary snorted.

Tony sighed. "Ha. Ha. But no, you don't need to find a professional athlete because I know one for you."

Delia froze. "Are you trying to set me up with one of your friends, Tony?"

"No! Hell, no. All of my friends need intensive therapy. This is more of an 'I know *of* him' situation."

Delia scoffed and pulled her shirt over her head, then reached for her favourite combed-cotton hoodie. "You know *of* an athlete, and you want me to, what, call him up cold and see if he'll date me for the press?"

"Exactly."

She threw her arms out in panic, and her head got stuck in the hood. As she scrambled to free herself, her clip flew off and shot toward Mary's head. She dodged, then picked it up and handed it back. Delia tsked. The clip had lost one of its teeth. "Hilarious, Tony, but I'm only twenty-five, and I've had enough blind date disasters to last a lifetime, thank you very much."

"That's the beauty of it. It wouldn't *be* a date."

Delia frowned, reaching over to the sink to wet her hands and calm her hair now that it looked like it'd been rubbed by a balloon. "You want me to date an athlete, but have it not be a date?"

"Right."

Mary finally stepped in. "Tony, I know your mother tongue is the language of love, but right now you're not making any damn sense."

Delia could hear his grin over the speaker. "You girls. *My* girls. I love how innocent you are." He clicked his tongue. "You do know it's entirely possible to have a relationship with someone—an intimate, soul-crushing love affair—and have the entire thing be for show, right? Did you think that Carson Hart and Lady V were together when she went to the Olympics? Or Emelio Sebin and Carrie Law? Darius and both his girlfriends? Celine Dion and René?"

"I'm pretty sure they had kids togeth—"

"Pshaw, all for show. It got them somewhere they couldn't have reached by themselves. And you, my dear, need to climb."

Delia's heart kicked into a gallop. Her dating life had been nonexistent the past six months, not only because she'd become more recognizable, but also because she'd sworn off all online dating after a guy she'd been talking to for three weeks turned out to be wanted in two states and their lovely province of Ontario for multiple felonies. Mary had helped her dodge that bullet.

Her instincts couldn't be trusted. Plus, she enjoyed her quiet house far too much to sacrifice it for another blah night of superficial conversation. Which meant . . .

She tapped her fingers from pinky to pointer on the makeup counter. It was a good beat. The way it grew in volume from one end of her hand to the other. What was she thinking about? Delia retraced her mental steps.

Right. Tony. His new idea.

If she wanted her own time and online dating was her personal hell, then a fake relationship was kind of a perfect solution. *Wasn't it?* She wouldn't have to talk to the guy outside of their arranged meet-ups. She wouldn't have to give up her nights at home, and Tony did have a point that love stories were selling big at the moment.

But who would have that kind of star power, and why would a guy like that be interested in her?

Delia sat back on the stool and crossed her arms over the counter. "Alright, Tony. I'm listening. Who is it?"

CHAPTER
Two

EACH PULL of Jack's laces spurred a slurry of bittersweet emotion. He sat in the dressing room of the ice arena that had become his home for the past five months. In one season, the Snowballs had become family, whereas he'd spent years with the Admirals and besides Flank and Rob, had never been excited to see any of them.

Now, he was leaving that newfound brotherhood. *Not forever*, he reminded himself. Though he'd be lying if he didn't admit he hoped for at least a few seasons.

"When do you sign your life away?" Brett tapped the side of Jack's skate with his stick.

"Nine tomorrow morning." He cinched the laces and tied a rabbit-ear double bow, then straightened his back.

The Snowball's captain, Sean, shoved his empty equipment bag into his locker. "Your emancipation will be complete."

Jack exhaled. "I wish I could do both."

"Bud, could you imagine Wheatfill's whining if we won the tourney this year with a signed NHL player on our roster?" André picked up his helmet off the bench. "He already pitched a fit on the league boards about us snagging you in the first place."

Sean huffed. "It was open season. It's not my fault Wheatfill's too busy sleeping with other people's girlfriends to round out his team."

Tyler laughed. "Good thing you don't hold grudges for ten years or I'd be nervous."

Sean shot him a look, then lumbered toward the door holding his gloves, helmet, and stick. The rest of the team followed like ducklings, and as the chilled arena air hit Jack's face, an overwhelming sense of gratitude washed over him.

He was going to do this. *Play hockey in the NHL.* Even if it was only for a few months, at nearly thirty, he'd be playing on the biggest stage in the world.

"You're one lucky son of a bitch, Jack." Boyd clapped him on the back as they poured out onto the ice through the gap in the boards.

Country pulled his helmet on. "Not luck. He earned that spot."

"With a little help." Jack wouldn't ever celebrate an injury, no matter who the player was. But if someone on the Blizzard was going to get injured, he was grateful it was their right winger. He'd never forget how the general public had rallied around him and clamoured for him to take the open spot on the roster, either.

"How could they not want to have your babies after that goal?" André spun in a circle on the ice, mimicking the play that Jack had watched on repeat. It was surreal. The move had been all instinct. *Some players study the game, and some feel it in their bones.* That was what his Juniors coach had always said.

Jack fell into a couple of laps around the rink, laughing when Country couldn't help but get competitive with the warm-up. Jack pushed faster, matching him stride for stride. "Compensating for something?"

Country grinned. "I have a huge penis."

"That's not what Jenna said last night."

Country knocked him into the boards, and Jack scrambled to catch back up. Probably not the best idea to get injured at practice before he signed an NHL contract in the morning. Jack paired up with Mike for passing drills, then wove with Brett and Tyler against Mike and Darcy in three-on-two.

"You find a new guy yet?" He asked Sean as they grabbed pinnies for a scrimmage.

"Nope. Especially not with your skillset."

"Well, impossible to match that."

Sean rolled his eyes, but before he could skate back to centre, Jack stopped him. "I'm sorry to leave you hanging, bud."

"Sorry? I'm not. You get to play for the Blizzard. Hell, I'd ditch every last one of you in a heartbeat to get that kind of opportunity."

When he was younger, that may have been true. Sean was now in his late thirties and probably hadn't considered a pro career since his first grey chest hair. Jack, on the other hand, hadn't ever stopped thinking about it. How he'd come so close, and the opportunity had slipped through his fingers. It was something every guy on the Snowballs probably went through at some point, but he hadn't ever arrived at acceptance.

Jack jumped into the scrimmage, immediately receiving a pass from Sean and darting toward the goal. He was met by a solid check from Darcy, sending him flat on his butt.

"Just prepping you now for the big leagues." Darcy stole the puck and took off.

Minutes later, Jack fought for a breakaway and deked Darcy so hard, his knees buckled. He took Boyd in goal one on one, faking to the left followed by a quick shot to the right. The puck slammed into the back of the net with a satisfying thud. Darcy muttered something under his breath as he skated past the blue line, which was all the win Jack needed.

He couldn't wipe the grin off his face as they finished up practice an hour later and retreated to the dressing room. Jack stripped off his equipment and base layer that stuck to him like a second skin. His feet slapped against the tile as he found a spot against the wall and started the shower.

He tested the spray and waited for it to warm up before stepping into the water, then hunched and dropped his head to let the stream wash over him. He never understood why shower heads weren't higher on the wall at the arena. The only people who used them were athletes.

"Where is the ink going?" Country nodded toward his left arm.

Jack flipped his wrist to reveal a patch of bare skin on the inside of his bicep. He was covered from wrist to shoulder with tattoos he'd collected since his first year out of high school, but this spot had always been saved for his first NHL team. Last Christmas, his dad had asked if he was going to fill it with something else.

"It's going to hurt like hell," Brett called out from the next shower slot down.

Tyler scoffed. "He's got about two hundred percent more tattoos than you, bud. I think he's aware."

Brett filled his hand with foamed soap from the dispenser. "Don't call Bowen to hold your hand. He's terrible with needles."

"I thought I'd call that girl from Curtis's party." Jack forced a smile, pretending he had the least bit of interest in some girl he'd met at a bonfire.

"Who? Rhonda?" Country asked.

Jack scrubbed soap into his scalp. "She was funny." That part was true. He'd met plenty of girls who were pretty and charming over the past three years. It didn't matter. His heart had been sealed up, and he wasn't planning to open it up to fresh air and sunlight anytime soon.

Country rinsed and shut off his water. "I think you're a little late. She's got a thing for this doctor who lives by Anne and Tina."

"But now I'm an NHL player. I think that trumps saving lives." He was good at playing the part. Making sure nobody worried about him. Even though the guys were solid, none of the Snowballs knew about his past. The desire to open up about his deepest, darkest wounds had never sparked at practice.

Country laughed as he wrapped a towel around his waist and stalked back to the benches. "Definitely lead with that."

Jack finished washing and stood under the hot water a minute more before turning off the shower and drying off. He inspected the uneven tiles with discoloured grout under his feet and inhaled the scent of the soap that was distinct to those dressing rooms. He searched for something else to laugh about.

That was his last practice with the Snowballs. His chest tightened as he walked back to his locker and started to dress.

André's voice lifted above the sound of splashing water and jostling of equipment. *"Tu voulais quelqu'un de solide, Quelqu'un qui sait où elle réside. Mais de ce qui suivrait, nous ignorions le pacte. Je suis désolé. Je t'en prie, c'est un fait!"* He whooped and swung a towel around his his head. "They never play the French version in Calgary, and listen!" He stood on the bench and pointed at the speaker buried in the ceiling tiles.

"Is that Delia Melise?" Ryan ran his towel over his long hair, then shook like a shaggy dog.

"Is it—?" André pursed his lips and planted his hands on his still-naked hips. "You ask like she's not the sexiest girl to come out of Quebec in a hundred years?"

"I thought she was from Toronto?" Boyd pulled on his shirt.

"She was born in Quebec City, and it counts." André stepped down off the bench, joining in at the chorus with abrasive volume and intermittent arm motions.

Jack chuckled. "I dated a girl from Quebec City once. I think she smoked more than you do."

André pulled on his pants, and his brow furrowed. "Not possible." As if to prove it, he pulled the carton of Marlboros from his pocket and slipped two behind his ear. Jack laughed and shook his head. He was going to miss the hell out of that dressing room.

He took time packing his equipment and zipping up his bag. When he had no other excuse to stand in front of his locker, he shrugged his black puffer coat on and slung the bag over his shoulder.

As he turned, Sean stepped over Ryan's gear on the ground and clapped a hand on his shoulder. "Not so fast, bud." Sean motioned to Tyler, who was in the middle of pulling something out of his locker. Everyone on the team, including André, quieted.

"Had to get you something to remember us by." Tyler lifted a swath of mustard yellow and teal green fabric.

Jack groaned. "Where did you get that?" It was the jersey he'd bought at the thrift store with Brett and Tyler the night of his initiation only a few months prior. He was ninety-nine percent certain he'd thrown that in the garbage after practice.

"We made some adjustments." Sean nodded, and Tyler turned it around. Jack's jaw dropped. His name was now stitched across the back instead of whatever player's name had been there before. Below the all-caps "Harrison" read the line, "Master at handling his stick."

Jack laughed out loud as Tyler strode forward to hand it to him. "How?"

Curtis snorted. "Sharla thought it was so nice we thought you were such an impressive stick handler."

The pieces clicked into place. Jack had been to enough Sunday Suppers to know Sharla Thompson, Sean's mom, was a seamstress and a talented one at that. He'd seen the eighties ski coat she'd crafted from scratch for Curtis's birthday. "She did this?"

Sean nodded. "If you ever let it slip that I made her stitch a masturbation joke on a jersey, I'll tell Rhonda you have a micro penis."

"More of a chode, don't you think?" André called out, and the whole team chortled like they were noticing pubic hair in grade seven gym class. Turned out penis jokes were still funny whether you were twelve or twenty-nine. Maybe by fifty, they'd all grow out of it. He hoped not.

Jack looked up from the fashion disaster of a jersey and opened his mouth to say something, but his words stuck in his throat. If he'd spoken, he probably would've expressed how depressed he'd been leaving the AHL without a contract. Or the relief that washed over him when Sean reached out with an opportunity to hold onto the sport he loved, and then his trepidation before meeting the team. He would've admitted how much he'd needed the Snowballs and how much he was going to miss their practices and games. In the end, the only words he could get out were, "Thank you."

Heads nodded around the dressing room, and Jack threw his free arm around Sean, clapping him on the back. As he walked down the narrow aisle, he fist-bumped the rest of his teammates until he found himself standing in front of the door. He turned, nodded one final time, then exited into the hall.

———

When Jack stepped into his sister's house, the aroma of roasted garlic potatoes hit him straight in the face. He took off his shoes, dropped his gear in the boot room, and walked into the kitchen to find his brother-in-law Oscar watching over slabs of meat sizzling in a cast iron pan.

"Hey." Oscar looked up and waved his spatula. "Any fans stalk you tonight?"

"Just two. They were waiting in the parking lot." Jack rounded the counter and rolled up his sleeves. It still felt surreal that people A, knew who he was, and B, cared enough to wait for him after practice to get his autograph. After his first pro game, he'd been recognized four times in the grocery store that same weekend. Now that word had gotten out about him officially signing with the Blizzard, he'd learned to expect that any stranger he interacted with knew his middle name and birthdate.

Jack washed his hands with soap and warm water. "How can I help?"

"You can chop some cucumbers for the salad. I already peeled them." Oscar motioned to the cutting board at his left.

Jack nodded and picked up the knife. It was Monday, which meant his sister Clara would've just gotten off her shift at eight. She should be home any minute. "How was work?"

"Worky."

Jack chuckled. "Tax deadline is coming up."

Oscar blew out a breath. "That's why we're having steak. I need something to remind myself that life is worth living."

"Plus, if you make steak on your night, I can get away with spaghetti on mine."

Oscar chuckled. "You made that last week, didn't you?"

"It was fettuccine. Keep it straight." Jack had barely sliced four cucumber rounds when his phone buzzed in his pocket. He dried his hands on the dish towel next to the sink, then pulled it out and, seeing Sean's name, answered.

"Miss me that much already?"

Sean grunted. "Nonstop weeping since you left the dressing room."

"I figured." Jack leaned against the counter and watched Oscar shake steak seasoning over the seared meat.

"Got an interesting call a few minutes ago."

Jack frowned. "What kind of call?" He couldn't think of a single reason Sean would be receiving a call involving him unless it was something he didn't want to hear. A league fine or complaint. He steeled himself.

"It was a publicist looking for you. He'd searched online for contact information and already sent you a Facebook message."

Jack shifted on his feet. "I don't check Facebook."

"Which is why he ended up calling me."

Jack connected the dots. "I'm listed on the Snowball's roster and your contact info is on the Elite league page."

"Bingo."

"What did he want?" Jack started to pace.

"Well, that's the thing. I'm not sure I'm buying what he's selling."

"And that is?"

"That he's the publicist for Delia Melise."

The furrow in Jack's brow deepened to a chasm. "The singer?" He'd heard her songs on the radio. André had been singing along to one in the dressing room.

"That's what he said."

"Why would he want to get in touch with me?"

Sean exhaled. "Your guess is as good as mine, bud. Said he had something he wanted to discuss. I didn't give him your number, but he left his contact info. I had Tyler do a quick search. The name he gave me matches up, but I didn't wait to hear if the dude actually works for her."

"Text it to me?"

"Yep."

"Thanks, bud."

Sean hung up, and Jack watched his screen. A moment later, ten digits showed up in a text from Sean. A few seconds after that, a text from Tyler followed.

> *The guy's legit. Found a picture of him with Delia at her show in Vancouver a couple of weeks ago*

"Everything okay?" Oscar asked as he transferred the now seared steaks to a cutting board.

"Yeah. I just need a minute." Jack couldn't quell his curiosity. He hit the number, then strode into the living room as the phone started to ring.

CHAPTER
Three

JACK'S BLOOD rushed as a voice answered on the other end of the line.

"Hello?"

He cleared his throat. "Hey, this is Jack Harri—"

"Jack! I'm thrilled you were able to get back to me tonight. How are you doing?"

"Uh, good. Thanks." Jack sat on his sister's creamy white sofa, which he never fully relaxed on. He held up his hands to avoid leaving a grimy fingerprint. She'd know it was his. "This is Tony?"

"Right, Tony Rusk. I head the publicity team for Delia Melise."

Jack's mouth went dry. "Mmm." He couldn't think of anything to say. He felt like he was in the middle of a nightmare-curious dream and any second he'd wake up, head to breakfast, and let Oscar analyze his twisted psychiatry.

"You know the name?"

Jack blinked. "Your name?"

Tony laughed. "No, Delia Melise."

Right, dipshit. Jack ran a hand through his hair. "Yeah, no. I've heard of her."

"Then you know she's got three singles in the top one hundred songs in the country at the moment."

Jack nodded. "I've heard them. They're good." He winced. *An overwhelming compliment.* He hadn't paid much attention to her songs, if he was being honest. He listened to music mostly when he was at the gym, and that usually required a specific level of pump-up energy. Not the best place for acoustic guitar.

"She's a rising star, and anyone in her orbit is going up with her, you know what I mean?"

Jack frowned. No, he did not know what Tony Rusk meant. He sounded like he was canvassing for a political party, even though Trudeau's Liberals hadn't called an election yet.

"Sounds like she's accomplishing incredible things." Jack squeezed his eyes shut. *What was this conversation?* Why would a publicist who worked for a pop star on the other side of the country phone him to talk about her singles?

"It looks like your career is skyrocketing, as well. Did you see your name was the number one search phrase in five provinces and one territory this week?"

Jack blinked. *What?* "I didn't know that." His head snapped up as the front door opened and Clara walked in wearing scrubs.

"Hey! Are you—?" She stopped mid-coat hang at the expression on his face. Her eyes shot to the phone, and she gave him a questioning look. Jack shook his head, which meant she immediately came to sit down next to him.

"Babe, is that you?" Oscar strode down the hall and found her perched on the sofa next to Jack. Clara waved him over and patted the cushion on her left.

"Impressive data, Harrison." Tony rapped his knuckles on something that sounded expensive. "Seems like the two of you are Canada's grad prince and princess this spring." Tony chuckled, and Jack scratched the stubble on his chin.

Maybe that was it. Tony wanted to get some visibility for Delia by bringing her to one of his games or something. His inbox, or rather Sean's, had been flooded with requests for interviews and appearances since his appearance with the Blizzard. Just yesterday he'd talked with Clara about her screening his media requests. With new products launching at work, he barely had time to eat and make it to practice.

Jack exhaled. "Listen, Tony, I'm not sure why you're calling, but if it's for an interview or—"

"Are you single?"

Jack blinked. "Barely." *Where had that come from?* That answer either read as an arrogant *I'm only single because I want to be,* or *I just got out of a long-term loving relationship, and I'm heartbroken.* Either interpretation couldn't have been further from the truth. He was single because he hadn't put forth a modicum of effort *not* to be, and the last relationship he'd been in had ended three years ago. *Had it ever ended for him?*

"I'm going to leave the psychoanalysis on that up to your therapist, but you're cis-gendered? Not that I care either way, but for my purposes tonight, it's an important question."

Jack's hackles rose. "Yeah. Not exactly loving these questions, bud." Clara's eyes widened, and she leaned in, trying to hear what was happening on the other end of the line.

Tony sighed. "Understandable. Here's what I'm getting at. You and Delia are both garnering plenty of attention on your own, but I think this could be an incredible opportunity for synergy."

Jack shifted until he was climbing the arm of the couch. When Clara nearly crawled onto his lap, he relented and turned it on speakerphone. Clara clapped her hands with glee, and Oscar gave an apologetic head shake.

Jack cleared his throat. "That word doesn't sound real."

"What word?" Clara mouthed. Jack dragged his thumb through the air in front of his throat as Tony chuckled on the other end of the line.

"Yeah, kind of sounds like I'm selling snake oil, doesn't it? It means that I think the two of you could be better together. That your combined energy could be more than the sum of its parts."

Jack nodded. "Listen, if Delia wants tickets to the next game, I'd be happy to talk to the coordinator, but I can't—"

Clara gasped out loud, her eyes darting between Jack and Oscar, then clapped her hands over her mouth just as Tony cut Jack off.

"No, no, we're not looking for a handout. More of . . . an agreement."

Clara grabbed the sleeve of his shirt and hissed, *"Did he say Delia? As in Delia Melise?"*

Jack snatched the phone from the table and stalked to the other side of the room, facing the wall so he could focus. "I'm not following, Tony."

"Delia's interested in a contractual relationship for publicity purposes. With you."

Jack laughed out loud. "Shit, Tony, at least buy me flowers before you whisper sweet nothings." *A contractual relationship for publicity purposes?* Now he was positive he was dreaming.

"I know it sounds cold, but people do it all the time. Think about Celine and—"

"Do NOT insinuate that Celine and René were in a contractual relationship," Clara burst out behind him.

"Who's that?" Tony asked.

"My sister, sorry. She just got home."

"Hi, Jack's sister."

Clara grinned as Oscar worked to keep her pinned to the sofa.

Tony continued. "On paper, it might not be sexy, but do you know what is? Bringing in more fans to the Saddledome for your games. Delia has thousands of followers. Specifically of the mid-twenties female variety, and they will flock anywhere Delia tells them to go. And you know who'll follow if their designer jeans are planted in those bucket seats."

Tony didn't wait for Jack to answer. "Guys. Beer-drinking, hockey-loving guys. Do you know who pays attention to stats like that? Team managers and owners. When they see the isolated variable that contributed to their ticket sales going through the roof was Jack Harrison being on the team, you better believe they're going to re-up your contract."

At the mention of strategy, Jack dropped into business mode. All day he ran cost-benefit and risk analyses on product lines and distribution agreements. This was in his wheelhouse. "If my name is the number one search term like you mentioned, why would I need anyone else to help me bring in more fans?"

This question shut Tony up but only briefly. "You're bringing in fans now, but if you've been paying attention to the NFL, you'll know exactly what a love story can do to ticket sales. Not only that, but I'm guessing your contracted rate isn't something to write home about. We're prepared to offer you an all-expenses-paid vacation. On us. You won't have to spend a cent while your contract with Delia is active. If you want, I can go into the social benefits of being seen with someone like Ms. Melise on your arm, but I'm sure you can do the math on that one."

Holy hell. The guy was serious. All expenses paid? Tony wasn't wrong about his pay with the Blizzard. He was only coming on to cover for the playoffs and had been offered a per-practice and game rate. He also worked for Big Rick, a ski and snowboarding company, and while his pay was good, he was recovering from ten years of making hockey his full-time priority without benefits. He wanted to buy his own place and avoid mooching off Clara and Oscar. With interest rates sky high, he needed to put twenty percent down, or he was going to eat it in his mortgage payments.

But all practical thoughts slipped as he realized what this would entail. Being out. On dates. With a woman. It didn't matter if it was real, just the thought of spending time alone with someone made his insides twist.

Jack turned to see Clara and Oscar staring at him like two baby birds. He knew exactly what they were thinking since they'd been pushing for him to get back on the horse and date since he'd moved in.

He tapped mute on the phone, then held out a hand, giving them the okay to give the advice that at least Clara was choking on. Oscar shrugged, then gave him a look like he'd eaten something bad at a Chinese restaurant. Clara, on the other hand, nodded emphatically and said, "You should at least meet her, don't you think? And take me with you!"

Jack pursed his lips. He was insane. A relationship for a publicity stunt? Three weeks ago he'd been the guy who was kicked off of two AHL teams, and now he signed autographs in the Ice Arena parking lot, slapped away media requests like mosquitos, and received requests from famous pop stars to be their contractually-obligated boyfriend?

He wanted to say an immediate no, but curiosity niggled at him. That and the pathetic plea in Clara's eyes won out. He turned off mute. "I'll need to think about it, and I'd need to meet Delia first. My sister Clara wants to come."

———

Delia sat glued to her phone screen, watching Jack Harrison in a post-game interview from a month ago. Or was it six weeks? Whenever he'd played the game that all of Canada seemed to be talking about. The one she'd only discovered hours prior, thanks to Tony. He was good-looking. Not in a traditional sense, more of a rugged, I've-been-working-on-car-engines-all-day kind of handsome, and she didn't trust those long lashes and mussed hair. He had an uneven nose, probably from breaking it in a hockey fight or something. His smile was nice—humble and almost shy.

She jumped when the video disappeared and her phone

buzzed in her hand. *Tony.* Delia answered the call. "Did you talk to him?"

"Waiting up for me, eh?"

Delia rolled to her side, folding her pillow in half so she didn't have to prop herself up on her elbow. "No, I was . . . writing lyrics." That wasn't a complete lie. She had been scribbling ideas in her notebook on her nightstand *before* she'd started stalking Jack Harrison online. The last thing she wanted was for Tony to think she'd been waiting up because she was nervous about this whole thing, or heaven forbid, that she was actually invested in the idea.

"I talked to him," Tony said, and Delia's mind splintered into a thousand directions. What had Tony said? What had Jack *thought* about what Tony said? Did he think she had proposed this idea, and if so, what did he think about her? Delia clutched her pillow tighter.

"He said he wants to meet you." Tony's words sank in like water over the soil of a potted plant. The sentence sat on the surface for a few seconds, then finally made its way to her roots.

He wants to meet you. Delia swallowed. "He's in Calgary, isn't he?"

"Yep, and he has a contract to sign and practice tomorrow, so there's no way he's coming to you. I've got tickets for you and Mary to fly out first thing in the morning."

Her fingers went cold. She hated flying. "Does Mary know?"

"I sent her the itinerary right before I phoned."

Delia tried to parse out the ramifications of this but couldn't see past the *YOUR GETTING ON A PLANE TOMORROW* neon sign in her head. She repeated the information back. "I'm flying to Calgary tomorrow and meeting this hockey player, Jack, after his practice?"

"Oh, you won't meet him till after the show."

"The show?"

"Right, I gave Mary the details. I called in a favour and got you a slot for your acoustic set at the Jukebox. You only need to pack your guitar, they've got the rest."

Delia clenched her jaw. She used to love last-minute gigs, but now there was so much more at stake. It was a miracle that people were finally paying attention. And also terrifying that people were finally paying attention. She no longer had to worry about jumping into a line-up and having nobody show, but her fans had expectations.

Thankfully, they'd done enough pop-up shows, people were used to her flying by the seat of her pants. They'd even come up with a secret code together on her socials. Every time she wanted to share info about a show, she posted about ice cream. She couldn't remember exactly how it had started, but it had caught on and stuck.

Delia put Tony on speakerphone and added a quick picture of the Humber Bay Bridge she'd taken the other night with the caption, "Just had the best ice cream for breakfast (don't judge). Yummy Yellowcake Confetti. Now to turn on the Jukebox and float till tomorrow." Delia grinned as she entered relevant hashtags, along with a few that had zero likelihood of being searched but brought her pure joy, like *#coldoncold* and *#ithaseggssoitcounts*.

"No comment?" Tony sounded beleaguered.

"Sorry, thank you. Just posting my ice cream code."

Tony laughed. "You found another fake flavour that corresponds with YYC? How have you not run out yet?"

"Well, if you'd stop booking me secret shows in Calgary, I wouldn't have to reach so far into the depths of my creativity. Can't you choose an airport code with a 'C' first? Cookies, Crumble, Cheesecake—the options would be endless."

"The double Y is problematic."

Analyzing letters helped her emotions settle. Until she remembered why she was going to YYC in the first place. The show was a bonus, but she had to be there to meet Jack Harrison.

Her heart did a weird jumping bean thing, then dropped so fast, she got woozy.

Jack seemed like a nice guy, and he was intriguing for a hockey-playing car mechanic, but she'd done enough online dating to know that none of that surface-level stuff mattered. If she was going to pretend to date someone for a few months, he had to be tolerable. Yes, she wanted to boost her visibility and get more streams. But would she be willing to smile and hold hands with just anyone? Especially when she knew there were men out there who could seem completely normal and then start begging for pictures of you rubbing lotion on your feet?

No. She wouldn't do that. No matter how much Tony—

The door to her bedroom cracked open, and her mom peeked in. "Mon chou, I'm heading to work." Her mother coughed. Delia hated it when she coughed.

She checked the time on her phone. *Ten thirty.*

"Is that Camille? Delia, say hello to your mother for me," Tony barked, and Delia held up her phone so Tony could see her through the camera.

Her mom laughed. "Allô, Tony. Comment?"

"Ah, super, surtout maintenant que je te vois."

Her mother blushed. "Tu me flatte, Tony."

Delia mouthed a "sorry" as she pulled the phone back, then deflated as her mom left for her night shift.

How long ago had Dr. Kemp told her mother she needed to slow down? Her Lupus had progressed to the point that she had permanent pleuritis—inflammation that couldn't be managed purely by pain medication. Since her mother had called corticosteroids "Upjohn poison," the only other option was stress management.

Okay, so maybe she'd agree to it. If Tony's idea got her royalty statements pouring in so her mom could quit her jobs and live ten more years, she'd hold hands with pretty much anyone. Hell, she'd do more than that if she had to.

"Did you tell Camille about this yet?" Tony asked.

Delia scoffed. "When would I have told her about this? I've known for all of five minutes."

"Well, more like three hours, but I'll accept your use of hyperbole. You *are* an artiste, after all."

"How generous of you." Delia pushed up on the bed and swivelled so her feet were on the floor. "Will you be there tomorrow after the show?"

"Absolutely. Someone has to convince this guy he wants to fake date you, and it's sure as hell not going to be you or Mary."

"Thanks for the vote of confidence."

Tony laughed. "See you in the morning. I'll wave from business class."

"Goodnight, Tony." Delia threw her phone on the bed, then walked to the closet to pull out her carry-on. She needed to talk to Mary, but outfits had to come first. She needed something new for tomorrow night, which meant a little research since she didn't want to pay for a stylist.

Clothing had always been an extension of her songwriting. A mood. A piece of herself that she displayed for public consumption. Mary always helped with her show fits, but this time it wouldn't be just the two of them in the green room. She needed something that would communicate her feelings to Jack loud and clear.

Business only.

The title of her non-existent sex tape.

CHAPTER
Four

DELIA WALKED down her dark front steps wrapped in the cocoon of a thick, oversized sweater. She never knew what to wear to the airport. She could count on the plane being either the approximate temperature of the sun, with the flight attendants instructing them to *please leave the window shades open* so they could be roasted and blinded, or a meat locker, where no combination of layers would keep her toes from turning into ice-cubes. She'd settled on a tank top under her chunky sweater, then a puffy jacket rolled up and stowed in her backpack for the half-frozen ham hock scenario.

On top of all that, she had to take recognition into account. It had only been within the past few months that she'd started to make a stir when she left her house. It had been shocking at first, then flattering, and then a little disconcerting. Typically if she could hide her hair, she was golden. Today's accessory would be a flat brimmed Hello Kitty hat with her hair pulled up.

Delia hauled her carry-on and guitar case to the back of the car that waited for her at the curb under the frosted glow of the streetlight. Mary was already in the passenger seat. The rideshare driver got out and loaded her case and bag into the boot. Delia checked the license plate just to make sure Mary hadn't been hoodwinked, then watched their driver close the trunk. Just in case he forgot to add one of her items and it was left sitting on the curb.

Delia got in the backseat and settled her leather backpack next to her before fastening her seatbelt.

"Early morning flight, eh?" the driver asked.

Delia groaned internally. *Please, Uber Gods, don't let this man be chatty at five thirty in the morning.* Thankfully Mary was feeling more chipper than she was. As usual.

"Yep, on our way to Calgary." Mary shot a look to the back-seat that said, *do you think he'll recognize you?* Delia pointed to the hat, and Mary snorted.

IndieLake had suggested she start using a private driver, but that cost more money than she was willing to pay. Yes, her popularity was growing, but she wasn't yet a household face. Especially not with the fifty-plus crowd, which this man with his grey hair and lined face seemed to belong to. Until it became a major inconvenience, she was happy to save money and get to the airport like everyone else.

Delia fixed her gaze on the blurring cityscape and breathed in the faint scent of mothballs mixed with sweat as a familiar knot tightened in her stomach. *Airports.* She hated the noise, the pissed-off travellers, the TSA agents that had long ago been converted to the belief that all humans were, in fact, idiots. And all of that happened before they were crammed into seats that were three-quarters the size of average chairs with backs that couldn't be angled at anything greater than ninety degrees.

She popped in her ear buds and opened the latest message from IndieLake.

What do you think?
   X Christian

· · ·

It was a stupid question because Christian didn't give a damn what she thought about new song concepts. She could write back, "This sounds like a jazzercise back up track, and I couldn't loathe it more," and Christian would respond with, "I forgot all about jazzercise! Super popular in the eighties." Or her personal favourite, "I bet it will grow on you."

Any response from him translated to one sentiment: learn to love it because it's going on your next album.

Delia pressed play on the attachment and, after thirty seconds, determined it wasn't the worst thing he'd sent over. She turned up the volume to drown out her rising panic as the car turned onto the highway.

The warped entrance to the chorus was intriguing. It sounded like someone had their fingers on a transposition slider. Like they thought about changing keys but then changed their mind at the last second. *Fun*. Almost whimsical.

But she hated the drums. It was trendy in pop songs to drop in a straight up soprano drum pad after the first stanza, but it grated. She had yet to hear a track where it enhanced the overall composition of a song. That track was no exception.

Delia blew out a breath. Hopefully the lyrics would be better than the last few, though it couldn't possibly beat repeating the phrase, "Fool me once, shame on you," twelve times plus in one song (not including the back up vocals fade out in the final measures). Thankfully, Christian had bent on that one, and it was currently sitting in Canada's Pop Top 100. Which Delia made sure to casually mention every time they were together.

"Isn't that in Terminal 1? Or is it Terminal 3?" Mary asked.

Delia blinked. "Sorry, Mares. I wasn't listening."

"Oh, I know, I was talking to Arpit." Mary waved her off and tilted her head toward their driver with an apologetic smile. "She's not a morning person."

That was generous. A more truthful statement would've been, *Delia enjoys people in very specific situations only.* Summer music festival? Yes. Restaurant week? No. Art in the Park or open mic night? Hell, yes. Maple Leafs game or the grocery store at six o'clock when everyone stops on their way home from work? Hell, no. A piano in an alcove at the airport where someone sits down and starts playing as you're passing by with your carry on? Conflicted.

They pulled up to the curb at Toronto Pearson International Airport at six fifteen in the morning, and it was already bustling. They walked into the terminal to travellers draped over their luggage and Delia's mind jumped to panic over flights being canceled. In the line to check their bags, she scoured the signs and couldn't find any delays. At least none that would affect their route to Calgary.

After checking in, Delia led Mary to the Tim Horton's where they each grabbed a coffee.

"You getting anything to eat?" Mary asked.

Delia shook her head. "I had a bagel at home."

Mary grinned and ordered a muffin. "You know, now that you're doing more shows away from home, you're going to have to learn to eat in front of people."

Delia rolled her eyes and moved to the other end of the counter. It was sticky with spilled coffee, and she was careful to keep her sleeves hovering as she grabbed a napkin. "It's not that I don't like eating in front of people—"

"It's kind of that."

"Only kind of. It's more that I don't like how my teeth feel."

Mary held her receipt like a ticket to an amusement park. "You know there are solutions to that, right? Portable toothbrushes?"

"Yeah, but then you have to carry a gross toothbrush in your purse."

"There are disposable ones—"

"They don't work! They accomplish the same thing as spreading mint gum on the end of your finger and rubbing it around your mouth."

Mary joined her against the wall as they waited. "So you're

saying that on top of everything else I do for you, I have to invent a travelling toothbrush that self-cleans?"

"Or a disposable with actual brushes—ooh! And built-in toothpaste. And it has to be affordable because I don't want to pay a dollar each time I use one."

"Simple. I don't know why it doesn't exist yet." Their numbers were called, and Mary retrieved both their coffees from the counter. She handed one to Delia, then turned back to grab the paper sack with her muffin.

They made their way to the gate, where Tony and his assistant Kels were already waiting. Kels groaned and handed a ten dollar bill to Tony.

Delia frowned. "What was that for?"

Tony folded the bill and tucked it into his wallet. "Kels didn't think you'd get here on time. But I knew Mary was picking you up."

Kels rolled his eyes. "He had to cough up a hundred last weekend when he bet me on the nationality of the pig during the Pig War."

Delia grimaced, though they likely couldn't see much of her expression under the shadow of her hat.

"It was American," Mary stated.

Kels pointed. "See? She paid attention in Social Studies."

Tony shoved his wallet back into his pocket. "I still think it's up for debate since Confederation hadn't happened yet, but whatever."

The flight attendant made the announcement for priority boarding, and Tony and Kels stood up. "See you in there, ladies."

"Enjoy the legroom," Mary muttered, and Tony flashed a cheeky grin as they walked up to the gate attendant.

"Why is Kels still working for him?" Delia shifted to the side so the rest of the VIP passengers could line up. A woman in a Nine Inch Nails sweatshirt and fleece pants did a double take, and Delia turned her back to the line.

Mary shrugged. "Because the pay is good, I assume."

"Yeah, but he has to be at Tony's beck and call. The guy's married, isn't he?"

"Maybe he's not happily married. Like *Dion*."

Delia groaned. "Ugh. Please don't remind me."

"How long did it take you to figure out that one? Three dates?"

"Four, and it wasn't my fault. He was lying through his teeth."

Mary scoffed. "Shouldn't it have been a red flag that he showed up with a bald spot when his profile picture flaunted hair like Justin Trudeau?"

"Hey, you know how bleak it is out there." Both of them had been on and off dating apps for the past couple of years, and neither had much to show for their swipes.

They moved into line as their boarding group was called, then joined the herd in the tunnel and boarded. Tony winked as they passed his seat, but Kels was already resting with a donut pillow around his neck.

"Don' mind us, govenah, just makin' our way back to steerage!" Mary announced, and Tony nearly choked on his coffee. Delia started laughing and couldn't stop since Mary had been loud enough to attract the attention of half the plane. Thankfully, her blotchy cheeks and squinched expression only did more to obscure her face, and by the time she'd taken her seat, nobody besides Fleece Pants Lady had come close to recognizing her.

"And this is why we travel at five in the morning," Mary whispered as she dropped down into her seat. At least IndieLake always purchased the whole row so they wouldn't have to sit next to a stranger. That was worth the extra cost.

Delia leaned in. "Why, so we can be obnoxious while nobody has the energy to speak up?"

"That and . . ." Mary motioned at the passengers in the opposite row. Two out of the three already had their blackout masks on.

"Speaking of which." Delia grabbed her mask from her bag and fished the Xanax she'd stowed in the pocket of her joggers.

Mary stroked her hair. "Go righ' t' sleep, love. I'll wake ye if the ship goes down!"

Delia laughed and shook her head. "I appreciate your commitment to this bit, but can we not talk about 'going down' right now?"

"Sorry, I thought ocean liners were safe for fodder."

Delia yawned. "Kate Winslet would say otherwise."

"Whatever, she lived. Leo's the one who should be complaining."

Delia arranged her blanket and travel pillow and settled in against the window. She pushed in her earbuds and closed her eyes, then pressed play on the meditation track she always turned to when she flew.

As waves crashing on a beach drowned out the hiss of air in the airplane cabin, Delia drew a deep, cleansing breath. She gripped her armrests during takeoff, but by then, the medication was kicking in. Delia slept and didn't wake until they were two hours into the flight, which was better than she could've hoped. Now she only had to survive the descent and landing, which was formidable but not nearly as nerve-wracking as takeoff. She hated any turbulence, but at least if it happened at the end of the flight, she knew they were getting closer to the ground, which was where she wanted to exist.

She was about to distract herself with the Ryan Reynolds movie where he lived inside of a video game when Kels appeared in the aisle next to them. Mary's head leaned straight back, her mouth open wide enough that Delia could've peered in and spotted her epiglottis.

"I don't know how flight attendants resist the urge to drop a sandwich in there."

Delia sighed. "Probably the fear of jail time."

Kels handed her a tablet. "Tony wanted you to look over the contract."

Delia frowned. She stared at the white screen filled with text, and suddenly it clicked. She lowered her voice. "For the thing. With Jack Harrison." Since Tony had put the guy on her radar, she was seeing him everywhere. On the front pages of newspapers, reels and stories in her social media feeds. His name was even popping up in conversations between announcers on the radio.

Kels raised an eyebrow. "The thing. Correct."

Delia rolled her eyes and took the tablet, and Kels returned to his seat. Her head was still blurry, and it took her a minute to fully focus on the words in front of her. She scrolled past the introduction, then tried to read through paragraphs outlining terms regarding public appearances and social media posts but kept losing her place. Then something made her pause.

Public Displays of Affection:

The Parties hereby consent to engage in a mutually agreed-upon level of public displays of affection (PDAs) to portray their status as a romantic couple to onlookers convincingly. Such displays shall include, but not be limited to, the holding of hands, the exchange of brief, non-prolonged embraces, and the occasional kiss if both parties consent beforehand. These acts of affection shall be performed in good faith during public appearances, social events, and any outings where the legitimacy of their partnership might be subject to scrutiny or question, all in an effort to fortify the perceived authenticity of their bond.

She imagined Jack reading through that and wanted to shrivel up and die. *Was she really doing this?* Forcing someone to hold her in a "brief, non-prolonged embrace?" Delia dropped the tablet in her lap and rubbed the bridge of her nose.

She thought of her mom. Her incessant cough. Her late work hours. Dr. Kemp's insistence that the only way for her to have a longer, better life was to slow down.

This was what she needed, wasn't it? But what had Tony offered Jack to make this worth his while? She could get Dion, serial philanderer, to go out with her, but Jack? He was Canada's golden boy. He had to have a million prospects.

Thoughts about the meeting that night and her impending humiliation eclipsed any anxiety over the plane landing. It helped that it was the smoothest landing she'd ever experienced. By the time she'd noticed her ears were popping in their final descent, their wheels were touching down on the runway.

————

Delia and Mary showed up to the Jukebox, and there were already a handful of people waiting outside on the street for the box office to open. As their car pulled around to the back of the theatre, Delia shifted in her seat. She didn't have to say anything for Mary to know precisely what she was thinking.

"You want to go out and do selfies?"

Delia nodded with childlike excitement. Those were the moments she loved. She would never forget going to an Avril Lavigne concert when she was in middle school and standing outside afterward praying she'd get an autograph. Avril had walked out and connected with as many fans as possible on her way to her tour bus. Delia still had that signed poster.

That was the role music played in her life. Not only transporting her beyond the current reality, but driving her closer to someone else. Filling gaps and soothing aches.

Since it had just been the two of them for so long, music had been a balm on both of their hearts after her father passed. Every morning, when her mom got home from her night shift, she'd start up one of her favourite songs in place of Delia's alarm clock. It was her cue to wake up and their neighbour Tenille's cue to vacate her mother's bed.

Tenille was in her fifties at the time with no living relatives that Delia knew of. She slept overnight at their apartment so that her mother could work and not worry about Delia waking up in the middle of the night to an empty house. Delia never noticed the exhaustion in her mother's face because, by the time she dragged herself out of bed into the hall, she was already dancing.

To that day, whenever she heard a song by Elton John or The Beatles, that invisible thread between her and her mother tugged. Now *she* had the opportunity to create songs that would pull people together and lift their spirits. Delia didn't take that responsibility lightly.

Which was why she was so anxious to push past that first year with IndieLake. None of the music on her first record or the new one about to be released was written by her, and she was dying to make that a possibility. But artists always had to sacrifice until they proved themselves, and she *was* grateful for the platform she had already. She just had to hold out a little longer, continue making the label happy, and continue to make herself invaluable to their bottom line. If agreeing to this fake relationship wasn't signal enough about her level of dedication, she didn't know what was.

Delia grabbed her guitar out of the trunk as Mary paid the driver. They'd already checked into their hotel for the night, so there weren't any other bags to retrieve. They walked to the back door, and Delia's stomach churned as they waited for one of the theatre staff to open it for them.

Waiting was never a good thing. It gave her too much time to think, and for the past twenty-four hours, her thoughts had been on a constant, aggravating loop. *Jack was going to be there tonight.* What did he think about this whole arrangement? What had Tony said to him to make him even willing to consider it? *Could it be that he was already interested in her?*

Delia mentally swatted at them like flies. *Who knew, she didn't want to know, and no, for the love, he was an NHL player.* Those guys fell hard for cheerleader types. Models. Perky, happy people who didn't write songs about the macabre thoughts that ripped them apart in the middle of the night.

Delia sat her guitar in the wings to the stage, then told the tech crew they'd be a moment. She grabbed Mary's hand and pulled her back to the door they'd entered through and was already giggling when they rounded the corner and strode toward the bundled up fans.

"This will be awkward if they're here for some totally different reason," Mary muttered. Delia elbowed her and didn't even have a chance to respond before one of the girls looked up and spotted her auburn waves. The girl screamed, and her friends scattered like someone had just dropped a cannonball in the pool.

"I'm dead!" The girl looked to be in her mid-twenties. Her blonde hair was piled on top of her head in two messy buns, and they bobbed as she swooned into the guy standing next to her.

"I told you it paid off to show up early!" Her friend, wearing a toque over her long, jet-black hair, grabbed the sleeve of her boyfriend's coat like a toddler trying to get her mother's attention.

Delia stopped next to them and grinned. "I'm always floored when people are willing to wait out in the cold for one of my shows. Just wanted to come say hi."

"Hi!" The blonde girl straightened, then jumped up and down, flapping her arms. "I saw your post last night and couldn't believe you were coming back to Calgary for an acoustic set. I missed the one you did last summer and was devastated, especially because they wouldn't shut up about it." She motioned to her friends.

"You were all there?" Delia asked. She searched their faces, trying to figure out if they looked familiar. When she was up on stage, she definitely noticed people and a few faces still stuck with her. A tween girl with tears in her eyes who looked to be there with her older brother singing every single lyric from the fourth row. A group of five women who had to be her mother's age wearing halter tops and getting sloppy drunk. They laughed maniacally at everything, and it was contagious.

And she especially remembered the weird ones. The guy who kept staring at her and flicking his tongue between his lips whenever her eyes landed on his side of the audience, or the couple she thought looked adorable swaying in each other's arms until she noticed that the guy's hand was down the front of his girlfriend's pants. She needed to get over her fear of making personal videos on her social media channels because stories like that had a good shot of going mini viral.

"I've been to two of your live shows. The one here in Calgary and then the one in Victoria," the girl with the toque said.

Delia beamed. "You travelled all the way out there?"

She shook her head. "No, I was visiting my parents. So yes, road tripped, but the show was a happy coincidence."

"Well, I'm honoured regardless." Delia motioned for Mary to pull out her phone. "Should we get some pics?"

The girls squealed with delight as Delia joined their group, and Mary started snapping shots. They passed over their phones and had her take a few more, then they all grabbed a few selfies.

"You're the literal best!" The blonde girl with messy buns stared at the photos on her phone.

Warmth bubbled up in Delia's chest. At home or before a show, she'd sit in front of a mirror and worry about whether her hair was too flat or her makeup washed her out. She'd agonize over the right outfit for a show and fret over how her mouth looked when she sang certain vowels. But when she was with her fans, she didn't think twice about what she looked like in her photos. It was easier not to care when she wasn't the only one standing in the spotlight.

When they finished, Delia waved and told them to enjoy the show while Mary reminded them to tag Delia's account in their posts, and the two of them jogged back to the rear entrance. They didn't waste any time in the green room. It was cramped and smelled faintly of wet cement, but the staff had stocked it with almonds, herbal tea, and freshly sliced lemons. She wasn't one to eat before a show—her stomach got tied up in knots, and she'd found it was better to stuff herself after a set so as not to Barden Bellas it on the first row. Not that she'd ever actually thrown up, but she'd come too close for comfort after eating a BLTA once. That moment still scarred her.

"Jack's ticket is waiting at Will Call," Mary started as Delia clipped in her in-ear receiver battery pack on stage.

"Mmhmm." She shielded her eyes from the glare of the lights, peering toward the sound booth to ensure she didn't miss the thumbs up for their sound check. Stagehands wrangled cords and equipment behind her, clearing out instruments and amps they wouldn't need.

"Are you nervous?"

Delia shot Mary a look. "If I were, would talking about it help?"

Mary held up a hand. "Hey, I just didn't want to sweep this whole thing under the rug. You get in your head about these things."

Delia scoffed. "These things? Like meeting a fake boyfriend is a regular occurrence?" The sound guy raised a hand, and she nodded, then began to pluck out a simple G-D-C-G chord progression on her guitar.

Mary planted her hands on her hips. "Don't pretend you aren't weird when it comes to guys."

Delia shook her head, then sang her next sentence to the melody of Mary Had a Little Lamb. "This is not a normal guy, normal guy, normal guy, this is not a normal guy, it's a business transaction."

"Now you just sound like a prostitute."

Delia grinned. "Or maybe he's the prostitute, prostitute, pros—"

"That's going to end up on TikTok, you know that, right?"

Delia laughed, sending her mic into a feedback fit. "Sorry!" She waved to the booth and cleared her throat, then started in on the chorus of Shiny People. She was a professional. She could complete a soundcheck properly.

Mary stepped off to the side so she wouldn't be a distraction, and after one verse of Dame Tartine, the song her mother always hummed around their apartment, the sound guy gave another thumbs up. Mary swooped in to put her guitar on the stand while she took out her earpiece.

They worked with the stagehands to get the piano placed where she wanted it, then met with the venue owner, who effusively praised her and shared his immense gratitude that she liked the Jukebox enough to return within a calendar year. Delia did like the Jukebox. She was sure that was why Tony had booked it because it definitely wasn't up to his standard of playability.

The Jukebox didn't have a website and only sold tickets at the door. They opened two hours before the live music started for the night and sold greasy bar food and craft cocktails. The drinks were good, or so she'd been told, and the food even better, if you were in the mood for heartburn and middle-of-the-night gastrointestinal distress.

Delia remembered the good 'ol days when she'd play a show then step off the stage and join her friends at the bar for hours afterward, since they were the only people who showed up to see her play. She'd never complain about her increased popularity, but it was a little anticlimactic going back to the green room with her ears buzzing and eyes mildly blinded to sit with Mary and drink Chamomile tea. Who was she kidding though? She loved that post-show routine.

"Ear pieces, Dels."

"Hmm?"

Mary spun her around and turned the switch to her receivers off. "What were you thinking about this time?"

"How I'm emotionally conflicted about what I do after shows."

Mary laughed. "You didn't take your medication?"

Delia shook her head as she set her guitar on the stand and walked into the wings. "I didn't want to feel more anxious on the plane."

"Understandable."

They descended the stairs and flopped onto the couches. They still had two hours, and Delia was about to suggest they take a nap when the green room door burst open.

Tony waltzed in with Kels on his heels. "I know you were all wondering where we were . . ." He taunted them with a garment bag on a hanger.

Mary smirked. "Tony, we agreed that you were going to pick up Delia's outfit. Neither of us was wondering."

"But you didn't know I was also getting a surprise." Tony hung the bag on the clothing rack against the wall and unzipped the protective cover. Delia had brought her burgundy high-waisted, wide-leg trousers that, when she wore them with her leather platform boots, made her look leggy and well beyond her five-foot-seven height. She would've just worn them here instead of packing them separately, but they tended to get creases through the crotch when she sat for too long in them.

Tony pulled out a vintage-inspired, flowy blouse with a delicate floral print that coordinated perfectly. That wasn't the surprise. Mary had found it on a local boutique's website, but even though she'd seen it online, it was better in person. Delia stepped forward and fingered the gauzy fabric.

"Voila." Tony pulled out a gorgeous tan suede jacket. "I couldn't leave this sitting in the window display. It was begging for you to wear it."

Delia's eyes lit up. She took the jacket from him, and it practically melted in her hands. So smooth and supple, she wasn't sure if she should put it on or cuddle up with it. "It's gorgeous. How much did this cost?"

Tony waved her off with a look that said, *It doesn't matter for something that good,* but it did matter to Delia. Any show expenses meant less take home, and she wanted to squeeze these shows for all they were worth.

Since she didn't want to crush Tony's kind gesture, she put on the jacket and smiled at herself in the mirror. It hit perfectly at her waist, and the sleeves looked like they'd been tailored to hit her wrists. It was stunning. "I'm a little disturbed at how well you know my size."

Tony laughed. "That was Kels. I don't keep track of measurements."

Delia gave them each a quick hug. "Thank you. I love it."

"Hot," Mary agreed.

Delia shrugged off the jacket and handed it back to Tony. It was pretty enough, she was tempted to wear it post-show, but she already had a particular outfit for that. Crew neck, black long-sleeve cotton shirt and straight-leg jeans. Nothing primpy or flirty. Plain. Professional. She couldn't let a pretty blouse and butter jacket knock her off course for the evening.

Delia mentally ran through her pre-show routine. An hour before showtime, she'd put on her blouse and start doing her makeup while Mary curled her hair. Then, thirty minutes before, they'd do a meditation along with stretches and a vocal warm-up. At fifteen minutes to, she'd put on the rest of her outfit, including her show jewelry, a gold locket from her mother and simple gold hoops, then Mary would do a last look, and they'd head to the wings to catch the end of the warm-up band. Tonight, it was a country singer who had gained popularity after performing at the Youth Talent Showdown at the Stampede the previous summer.

Having Tony there was an anomaly but a welcome one. His stories always made the time fly by. This time, he regaled them with a tale about a woman who tried to use a clipped coupon at the register of the boutique. *"It wasn't even for the same store!"* Then he showed them pictures of the line down the street and wrapping around the corner for the show. By the time Kels finished with how they didn't know they'd parked in a staff space until a homeless guy yelled at them for taking "Pete's spot," it was time to get moving.

Delia turned on her playlist, and she and Mary got to work. She applied foundation and bronzer, then blush and a smoky eyeliner. She darkened her eyebrows and applied the only lip stain she'd found that didn't make her feel like she was wearing a mud mask halfway through her set. For all her normal anxieties, this part was seamless. It felt like being strapped into a roller coaster—she knew the process and the eventual walk on stage was inevitable. The ride was going to start, and she could either be ready for it or get whiplash.

Tony and Kels left before they started their meditation, stating he was going to wait for Jack and make sure he found their reserved table. The Jukebox had a broad dance floor that was standing room only, but raised up around the periphery of the room were high-top tables and chairs. It was first-come first-served, and those spots were coveted. She hoped their selfie friends staking out the box office were smart enough to snag one when the doors opened.

Before Delia knew it, she was standing in her maroon trousers, the floral blouse, and suede jacket in the wings, listening to a woman sing her rendition of *I've Got Friends in Low Places*. She had a decent voice, even if it was a bit twangy for Delia's taste.

As the final chords resolved, her heart picked up speed. No matter how many times she prepared herself for this, her insides flipped like she was about to dive headlong off the edge of a cliff. It was a love-hate relationship. She adored filling any venue with music. Hated that initial step on stage, especially on nights like this when she was walking into the spotlight alone.

Strapped in, Delia reminded herself. She placed her earpiece as Mary flipped up her shirt to ensure the receiver for her in-ear monitors still had full battery strength.

The warm-up act thanked the crowd, then shouted, "Who's

ready to hear Delia Melise?" The cheers and applause were deafening even there in the wings. Mary rubbed Delia's shoulders.

Delia clenched and unclenched her fists, whispered a silent prayer, then took that dreaded first step into the light. She smiled and waved, scanning the shadowed, faceless blobs in the crowd until her eyes adjusted. She pulled her guitar off the stand and slipped her head under the strap, then plugged in the cord connecting it to the amp.

"How are you tonight?" she asked, getting another roar in response. "Can we raise the house lights a bit? I'd love to see your faces before we start." The cheers grew louder as the lighting crew did as she asked. People lifted their drinks into the air, and she spotted the two girls they'd met out front earlier. She winked, and Messy Bun Girl's face went slack.

Then Delia found Tony and her heart skipped a beat. Kels sat next to him and—

Nobody.

There was nobody else sitting at the table with them.

JACK PARKED NEARLY five blocks from the Jukebox after circling around the area twice. He'd been there once before to watch a band Clara was into when he first moved back to Calgary, but it hadn't been even close to that packed.

He waited for Clara to hop down from the passenger seat, then locked the Chevy and shoved his door closed. The icy air stung his cheeks. March in Calgary meant the weather had a perpetual mood disorder. Earlier that week, it had been nearly fifteen degrees, and now they were back at minus twenty with a bonus biting wind that had kicked up on the drive over. Jack pulled up his collar and buried his hands in the pockets of his heavy coat.

For the first time in months he'd put thought into what he was going to wear. Clara had insisted he don a Henley. She said buttons made a shirt look way more upscale than a plain tee, and though that made zero sense to him, he'd trusted her. She'd approved of his decision to pair the dark blue shirt with a pair of natural wash jeans, but then balked at his choice of shoes. *"Slip-ons or loafers, no laces please."*

When she found the pair of burgundy slip-on Vans in his closet, she looked physically pained that she'd never seen them on his feet before. They were an inside joke between him and a few friends in Toronto after he found them on clearance for fifteen dollars. Otherwise, he would've donated them years ago. Clara said they were perfect, and now here he was, walking down the frozen sidewalk in clown shoes.

"I can't believe we're doing this!" Clara fell into step next to him, burying the bottom half of her face behind her coat collar.

"I love how you're pretending we're in this together."

Clara scoffed. "We *are* in this together. I've got your back."

If she meant *a hand on the back shoving him toward Delia so she could meet her pop idol*, then yes. That statement was true. Jack winced as Clara bumped into his arm, pressing his newly tattooed skin against the rough hem of his coat.

"Sorry. I keep forgetting you're delicate right now." Clara moved further to the left. "Is it doing okay?"

Jack nodded. "It's great. I just have to be careful with it for the next few days."

"It's going to scab, right? Peel?"

"This one was small, so it won't be too bad." He'd gotten the Blizzard logo in silver and blue that morning, and Brett was one-hundred-percent correct. It hurt like hell on that sensitive skin on the inside of his arm. But the burn had been worth it. He'd waited twenty-nine years to fill that spot. Now the ink was permanent. He only needed to make the ink on his contract match.

Downtown Calgary buzzed with activity despite the hour. People wrapped in layers, scarves, and toques moved between restaurants and bars, their breath creating transient clouds in the air.

Jack kept his head down. In the dark, it was less likely that anyone would recognize him, but the frequency of people asking him for photos or autographs lately made him twitchy. He'd never considered himself an introvert, but he'd found himself seeking out alone time more in the past three weeks than ever in his life.

The neon sign for the Jukebox buzzed ahead and the windows were already steamed up. As he approached Will Call, a large "Sold Out" sign was posted on the glass. The woman in the booth shoved a bite of poutine into her mouth with a fork, then reached for a napkin and hurried back to her stool.

Jack nodded. "Hey, I'm here to pick up two tickets."

She scanned his face, gave Clara a passing glance, and didn't even ask for his name before handing him the tickets. "They didn't think you were going to show."

He thanked her, then pushed through the glass doors to an instant immersion of his senses. The heat and humidity, the smell of fries and chicken wings, the sound of loud conversation humming under the strains of a guitar, but floating above every-thing else was *that voice.* He'd heard Delia sing countless times on the radio, but now that version of it seemed like an echo. Her voice drifted through the entry, lilting with ethereal dexterity, so clear and pure he shivered.

Clara grabbed onto Jack's arm as he wove through the crowd, fighting upstream until they were past the bar and in the main ballroom. They nestled into a corner behind the ring of tables surrounding the large dance floor.

And there she was.

Standing on stage with her guitar, her auburn waves brushing her shoulders as she strummed. She was taller than he'd expected, which didn't make any sense because he'd never once thought about how tall Delia Melise was. She wore a soft blouse and pants that were . . . Jack smirked. They were almost the exact same colour as his shoes.

"She has good taste," Clara called to him, winking.

"Excuse me, are you—?" A woman with chunky black glasses slid off her stool, peering closer at him. "Holy shit, you *are* Jack Harrison, aren't you?" He nodded, hoping nobody else had heard the woman over the music. "Can I get a selfie?"

He nodded again, but didn't put his arm around her as she leaned in close and snapped a photo. It was beyond awkward.

Where was he supposed to put his hands? One time he'd tried to look friendly by putting a hand on a woman's back, but she'd unexpectedly turned and he'd nearly felt her up. Now he kept his hands at his sides and tried not to look like a robot.

"Jack!" a voice called out, and he turned as the woman wobbled back to her table. A man in a crisp button-up shirt and hair like the models in a "Top 100 Men's Haircuts" magazine pushed through the crowd toward him, smiling apologetically. Jack frowned. He had no idea who the man was but had a sinking suspicion he was supposed to. *Could he be someone from the Blizzard administration? A journalist he'd spoken to?*

The man stopped in front of him. "Damn, this place is packed tighter than a can of sardines." He straightened his sleeves and held out a hand. "I'm Tony. Sorry I didn't find you sooner, we were expecting you about forty minutes ago."

The pieces clicked into place. *Tony.* The publicist he'd talked with on the phone who'd set this whole thing up. Jack's heart picked up speed as the crowd erupted around him.

This was real. He was here watching Delia Melise perform and talking to her publicist who wanted them to pretend get together. *What the hell had he been thinking agreeing to this?*

"Is this your sister?" Tony leaned in and put out a hand.

"Hi, I'm Clara!" Her voice was barely audible over the audience singing along with Delia's lyrics. Tony motioned for them to follow. He guided them to a table where a man sat nursing a beer. "This is my assistant, Kels." He was wearing a T-shirt and vest with artistically messy hair. Apparently, he didn't get the Henley memo.

Jack and Clara shook his hand, then took the seats opposite him.

Tony motioned for a server who looked more frazzled than a Co-op employee after a Blizzard home win. "What are you drinking tonight, Jack? Clara?"

"Whatever he's having." Jack pointed at the beer across the table.

"Just soda water, cranberry, and lime for me," Clara said.

The server nodded and whisked back into the crowd. Jack turned to the stage. Delia had started another song with a chorus he recognized, but he still felt a little like he'd shown up to take a provincial exam without cracking a book. Everyone around him, including Clara, was riveted, chanting every word.

Tony leaned in. "She's something else, isn't she?"

Jack nodded, not sure what he was supposed to say to that. Would it be better for him to make it clear that he was totally uninterested so her team wouldn't worry he was going to try something skeezy? Or would that come off as pompous, considering any hetero guy with a pulse witnessing this would consider the possibilities?

Delia was the definition of attractive, her feminine curves on full display as she curled around her guitar. It wasn't so much her particular features but how she moved—the way her arm flexed as she strummed, how her brow furrowed as her glossy lips shaped each syllable, how her collarbone cast shadows in the stage lights. *Did he finally understand why women threw their bras at heroine-addict-looking rock stars?*

He settled on, "I don't go to concerts often. This is impressive." Compliment her skills and ability to bring in a crowd. That had to be safe.

When the server brought their drinks, he tried to relax and enjoy the show, but his head wouldn't stop spinning. It felt all kinds of wrong to be ogling a woman he'd never met but was hoping to for monetary gain.

When he'd expressed his concerns to Clara and Oscar, they'd related it to any other business deal. *"Would you feel weird about going to a meeting with SportChek? If you were hoping for them to carry your brand and make your company money, would it be wrong to meet and sign a contract?"* Clara asked.

He'd argued that he wouldn't have to wine and dine anyone to seal the deal, and Clara said he better not ruin anything for her. So now he was here. Watching Delia Melise in person and trying not to sweat through his shirt.

"Your shoulders aren't supposed to be earrings." Clara put a hand on his arm. Jack drew a deep breath and held it. "What are you so nervous about?"

He leaned in. "You know what I'm nervous about."

"No, I don't, actually, because this isn't a real date."

Jack opened his mouth, but Clara scooted closer and continued. "Yes, I get that she's a woman, Jack, and I'm not trying to minimize what happened with Angie. I know you're still hurting, and I wish I could take that away. You have no idea."

Jack shifted in his seat, nodding in the hope that anyone watching them—specifically Tony and his assistant—would assume they were talking about a meeting tomorrow or family drama. Anything but his inability to jump back into dating after losing the love of his life.

"You don't know what this contract will entail," Clara continued. "If you hate it, you can say no."

"Only after you meet Delia, though."

"Obviously." Clara patted his arm, then leaned over the table and sipped her pink non-cocktail. Jack eyed her suspiciously. Clara had never been a big drinker, but he hadn't seen her take a sip of alcohol for months. Was it possible—?

The crowd erupted around them, and Jack straightened and clapped. Clara whistled next to him, fangirling with the best of them.

Delia grinned and looked out over the crowd. Jack was in the middle of ruminating on how much she could actually see into the dark when the lights dimmed from bright white to soft purple, and her eyes landed on him. Her smile slipped a bit at the corners, and her quick intake of breath was visible. As quickly as it happened, the moment passed, and Delia was pulling a stool up to the mic. She sat and lowered her mic stand, then propped her guitar on her thigh. "Thank you for coming out last minute, it's been a joy playing for you. I've got one more song for you, Calgary."

More cheers mingled with "We love you Delia!" and various song requests built to a low roar then silenced in seconds as Delia started to strum. Jack knew nothing about music, but the melancholy chords instantly drew him in. They reminded him of the jazz albums his mom used to play on Sunday mornings.

"Interesting choice," Tony murmured.

Clara sighed, folding her arms over the table. "I love this song. Does she not normally play it?"

Tony shook his head. "I've never heard her play it live."

Clara leaned into Jack. "This isn't on her album. It's from her TikTok channel. Before she got signed."

"You have a TikTok account?" Jack eyed her skeptically.

"'Kay, I'm not that much older than you, so don't look at me like I'm Mum or something. Though I think she has one, too. She wanted to watch the Pro Dance-off highlights and hates doing it on—" Clara held up a hand, cutting herself off as she turned mesmerized to the stage.

Delia started singing. She began in French, then switched to English with the words, *I've never been one to reach for the stars because flying has never felt safe.* Jack had never been one to listen to lyrics. He wanted beats that made his adrenaline spike. Rhythms that matched his reps. But at that moment, the room seemed to shrink until everything was blurred at the edges. It was just him sitting at that table with Delia in front of him, holding her guitar at the mic.

"They say it's a door only I can open, but I don't want to let out the heat." Her voice was nimble. Like it barely touched each note before floating on to the next. Jack's breathing quickened. The lights glinted off her hair, the shimmer in her eyes, the polished wood of her guitar. Every sentence struck deeper, breaking into a shell he wasn't aware he'd built inside himself. Memory seeped like molasses through the cracks.

· · ·

"Jack?"

"Hey, Melanie. What's up?" He'd only ever gotten a call from Angie's mother twice in the time they'd been together. Once about a surprise birthday party for Angie's twenty-fifth and once because she had a snake in the yard and didn't know how to phone the fire department.

Melanie's voice shook. Her breath hiccupped. "There was an accident. Angie was—she's gone, Jack."

Jack sat up, gripping the phone tighter against his cheek. "Who's gone?" Dread slid down his throat like sour wine and ate at the inside of his stomach.

"There was an accident. She was driving over to drop off the ladder she'd borrowed from the garage, and when she didn't show up—"

"Slow down, Melanie. Angie was driving over?"

A sob punched through the speaker. "Yes, she was driving over to return the ladder, and I had chocolate lava cakes ready on the counter, and when she didn't show up, I phoned her, but it went straight to voicemail. We waited for another hour and still didn't hear anything, so then I phoned the non-emergent line like you showed me and—"

Her voice had snagged then, and she broke into rough, guttural weeping. That's when he knew. Even though she said the words, it was only then that he understood what his fiancée's mother was trying to tell him. Angie was dead, and even after three years, that wound still festered. It had hurt to be traded from the Admirals to a different AHL team, but living in Calgary was a breath of fresh air.

Jack looked around, searching for an easy exit. He didn't want to feel this—didn't want to remember this—and every word out of Delia's mouth was dredging all of it to the surface. Clara grabbed onto his arm and mouthed, "Just wait for the ending!"

He didn't want to wait for anything. He needed to get out of there, but Clara held on, swaying with her eyes closed. Maybe if he'd talked to his sister about Angie's death, he would've been able to pull his arm away and walk out, but he hadn't. He hadn't talked to anyone about it, really. She and his parents had given him plenty of opportunities, but when he didn't open up, they'd stopped asking.

Clara and Ange had been close. She must've missed her just as much as he did. But then she'd met Oscar and gotten married two summers ago. She'd moved on.

He had not.

Delia continued, "If there's ever a day when I don't see your face, I'll be right here on my knees. Dans le soulagement et le regret, de toi, je n'ai point oubliet."

Jack held his breath, which only made the pressure in his head worse. When they'd entered the venue, it had been filled with chatter, laughter, and clinking glasses. Now, every person, including those squeezed into the foyer near the bar, was silent. Delia's fingers were frozen in the air above her guitar strings as her final strain reverberated through the room.

Finally, she dropped her hand and silenced it, sending a metallic whisper through the amp. The room erupted. The people sitting at tables around them pushed back their stools and jumped to their feet. Clara joined them, shouting, "Wasn't that gorgeous?" in his direction.

Jack grunted, not trusting himself to open his mouth. He didn't understand half the words of the song, but it had shifted him on his axis. He didn't need to know the lyrics to feel the grief. The longing. That sank into his bones like vinegar.

Clara turned, and Jack was about to beeline for the washrooms in the back corner when Tony clapped a hand on his shoulder. "This way."

Tony strode ahead, expecting Jack and Clara to follow him and his assistant. Clara's eyes grew wide with excitement, looking like she was five years old and about to meet Santa Claus for the first time. He couldn't back out now.

Pull it together. Jack clenched his hands into fists and gritted his teeth, forcing air into his lungs as he started walking. They wove through the still cheering crowd, who were probably hoping Delia would come out and do an encore. *Would she do an encore?* He hadn't been to enough concerts to know whether that was still a thing.

Tony nodded to the security guard standing at an unmarked door down a narrow hall past the staff entrances. They walked down an only slightly murderous-looking hallway. Clara leaned in and whispered, "Where do you think they'll hide our bodies?" when they reached the landing. And comments like that made him positive neither of them were adopted.

They reached the basement that smelled of damp garage floor mixed with stale cigar smoke. Tony knocked on a door painted half teal and half coral as if someone couldn't decide between bubblegum and cotton-candy sponge paint. The door swung open, and a woman with hair like Jennifer Anniston in the nineties stood in front of them. Jack's heart sank. He hadn't realized he'd been hoping for that face to be Delia's until it wasn't.

"Couldn't wait for her to mop up her sweat first?" The woman raised an eyebrow.

Tony laughed. "Jack, Clara, this is Mary. Delia's manager."

"I like to lead with the title of best friend." Mary held out a hand, and Clara's hand shot up first. After Jack shook her hand, Mary stepped back to let them into the room.

Delia sat directly ahead, seated on a stool across the room, leaning close to a mirror. She looked up, and her reflected eyes stopped on him just as they had in the ballroom. Now that he was closer, he could make out more details. The lights surrounding the mirror washed out her already fair skin, but she had light freckles across her nose. Her irises seemed to be three different colours—rings inside of rings—and her hair was less red than it had appeared on stage.

Tony nudged his elbow. "Jack? Would you like to take a seat?"

CHAPTER
Six

DELIA DROPPED her gaze from the mirror and grabbed a make-up wipe from the half-empty pouch to clean off her lipstick. She swivelled away from the tall, dark, and handsome man standing in her green room doorway and swiped her lips.

This had to be the most awkward experience of her life. Worse than the time a singing telegram showed up in her office and performed for her alone—dressed as a sexy Mountie—while the accounting team waited with a very confused Barb, the actual birthday girl, in the boardroom on the next floor up.

"Incredible show as always." Tony pulled a stool from the opposite wall and set it on the other side of the low coffee table for his assistant, then grabbed one for himself.

Delia turned from the mirror before she rubbed her skin raw. "Thanks."

"When did you start playing 'Oubliet' live again?" Tony asked.

She tensed. Why *had* she played "Oubliet"? It definitely hadn't been an intentional choice. She'd planned on ending with "Trial" like she usually did. It was high energy and one of her top-streamed singles, but tonight . . .

Delia stole a glance at Jack who sat next to a woman with

dark hair pulled into a low bun. They were obviously siblings, with the same dark eyes and features, but Jack had a stronger jaw and a deeper furrow to his brows. She wondered if their noses used to be the same before hockey.

Why was she looking at Jack? Right. Because something she'd seen in his expression had made her change the song. *What had she seen there?* Delia forced her gaze back to Tony and Kels. "You're not going to pass that on, are you?"

Tony shot her a look. "I'm not a nark, but I don't have to be. You know a hundred people recorded that performance and are already posting to their TikTok accounts."

Delia pursed her lips, and Mary jumped in. "IndieLake knows you built a following on those old songs. Christian has never said you couldn't play your personal stuff."

"You wrote that?" Jack's voice was low, but not a full bass. More in a baritone register with a bit of fray around the edges. She loved a raspy voice. There was a TikToker, Ethan Hayes, from Calgary that had popped up on her feed a few weeks ago who sounded like a mix of Teddy Swims and Brian Adams. She was still working up the courage to message him and see if he wanted to collaborate. Of course, that would be a lot easier if IndieLake was open to any of her own music instead of purchasing songs from other writers.

Delia looked up. Jack was watching her. *What was the question again?* Right. He'd asked if she'd written "Oubliet." She nodded. "It was one of my first."

Jack's eyes stayed locked on hers, and just when she thought he was going to open his mouth, Tony cut in. "This is Jack Harrison and his sister Clara . . ."

"Renault." Clara gave a small wave.

Delia tried to keep her lips from twitching. *Was she smiling normally?* "Nice to meet you."

Mary coughed next to her, and Delia was ninety-nine percent sure she was covering a laugh. If she'd been in Mary's position, she sure as hell would've been laughing. How ridiculous was this? To be checking out a fake hockey player boyfriend with her publicist and manager along with his sister?

Dread dropped in her stomach. Jack knew it was fake, didn't he? *Did Clara?* Her eyes darted to Tony, as if he could read her mind and answer her. *What had he said about his conversation with Jack?* Her memory was a blur, and she couldn't remember his exact words.

Clara shifted on the couch. "Why haven't you recorded that song? It was a total showstopper tonight. One of my personal favourites, for sure."

Delia's chest warmed. If it was one of her favourites, she must have known her music before IndieLake. That or gone down her TikTok rabbit hole after the fact. "Maybe someday it'll be recorded. Right now I'm focused on finishing up a new album," Delia answered, noting the look of approval from Tony.

She gave him a *See? I'm trying to be diplomatic* grin. He knew her well enough at that point to predict what she wanted to say instead. Something like, *My contract screwed me out of any creative control over my music* or *My label doesn't give a rat's ass whether I like the songs I'm producing as long as it makes them money.* Something like that.

Tony slapped his hands down on his thighs. "Well, I really appreciate you coming down, Jack. Do either of you want tea or —Delia, why don't you have any snacks in here?"

Mary pointed to the counter. "There are almonds."

Kels frowned. "No Tim's or pizza or something?"

Mary laughed. "Since when does she eat donuts and pizza?"

"Since when do we have guests in the green room?" Tony turned back to Clara and Jack. "Sorry, apparently we only have squirrel food and tea."

Jack reached out and pulled a bottled water from the basket on the table. "This is perfect for me."

His shirt sleeve pulled up on his arm revealing a swirl of black ink. *Interesting.* It didn't look like a small tattoo, and Delia instantly wanted details. What was it? How far did it go up his arm? How long ago did he get it? When someone committed to a permanent mark on their skin, it usually had a story. And Delia loved stories.

Jack pulled up his sleeve a little higher before unscrewing the cap, and Delia realized she'd been staring. She tore her eyes away, but not before she noticed the side of Jack's mouth curl up. *It was too hot in here.* She needed fresh air after performing in that hot box upstairs and then sitting with five other people in a space barely bigger than a basement bedroom.

"Here." Mary grabbed a portable fan from the counter and plugged it in, then turned it toward Delia's face. How did she always know?

"Thank you," Delia murmured and reached for a bag of squirrel food. She wasn't going to eat it, but at least then she had something to hold.

Tony hunched and grabbed a tablet from the bag sitting next to him on the floor. "Alright, then—" He started, then froze and looked between Jack and Clara. "Did you want your sister to be here for this?"

"For—" Jack glanced down at the tablet. "Oh, right. Umm, yeah. That's fine. She can be my lawyer."

Clara's eyes widened, and Mary asked, "Wait, *are* you a lawyer?"

Clara laughed. "Only if you count watching *Better Call Saul* on slow shifts. I'm a nurse." She shifted on the couch. "I kind of forced Jack to bring me. I love your music, Delia, and couldn't believe he was going to get to meet you when he didn't even know who—" She stopped mid sentence and back pedalled. "I didn't mean—of course he knew who you were, but—"

Jack's face was turning red, and Delia didn't know whether to be amused or jealous. When she blushed, her face went splotchy like she was about to break out in hives. Jack's skin was bronze and even, and when blood rushed to his cheeks, it only made him look . . . hot. *Very hot.* Possibly bothered. Especially when he reached up and rubbed his neck and—

"I did know who you were," he clarified. Jack looked up, and Delia's heart stuttered.

She waved him off, pretending she'd been thinking *at all* about what Clara had said. "It's fine, I don't expect everyone to be fans."

"It's not that I don't like—"

"It's seriously fine." Now Delia's cheeks were on fire with him watching her, and she planted her face in front of the fan.

"Sorry," Clara groaned. "I only meant to say that I'm a massive fan, and it's impossible for Jack to match that energy. I wanted to meet you, but I don't have to stay for—"

"Clara, you're staying." Jack set his water bottle on the table, then motioned for Tony to continue.

Mary shot Delia a look that said, *This is already the highlight of my day.* Delia mouthed, *"I hate you,"* and Mary's grin grew even wider.

Tony flipped open the case on his tablet. "Okay, then. I've got a contract right here for both of you to look over."

"A contract?" Jack cut in. His hands were on his knees, his knuckles white.

"Right, we can make any changes the two of you want, it's just the safe way to do things. Make sure everyone knows what they're signing up for."

Delia's palms started to sweat. *Public Displays of Affection.* She didn't even know this guy, besides the fact that he had a tattoo, a story behind his eyes, and a decent relationship with his sister.

But . . . what was the difference between this and meeting with a writer or producer in a booth for the first time and being expected to pour out her soul through vocals? At least with Jack she wouldn't have to open up anything other than her hand and her wallet.

Jack nodded. "No, I understand that, it's just—" He paused, his brow furrowing. "I guess I thought there would be more . . . I don't know. Time."

"Time?" Tony repeated.

"Right." He glanced at his sister, then looked up, fixing his gaze on Delia. "I'm sorry, but I don't think I can do this. The concert was . . ." He didn't finish his sentence, and something bubbled up in Delia's chest. *The concert was what?*

She was suddenly desperate to know the words he would've chosen to describe her performance as a revealed non-fan. After her first single hit big, all she heard from her team of producers was how ground-breaking her music was. Delia wanted to believe them, but zero part of her could. Adding French lyrics to repetitive pop songs didn't constitute trailblazing. If she hadn't seen her mother's French birth certificate, she would've accused herself of cultural appropriation.

Jack stood, straightened his shirt, and moved toward the door. So many questions she wouldn't get the answer to. So many stories she was already hoping to hear. But that wasn't why Delia panicked and jumped from her stool.

"Why not?" she asked. Delia's mother had just started her night shift. She didn't like the idea of a publicity stunt any more than Jack did, but ever since Tony brought it up, she couldn't deny its brilliance. Celebrity couples were making waves everywhere. Mary had shown her an article the other day that estimated a five-hundred-percent increase in streams and record sales for female singers and songwriters who dated famous athletes. Especially if they were beloved or intensely controversial, and Jack was both of those things. Tony could probably find someone else to fit the bill, but they wouldn't be as hot of a commodity as Jack. And Delia needed to earn out that advance.

Jack stopped in front of the door. His shoulders were tight under his cotton shirt, his coat looped over his arm. "I just can't."

Again with the unfinished thoughts. That time, Delia's mind went straight to her own jugular. *He hated the concert. He'd been game over the phone, but now that he saw her in person, he was underwhelmed.* Every shit date she'd gone on over the past year and a half coagulated into a wrecking ball that swung and hit her square in the chest. *She hadn't been exciting enough on her own, and now she couldn't even pay a guy to pretend to date her?*

Delia clenched her hands into fists as her cheeks flamed. "Am I not good enough for you? Not enough of the skinny, hot cheerleader type?"

Mary stepped forward. "Delia—"

"No, I want to hear what he thinks. If he's going to walk out that door and spread the word that Delia Melise wanted him and he turned her down, I want to at least be privy to his reasoning before it hits the tabloids."

"I signed a non-disclosure." Jack's eyes were dark as he turned to face her.

There it was again. That flicker she'd seen in the ballroom. Delia stared him down. "Well, *thank you* for that."

"I've got a lot on my plate," he said crisply.

"What, playing a game? This would require next to zero effort and it would benefit both of us." Delia folded her arms over her chest.

Jack's eyes hardened. "Unlike you, my career isn't exactly solidified at the moment. I need to focus."

"If the Blizzard want to sign you for another year, this kind of publicity would give you leverage for your pay scale," Tony interjected.

"If I'm distracted and don't play well, I won't get signed."

Kels adjusted his glasses. "The data shows that having a new girlfriend present at a game can improve your stats by nearly thirty percent."

Jack raised an eyebrow. "How's the data on fake girlfriends?" Kels pursed his lips, and Jack exhaled as he turned back to Delia. "It's not personal—"

"Then what is it?" she asked, and this time Mary put her hand on her arm.

"Dels—"

"I feel like a gigolo," Jack snapped.

"But there's not even any sex!" Delia reached for the tablet and held it out to him.

The corner of Jack's mouth quirked. "You sound disappointed."

Delia hive-flushed. "No, I didn't mean it like that. I just meant . . . you don't have to do anything you don't want to."

"Right, which is why I'm walking out."

"Because you don't want to meet up with someone at regular intervals for money?" She heard it then. "Okay, I get that it doesn't sound good, but—"

"Not someone. You." Jack clenched his jaw.

Delia slapped a hand to her hip. "I thought you said it wasn't personal."

"Just clarifying."

She chewed on her lower lip. *What were they even arguing about at that point?* "It's basically the same as you getting paid to play a hockey game. We meet up, play a game, and we both get paid. Probably less physical contact than the NHL, actually."

"A lot more lying."

"You don't have to lie." Delia scrolled to the paragraph under media appearances and turned the screen to him.

When asked about the relationship in interviews, both parties agree to provide affirmative but vague responses that confirm their relationship without delving into details.

Jack scanned the text then looked up. The top of the tablet was touching her chest and the bottom was nearly pressed against his. *When had she gotten that close?*

He stared at her. Hard. Delia hated prolonged eye contact, but she couldn't force herself to look away. Jack finally broke. "Why do you care? Couldn't you find some other hockey player?"

"Not one who people are obsessed with." Delia swallowed

hard. "Not one who was willing to come here even though he didn't want to just so his sister could meet me."

Jack laughed through his nose. "You think that makes me a nice person?"

"I hope it makes you not a psychopath."

Jack gave a pointed look in Tony's direction, and Delia didn't have the mental energy to parse that out. She was exhausted. Bone-deep tired after waking up early, holding herself together on the flight, then doing the show.

She wobbled a bit on her feet and tried to bite back the words pouring onto her tongue, but couldn't. "I care because I bought a house for myself and my mom. I used my advance to pay off some of her debt, but she's sick, and the answer isn't in better medical care, it's in lowering her life stress, which means she needs to not be working. That means I need to sell enough to be in the black. I've busted my ass releasing new music, and if Tony thinks being seen with Jack Harrison will push me over the edge, then I'm in."

Delia took a step back, but before she could hand the tablet back to Kels, Jack took it from her. There were those eyes again. That furrowed brow. Finally he dropped his gaze to the screen and swiped.

"I'm going to need to read this."

Tony ran a hand over his face. "We're all leaving on a flight first thing in the morning, so—"

"I'm not saying I need a week," Jack murmured.

"All I know is that I need food." Mary pouted.

Tony looked between the two of them. "Can I recommend you look that over at the restaurant on the corner?"

Delia shook her head. "Tony, you know what's going to happen. We're going to get there and—"

"Already taking care of that." Tony pointed to Kels who was now holding his phone to his ear. "You know you're not the only one in this group who gets swarmed in Calgary, eh?"

Delia looked at Jack who still had his hand on the door handle. He shrugged. "I'm not used to it yet, that's for damn sure."

CHAPTER
Seven

JACK HAD BARELY STEPPED onto the street when Clara grabbed the sleeve of his coat. "I'm *not* going to dinner with you and Delia!"

"It's not 'going to dinner.' I just want to talk for a minute to see if this is even—"

"Yeah, still not coming." Clara dropped his arm, then looked both ways and darted across the street.

"Clara!"

"I'll be in the pub!" She pointed at a sign with a Union Jack and flashed a grin before turning her back on him and heading down the sidewalk on the opposite side of the street.

"Where's she going?" Mary stopped next to him and wrapped a scarf around her neck.

Jack blew out a breath, sending a cloud into the air between them. "She didn't want dinner."

Mary laughed. Delia, Tony, and his assistant appeared in the parking lot behind the venue. Delia looked around. "Where's Clara?"

"She went for a pint." Mary linked arms with Delia and followed Tony's assistant to the corner, leaving Jack to walk with the big man himself. Tony was large. Surprisingly so, considering Jack spent most of his time with professional athletes.

"Did you used to play?" Jack asked.

"Hockey?" Tony shook his head. "No, I've got zero coordination. My PE teacher in high school begged me to try out and within ten minutes of seeing me on the ice, he asked if I was actually Canadian."

"Ouch."

"I'm not. I was born in Boston."

Jack laughed. "Don't usually hear of people from Mass coming this direction. Usually the other way around."

"Parents were both from Ontario. My dad was finishing his doctorate at Berklee."

"Isn't that in California?"

"No, the Berklee College of Music."

Jack nodded. "So you came by this line of work honestly."

"Never thought I'd be on the promotional side of things. I always thought I'd be the pop star."

"Still time, bud."

Tony grabbed the door from Kels and held it while Jack walked into the airlock. "You seem like a nice guy Jack."

"Thanks."

"I've met plenty of assholes that seem like nice guys."

Jack paused with his hand on the next door. "Probably something you should've asked about then. Before the contract was drawn up."

Tony's jaw flexed. "I have a job to do, and I'm damn good at it. I'm not her father or anything—"

"But you're now realizing that this could go south if I'm a dick?"

"Exactly."

Jack pulled the door open. "It's a good thing I'm not, then." He strode into the restaurant to heads already turning their direction.

"Isn't that what a dick would say?"

"Probably." Jack followed the waiter to a back room. Mary and Kels took a table in the far corner as the waiter motioned Delia to a two-seater next to the window. His step faltered. He hadn't meant he needed to talk to Delia solo, but now didn't see a way out of it. Jack strode forward and shrugged off his coat then hung it over the back of his chair. Delia did the same but didn't sit.

Jack stood next to the table. "I didn't mean to make this even more awkward."

She breathed a laugh. "And yet somehow you succeeded." Delia looked up, her eyes wide. "I'm sorry. I didn't mean to say that." She looked genuinely repentant.

"I think you *did* mean to say that."

She glanced down at the menu on the table in front of her, and her eyes shifted to the tablet Kels left in Jack's spot. "It was a thought that wasn't supposed to make it into the real world. Normally, I'm crashing on a couch by now. After a show."

Jack nodded. He understood that. In his early twenties, all he wanted to do after a game was party. Even before his increased popularity, staying out late had been a harder sell.

"Do you mind if I—" Delia held up her phone. Jack shook his head and glanced out the window next to the table. He and Delia, though protected from the rest of the diners, were in prime viewing position from the sidewalk. A small group had already stopped to take pictures.

Delia set her phone down. "Sorry. Just needed to text my mom."

Jack felt like a dick for momentarily judging her phone habits. He rapped his knuckles on the back of the chair. "Tony's a genius."

"Why? Because he found a way for us to make headlines without you even signing the contract?" Delia sat, and Jack suddenly wondered what had happened to the outfit she'd worn onstage. All his senses were playing catch up. He'd been so amped up in that dressing room, all he'd seen was her face.

Her expressions. He hadn't even noticed what she was wearing.

"Jack, can you sit down? You're making this awkward," Tony called from the back of the room.

Delia pursed her lips. Jack pulled out his seat and did as he was told.

"I apologize for Tony. He's not exactly sensitive." Delia pulled the menu closer, and Jack noticed her nails were cut short. Her fingers long and slender.

Jack gripped his chair and scooted in. "Has he always been your publicist?"

"Only since I started with IndieLake last summer." She kept her head bowed, scanning each line of the menu like she was going to be tested on it. Based on her flushed skin and panicked breathing back in the room, she didn't enjoy making eye contact, but Jack was dying for her to look up.

"You've only been signed with a label since the summer?" He asked.

Delia nodded and finally lifted her chin, crossing her arms on the table in front of her. "Is that off-putting, Mr. 'I only got signed three weeks ago'?"

Jack grinned as shock flitted over her expression a second time. "Another inside thought?" he asked. She was about to apologize again, but Jack held up a hand. "Just a second."

He inspected her eyes in the softer lighting of the restaurant. In the dressing room, the garish fluorescent bulbs had created strange shadows, and he hadn't gotten a good look at them. Not for lack of trying. They'd captured his interest the second he'd turned from the door and she'd marched up to him brandishing that tablet.

Her irises had a ring of almost fiery red around her pupil that faded into a thin stripe of gold, then bled into pale blue, finally edged by a ring of navy. It was like someone had pressed pause on a kaleidoscope. On top of that, her left eye had two black freckles at ten o'clock. Like drops of midnight ink.

"They're weird. My eyes," Delia's throat was flushing again.

Jack cleared his throat and looked away. "Not weird. They're unique."

Delia scoffed. "That's what my mom used to always tell me. About my eyes, my hair. Everything. Even when I came home from school wearing bright pink tights with snake skin boots and an olive T-shirt—not the color, an actual olive on the front—with my dad's tie to round out the ensemble."

Jack chuckled. "I'm sure it suited you."

A smile played at the corner of Delia's mouth. "It was disgusting. I have pictures to prove it."

"Well. Your eyes aren't disgusting."

Jack had chosen the word "unique" because he didn't think telling Delia that her eyes were stunning or breathtaking was the right play. Though, was it ever a bad idea to give a woman a compliment? It had been so long, he didn't remember the rules.

Jack ran a hand through his hair. "I don't do this often."

"What, gigoloing?"

Jack laughed out loud. "I don't think that's a verb." Delia looked pleased with herself, and his smile slipped. "I meant sitting down at a restaurant with someone. The dating thing in general." The last time he'd eaten out was at One Place, the bar across from the Snowball's practice arena, and within an hour, it'd been swarmed by people looking to get his autograph. He'd left just so the other guys could get appetizers in peace.

Delia raised an eyebrow. "I find that hard to believe."

"I know. I'm funny, charming as hell—Oh wait. You know nothing about me."

Delia shrugged, her shoulders pushing up on her soft waves, compressing them like an accordian. "I meant it was hard to believe because of the whole famous-hockey-player thing." She looked back at her menu, though based on her eye line, he was pretty sure she was staring directly at the kids' meals.

"I've only been famous for three weeks, so I have yet to reap any of the benefits." Jack looked down at the list of entreés, and his attention snagged on the Birria tacos. Then he remembered Clara was waiting for him at the pub down the street.

He slid the tablet over, flipped open the cover, and started to read. He'd told her he needed a minute to look over the contract, so that's what he'd take. Jack skimmed the sections. Number of public appearances. Types of appearances. Documentation of appearances. "You have social media accounts?" he asked.

"I have *all* the social media accounts."

Jack glanced up. "Do I have to get them?"

Delia shook her head. "Not as long as you don't mind me posting pics on mine."

"What kind of pictures?"

Delia pulled out her phone and spun in her seat, then snapped a selfie shot of them at the table. She turned the screen for him to see. "Like that. Not a big deal."

"I look pissed."

Delia deleted the photo. "Then try not looking pissed."

"Perfect. I'll work on that." Jack lowered his voice as their server arrived with an overly broad smile and droplets of sweat forming near his temples. One of the most puzzling things to come out of his newfound celebrity was how hard people had to try to act normal around him. It had to be ten times worse for Delia.

The server put down two glasses of water, both with lemon slices floating amidst the ice cubes.

"Thank you." Delia reached for the glass. "I'm ready to order, if that's okay?"

The server nodded. "Of course. What can I get—get for you?"

Delia didn't even blink as the poor kid's eyes bugged out of his head. "I'd like the Birria tacos, please." Jack gave her a look, and Delia slid her hand up her arm. "What?"

"That's what I was going to order." Never mind that he'd planned not to order and get the contract review over with. What were the chances that from a menu with a hundred different items on it, they'd choose the same thing?

Her lips quirked. "Then I guess we'll get two." She handed the server the menu.

Delia waited for him to walk away. "Did you do that on purpose?"

Jack frowned. "What?"

"You made it seem like we were having a moment."

He leaned back in his chair. "A moment? Ordering tacos?"

Delia dropped her phone in her bag. "You know that's all that waiter is going to be talking about, right? He's going to tell all his server friends some version of how we both accidentally ordered the same thing, and it's going to show up all over the internet."

Jack exhaled. "And that's why I don't go out."

Delia considered him a moment. "This is nice. Better than I thought it would be."

Jack squirmed in his seat. *Nice?* Was he somehow giving her the wrong impression, because—

"I don't even have to pretend around you since this is just business, but not even real business, you know?" Delia smiled up at him. He blinked. "You don't have anything to do with my music, so I don't have to impress you there, and this isn't going anywhere past April, so I don't have to worry about you wanting to keep me around."

"April?"

Delia motioned to the tablet. "Keep reading. There's a breakup clause."

Jack scrolled. Sure enough. *Staged Breakup.* He scanned the next few paragraphs taking in the details. The breakup would occur after the NHL playoffs, exact date determined by whenever the Blizzard either got knocked out or won the Stanley Cup. Not likely, but he wouldn't write it off just yet. The breakup would be attributed to the pressures of their careers and difficulty of maintaining a relationship in the public eye. They would only talk positively about each other and avoid negative connotations or blame. Their last appearance as a couple would be at a playoff game or one of Delia's shows, whichever they agreed on at the time.

"I don't do the dating thing either. Just so you know." Delia took a drink of her water.

Jack swiped up to read the paragraphs he'd skipped. "I find that hard to believe."

"Hilarious."

He lifted his head. "Now I'm just disappointed. A few minutes ago you made it sound like I had something to look forward to, but if you've been signed since the summer and dating isn't looking up . . ."

"I think it's a little different for women versus men."

"You mean easier?"

"Hell no, I don't mean easier! Normal, well-adjusted men were difficult to find when I wasn't . . . well-known."

"You mean a celebrity?"

"I'm not—I don't like using that word."

"Why not?"

"Because it's pretentious." She sat back in her chair and folded her arms in front of her. Her shirt sleeves came past her wrists, and she gripped the hem against her palms. It was cute.

Jack closed the tablet cover and slid the device to the side. "Isn't it factual?"

"Do you think you're a celebrity?"

"I think I'm probably a fifteen minute-er."

"That's a long time depending on the circumstance." Delia muttered, then froze as she reached for her water cup. "I'm sorry, I—"

Jack didn't hear the rest of her stammered apology through his laughter. How did she keep doing that? Taking him completely off guard and making him forget why he was there or why he should be walking away and collecting Clara from the pub.

"I don't know what's gotten into me." Delia pushed her hair out of her face. "Maybe we just shouldn't talk anymore."

"Because it's after a show and you should be introverting?"

Delia nodded. "Exactly. Right now I have no filter."

Jack took a drink of his water. *Lemony.* "So normally you won't be joking around?" Even as he said it, something told him there was no "normal" with Delia Melise.

She nodded stoically. "Right. All business. I won't talk much. I won't annoy you, if that's what you're worried about."

"It's not." He held her gaze a moment and saw that flush creep up her skin.

"What is your tattoo? On your arm?" she asked. He'd noticed her eyeing his ink back in the dressing room and glancing at his arm when she thought he wasn't watching.

"I thought we weren't talking?"

She exhaled. "You don't have to tell me, I just—"

Jack pulled up his sleeve and pointed at his forearm. "This was my first one."

"Pinecones?" Delia frowned.

"They're serotinous cones. From the Lodgepole pine. They only open after a wildfire melts the resin so they can open."

Delia's finger twitched, and for a moment he thought she was going to reach out and trace the lines on his skin. Instead, she balled her hand into a fist. "What was next?"

"Then I decided I wanted this to be a full sleeve, so I had an artist work in the Rockies, hockey—"

"What's the owl?" Delia's hand got closer, but she didn't touch him.

"Head on a swivel." Jack waited a beat to see if she understood. When she obviously didn't, he explained. "We have to see everything on the ice. One of my coaches had this pre-game thing he did about barn owls."

Delia's lip twitched. "And . . . is that a praying mantis?"

Jack's heart skipped a beat. "Yeah." He rolled down his sleeve, careful to keep the fabric off his bandage. Jack hoped when he covered up his arm, she'd get the hint and let it go. She didn't.

"What does it symbolize?"

"That one's personal."

Delia's lips parted, then she pulled her hand back and nodded. "Sure. Thanks for showing me." She searched for something to stare at, but since their menus were gone, all they had were condiments. "Did you hurt yourself?" Jack frowned as Delia grabbed the ketchup bottle and started reading the ingredients list. "You had a bandage on your arm."

"Oh, yeah. No, that was a tattoo I got this morning." He didn't think she'd noticed it since his sleeve had barely come up that far.

Delia's eyes snapped up. "You got one this morning? What is it?"

Just then, the waiter arrived with their tacos. The scent of slow roasted meat along with chilies and onion made his mouth water, and Jack wasted no time before digging in. He took a bite, barely avoiding juice dripping under the sleeve of his shirt with a quick lift of his elbow.

Delia stared at her plate.

"Is something wrong?" he asked, still holding his taco.

Delia worried her bottom lip. "I don't usually eat while I'm out. I think I impulse ordered."

Jack looked between her and his partially eaten taco. "But you're hungry." She nodded. "So you should eat." She didn't make a move, so Jack took another bite. When he finished the taco, he used a napkin to wipe his fingers.

Movement outside the window caught their attention. When Jack's eyes focused beyond the glass, he saw a girl and her boyfriend recording them from the sidewalk. Delia smiled and gave a small wave. "I'll just ask for a box—"

Jack stood and jerked the table away from the wall, and Delia gasped. He sandwiched his chair between the window and the end of the table, moving as close to the corner as he could to block the view of any onlookers. "There." He picked up his second taco and took the messiest bite he could muster. "I'll eat like this so no matter what pics they're able to get, nobody will be looking at you."

Delia clapped a hand over her mouth, but it couldn't hide the smile stretching from ear to ear. "*What?*"

"You can't understand me?" Jack shoved the food into his right cheek until it bulged. "I said—"

Delia snorted and grabbed her napkin. "No, stop, I get it." Her eyes squinched, and she grabbed onto herself like she didn't know what would happen if she let her laughter out in full force.

Jack wished he could see what that looked like. "The tacos are really good." He licked his lips.

"I can see that."

"You should try them."

Her eyes flicked to his. "I'm working up to it."

"Just—"

"Fine!" Delia picked up her taco like she was trying to remove a plastic femur without hitting the buzzer in the game *Operation*.

"Shove it on in." Jack spread his elbows on the table and hovered to make sure nobody could get a glimpse of her leaning over her plate. Delia took the most dainty bite known to humankind, but her eyes lit up. "See? Better fresh than to-go."

"Yeah." She nodded and took another mouse bite.

Mary appeared at the end of the table, her eyes wide. "What the hell is happening here?"

Jack felt like a kid caught with his hand in the bag of chocolate his mom hid behind the cereal. "We're eating?"

"Yeah, I can see that." She shot Delia a look. "You'll eat for *him?* The stranger you met ten minutes ago? Really?"

Delia chewed and swallowed. "No, it's late, so I know I'm going right back to the hotel room and won't have to deal with fuzzy teeth."

Fuzzy teeth? Was that what this whole thing had been about?

Delia pointed to the glass. "Plus he blocked the—"

"That's all I had to do to get you to eat a proper meal? Put my ass between you and the cameras?" Mary put her hands on her hips.

"Only if it's a nice ass," Jack quipped as he picked up his last taco.

Delia stifled a smile, and Jack's stomach flipped. And that was the exact moment he knew he couldn't, in fact, sign the contract.

CHAPTER
Eight

"YOU DIDN'T SIGN IT?" Clara hissed as they got back into his truck. Jack hit the start button and turned on the seat warmers. "Jack, seriously? Was there something terrible in one of the clauses?"

"You'd know if you came with me."

Clara rolled her eyes. "I wasn't going to be a third wheel on a *date*."

"It wasn't a date. It was—"

"A business meeting, yeah, I know." She slumped against the seat and clicked in her seat belt. "She was so *nice*, though. And beautiful and talented." Clara sighed. "She could've made a great fake girlfriend."

Jack shot his sister a sidelong glance. "I don't need a fake girlfriend."

"True, you need an actual one," Clara muttered as she pulled her lip balm from her purse. She smoothed it on then rubbed her lips together. "Want any?"

Jack shook his head. The oil from the tacos was still soaking into the skin around his mouth. *He'd flirted with her.* What the hell had he been thinking? The little sound she'd made when he pulled on the table had lodged in his brain like a goat's head burr. It pricked when he moved.

"I'll find a girlfriend when I'm ready." He clenched the wheel as they waited at the stoplight. Clara and Oscar, along with half the players on the Snowballs, had been trying to set him up for months. He'd have been lying if he said he didn't think about companionship. There were nights where he craved it. The problem was that the one person he wanted by his side was buried under a metre of earth.

Clara sighed. "She was right, you know."

"Who was?"

"Delia. About you being a nice person."

The light turned green and he turned left. "I didn't just go for you. I was curious about the whole thing, too."

"But you wouldn't have gone if you didn't know it was important to me."

He shrugged. "Maybe I would have."

Clara smirked. "Don't pretend to be too cool for school. You can't pull it off." The corner of Jack's mouth lifted as he adjusted his grip on the wheel. Clara looked pleased. "Are you working from home tomorrow?"

Jack nodded, already skipping ahead to the insane schedule he had to keep. *Work. Meetings. Practice. Lifting. Somehow get in his nutrition. Sleep. Rinse. Repeat.* "I'll be home for the morning, at least. I should be getting some samples in the mail. If they arrive on time, it would be good to meet with Xander in person."

"Xander? That's the designer?"

"Yep. He's ready to make mock ups." Big Rick, the company he worked for, was redesigning one of their least popular men's coats for the next ski season, and Jack's deadline to get the portfolio options was looming.

"Isn't that a pretty fast turnaround?"

Jack turned onto the exit for Deerfoot and sped up to merge. "Yeah, the samples are usually the bottleneck."

"Then you have practice . . . with the BLIZZARD!" Clara cupped her hands around her mouth and mimicked a crowd cheering his name.

Jack laughed. "Right."

Clara dropped back against her seat. "I still can't believe this is your life! My little brother . . ." She shook her head and grinned at him. "You like the guys?"

"I feel old."

"You are old, and don't even say it." Clara stuck out her tongue. Jack bit back his comment about her being eighteen months older. Everyone assumed he was the oldest sibling anyway because of their size difference. And because there was a bit of salt and pepper starting to appear when he grew his beard out.

Clara yawned as they pulled onto her street. "That was amazing. Truly. Even if you don't want Delia as your fake girlfriend, which I still think you should reconsider, I'm glad we went tonight. Thank you so much, Jacky." She reached over and tried to ruffle his hair, but he blocked her arm and nearly swerved onto the sidewalk.

———

Jack stepped into the Saddledome, and as the chill of the arena pressed against his skin, the weight on his shoulders immediately lessened. All morning he'd been getting texts and screenshots with pictures of him and Delia at Malley's the night before. Most of them had, in fact, been of his ass. Apparently, the whole country thought it was adorable that he'd stepped in to protect Delia from view as she ate. There were also pics of Mary standing in front of the two of them with a stern look on her face.

The headline "Someone's Been Pucking Naughty" was his personal favourite.

In the past six hours, he'd received an education. Clara had informed him that the video taken of them was going viral on TikTok, where an online community of avid book fans were next to rabid at the news that he'd been spotted out with Delia. #real-liferomcom was trending on three different platforms. The whole thing was insanity.

There had been a group of people staking out spots by the Saddledome when he'd arrived, but security there was good. He'd given a wave toward the fence as he walked into practice, wishing he'd worn something better than his typical joggers and a hoodie.

Something had definitely shifted since the night before, and he was working to grasp the scope of it. Would it all blow over in a day or two? A week? It would have to die down at some point since he had no intention of stoking the fire with more photo ops. His time with Delia Melise was a one and done.

Jack walked down the hall, then pushed through the doors into the dressing room. Instead of being met with André powdering his balls on the bench, there was low chatter humming beneath pump-up music. The dressing room itself was pristine. Better than the facility in Springbank, which was saying something.

There were spacious, personalized lockers for each player, constructed from polished wood instead of cheap metal. His name plate wasn't up yet, but their manager had assured him multiple times it was coming. The floors were covered with durable, non-slip rubber matting instead of bare concrete, and to one side, there was a large, logo-emblazoned carpet with the Blizzard's emblem. Besides the state-of-the-art speakers, there was a high-tech video system set up for game analysis and strategy sessions, a medical and training room with the latest in rehabilitation equipment, and a nutrition center. Since he worked a full-time job, he had yet to take advantage of any of it.

Jack wound his way through the equipment and half-dressed players to his spot.

"Hey, Jack. Good to see you." Nathan Pelletier put out a fist, and Jack bumped it before setting his gear down on the bench.

"Good weekend?"

Nathan nodded. "Chill. Spent it with the wife and kids." At twenty-seven, he was two years younger than Jack and already had a three-year-old and a six-month-old baby. "You?" Before Jack could answer, he snorted. "I'm sorry, I can't do it, bud. I was going to try and play it cool, but you have to tell me how you met Delia."

The second the word "Delia" left his lips, hoots and hollers sounded out through the room along with *"Robbing the cradle, eh, bud?"* and *"Did you smash?"*

Jack's ribs ratcheted around his lungs. "My sister's a huge fan. She was nice enough to say hi to us after her show."

"I didn't see your sister in the picture," Monahan, the Blizzard's center noted, and Jack wanted to pinch himself to make sure this was real. His NHL heroes were standing there in the dressing room digging for information on his night?

"Was she the Karen chewing you out, bud?" Lindholm asked.

Tkachuk grunted as he pulled on his pads. "Are you a fan of her music?"

"No, that was Delia's friend, and yes, I think her music's great." Jack turned to unzip his bag, ignoring the groans of his teammates. He knew what he'd have to do to keep their attention, but the idea of saying anything else about Delia when he'd talked with her for a total of forty minutes seemed asinine. Maybe they had the luxury of getting distracted by a pretty face, but Jack didn't. Coaches and management were watching him like a hawk at practices and games, and he had to look his best out there.

He dressed on autopilot as banter swirled around him, catching bits and pieces about the threesome Nils Johanssen had on Saturday with best friends he met at the Stampede last summer. They were either from Amsterdam or loved to visit Amsterdam. Or wanted to pretend Calgary *was* Amsterdam for the night. Either way, Nils was a big fan.

"How did you meet up with her, though?" Monahan's voice cut through the machismo as Jack pulled on his jersey.

He grunted. "Happened to stand next to her publicist. Someone asked for my autograph, and he recognized me." *Even without signing the contract, he was lying for that girl.*

"And you went out for dinner?"

Jack replayed Delia laughing as he made a mess of his taco. "Yeah, everyone was starving after the show."

Nathan chuckled. "Keeping it low-key. I get it."

"There's nothing to—"

"I get it, bud." He patted Jack's shoulder, then sat to lace his skates.

There was no good explanation for why he wouldn't be trying to pursue a famous singer, so he didn't bother pushing it. Instead, he finished getting dressed while trying to keep his mind from launching into comparisons between him and the other wingers on the team.

Lindholm, with his electrifying pace, had been a first-round pick, twelfth overall, in the 2021 draft. Last season, he boasted an impressive tally of twenty-four goals and thirty assists, but his defensive game still needed work

Then there was Owen Monahan, drafted in the second round, thirty-fifth overall in 2019. He'd become known for his physicality, amassing two hundred hits in the last season alone. His offensive numbers were modest with fifteen goals and twenty assists, but his plus-minus stood at +12.

Liam MacDonald, the latest addition, was chosen eighteenth overall in the most recent draft. His rookie year had been a roller coaster, but he managed to notch ten goals and fifteen assists, a respectable start with a plus-minus of -2. If the last six weeks were any sign, though, Liam's career was on the backslide. He'd been showing up late to practice. Getting less ice time. Jack had never shirked his responsibilities, but he couldn't help but see something of himself in the kid.

After a brief team meeting with Coach Novak and Assistant Coach Kreviasuk, the Blizzard charged down the tunnel to the ice. Practice kicked off with speed drills, then endurance conditioning. Jack leaned into the burn, glad to have a reason not to be in his head.

They moved into passing drills, and Jack dug in to keep up. Lindholm and MacDonald were fast. Strong. He was used to playing with the Snowballs, and while Tyler, Sean, and Country had intensity, they were ten years older than the guys here. Jack had to push, and it felt good.

It also scared the hell out of him. One dream game wasn't enough to clinch his spot on the team, especially since the player he was replacing wasn't out permanently. He had to start putting up stats. ASAP.

The whistle sliced across the arena as they circled up for a scrimmage.

"Harrison!" Coach Kreviasuk called from the boards. "Management needs a minute."

Jack pressed his blades into the ice, pulling to a stop. "Should I—"

"Go ahead and get changed."

Shit. Jack's stomach churned like it was filled with rocks. That was it, then. They'd decided to bench him or pull out of his contract. There were enough contingencies built in, it wouldn't be difficult.

Jack tromped to the dressing room and peeled off his gear. He showered as fast as he could to minimize the dread and avoid running into his teammates as they finished practice. He cleared out his locker, which didn't hold much anyway, and trekked to the upper levels of the Saddledome. The rubber on the soles of his shoes squeaked against the polished floors.

Jack was ushered into a meeting room that smelled of new paint and a vanilla scented candle. There was a mini fridge and bar along the far wall and an oval table in the center surrounded by high backed chairs.

The team's General Manager, Alex Renard, and the Head of Marketing, Lisa Carter, who he'd met upon his initial signing were already seated, their expressions unreadable. "Jack, take a seat," Alex began, his tone cordial. Jack was already on edge, and the clinical greeting didn't help.

"Wasn't expecting to be back here so soon." Jack pulled out a chair and sat.

"Sorry we had to interrupt practice, but I've got a flight to catch tonight." Alex tapped his phone screen as if to emphasize how little time he had to deal with the situation. He glanced up. "Why are you carrying your game gear?"

Jack frowned. "I wanted to thank you for the opportunity to —" he started, but Lisa cut him off with a wave of her hand.

"Jack, we appreciate that, but we wanted to have a quick discussion about the buzz you've been generating. Our ticket sales for Saturday's game went through the roof this morning. Seems like your little escapade with Delia Melise has caught everyone's attention."

Jack blinked. *This was about his dinner with Delia?* He could think of a hundred other reasons for ticket sales to fluctuate. Good weather or the fact that they were playing the Oilers being his top picks. "You're sure it's not because it's Edmonton?"

Lisa clicked around on her laptop, then turned the screen to face him. "These were our ticket sales for our last rivalry game. About ten percent higher than normal season sales. And this—" She clicked again. "Is our gross ticket sales as of thirty seconds ago compared with where we sat last night at seven."

"Holy. Hell." Jack ran a hand through his damp hair. The sky-high bar on the chart dwarfed the one next to it. *How was that possible?*

"The fans are rallying, the media is buzzing, and obviously, that's been a boon for the franchise. But we're wondering . . ." Alex paused, eyeing Jack with a mix of curiosity and calculation. "Is this going to be an ongoing thing? Just so we can plan accordingly."

Jack's mind raced. He'd walked into this room expecting to face a dissolution of his contract and instead found out that his hour of sitting across from Delia eating Birria tacos had nearly doubled the ticket sales for the Blizzard that weekend.

Exactly like Tony had told him it would.

Jack cleared his throat. "Uh, I'm not sure. The whole thing is pretty fresh."

Lisa's laugh was light, but her eyes locked onto his like a bird of prey. "Well, we're fans of whatever this turns into, and while we're not in the business of managing your personal life, we did want to make it clear that this kind of press is exactly what we want to encourage. It's good for the team, and what's good for the team is good for all of us, right?"

Jack nodded. "Right." He spun the pen sitting in front of him on the table a half turn. "Delia lives in Toronto, though, and—"

"In situations like this we're happy to make accommodations. Just keep us in the loop, and we can make adjustments as needed. I'll talk with your coaches." Alex pushed out his chair and slipped his phone in his pocket.

Accommodations? What kind of accommodations?

Lisa slipped a card across the polished wood. "It would be best if you contacted me directly, and if this becomes more than something *fresh*, if Delia has a publicist, I'd love to be introduced." She stood and motioned for him to exit as Alex gathered his personal items into a leather messenger bag.

Jack stalked back into the hall feeling like his head had just been plunged in a bucket of ice water. He wasn't being fired. Not even close. He was . . . getting accommodations? Encouragement? Special treatment?

How the hell had a few pictures made this kind of impact? It didn't seem possible, though nothing in his life over the past month had seemed possible. If someone would've told him that by March he'd be playing in the NHL, getting phone calls from famous pop stars, and selling out the Saddledome, he would've laughed in their face. The whole thing sounded like something he would've written on his vision board in grade three.

Jack walked to his truck in a daze, barely noticing the crowd that had gathered by the entrance to the lot. *Do you have more plans to see Delia?* The implications were obvious. He'd put butts in seats after his first appearance with the Blizzard, but those numbers were next level.

He threw his gear in the back, realizing he should've returned it all to his locker, then slumped into the front seat. He drew a deep breath and rested his forehead on the steering wheel.

After a few moments, he pulled out his phone. *What's good for the team is good for all of us, right?* If he'd felt like a money grubber looking over the contract last night, it was nothing compared to dialing Tony's number now.

"Let me guess, management is thrilled with you right now." Tony sounded smug, and Jack didn't have one gram of leverage.

"Yeah, you could say that." Jack started the truck, but didn't pull out of his spot.

Tony chuckled. "I've got to be honest, I expected this call a lot sooner than ten o'clock. Though I guess it's only eight in Calgary, eh?"

"Sorry, forgot about the time change."

"No, I'm always up late." He grunted like he was pushing up from an easy chair. "Any changes you want to the contract before I have Kels send it over for you to sign?"

"I don't think so." Jack felt like a dog skulking back to his owner with his tail between his legs. "I guess I don't fully understand how this will work. Delia's recording a new album there. I'm playing here. My management team says they can make some accommodations—"

Tony laughed out loud. "Damn right, they can. Listen, it will take creativity, but we'll make it work. Do you have an agent or—"

"Head of marketing. Her name's Lisa."

"Perfect. Send me over her info and we'll take care of it. At this point, you just need to sit back and enjoy the ride. And get to the damn airport on time, Kels hates rescheduling flights."

CHAPTER
Nine

DELIA CHUGGED an entire glass of water with lemon, then sat down at the table and stared at the string of headlines on her phone. Mary had helped her set up a browser extension to notify her whenever her name or song titles appeared on the World Wide Web. That morning she'd woken up to twenty-two hundred notifications.

Offstage: Delia Melise turns heads with Harrison

Hope for Harrison's sake Delia's love isn't as fleeting as her last hit single. 🏒💔

Someone tell Jack Harrison he's supposed to dodge the pucks, not date them. #DeliaMelise

Did they or didn't they? Delia Melise caught doing more than dinner with NHL Star Jack Harrison!

Delia groaned. *Let the circus begin.*

"Everything okay?" Her mother swooped into the kitchen and grabbed a Tupperware from the fridge with a salad she'd prepped for herself over the weekend.

Delia nodded. "Yeah." It was better than okay, which didn't explain why she needed to chew an antacid. A media explosion was exactly what they'd been hoping for, wasn't it?

Her phone buzzed.

MARY

> Check out these streams 😜

Mary had included a screenshot of her Spotify dashboard. Jack's butt in the window had definitely made the impact they'd all hoped for. Scrolling through her social media feeds she'd already come across four different reels with captions like, *OMG the way he kept her for himself* or *Bu-bye bodyguard, hello Jack Harrison.*

Delia, of course, knew that every one of those stories about him being protective of her was false. Jack was a nice guy. And he felt strongly about tacos. Or not wasting food. Possibly a combination of both. Still, she found a small part of herself wondering what it would be like to have a guy who would put himself between her and the cameras.

"Delia, is that a picture of you?" Her mother leaned over her shoulder.

Delia dropped the phone on the table. "It—yeah. From the show last night."

"That didn't look like your venue."

Her cheeks flushed, and she reached for a banana from the fruit bowl. "Mary and I went out for dinner after."

Her mother raised an eyebrow. "I know how to Google too, you know."

Delia pressed her thumbnail into the peel and snapped the stem back. "There may have been a hockey player there. Tony thinks it would be good to have a bit of a public relationship."

"Since when do you know hockey players?" Her mother looked either affronted or impressed.

"Since Friday night." She peeled the banana and took a bite.

Her mother's hand lifted to the neckline of her sweater. She looked far too pleased about this turn of events. "So . . . you met him on Friday and now you're in a relationship?"

"It's not real, Mom. It's just for exposure. For both of us." The media headlines had been a surprise, but the biggest shock? The message from Tony saying that Jack had signed the contract the night before without any additions or changes.

After he'd left abruptly from the restaurant the other night, she thought it was dead in the water. It was all so confusing. They'd seemed to get along just fine, which was best-case scenario. Most of the hockey players she'd known growing up were arrogant assholes, though that could've had more to do with the fact that they were sixteen and obsessed with their newfound abs and biceps. *Maybe the problem had been her?*

"Would I know him?"

Delia raised her eyebrows. "I thought you already saw the headlines?"

"I saw the pictures. I didn't have time to read about them."

Delia finished the banana, then stood to throw the peel in the trash. "Do you follow hockey?"

Her mother scoffed. "I'm Canadian, aren't I?"

"Not officially." Delia grinned. Her mother had her test scheduled in April to gain Canadian citizenship in addition to her French, but until then, Delia was going to take every opportunity to rub in her immigrant status.

Her mom didn't look impressed. "Name, please."

Delia pursed her lips. "Jack Harrison."

Her mother's eyes widened. "Jack Harrison? As in the man who played one night for the Blizzard last month?"

Delia nodded. "He signed an official contract for the rest of the season."

"Aurelia has his face as the background on her phone."

"Aurelia? Your manager? Isn't she, like, fifty?"

Her mother laughed. "I'm fifty!"

"Are *you* thirsting after thirty year old men?"

"No, that's your job." She booped Delia's nose. "I love this, Delia. You need to let loose. Live a little. None of this publicity stuff, have a real affair—"

"Mom!" She groaned as her mom walked toward the front entry.

"I'm just saying. If not with Jack Harrison, you need to have a strong, capable man sweep you off your feet."

Delia sighed. "I don't think that's a thing anymore. Guys now just lie about their stats online and ask for topless pics before your first date."

Her mother set her Tupperware of vegetable soup on the stairs and pulled on her coat. "It might require you to meet men in real life."

"Perfect. I'll get right on that. It'll be super easy to find someone while I'm being swarmed by photographers."

"I think paparazzi were waiting outside our gates the other day." Her mother slipped on her runners.

"I'm sure they were. Christian said they're working with the HOA to beef up the security."

Her mother motioned for Delia to meet her at the door. "I know this is strange. We'll navigate this together, mon chou. But please, eat more bread and don't give up on romance." She wrapped Delia in a hug.

Delia breathed her in. Her soft floral perfume, the clean scent of the lotion she'd always used on her face. She pulled back and met her mother's eyes. "Have you? Given up?"

Sadness tinged the edges of her mother's expression as she put a hand on Delia's cheek. "Never."

. . .

———

Delia walked into the studio after shielding her face from the dozen photographers camped out past the security guards. She didn't mind it most of the time, but that morning felt more abrasive than usual. Probably because she hadn't been able to escape blurry pictures of her next to Jack's all morning.

She'd seen pictures of herself waving through the restaurant window. Her profile obscured by Jack's shoulders. The back of her head as she listened to Mary chastise her. But the one that she'd looked at the longest showed half her face looking up at him squinched with laughter. She'd legitimately *laughed* Friday night. With someone other than Mary. She'd eaten tacos. *In public.*

"Delia, my love, are you ready to make magic?" Finn Gallagher grinned as she dropped her purse in the chair against the wall of the booth. Why did everything sound sexy in his Irish accent?

She blew out a breath. "Not going to lie, I'm a little distracted this afternoon."

"Does that have anything to do with a certain hockey star?" Finn waggled an eyebrow. And there it was. Of course Finn had seen everything. Delia was about to blow him off when she remembered that Tony, Kels, and Mary were the only people on her team who would be privy to the knowledge that her relationship with Jack wasn't a true burgeoning romance. Well, and her mother. She hadn't officially gotten permission from Tony for that breach, but he had to know by now that she told her mother everything.

Delia plastered a smile on her face. "More like the media frenzy that came along with him."

"You threw chum in the water, love. What did you expect?" Finn grinned and swivelled on his chair. "How did you and Jack meet?"

Delia took a drink from her water bottle. "He came to the Calgary pop-up. His sister's a big fan." *Not him, though.* She stifled a grin remembering the flush of his cheeks when Clara announced he didn't know who she was.

"Convenient." Finn tapped his fingers on the edge of the mixing board. "You had a good time?"

"I . . . had tacos."

Finn nodded. "A good start."

Delia pulled out her tablet and cleared her throat. "Is there anything in particular you want me to pay attention to with this song?" She opened the sheet music to a bubbly pop number titled "Heartbeat on the Dance Floor." It was penned by a well-known songwriter named Jessie Harlow, and IndieLake had it poised to be Delia's next single. She scanned the lyrics.

"In the club, our eyes lock,
Magic in the air, tick-tock,
Feel the bass, let's rock,
With your heartbeat on the dance floor."

Delia sighed inwardly. A night club encounter. *So hot right now.* And so far from reality. Her lyrics definitely would've included lying about hair plugs and venereal diseases.

Finn fiddled with settings on the soundboard. "Let's play around and see what we get. You listened to the backing track?"

Delia nodded. "It's a little synth heavy."

"It *is* a dance track."

"Right."

Finn smirked. "You don't have to pretend it's your favourite."

"Good, because I wasn't going to." Delia glanced at the clock hanging on the wall above Finn's head. "Mary should be here soon, but we don't need to wait for her." She stood and took her tablet with her into the recording booth.

"Please, your enthusiasm is staggering." Finn's voice piped in through the speaker.

Delia held up her middle finger, then smiled to make sure he knew she was joking. Finn had always been on her side. Yes, he worked for IndieLake and had to give them what they wanted, but he wasn't a lackey. He owned their pandering fully and was more than willing to poke fun at the sellouts. Even when they were part of that group.

"From the top." Finn hit play, and the upbeat instrumental filled the room. Delia drew a deep breath and started to sing. She focused on her vocals. Her breath. Pretending she was singing something other than a cheesy pop anthem.

As the last notes faded, Finn rubbed his chin behind the glass. "Lovely. I know this was a warm up, but you're holding back, darling. This song is about letting go, feeling sexy in the moment."

Delia snorted. "Right, I'll just tap right into that energy."

"Delia, you're a sexy beast." Mary's voice came over the speaker. "Do I need to force you into a club wearing a halter top this weekend so you can remember what it's like to get your hair sweaty and leave with unexplained glitter on your neck?"

Delia shuddered. "Hi, Mary."

Mary waved and almost spilled her coffee. Finn looked horrified and forced her away from the sound equipment.

Delia stretched her arms over her head. "Okay, channeling horny club energy."

Finn laughed silently behind the glass then pressed the speaker button. "Excellent. Take two."

They ran through the song four more times with Finn adjusting levels and adding to the backing track. At four they took a break to eat. Mary had Cobb salads brought in, Delia's favourite recording food. It didn't make her mouth smacky but kept her stomach from grumbling.

Delia picked up her guitar while she waited for Mary and Finn to get back from the washroom. She plucked out the most recent melody she'd been working on. Meandering and dissonant. Decidedly nothing IndieLake would ever be interested in publishing. She whispered the lyrics under her breath.

"Underneath the willow tree,

Whispers of you come to me,

In the silence, I find peace,

Echoes of what used to be."

"Sounds a little sad for a club vibe." Finn winked at her from the booth. Delia set the guitar back in the stand. "You'll be able to record that someday. You know that, right?"

Delia nodded. "When I'm old and grey."

Finn made a pouty face. "Are you feeling sorry for yourself, Ms. Melise?"

"Me?" She shot Finn a scandalized look. The idea that she could sit here with any complaints inside her head made her feel like the girl who was thrown down a walnut shoot in Willy Wonka. A year ago, all she'd wanted was a recording contract. Now she had it and still wasn't satisfied?

She winced. "I'll stop being a baby. Let's go again."

Finn grinned and hit play.

By seven, they had plenty of vocals to work with, and Finn called it a wrap. Delia stepped out of the recording booth, massaging her jaw muscles.

Finn pulled one side of his headphones off. "Beautiful work, love. I'll have a master to you by the weekend."

Mary yawned. "It sounded great. I think Christian is going to be obsessed with it."

Delia nodded and rifled in her bag for her phone. She paused when she saw a text message from an unknown number, then clicked on it.

Hey, this is Jack. Tony said I should reach out.

Looks like I'm coming out tomorrow night after practice

. . .

She read it twice, then turned the phone so Mary could see.

Mary's eyes lit up. "Wow. That was fast."

"Whatever she told you, it isn't true." Finn leaned back in his chair, and Delia rolled her eyes.

"Not everything's about you, Gallagher."

"Most things are, though, eh, love?" He set the headphones on the desk.

Mary stood. "Delia might have more energy for our session on Wednesday. Or less. Depending on how tomorrow night goes."

Delia smacked her arm, and Finn's eyes widened.

"Hockey player?"

Delia turned off her phone. "Looks like he's coming out to Toronto."

Finn scrubbed his hand over his chin. "Do they have a game against the Leafs?"

Mary shook her head. "He only has one reason to be here."

"Damn, Delia. Those must have been some tacos."

Delia ignored her flaming cheeks and grabbed her coat and purse. "Thanks for making me sound good, Finn. Wednesday?"

"Bring Jacky boy. My sister'll be a narky hole if I get a picture with him before she does." Finn swivelled in his chair, his hands laced behind his head.

Delia laughed. "I highly doubt he'll be interested in any of this."

Finn picked up the headphones and winked. "Well then, I'll at least look forward to an explanation of the glitter on your neck."

CHAPTER
Ten

JACK'S FLIGHT out of YYC had been late, but thankfully he didn't have to work too hard to keep a low profile. Most of the people on his plane were too tired to try to introduce themselves even if they did recognize who he was. When he woke from his two hour nap, he connected to the free onboard WiFi and found messages waiting for him on the Snowballs' chat.

TYLER

> I don't know about you, but I could use more Harrison on my Instagram feed

COUNTRY

> Hope you don't mind, Jack, but I'm milking Jenna's footage for all it's worth. Reposted a video with you in it and it's already at 100k views

. . .

J ACK

> Use and abuse my dude

A NDRÉ

> You're worse than Country, you know that?
> Need details on this Delia chick

J ACK

> We had tacos

A NDRÉ

> Like YOU had a taco?

S EAN

> Shut the hell up André. And I blocked the word
> "crema" from the chat, FYI

Jack laughed, grateful he didn't need to respond to that. Joking about women and sex? Easy. Actually getting in a relationship? Not so much.

How long had it been? Clara had been relentless about him getting out of his apartment after he'd moved in, and he had tried initially. But no matter how many women approached him, the idea of "getting over" Angie always slammed him down to the same place. Regret. Anger. Guilt.

He hadn't even come close to bringing someone home for the night because any kind of fling felt pointless after what they'd had. All the conversation and flirting was cheap, and sleeping with someone for the hell of it didn't equal fun.

Holding someone close after laughing until you were sick was fun. Climbing into the shower with her and helping her wash her hair after she'd been knocked out by a cold all weekend was fun. Cuddling up and eating nachos in underwear and a T-shirt to watch the latest *Survivor* episode was fun. And "fun" didn't begin to cover it.

"Excuse me." A woman with a brunette bob and a sleep mask holding back her hair like a headband tapped his shoulder as he pulled his carry-on bag from the luggage compartment. "Would you mind grabbing mine? It's the silver one." She pointed to the bag that had been sitting next to his.

"Sure." He reached up and grabbed the suitcase, then set it in the aisle in front of him and motioned for her to go first.

"Thanks." She gathered her things and slipped into place, waiting for the doors to open.

He hated that he wondered if she knew who he was. Hated that he was already thinking about that interaction showing up in a headline somewhere. He wouldn't ever complain about where life had taken him over the last month, but sometimes he wondered if he was a good enough person to handle it.

It was easy to see how athletes became pricks. Being fed a constant diet of praise and public interest could turn even the most humble soul into a narcissist.

His phone buzzed.

Clara

> Landed yet?

Yep. Just

He didn't ask why she was up at eleven o'clock on a Tuesday. She was either at the hospital on shift or had just arrived home.

Clara

> I don't think you're a prostitute.

Phew. I was worried

> Even if you slept with her, I wouldn't think that

I'm not going to sleep with her. Sorry to crush your dreams

> Then who are you going to sleep with Jack? It's been three years

This isn't a normal conversation to have with one's sister

> This is a matter of health, of which I'm an expert

You're a sex therapist now?

> Jack, I loved Angie. You know that. She wouldn't want you to be alone the rest of your life

. . .

Jack rubbed the back of his neck. This wasn't a conversation he wanted to have in the aisle of an airplane at one o'clock in the morning.

CLARA

> Maybe a fake relationship could be good.
> Could remind you that women are fun?

There was that word again. Jack clicked off his phone and put it in his pocket.

The woman in front of him turned her head. "You think you'll beat the Oilers Saturday?"

Jack exhaled and forced a smile to his face. "You better believe it."

The doors opened, saving him from having to stand there awkwardly or answer more questions he didn't have the energy for. Instead, he walked down the connecting bridge and into the terminal to an immediate entourage.

Tony's assistant, Kels, was there, along with two men who looked like they were straight out of Men in Black.

"Is this a thing?" He pointed to their earpieces.

Kels tapped something into his phone. "You're with Delia now. We have to take precautions."

Jack fell into step with them. *Was this how she travelled?* The idea of being escorted everywhere he went left him conflicted. He had to admit, it was cool as shit to walk through the terminal with dudes wearing indoor sunglasses. Less cool to think about having to coordinate with someone else every time he left the hotel.

"Glad you made the flight." Kels typed away on his phone and somehow still made it smoothly onto the moving walkway.

"Tony threatened me."

Kels laughed. "Such a softie."

Jack followed the men through the mostly quiet airport, following signs to the LINK train. "How did you end up working for him anyway?"

"I was sleeping with his sister."

Jack chuckled. He'd wondered more than once if Kels was more to Tony than just his assistant. "Makes perfect sense."

Kels stopped on the platform. The digital sign announced the next train would arrive in four minutes. "I was working a soul-sucking sales job. Tony's sister Linda was a bit of a mess, and I helped get her organized. When Tony came over and saw that I'd labelled plastic bins in her pantry, he asked if I was open to a career change."

"Are you still with Linda?"

Kels shook his head. "No, she's living over in Ireland or something now. Met an artist after we broke up. I've been married for a year and a half now."

"And you like working with him?"

Kels nodded. "Best job I ever had. It's a lot of hours, but all I do is take chaos and turn it into order."

"Does Tony only work for Delia?"

Kels shook his head. "He represents everyone signed to IndieLake between 2022 and 2024. They just signed a new band out of Portage la Prairie this weekend."

"Wasn't that where a guy ate someone on a bus?"

Kels grimaced. "They're hoping to change their town's one claim to fame."

The train arrived and they travelled in silence to the car waiting for them in the parking garage. Kels sat in the back seat of the luxury sedan with Jack and pulled out a tablet as one of the secret agents backed out.

"Alright, schedule for tomorrow. Do you have a Google calendar?"

"Uh, no." Jack grabbed his phone.

"But you have a Gmail account?" Kels asked with more than a tinge of judgment. Jack nodded. "Perfect, then let's get you set up. It'll be easier for me to send you invitations that way than having to copy everything over to a different app."

Kels walked him through accepting his invitations in the app. By the time they pulled up in front of the Radisson, Jack had three appointments set for the following day.

"So, meet Delia for breakfast at the bakery in the morning."

Kels nodded. "Then you two can decide what you want to do the rest of the day. She has a recording session, but that's optional. Nobody will be there, though she has been getting papped out front lately."

"Sounds like a gynecology appointment, but got it."

Kels closed the cover on his tablet. "Madden will escort you in."

The Tommy Lee Jones of the partnership unclicked his seatbelt and stepped out onto the sidewalk. Jack pushed the door open. "Is he staying in my room?"

"Only if you ask nicely," Kels said without any hint of a smile.

———

Delia stood at the hostess stand trying not to tap her foot. She'd tossed and turned until three, then had a middle of the night anxiety-ridden text conversation with Mary before finally falling asleep until her alarm woke her at eight-thirty. The closer she got to seeing Jack again, the heavier her questions landed in her head. Why had he left the restaurant? Why had he suddenly changed his mind about the contract?

It didn't matter. Mary had reiterated that point at least five times during the night. She was right. This was an agreement, nothing more. It didn't matter why he'd changed his mind, only that after today, her numbers would hopefully skyrocket again like they had last Saturday.

Delia couldn't help but get her hopes up. Her last single had jumped thirty spots on the charts after being spotted *one* time with him, and her imagination ran wild with where another public appearance could take her numbers. For the first time, that earn-out hovered so close she could taste it.

Tony had texted her that morning with homework: she and Jack needed to come up with a narrative about their relationship. According to him, intrigue was good to a point, but then people needed something to sink their teeth into. She was glad to have a purpose for their meeting. Especially since she was already thinking about that praying mantis on Jack's bicep.

"Right this way, Ms. Melise." The hostess took her past the other diners, who were trying to look at her without blatantly staring, and sat her in a booth in the far corner of the restaurant. The tables in the immediate vicinity were notably empty. *Thank you, Kels.* "If you need anything, please let me know."

The hostess turned, then paused as the bell above the door jingled. Delia's breath caught in her throat. Jack stood in the entry in jeans and a long-sleeved cotton T-shirt with his down puffer coat slung over his arm.

"Is that—?" The hostess swallowed hard, then flushed crimson when she realized she'd spoken out loud. Jack scanned the restaurant and stilled when his eyes landed on her. Delia reached up and swept her hair behind her ear *like a loser.*

"He's walking this way," the hostess whispered, then turned to face Delia. Her eyes widened as if just putting two and two together. "Oh! Right. I—I'm sorry, I didn't—" She snapped her mouth shut and stepped back from the table, running directly into Jack. The hostess spun, then squeaked an apology before scurrying back to her post.

"Hey." Jack slid into the booth, stuffing his coat against the wall.

Delia sat across from him. "Gello." She winced. "I was going to say good morning, but then thought 'hello' at the last second."

Jack's lips curved into a half smile. "If you didn't say anything I would've assumed it was Ontario Gen Z slang."

"Would you have used it in conversation?"

"Definitely. Would've tried to seem less geriatric with my teammates."

Delia laughed. "You're not that old."

"Pretty sure our contract doesn't stipulate you have to lie to protect my feelings."

Delia's pulse pounded against her eardrums as she searched the table for the menu, then realized there was a QR code on a stanchion next to the condiments. She pulled out her phone and scanned it.

Jack was twenty-nine. Four years older than her. She'd discovered that along with strings of stats from his time in the AHL league. The specifics of his numbers were lost on her, though she'd absorbed enough from being steeped in hockey culture her whole life to know they were impressive.

Delia scrolled the menu on her phone and said nothing since stating she knew his exact age would reveal she'd been reading up on him.

"What's good here?" Jack asked, lifting his phone to the code.

"I don't know. I've never been."

Jack peered at his screen. "Tony said it was close to the studio you record at."

"Yeah, it's just around the corner. Your hotel is a few blocks away?"

"The Radisson. They upgraded me to the Concierge level." He grinned, and Delia's insides fizzed. Jack looked like a kid who'd just been given a full-sized chocolate bar on Halloween.

"Has that never happened to you before?" she asked, trying to keep her eyes on the food descriptions in front of her.

Jack shook his head. "First time in a hotel since . . ." he motioned in the air, and Delia understood. *Since the whirlwind hit. Since people knew my name.* "I guess I should thank you for that."

Delia shook her head. "I think you did that all on your own. Even my mom knows who you are."

He looked up with an unreadable expression. "You talked to your mom about me?"

"No, I—she asked about the pictures, so . . . she knows. I don't think Tony knows she knows, but she knows."

Jack laughed and looked back at his phone.

Delia frowned. "What's so funny?" Jack shook his head. "No seriously, what's—"

"It sounded like that rhyme." He set his phone on the table, and it seemed like an invitation.

Delia took it and set her phone down on the bench. She already knew what she wanted. "What rhyme?"

Jack glanced around the restaurant, then shifted so he wasn't as visible from the rest of the dining room. He put his finger on his nose, then started touching various body parts as he whispered, "Tony Chestnut knows I love you, Tony knows. Tony knows."

Delia pursed her lips and blinked. "What *the hell* was that?"

Jack's cheeks flushed. "You've never heard that before?"

"No. I have not."

He exhaled, and his olive skin did that hot and bothered thing again. Delia squeezed her thighs as he ran a hand over the barely-there stubble on his jaw. "Well. Now I feel like an idiot."

Delia couldn't hold it in. She burst out laughing. Guttural, side-splitting laughter. Jack Harrison—hockey player tough guy and presumed panty dropper—had just recited a Mother Goose rhyme to her. It was the most adorable thing she'd ever seen, and the swoop in her midsection made her wildly uncomfortable. "I'm sorry, I'm not laughing at you—"

"You're laughing *with* me, right. I've heard it all before." Jack pretended to be pissed, but she saw the corner of his lips twitching.

Delia sucked in a breath. "You have to teach it to me."

"Absolutely not."

"Please?"

"After you just publicly mocked me?"

Delia pursed her lips as her eyes filled with tears at the effort of keeping another bout of laughter from escaping.

Jack doubled down. "I travelled across the country to have breakfast with you, and within two minutes of me sitting down, you treat me like this?"

Delia was dead. Tears streamed down her cheeks. She was making an absolute spectacle of herself, but she couldn't help it. It was stupid, but that was the funniest thing she'd seen in months, and because of the impeccable replay function in her brain, she was watching it on repeat.

A server with her hair pulled into two Instagram-worthy French braids appeared at their booth. "Hey, can I get you two anything to drink?"

Jack turned away from her, acting as if nothing out of the ordinary was happening while Delia dropped her head into her arms on top of the table to hide her breaking face. His voice was smooth as honey. "Hi there, I'll have the Morning Meditation and the skillet with scrambled eggs and extra bacon."

The server scribbled his order down in her notepad. Delia tried to pull it together. When she was little, she'd been kicked out of dinner for having giggle fits at the table, and it was only after her mother had found her sobbing in her room wailing, *"It's not my fault I feel so happy!"* that her parents had reconsidered their strategy. Then their family had gone from three to two. She didn't think she'd laughed at the table since.

That memory sobered her, and Delia lifted her head. "Uh, I'll take the same."

The server blinked. "The same thing?"

"Right." Delia grabbed a napkin and dabbed at her eyes, her giddiness transforming into embarrassment.

"I'll get that right in for you." The server bounced back toward the kitchen, and Delia slumped against the back of the booth.

"I'm sorry. I have no idea what got into me."

Jack watched her curiously. "Is this another no-filter moment?" Delia nodded, wishing she could blow her nose. He leaned in. "It's not midnight after a show."

She sniffed. "I didn't sleep well last night."

"No?"

She shook her head.

"Me either."

Delia set down her napkin. "What time did you get in?"

"Just after one."

She winced. "I'm sorry."

"It was the only flight that worked with my practice time."

"Are you missing practice today?"

Jack nodded. "I'll do my lifting sets in the gym at the hotel later."

Delia imagined him in shorts and a T-shirt with a squat bar and her face flushed deeper. Again, she tried to sort out what it was about him that both put her on edge and made her feel like she was putting on her favourite sweatshirt. She shifted on the bench and lowered her voice. "Can I ask you something?"

Jack fiddled with the salt shaker. "Sure."

"Why did you change your mind?"

Jack thought for a moment. "Because Tony was right."

Delia swallowed her disappointment. What had she wanted him to say? That he couldn't stop thinking about her? *Business only.* "About what?"

"The Blizzard saw an influx of ticket sales for the weekend."

She smiled. "That's great." Delia was about to go on and talk about her streaming numbers, but the last piece of her question blared like a foghorn. "Actually, there's one more thing I was wondering."

"Yeah?" Jack straightened, and Delia shoved her hands under her thighs to keep them from trembling.

"Why'd you leave the other night?"

A muscle in Jack's jaw flexed. "Clara was over at the pub."

Delia nodded. "Right." It was a stupid question. Even if she had done something to make him second guess everything, he wouldn't—

"And I got nervous."

Delia looked up, her blood pumping faster. Hearing that sentence hang in the air between them hummed like she'd finally sung something real after repeating Heartbeat on the Dance Floor a thousand times. "Why?"

Jack shrugged. "It started to feel . . . I don't know. Like an actual date."

"Which you don't do."

"Right."

The waitress walked back to their table with two tangerine drinks swirled with deep magenta beet juice. Delia smiled and thanked her, then opened her paper straw. Jack took a sip straight from the glass.

"You're going to get all the orange and none of the red." She dropped her straw in the drink.

"You're going to get all the red."

She swirled her straw until the two colours started to mix. "Not if I go like this."

Jack scoffed. "Now you won't know which one you like better."

"That's not the point."

"It was the point until you ruined it."

Delia stopped and took a sip. She grimaced. "Orange is best."

"You didn't even try the orange."

"Well, it has to be better than that."

Jack laughed and took another drink. "Orange is pretty damn good."

Delia mixed until her cup was the colour of pink grapefruit. "Why don't you date?" She paused, thinking again of the mantis tattoo. "Sorry, is that too personal?"

Jack didn't answer for a moment, and Delia was about to come up with something else to change the subject when he finally said, "I lost someone close to me a few years ago."

The air she'd been holding whooshed out of her lungs. Responses swirled in her head, none of them satisfactory. Whenever people asked about her dad and she told them that he'd passed, they were always so quick to jump in and say something like *"I'm sorry for your loss,"* which was impossible because they couldn't be sorry. Not in the way they should be. They didn't know him. They didn't know what it was like to be without him. Then they'd move on to questions like, *"How long ago? How did it happen?"* like she should be able to give them a play-by-play. *"Well, first the left ventricle in his heart started leaking, and then he got dizzy, and—"*

Jack coughed. "She was my fiancée, actually. She died in a car crash on the 401."

That was a straight punch to the gut. "Shit, Jack." She reached out for his hand without thinking. He pulled back before she made contact, and her stomach dropped out from under her. "I'm sorry, I just—"

"No, it's okay. I'm—if this is going to work, you have to know I have some . . . things."

He didn't have to clarify. She knew exactly what he meant. Things like wondering whether she remembered her dad's face right. Or thinking about whether she'd ever told him she loved him. Wondering if the version of him in her head was the reason why she balked at any other man she met because none of them could measure up. Things like staying up half the night reading about praying mantises and worrying about whether a perfect stranger secretly hated her, or buying a hotel lock for her front door at four in the morning when she heard a rustle on her porch. "Yeah. I have some things, too."

"Like public displays of affection. That's . . ." Jack ran a hand over the back of his neck.

"Sacred?" It was the first word that came to her head.

He paused, his eyes dragging to hers. "What?"

Delia's hands started to tingle, though it could've been the lack of blood flow since she'd been smashing them against the bench for the past five minutes. "Sacred. Special. I know people don't think it's a big deal, but I do." She drew a shaky breath. "I told you my mom is French, and she's all about romance, embracing life and enjoying her body, but I think it's because she had love, you know? She knew what it felt like to be safe, and I've never had that. So why would I let random guys put their hands on me? They haven't earned that."

Delia stopped. She hadn't told anyone that, not even Mary. Her thoughts hadn't ever been that clear in her own head. Jack was still staring at her, and she dropped her eyes, letting her hair fall like curtains. "Anyway, we don't have to do any of that. We can tell the media we're both private people. Maybe it will add more intrigue, and Tony will be thrilled."

Jack nodded and took another drink. "Had?" Delia's brow furrowed, and she looked up. "You said your mom *had* love."

Delia's shoulders curled. "My dad died when I was seven." Had she not told him that already? No. She'd sung it to him. But of course he hadn't been able to read her mind.

Jack exhaled, his breath hissing between his teeth. He wrapped his hand around his drink. He tapped his finger on the glass. "That's the song. The one you sang at the end of the concert."

Her heart stumbled in her chest. He'd listened. He'd felt it. *If there's ever a day when I don't see your face, I'll be right here on my knees. Dans le soulagement et le regret, de toi, je n'ai point oubliet.*

In relief and regret. I have not forgotten you.

It didn't feel strange that they were sitting in silence when the server brought their skillets. Delia thanked her, then took in the monstrosity in front of her. "Wait, did you ask for extra bacon?"

Jack picked up his fork. "Guess you should've been paying attention during your giggle fit."

Delia rolled her eyes and reached for her napkin wrapped cutlery. She'd made arrangements so that she didn't come across as a head case this time. She'd be at the studio after this, and Mary had already put extra toothbrushes in the washroom there. *I have things.* Oh, did she have things. "What are your plans for the rest of the day?"

"I was thinking day drinking. Then the strip club." Jack answered with a straight face.

Delia continued the bit. "Excellent choice. I think there's a Star Wars cabaret thing in town. Sexy Storm Troopers or something."

"Perfect. I'll text Kels and see if he can get me a single ticket." Jack took a bite of eggs, then watched her while he chewed, daring her to laugh.

Delia picked up one of her ten pieces of bacon and bit into it with a crunch. "So. Recording studio?"

"Yes, please."

"And then you'll teach me that creepy Tony song?" She snuck that in there, hoping he was saying yes to everything.

"I'm going to revoke my signature."

She scoffed. "Not possible. Didn't Kels make you sign it in blood?"

Jack wiped his mouth with his napkin. "Ah. But you see, it wasn't exactly mine."

CHAPTER
Eleven

JACK STARED at the crowd that had gathered outside of the restaurant. "What's the plan?"

Delia blew out a breath. "I'm texting Mary. This is insane."

"Not normal, then?" Jack glanced toward the back of the restaurant, watching for their server. He'd insisted on getting the check, especially since Tony had already deposited a week's worth of per diem into his bank account.

Delia typed out the message on her phone. "Not normal."

"Do you have security or anything?" Jack folded up his napkin and set it on the table, thinking of his trip from the airport.

She set her phone down. "I haven't needed it. I bought a home within a gated community, and I always have a security guard at the venues when I do shows. My label pays for that . . ." Delia trailed off as her phone screen lit up. She frowned, and her right eyebrow dropped lower than her left.

Delia clicked her tongue. "Okay, Mary says she has a car pulling around to the back alley. She's going to meet us at the studio." She set her phone in her lap. "I'm sorry about this."

Jack shook his head. "No, I was going to apologize. The same thing happened to me outside of practice last night."

"Really?"

Jack grinned. "Don't look so shocked."

"I'm not shocked, just relieved. Or grateful?" Her cheeks flushed, and she grabbed her glass, coaxing the last trickle of pink juice from around the ice cubes at the bottom up her straw. "Not that I want anyone else's life to be disrupted, but it can be a bit lonely."

"I guess that's why celebrities are all friends with each other," Jack said. She gave him a look, and he smirked, knowing exactly what word she took issue with in that sentence.

She crunched the ice with her straw. "Nobody tells you how to start that, though."

"Start what?"

"Friendships. It's like, all the people you knew before don't get that you have to dive headlong into this new career, and you can't be at the parties or go on that trip to Europe with everyone, and then when you do make time to get together, you find you don't have anything to talk about because nobody else has any idea what your life looks like on a day-to-day basis and you feel like a narcissist talking too much about it. Especially because some of your friends are musicians, too, and they didn't get a record deal. And—" Delia's phone buzzed. "Ooh. Car's here." She looked up and blinked. "Sorry, that was a lot."

Jack grabbed his coat and stood, trying to process the thousand thoughts running through his head after Delia's monologue. He resonated with it. Every part of it, but for very different reasons than hers.

Delia whispered something to their server who nodded and led them down the hall to the washrooms, then opened an employee-only door. Jack barely registered the stacks of supplies on shelves or the bustling staff as they pushed through to the back of the establishment. His thoughts were still spinning.

When Angie had passed, he'd been immediately isolated. Conversations stopped when he entered the room. Hockey teammates stopped phoning, and when they saw him at practice, they acted like they weren't sure if he spoke English.

They were afraid, he understood that now. Afraid of saying the wrong thing. Worried he'd need something they couldn't give. But at the time, he may as well have lived on a different planet. His old life was still rotating on earth, and he'd been plucked up and dropped onto an orb of dark nothingness. Nobody wanted to buy a ticket there, and he couldn't figure out how to travel back.

Clara had tried to help. So had his parents. But the best fix had been moving to Calgary and meeting new people who didn't know his history. Most of his teammates on the Snowballs still didn't know about Ange. Not because he didn't trust them with the information, but because he wasn't willing to risk being booted out of normal life again.

Then he'd gotten the contract with the Blizzard and knew that every single one of his Snowball teammates had to harbour a bit of jealousy. He would've, had one of them been called up. He liked to think his envy would've been outweighed by legitimate happiness for his teammate, but that was a generous theoretical.

All of them had wanted a place in the NHL at one point, and too few of them had gotten a shot. Now he was the one trying to avoid talking about the elephant in the room on the team chat, which was becoming harder to do with his face being plastered over every media outlet in the country.

"Ready?" Delia paused at the back door of the restaurant and looked back. When Jack nodded, she pushed through and hopped into the car idling next to the dumpsters. Every admonition from his mother about not getting into cars with strangers flitted through his head, but he jumped into the backseat. He couldn't in good conscience let her get kidnapped alone.

The car took off as soon as his door slammed shut. Delia fastened her seatbelt, then turned to stare out the window. She was being oddly quiet considering they'd just made an epic escape from brunch.

That's when Clara's words came back to bite him. *"Jack, maybe you'd have more luck with women if you didn't expect them to be mind readers. You have to actually say words out loud for us to know what you're thinking. Or, you know, not assume you think we're annoying as hell."*

Jack cleared his throat. "I get it. What you said back there."

Delia turned. She was chewing on her bottom lip. "Which part?"

"All of it. I played for two different AHL teams, then when I didn't make the NHL, I joined an Elite League team—"

"Wait, like Country? That YouTuber?"

Jack couldn't contain his amusement. "Yeah. Exactly like him. Country's on my team." Delia's eyes went wide. "I'd offer to introduce you, but he already has a girlfriend."

She shot him a look. "That was a fangirl reaction, not . . . attraction."

"Uh-huh."

Delia ignored the comment and motioned for Jack to continue.

"So, I'm playing with guys that feel more like family than anything else, and then I get a miracle. I have to leave them mid-season to follow my dream, which also happens to be their dream, too." Jack held up his phone. "They have it rubbed in their faces on a daily basis."

"That you're in the NHL?"

He nodded. "And . . . everything else."

She tucked her hair behind her ear. "You and me?"

Jack flattened against the seat as they passed the hoards of people outside the cafe. "They don't know it's not real. Which means they think I not only got my dream job, but also immediately hooked up with a girl they fantasize about." Delia's cheeks stained pink, and Jack backpedalled, "Not fantasized in a creepy way, just—you know."

"No, I don't know, Jack. Please, explain it to me."

Jack scoffed. "Stop. You know men find you attractive."

"What's funny about that is they never used to. Now they hear my music on the radio and assume I have money, and suddenly I'm a ten out of ten."

Jack raised an eyebrow. "They never used to?" He glanced out the window over her shoulder to make sense of where they were headed. He'd scouted out the location of the recording studio in relation to their breakfast spot that morning, and it seemed like they'd already gone too far.

"I think he's circling. Leading off any people who might've followed us from the restaurant," Delia said. "And no. Men have always gravitated more toward Mary than me, which is why it was so exciting to get that kind of attention at first. But then it became obvious what they were after. Ironically what you *didn't* want initially."

"What, a contract stipulating mutually consensual PDA and no sex? I didn't know those were such hot commodities."

Delia snorted. "Status, Jack."

"I'm betting it was actually sex."

"You don't ask if you can take nude pictures with someone on a first date unless you're hoping to get mileage out of your experience."

Jack looked skeptical. "A guy did that?" The idea of walking up to a girl and asking for naked photos made him want to throw up. Growing up with a sister and a few years of being engaged had that effect.

"Not one guy. All of them."

And with that comment, Jack started to get pissed off. "How are you meeting these douchebags?"

"Online."

Jack drew a breath and unclenched his fists. "Well, there's your problem. You need to wait until people's publicists phone you up like the rest of us."

Delia laughed out loud. "If I only would've been patient, I

could've signed my own contract for PDA and no sex. Instead, I had to write one myself."

"We're the lucky ones." He grinned, and Delia settled back in her seat, a smile still on her lips.

The car pulled up to the curb, and Jack scanned the lot next to the studio. That was becoming automatic, especially with Delia there next to him. There were people sitting in cars, a few people with cameras standing next to the corner. Jack reached for the door handle. "If we go fast, they might not realize we're here until all they can shoot is our backs."

Delia nodded, but before she could push open her side of the vehicle, Jack opened his. There was no way he was going to let her step out alone. "Follow me. I'll block you." She did as he said, allowing him to stand between her and the paparazzi to their right. Without thinking, he put an arm over her shoulder and angled his body around her. They rushed forward together toward the building, and the shouts and shutter clicks barely caught up when they were a few paces from the entrance.

Mary pushed the doors open from the inside and ushered them through.

Jack pulled his arm off Delia's shoulders. "Sorry if I—"

"No, thank you. It was . . . logistical." She straightened her jacket.

Logistical. Right. He would've done something like that for anyone, wouldn't he? Jack thought back to the time he shared a ride with a woman in Boston back from a restaurant after a game. It had started raining, and he'd pulled his jacket over both of them as they ran into the hotel.

That counted. He didn't know the woman and hadn't been looking for any kind of reward for that act of kindness. True, she'd walked with him to the elevator and didn't hit the button for her own floor, but that had seemed like a coincidence. It wasn't until she tried to hold his hand that he'd panicked and picked up his phone with a loud, "Hey babe, I'm almost to the room."

Smooth.

Jack shoved his hands in his pockets, and Mary reached for Delia's coat.

"Ugh. So glad you made it! I was starting to worry there for a second, especially since you didn't text me back."

Delia pulled out her phone. "Oh, I didn't even check. Your hired driver was quite thorough."

"You enjoyed your city tour?" Mary grinned. "Sorry, I just didn't want to add to the mayhem over here by making it obvious you were recording, and, before you ask, I did just hire a company to provide security from here on out. For both of you. I think Jack met them at the airport?"

Jack nodded, but Delia winced. "How much is that going to cost?"

Mary looked between her and Jack. "Probably something we should discuss later?"

Jack thought back to their conversation in her dressing room after the concert. How Delia needed the money to earn out her advance and retire her mom. That had definitely tugged at his heartstrings.

Delia nodded and gave Mary a hug. "Later. Thanks so much for figuring all that out. I can't believe how much this is ramping up."

"Exciting, though, right? Have you seen your streaming numbers?"

Jack was intruding on a moment, so he turned and looked for the washroom. There was a hallway off to the left. He figured that was his best bet.

He strode forward, and sure enough, there one was. He reached out for the door handle just as it turned. The door opened into the hall, and Jack stepped back as a man with dark, wavy hair, wire-rimmed glasses, and a V-neck black T-shirt appeared in front of him.

"Sorry, mate. I . . ." The man frowned, looked him up and down, then glanced past him into the hall. His eyes lit up.

"Delia, love! I wasn't aware you'd already arrived." He didn't look back or introduce himself, and Jack fought the urge to mutter something about how it was nice to meet him, too.

Jack stepped into the washroom and unzipped his slacks. *Who was that guy?* Someone who knew Delia well. His jaw tightened. The dude was Irish. He probably called everyone "love."

Jack had never known someone in the music business, and that meant he knew nothing about what was going to happen there at the studio. His childhood music career had been short lived, punctuated by a year and a half stint of forced piano lessons at age six.

The few things he knew about music came from that teacher, Mrs. Montgomery. He technically had a music teacher at school, but she was mousy and dull. Mrs. Montgomery, on the other hand, had worn sleeveless silk blouses and high heels *inside* the house. She had art on her walls, fresh flowers on the table, and she always sucked on tiny, perfectly round mints. She was a sophisticated fish out of water in Moose Jaw, and Jack might've had the tiniest crush on her. It didn't mean he practised, but he did listen with rapt attention whenever she leaned over and put her hands next to his on the keys. He still knew a C major scale because of her.

Jack zipped up and washed his hands, then pulled out a small tube of petroleum jelly from his pocket. He pulled up his shirt sleeve and applied the ointment to his still-healing skin, then put it away, wiped his fingers on a paper towel, and walked back into the lobby. Only Mary was left standing in the hall.

"Hey, Jack."

"Mary."

"Do you want to come back and watch the recording session or hang out here?"

Jack scanned the tiny meeting room. There was an armchair that looked like it could've only held him until he hit a growth spurt in grade ten and a water cooler with paper ice cream cone cups. "Does Delia not want me there?"

Mary shook her head. "No, she just went back to the staff lounge to brush her teeth. She told me to ask you."

"Oh, okay. Yeah. I'll come back and watch, then." Jack followed Mary down the dark hallway and into a small, narrow room bathed in a soft, ambient light. Mary took a seat next to the man he'd run into in front of the washroom.

"Jack, this is Finn Gallagher. He's producing the album." Mary leaned back so Finn could put out a hand.

"Nice to meet you, Jack. I thought we could get a picture after, if that's okay." Finn shook his hand, then grinned and looked past the left side of his head. "Happy with your teeth, Dels?"

Jack turned and barely caught Delia rolling her eyes. "Don't pretend you aren't thrilled I'm only breathing minty fresh air onto your pet mic."

Finn laughed. "I don't believe food breath sticks."

Delia swept her hair behind her ears. "Any fixes from the other day or are we moving straight into 'Choose Me'?" They spoke so smoothly to each other, like they were fluent in a different variation of English.

"I have a bit more blending to do on the splices, but all in all, it's a good cut. I'll send it over to both of you this weekend." Finn put on his headphones as Delia entered the studio, and for a few seconds, Jack could only see Delia's lips moving. Then Finn flipped a switch and turned on the speakers.

"—assuming you want more of a breathy feel there," Delia finished.

Finn nodded. "Yes, exactly. I want it breathy and sexy. Like a 'Happy Birthday, Mr. President' moment, then we'll punch it on the bridge."

Delia nodded, then put her own headphones on and set her tablet on the stand. Finn started the backing track and his hands roamed over the control panel in front of him, adjusting dials and pushing sliders until he was satisfied with whatever was showing on his computer screen.

Then Delia began to sing, and just like in the club in Calgary, Jack's world narrowed to that sound. This time there weren't conversations and clinking glasses or fans shouting out her lyrics to dilute the sound of her voice. It was raw, floating over the slow guitar. Jack couldn't categorize the song, but it made him think of speakeasies in the forties with red lights and cigarette smoke.

Whatever Finn had said earlier, Delia didn't have to do anything to make her voice sexy. Every word that came out of her mouth was a marriage between Norah Jones's rasp and Adele's soul.

"Pick me, let me be the one,
   To dance under the moon and sun.
   In this maze of hopes and fears,
   Let me be the one you hear."

Jack listened in awe, then gaped as Finn stopped her and pretended something she was doing wasn't flawless. Delia started again, then they both repeated the entire process over and over until the first verse and chorus were complete.

Mary leaned over. "Bored yet?"

Bored was the antithesis of what he was. Even after Delia had sung the same lyrics twenty times, he was still on pins and needles waiting for her to open her mouth again. It had to be a reaction to seeing something so wildly outside of his life experience—something behind the scenes. That warmth in his chest. The tingling in his hands. That would happen with any artist creating music in such an intimate setting. *It wasn't just Delia.*

Jack shook his head. "Not bored. Is this how every record is made?"

Mary shrugged. "I've only worked with Delia, but other managers talk about artists holing up in a studio for a week at a time. Recording straight. Usually that's when they're writing all their own stuff. Or working as a band."

"Doesn't Delia write?"

"She does, but that's not what the label signed her for."

Jack's brow furrowed. "So she doesn't record any of her own songs?"

Mary shook her head. "Not yet. Maybe someday."

That was a travesty. Yes, her voice was otherworldly—she could probably sing movie credits and he'd want to listen—but the one song he'd heard of Delia's that had struck him to the core had been the one at the end of her concert. The one she'd written. Maybe the reason he didn't connect with lyrics was because he'd never heard any good ones until that moment.

Finn clapped his hands. "Brilliant! Let's take a minute. I'd like to get these tracks sorted before we move on to doubling and harmonies, yeah?"

Delia set her headphones on the stand and pushed through the door into the booth. Finn sat hunched over the board with his headphones on.

Mary stood and stepped out of the way. "Here, sit for a sec."

"You should take my seat." Jack stood, but Mary was already pressed against the back wall.

She folded her arms in front of her. "You're our guest, Jack. Sit down. I'm not too feeble to stand for ten minutes."

Delia sat in Mary's chair and swivelled to face her. "How's it sounding?"

"Like another hit."

Delia raised an eyebrow. "Are you being sarcastic?"

Mary laughed. "No, I'm not being sarcastic."

"But the lyrics . . ."

"Nobody listens to the lyrics." Mary waved her off, and Delia turned to Jack with a questioning look.

He looked between the two of them. The song hadn't hit him like the one at the concert, but he'd definitely been more focused on the way her lips moved around the words rather than the words themselves. He wet his lips. "I don't usually listen to lyrics."

"But?"

But I listened to yours. Jack shook his head. "I also don't listen to this kind of music."

Delia's expression fell, and he wished he could take his response back. She sighed. "He doesn't count because he's not my target audience."

Mary grinned. "How much time left?"

Delia rubbed her temples. "Probably a half hour or so? Why, do you want to do something?"

Mary nodded. "It's been crazy. I thought we could go for dinner? Talk about this collab with Ethan Hayes?"

Delia's expression brightened. "Do we *have* a collab with Ethan Hayes? Did IndieLake actually set it up?"

"They're still talking with his manager, but I think it's moving along."

Jack thought back to all the conversations he'd had with his coaches and agent back in the day. How in high school and college they were always working behind the scenes to get him in front of the right people, to give him opportunities to learn from players who were just ahead of him on the NHL-hopeful path. That part of the business made sense to him. No matter what industry you were in, networking and locking in resources were imperative to levelling up.

Just that tiny slice of his world slammed Jack back into reality. He was there for just over twenty-four hours to make a buzz, then he'd fly back to Calgary first thing in the morning and do what he knew. Hockey. After practice, he'd have a game—where he'd hopefully perform better than the last one—and with all the press, he'd be one step closer to nailing down a contract for next season.

Delia stood, and Jack caught the scent of her shampoo as she stepped back into the booth and slipped her headphones back on.

"Alright, love. Try something new on that last bridge, yeah? Maybe a small run—something fanciful." Finn ran a hand through his hair, and Delia laughed.

Jack clenched his jaw. This wasn't his world. They were comfortable with each other here. Finn and Delia were a little more comfortable than he preferred. And just like in the restaurant, that tightness in his chest and the swoop in his belly told him he needed to leave. There was zero reason for him to be in the booth and one very pressing reason for him not to be. He was enjoying this. He wanted to keep watching her, and he didn't appreciate that Finn kept grinning and calling her "love."

The paparazzi had gotten pictures of him at breakfast with Delia. They'd snapped some shots as they entered the recording studio, which meant his job there was done. This wasn't a relationship, and the more time he spent with Delia, the easier it would be for that line to get blurry.

Jack leaned over to Mary. "I'm going to head back to the hotel. I have an early flight."

She frowned and looked at her phone. "It's only two in the afternoon."

He stood. "I'm old, remember?"

Mary laughed, and Finn held up a hand for quiet. She motioned for them to step out of the room. "Don't you want to wait until she's done?" Mary asked as soon as they were in the hall.

Jack shook his head. "No, I think Tony's in touch with the marketing person with the Blizzard. I'm sure they'll figure out our next photo op."

Mary's eyes narrowed. "Right."

"Thanks for letting me tag along. I'll just . . ." Jack motioned to the door, and Mary nodded. He turned and walked down the hall, then pushed out the front doors and froze as a barrage of arms and cameras accosted him on the sidewalk.

"Jack! Over here!"

"Jack, where's Delia? Are you in love?"

"Jack! Give us a smile!"

He scrambled for the door handle and fell back into the studio foyer.

"Forget something?" Mary still stood in the hall, looking at her phone.

"There are at least fifty reporters out there."

Mary cursed under her breath. "Do you have security through your team in Calgary?"

"I haven't thought twice about it."

"You might need to. But don't worry, I'll take care of it." She tapped something on her phone screen.

Delia burst out of the recording studio and walked down the hall. "Mary? Finn says we're finished, and—" She pulled to a stop when she saw Jack. "Oh. I was just going to ask where you went."

Something fizzed in Jack's chest. She was looking for him. "I was going back to the hotel, but it seems we've attracted some attention."

Delia walked to the window and peeked out through the blinds. "Oh." She backed up. "Do you still have that driver, Mary?"

Mary nodded and turned to Jack. "He's on it. We can drop you at the hotel on our way home."

"See you, Finn!" Delia yelled down the hall as she grabbed her coat. It looked like it had been taken from a recently shorn sheep. Jack noted how the soft cream colour brought out the blue in her eyes. And that she didn't go back into the studio to say goodbye to Finn in person.

Mary gasped and gripped her phone like a venomous snake. *"Shit!* Shit, shit—" She looked up, her eyes panicked. "I'm supposed to pick up my niece after school *right now* and take her out for tea today. It's our birthday thing."

"What time?" Delia didn't bite on the panic.

"Her school is out in half an hour. I don't have my car. I came with the driver." Mary pressed her thumb and forefinger on either side of the bridge of her nose. "Let's go. I'll phone the school in the car, and—"

"You could make it, couldn't you? If you went straight to the school?" Delia shoved her arms into her fleecy coat sleeves.

"Probably, but I wouldn't have time to take you home, Dels." Mary glanced at Jack. "The hotel's on the way, at least."

Delia let her coat slip off her shoulders. "No problem, I could just hang out here. I'm sure Finn wouldn't—"

"Or you could come to the hotel." Jack blurted as he pulled off an ice cream cone cup next to the water tank. Mary and Delia blinked at him. He held his cup under the dispenser and pressed the blue button.

Where the hell had that come from? He didn't want Delia to come with him anywhere, especially not alone to his hotel room. But the idea of her taking off that coat and walking back into the room with Finn Gallagher tied his stomach in knots. He backpedalled. "Not that you have to. There are probably better places to kill an hour."

Mary chewed on her lower lip. "It would be more than an hour. Unless I sent the driver back to get you after dropping me and Alice off at the Palace Hotel, but then he wouldn't be able to get back for us until—"

"It's fine, Mary. I'll hang out at the hotel with Jack until you're done, then we can head home together." Delia turned her eyes on him. Her tongue flicked over her lips. "You sure that's okay?"

He nodded, ignoring how it suddenly felt like he was standing on the deck of a ski boat going full speed.

Mary exhaled. "You two are the best." Her phone screen lit up. She tapped something and slid it into her jacket pocket. "Okay, ready to face the masses?"

CHAPTER
Twelve

DELIA'S MOUTH was dry by the time they pulled up to Jack's hotel. She was coming down from a mountain of hypochondriac-ish thoughts after searching through articles about the benefits of corticosteroids. Even though she didn't have an inhaler, dry mouth had been listed as a complication, and a part of her was positive her cotton mouth was a symptom of something related. Hashtag worth it since she'd stumbled upon an article stating that chronic inflammation could be as damaging as drugs. Which she'd promptly forwarded to her mother.

Delia grabbed a bottled water from the side door of the car and snuck a drink before the driver pulled to a stop in the circular drop-off zone. *No waiting fans.* That was a relief.

"Looks like they haven't figured out you're staying here. Bets on how long that will last?" Mary winked. "Thanks, you guys. I'm so sorry I didn't bring a separate car."

"It's almost like you've never been a manager for anyone before." Delia laughed at Mary's expression and squeezed her friend's knee. "I'm kidding, Mary! I'd way rather have you working with me than somebody who's been in the business for twenty years. You still have light in your soul."

Delia met Mary in Vancouver at a music festival back in 2019 before the shutdown, and since they were both living in Toronto at the time, they'd gotten together when they were back in town. Mary had been working for some band from small-town Alberta that broke up a week after the festival because one of their guitarists had to go into rehab.

Mary grinned. "I'm fooling everyone, then." Mary had signed on with her during COVID when Delia dove headlong into social media music creation. It wasn't anything official, Mary had simply started promoting her for fun. Delia kept going to Mary for answers to her music industry questions and sending her coffee money through PayPal as thanks. When her actual agent had been less than impressive during her contract negotiations with IndieLake, she'd asked Mary to be her official manager. So far, Mary had been outstanding.

Delia blew Mary a kiss and slid down the leather seat as Jack pushed out of the car. She trailed him through the glass doors, then through the lobby to the elevators. There weren't many people checking in, but a few of the workers did double takes.

The whole thing felt like some cosmic experiment she'd been thrown into and was directly benefiting from. It made her watch herself from two different angles. Inside and out. *Will they notice me here? Will they love my music if it sounds like this? Will they know me in this province? Do they recognize me outside of Canada?*

It was like having a split persona. She had an insatiable drive to be a household name, to blast her music to the stratosphere, but also wished she could do it anonymously. Delia wanted a "fame" switch that she could turn on and off when it suited her, and that was likely the most spoiled, entitled thought she'd ever had. She kept it to herself as she and Jack stepped into an open elevator.

Jack hit the number twelve, and that's when it hit her that she was going with him *alone* to his hotel room. The car ride from the café and then the walk from the car to the elevator was the only alone time they'd ever had, and they'd still had a driver present. Inside the room, it would be just the two of them.

Delia's heartbeat pulsed in her armpits, and she unzipped the front of her coat. Just as the doors were about to close, someone stuck their hand through. "Ooh! Sorry, do you mind?" A plump woman who looked like a stay-at-home mom who'd gotten her first taste of freedom with hair appointments and shopping trips lumbered into the elevator dragging two monstrous designer suitcases.

"No problem. What floor?" Jack asked.

"Ten. Thank you . . ." The woman trailed off as she registered Jack's face. She worked to catch her breath. "Oh you *are* more handsome in person. And tall. And . . . big."

Jack chuckled. "Thank you, I think?"

The woman's eyes lit up. "My daughter is a dancer for the Stampeders, did you know that?"

Delia pursed her lips, watching the scene play out with someone else for once. It was so much more fun being on the sidelines.

"Sounds like a dream job." Jack leaned against the wall, and Delia grinned. Did he not see where she was going with that or was he trying to act daft?

The woman pressed on. "Oh, yes. She auditioned twice and finally got it. She's gorgeous—long blonde hair and green eyes—and shockingly flexible."

Jack kept his expression serious, and it made the whole thing even more hilarious. "You'd have to be. Those routines are demanding."

Delia couldn't do it anymore. She turned to hide her smile. *Demanding?* The elevator dinged and the woman tried to beat her bags into submission so she could exit onto her floor.

"Here, let me help." Jack grabbed one of the suitcases and hoisted it over the other, then reached for the second one and dragged it out onto the blue swirled carpet.

"Well, aren't you just the sweetest." The woman stopped between the doors with arms out like a bouncer, blocking Jack's path back to the elevator. "Can I give you Allison's number? I have to tell you, she's talked about you—well, she and her friends talk about you all the time. Hoping they'll run into you at the bar in Calgary or something. They see other Blizzard players there sometimes."

Jack smiled like he was meeting his girlfriend's parents on grad night. "Well, maybe we'll run into each other—"

"Let me give you her number and maybe—" The woman stopped as Delia tapped her arm.

"Ma'am, do you mind letting my boyfriend back onto the elevator?" She smiled sweetly as the buzzer on the elevator started to complain.

The woman's eyes widened. "Oh! I didn't even see you there." She turned back to Jack. "I'm sorry, you're dating some-one?" she asked, like she couldn't believe he'd two-timed her Canadian-Football-League-dancing daughter.

"I am." Jack slipped past her outstretched arm to stand next to Delia again in the elevator. It was all instinct that sent Delia's arm around his waist. Jack was still in his coat, so it was like she was holding a marshmallow, but her heart still doubled its beats.

The woman watched in dismay as the doors closed, and once they started to move, Delia stepped away and dropped her arm. "Sorry, I—"

"No. It was logistical." Jack smirked, parroting her words from earlier.

"Right." Delia nodded. Once she saw that Jack wasn't put off by her little show, she finally let out the laugh she'd been holding in. "Can you believe she just tried to set you up with her daughter? By telling you how *flexible* she was?" Jack raised an eyebrow, and Delia's laugh turned into a groan. "Right. Hockey player. You have irrational confidence."

Jack snorted. "What is that supposed to mean?"

The elevator doors opened on their floor, and Delia stepped out only to realize she didn't know which room they were heading to. She waited for him to take the lead. "It means you guys all believe the sun shines out your asses. *Of course every mom would want their daughter to sleep with me.*"

"Please, tell me more." Jack walked past her and turned right. "And that was a terrible impression, by the way."

Delia ignored him. Her impressions were excellent. "Every hockey player I've ever met thought he was God's gift to women, that's all I'm saying."

Jack stopped in front of room 1228. "You sound a little jealous." He fished in his pocket for his key.

"Jealous? Uh, no. Annoyed, maybe? Here are all these attractive men who aren't emotionally available because they've had boobs in their faces since high school. Maybe if women ignored their thirst for men in uniforms or their twisted biological propensity for latching onto anything resembling toxic masculinity—" She stopped, realizing that Jack was leaning against the doorframe, watching her. The walls pressed a little too close.

"No, please. Tell me how you really feel."

Delia pursed her lips. "I think I'm done."

"Are you?" Jack smirked. Delia nodded, then glanced down at the key in his hand. He swiped it over the door handle.

As the door clicked open, any remaining thoughts jumbled together and lodged in her throat. *She was going into a hotel room with Jack Harrison.* Her fake boyfriend whom she'd just touched in the elevator because she didn't want some mom to set him up. *Maybe he wanted to be set up with a CFL dancer, had she considered that?* This wasn't a real relationship, and she'd prevented him from meeting some woman who was apparently quite flexible.

She on the other hand was *not* flexible, not even after doing pilates and yoga in her living room twice a week for the last month. She'd pulled a hamstring trying to lower her heels in downward dog, and it still wasn't fully functional. Then she'd berated him for *liking boobs* and—

"Delia?"

"Hmm?"

Jack waited, holding the door open for her. Delia clenched her hands and walked through.

"Have you ever dated a hockey player?" he asked, shrugging off his coat.

"Uh, no."

He threw his coat over the back of the armchair. "Well, there's your problem."

Delia gave him a skeptical look. "I don't need to have first-hand experience with a hammer to know it pounds nails."

Jack leaned on the kitchenette counter, and Delia took in the space. It wasn't just a regular hotel room, there was a living area and separate bedroom. A T-shirt and possibly a pair of boxers sat rumpled on the couch. "Okay. Maybe I am a little jealous."

"Of which part?"

"Of that." Delia pointed at the clothes. "Of the fact that you had no hesitation inviting someone over to your hotel room even though you knew it wasn't perfectly clean."

"It needs to be clean?" Jack took a step toward the couch, but Delia stopped him.

"No, it doesn't need to be clean. That's the point." She took off her coat and dropped it next to his. "But I'd have thought about it for a solid few minutes, trying to figure out whether it would make me look like a slob if someone else saw my clothes out. Then I'd worry about what we'd do once we got there and how I could be a good host so whoever I was inviting wouldn't be bored, or worse, think *I* was boring.

"I would've thought about snacks, whether it smelled funny, or if it was a guy I was interested in, all of that would be multiplied by ten because I'd also be wondering what his expectations were or whether he'd find me attractive—" Delia stopped, realizing Jack hadn't moved. She bit her lip. "You just get to give out hotel invitations willy-nilly. And get asked in an elevator if you want to sleep with flexible girls. So. That was all information you probably never wanted to know."

Jack shifted on his feet. "You go through all of that anytime you invite someone over?"

Delia swallowed. "Yeah. So that's what I'm jealous of. It would be really nice to only think,'Of course he's into me, why wouldn't he be?' or 'My house is great as it is, take it or leave it.'"

Jack considered her for a moment, then strode forward. His arm brushed hers as he passed, and the hairs there stood at attention. "It's not that we don't worry, or at least I do. We've just had a lot of practise pretending like nothing ruffles us. It's necessary on the ice. And in the dressing room." He picked up his boxers and shirt and tossed them through the open door to his bedroom.

"You didn't need to do that."

Jack sat down on the couch. "Just give me a sec. I'm thinking of options for how to keep you from getting bored."

Delia groaned. "And I'm never going to let my inside thoughts out again."

"Doubtful. I'm at three for three." Delia's cheeks warmed. *He'd been counting?* Jack looked up. "I'm kidding. I like your inside thoughts."

"I don't think our contract stipulates you have to lie to protect my feelings."

A smile spread across Jack's lips, and it was like the sun peeked out through the clouds. Had she noticed how long and thick his lashes were? Had she seen those smile lines at the corners of his eyes?

He looked away and grabbed the remote. "I already had a boredom plan, by the way."

"Which was?"

"We go down to the concierge lounge and get snacks and then watch a movie." Delia winced, and Jack held up a hand. "I have an extra toothbrush in the washroom. I forgot mine, and when I phoned the front desk last night, they sent up two."

She opened her mouth but nothing came out. *How had he known what she was thinking?* Her mind buzzed with an explanation. She'd talked about it when they'd eaten together in Calgary, but hadn't said anything that morning, had she? "You must think I'm crazy."

"A little. But I'm the one who rubs his hockey stick three times on both sides before a game, so . . ."

"Is that a euphemism?"

Jack laughed and stood. "Let's go make your teeth fuzzy."

———

Delia popped a mini quiche into her mouth and pulled the blanket higher on her legs. "This is so classic. Every Bond girl is like that, and you know she's going to die. Like, how did the Hero's Journey even become popular? It's all about some macho guy losing everything he's ever loved and being so strong he can live a life of isolation and sadness. How is that a fun story?"

Jack broke a chocolate chip cookie in half. "Probably because he saved the world. It's the price he has to pay."

"So he can't save the world and have a healthy relationship?"

"They kill anyone he's with, so why waste time on a relationship?"

Delia scoffed. "So you think he knows those women are going to die? He just has to hurry and bang them first?"

Jack shrugged. "I mean, saving the world is stressful. Gotta blow off some steam. Plus, if you knew you were about to die, wouldn't you like to go out with a bang?"

Delia snorted. "So he's doing *them* the favour?"

"God's gift to women, right?"

Delia was about to launch into another diatribe, but her phone buzzed and she hunted for it underneath the blanket. She grazed Jack's hand and jumped. "Sorry."

Jack didn't say anything, but her fingertips burned as she

finally located her phone between the seat cushions. *It was Mary.* Delia checked the time. *Had it already been two hours?* Yeesh. Almost three. She answered. "Hey, are you all done with tea?"

"Yes, it was perfect. The egg salad sandwiches were the winners. Thank you again so much for being willing to put your day on hold so I could do this."

Delia looked up to see double-oh-seven double-oh-doing it on the counter of his washroom. She rolled her eyes extra dramatically so Jack wouldn't miss it. He laughed, and she couldn't keep from grinning. "It was totally fine. Jack and I are watching old movies."

Mary was silent for a beat. "What kind of old movies?"

"We watched the last half of 'Sleepless in Seattle' and now we're onto one of the Bond movies with that British guy."

Mary laughed. "They're all British guys, Dels."

"Yeah, but you know the one."

"Pierce Brosnan?"

Delia laughed. "Yes, see? Perfect description."

"She got Brosnan off of 'that British guy?'" Jack shook his head and reached for a can of Coke.

"Is that Jack?" Mary asked.

Delia pulled off the blanket and stood, then walked past Jack to the washroom so she could brush her teeth. Again. "Are you here? Should I get my coat and come down?" She turned the phone on speaker and used some of Jack's toothpaste. It was straight peppermint. Different than her typical, but she liked it.

"Is that water running? Are you on the toilet?"

Delia shoved the toothbrush into her mouth and scrubbed. "No, just brushing my teeth."

"You're using *Jack's toothbrush?* What the hell, Delia?"

Delia laughed and sprayed a bit of toothpaste on the mirror. "No! He had an extra!"

"I don't even know who you are right now."

Delia finished and rinsed her mouth and the toothbrush, then used a square of toilet paper to clean off the mirror. "He had an extra toothbrush from the front desk." Another silence. "Mary, are you still—"

"Yeah, I'm here. Like, on the phone but also at the hotel. I'm just at the roundabout where I dropped you off."

"Okay, I'll be down in a sec." Delia ended the call and slipped her phone into her back pocket, then walked back into the living room.

Jack craned his neck. "You missed it. She's already dead."

Delia laughed. "Damn it, I was hoping for one more non-committal lay."

"Title of your sex tape." Jack looked up with an almost repentant look, but couldn't quite get the corners of his mouth to lay flat. Delia almost succeeded in convincing him she was offended, but couldn't keep the laugh from bursting out of her. She reached for her coat but hesitated with it in her hands.

"Mary's here?" Jack asked.

Delia nodded. "Thanks for letting me crash."

Jack sat straighter on the couch. "What are fake boyfriends for?"

Delia twisted the coat around so she could find the arm holes. "Your flight leaves early?"

Jack nodded. "I have meetings in the morning."

"With your team?"

He shook his head. "No, for my actual job."

Delia frowned. "Wait, your actual job?"

He laughed and ran a hand through his hair. There was just enough light filtering in through the closed curtains to make the motion look almost erotic. Delia looked down at her coat even though she already had a finger on the zipper.

"I do product distribution and development for a snowboarding company," Jack said. "I have no idea if I'll last through this season with the Blizzard, let alone next, so I'm doing double duty."

"Double-oh-duty," Delia murmured, and Jack's brow pulled together.

"What?"

She shook her head. "Nothing." Delia pursed her lips. "So you'll just be hanging out, getting some sleep tonight?"

Jack nodded. "I was thinking about reaching out to some friends while I was here, but I realized anyone I would want to see isn't around anymore. It's been a few years."

A banner popped up on Delia's phone. Mary was texting, but she ignored it. Her arms were jittery. "Do you—I don't want to be presumptuous, but do you mind if I stay and finish the movie?" Her heart pounded like a gavel. What if Jack was waiting for her to leave so he could be alone? Or maybe he hated that movie and didn't want to watch the ending?

Jack leaned over his knees. "Yeah, of course. I mean, no, I don't mind, but is Mary—"

"I was going to invite her up." Delia started typing. "I think we pay the same for the car service today no matter how long we have it. So maybe she could join us for a bit? She wanted to go out for dinner, but I kind of . . . I don't know. I don't feel like going out right now. Maybe we could order pizza or something."

"I was going to order from One Night Only. It's been forever since I've had their pies."

Delia sent the text, and Mary responded instantly.

You want . . . to keep hanging out with Jack?

No, he's just by himself. He was thinking of ordering pizza, so I thought we could keep him company

She left out the part about her asking to stay before she knew he didn't have plans and wanted to order pizza.

. . .

MARY

> Since when do you want to keep people
> company?

> If you don't want to, it's fine. I can come down

> Is this because he got you a toothbrush?

> MARY

> I'm coming up. Chill. What room?

Delia gave her the information and was about to put her phone away when she saw one last text come through.

> I know you're trying to be nice, but he's not
> your boyfriend, Dels

Shame washed over her. Deep down, she knew she didn't care how Bond ended.

> Well aware, thanks

Delia clicked off her phone and slid it into her back pocket, then set her coat back on the chair.

"She's coming up?" Jack kicked his feet up on the coffee table.

He could sit there like nothing was amiss. Like it was normal for a girl to choose to stay here rather than make other plans. *Jealous.* Delia nodded. "Yep."

"Everything okay?"

Delia smiled tightly and took off her coat. "Mmhmm."

"I'm glad you're staying," Jack said, and Delia looked up. "One Night Only has a better deal on full pizzas and I wanted two flavours, but I definitely can't eat two pizzas by myself."

Delia's heart dropped as she walked back to the couch. "Have you ever tried to eat two?"

"Once. Didn't end well."

Delia sat down in her spot and picked up her glass of water. "Pictures or it didn't happen."

———

At just after midnight, Delia yawned, waved to Mary on the curb, then walked in her front door. There weren't people parked outside her gated neighbourhood, probably because of the hour. Also possibly because the paparazzi were all at the hotel when she and Mary left Jack's room. They hadn't intended to watch a second Bond movie and then play beer pong after eating enough of those two pizzas that Delia was already gassy, but it was what the night had demanded.

Jack was cool. Just like the first night they met, it seemed impossible to have a filter with him. She couldn't help but blurt out what she was thinking, and somehow he didn't think it was weird or off-putting. Or if he did, he was excellent at not letting it show on his face. *We've just had a lot of practise pretending nothing ruffles us.*

Earlier, Delia admitted she didn't love watching hockey, but she hadn't thought twice about it since Jack had already admitted he didn't listen to song lyrics and wasn't a fan of her music. Maybe he still wasn't? *Maybe he wasn't a fan of her?*

Maybe he was just pretending. Getting a kick out of her. Texting his teammates about the ridiculous things she said.

A rock settled in her stomach as she hung her coat and took off her shoes. *No.* It didn't track. She'd seen his face during the recording session that afternoon. She'd tried not to look at him so she wouldn't get distracted, but she couldn't help it. Even through the tinted glass, she saw him sitting off to the side watching her. His brow had been furrowed, not in anger, but in concentration. Like he needed to make sense of it. Make sense of her.

He liked her singing. She knew it like she knew what word should come next in a poem. And he'd been the one to invite her to the hotel. Maybe it was so he could mock her in private, but she was going to try and erase that possibility so she could sleep at night.

Delia shivered as she walked into the kitchen and set her bag on the chair, then filled the tea kettle with water. The idea of eating anything after all that pizza made her want to die, but some lemon tea sounded like just the thing before bed.

She thought about asking her mom if she wanted anything, then realized she would've left over an hour ago for her night shift. *Not much longer.*

Every time she thought about how her mother had kept food on their table and a roof over their heads for twenty-five years, solo, her commitment redoubled. Her mother had made whatever sacrifices she needed to to get Delia lessons or opportunities in summer music camps. Now it was she who needed help, and Delia would give whatever it took to get her healthy.

Singing and performing didn't feel anywhere close to the same level of sacrifice her mother had made, but recording IndieLake's music did require her to give something of herself. Would she have signed with them had she not needed that advance? Could she have taken her time and worked her way up with her own songs? Maybe. But maybe not. It really didn't matter at that point.

The teapot started to whistle, and just as Delia was about to take it off the heat, her phone buzzed on the table. Her heart leaped, and she only realized she was hoping it was Jack when she saw Tony's name at the top of her screen.

"You know it's after midnight, right?"

Tony exhaled. "I was planning to leave you a message. I didn't expect you to pick up, I was just too lazy to type everything out."

Delia pinned the phone between her shoulder and ear and walked back to the stove to make her tea. "What's going on?"

"Well, first of all, you and Jack are absolutely killing it with your public appearances. Kels sent me a picture of him wrapping you in his arms and walking you into the recording studio. Insert *awwws* heard around the world."

Delia grinned, then tried to sound nonchalant as she said, "That's already up?"

"Definitely. Oh, and I also found a TikTok from someone working at the Radisson. They saw you two walk in together and head to the elevators."

Delia poured the hot water into a mug. "Right, that was an extra bonus we thought we'd throw in." *It had been all strategy.*

"I heard about the media frenzy at the recording studio and at the hotel when you left, but Delia, you were there till midnight?"

Delia sensed the judgment in his tone. "Mary was there, too. We were hanging out and eating pizza."

"But you didn't have to spend more time with him, you know that, right? Your contract only stipulates—"

"I know, Tony. I was being nice. He was all alone for the night." Delia ripped open the tea bag and plopped it in the mug, then threw out the paper wrapping. "Is this why you phoned? To make sure I understood the contract?"

Tony blew out a breath. "No, though I'm glad we hit on that. I wanted to leave you a message about two things. First, I got you a spot on 'Late Night with Ken Massey.' Films there in the city, so it's easy enough to get to for tomorrow night."

Delia froze. "*Tomorrow?*"

"Breathe, I'm not finished. I also heard back from Ethan on that collaboration."

Delia wrapped her hands around her mug. "And?"

"He's in. But, he doesn't want to work together online. I told him that was perfect because . . . you're moving to Calgary for a bit anyway."

"*What?*" Delia nearly sloshed hot water onto her jeans.

"Think about it, Delia. Your popularity is skyrocketing, and every time you and Jack are seen together, we reach a new shelf. Plus, it might be good for you to be seen supporting him in his endeavours."

Her head spun. A late-night appearance. A collab with Ethan. Moving to *Calgary?* "Does Jack know?"

It sounded like Tony was rubbing his eyes. "No, I'm working with the Blizzard's marketing lead on this. It's a win-win. They're hitting him with a bunch of media opportunities which will compliment our efforts."

What about her mom? Delia was already running the logistics of leaving her home. She'd have to talk to Finn. See if they needed any retakes before she left, and *what about her mom?* "How long would I be there for?"

"Just until the NHL playoffs are over. Maybe a little less if the Blizzard are knocked out early. At which point you and Jack will publicly break up, and you'll start your promo for the album."

Delia blew on her drink and inhaled the scent of peppermint. "And Mary?" She scrambled for anything to talk about until she could come up with an appropriate ask. She couldn't leave her mom there working by herself. She needed someone to at least check in on her, and that was the bare minimum.

"Mary will come with you. We already have our eyes on a bed and breakfast on the north side of town."

"Okay. Okay." Delia blew out a breath. "Tony, we'll need to hire someone here at the house. Someone to grocery shop and clean once a week."

"That's money, Delia."

"I know. But it's not optional if I'm leaving." Delia bit the inside of her cheek. She could post more on socials. Get more pics out and about. With the collaboration official, Ethan's audience could be tapped as well.

"Fine, have Mary set it up. We still have a few logistics to work out. I was thinking you could wait until tomorrow night to shout this turn of events from the rooftops. Preferably on national TV."

CHAPTER
Thirteen

JACK WALKED into the dressing room. He felt oddly naked not carrying his stuff with him. No clanking of his equipment, no musky scent of sweat-soaked pads. When he practiced with the Snowballs, they always had to hustle to clear out of the dressing room, and the routine was ingrained in his muscle memory. Now, all his equipment had a home in the metal lockers. They even had a guy who cleaned and sanitized their equipment. After this, he was never going to play so clean again in his life.

"Look who decided to show." Johansson shot him an unimpressed look while he applied tape to his left knee.

Jack didn't respond to that. He knew better than to stoke the flames with excuses or explanations. He doubted there had been an announcement from management in the dressing room about how he was allowed to miss practice for a girl. The truth—his truth—seemed insignificant against the backdrop of rumours that must have been circulating like norovirus. The guys had all seen the headlines.

He imagined what he'd be thinking about himself had he been on the other side, and none of it was good. He'd known plenty of F-boys in his time with the AHL. The second they miffed it on the ice, every guy on the team was thinking the same thing. It meant he had to kill it out there to prove his priorities were lined up. To prove he belonged there with the rest of them.

Jack stopped at his locker and opened it. The door slammed with a clang as he wrestled with his bag and pulled out his gear.

"Special privileges if you're making press, eh?" Nathan said next to him. He smiled to make the comment seem like a joke, but Jack knew it wasn't.

"I'm here to play." Jack stripped off his sweatshirt and pulled on his base shirt.

"Which game, though, bud?" Tkachuk shot him a look, then sat on the bench to lace up his skates.

Nathan nudged his shoulder. "It's bringing people out to the games, so it's good for the team. These assholes are just jealous you were with Delia last night and they were left tugging chubs in the shower."

Jack chuckled and left that alone. He didn't love that they were all making assumptions about his sex life, but the idea of setting the record straight was worse. He flew out to Toronto to see her, and the whole world knew she'd been with him at his hotel. When he'd seen the pictures at the airport the next morning, it hadn't registered that it was him. He looked confident. Cool next to Delia with her auburn waves. It was like there was a version of himself with rizz that he was only privy to through camera lenses.

Jack finished suiting up and was just starting to lace his skates as the buzz of the dressing room tapered into a focused silence. All attention converged on Coach Novak, who stood on top of the Blizzard logo, clipboard in hand.

"Morning, gentlemen," he began. "Today, we're going to focus on refining our power play strategies. We've got a chance to turn the tide this season, but it's going to require every single one of you to push harder, think faster, and work together more seamlessly than ever before."

Assistant Coach Kreviasuk took over, diving into the tactical nuances, dissecting video clips of their previous games with critique. "Here," he pointed at the screen, "is where we need to adjust. The Oilers won't let that pass." He outlined a few play adjustments, then sent them to the ice. Before Jack could exit, he heard his name and turned.

Lisa Carter was there next to the water station. She motioned for him to leave the flood of players and join her. He set his helmet on the bench and leaned his stick against the lockers as she handed him a paper.

"This is a preliminary press schedule for the next week. It's built around your training and game commitments, of course. We were also hoping you could set up a time to film with Country—you're still on good terms from your time with the Snowballs, yes?"

Jack nodded. "I didn't realize you knew anything about my past team."

Lisa smiled. "We're careful about who we bring onto this team, Jack. Even when the fan base is clamouring for movement."

"Yeah. I can reach out to Country." Jack had already told him he'd come on the show when he didn't have a game, he just hadn't put a date on the calendar. He'd been a bit distracted the last week.

"We think it would be best if that was filmed with Delia present, too."

Jack lowered the paper. "That's not up to me. She's recording a new album in Toronto."

"Don't worry about the logistics. I think we've almost got that covered."

Jack frowned. *Almost got what covered?* It should've been off-putting to be a pawn in a game when he couldn't even see the chessboard, but it didn't. The sensation was normal. That was almost more disturbing than being blindly obedient.

How many times had he shown up to practices and worked his ass off knowing he had no control over what decision would be made behind the curtain? The idea that he could only perform to the best of his ability and then he'd have to cross his fingers and pray for the rest had been ingrained in him since the time he could barely skate.

"Okay, I'll rearrange my schedule to make sure I'm available." Jack folded the paper and walked back. A metal clank made him jump. He opened his own locker and slipped in the paper, then went down the front aisle to see what the ruckus was.

Jack smiled to himself. Liam MacDonald, a Rookie from Boise, Idaho, scrambled to put on his clothes. "You need anything?" Jack asked.

Liam grunted. "I don't need smug-ass comments."

Jack stopped on the other side of his locker. "I was a hardship claim, bud. I'm the last person in here who's going to judge you for showing up late to practice."

Liam looked up, then shoved his head through the neck hole of his jersey. It was enough for Jack to see the whites of his eyes were bloodshot and watery. He was either high at the moment or severely hungover. A pit opened up in Jack's stomach. Liam had to be nineteen, barely, and Jack remembered what that looked like. He hadn't even been signed to an NHL team and he still could've been at parties four nights a week if he wanted to. The drugs. The women throwing themselves at him. *Here are all these attractive men who aren't emotionally available because they've had boobs in their faces since high school.* That comment out of Delia's mouth had stung.

The truth was, Jack would've been sucked in like the rest of them without Brad and James to keep him on the straight and narrow. They were at the gym religiously every morning at six, and since he was rooming with them, the peer pressure to get his ass out of bed and join them was intense. Especially since they were all competing for the same NHL slots. Then a few years later, Brad introduced him to his cousin Angela. At that point, any speck of desire that had existed for him to party had been extinguished. The boys kept him focused, and Ange had kept him safe. He'd seen plenty of guys burn out, get DUI's, OD, or stop caring because they liked weed and porn more than working till they puked at practice.

"I'm Jack Harrison." He put out his hand, but Liam didn't take it.

"Yeah. I know who you are."

"You're strong out there on the ice. It's impressive." Jack wasn't pandering. He'd noticed MacDonald at his first practice. The kid was as quick as a loon taking flight over Muskoka and almost as graceful. Plus he had a shoulder on him. And enough angst to fuel it.

"Thanks, Gramps."

Jack chuckled. "You're a little shit. That's okay, though. I was, too." He clapped him once on the shoulder pad and exited the dressing room.

Practice went fast, especially because Jack felt like he was huffing paint. His lungs burned, which made no sense. He'd only spent twenty-four hours at lower altitude, and even though he took the evening off to hang out with Delia and Mary, he'd still done sets at the gym before his flight. He was going to have to find a way to squeeze in more conditioning, especially if his media appearances were going to take him away from practice.

After he showered, Jack looked over the sheet Lisa had given him and compared it with his calendar. He'd gotten to the following Monday when a message popped up. His heart snagged when he read Delia's name. He clicked on the message.

> You get home ok?

> Yep, just finished practice

Jack typed out a few options for what he could ask her but then deleted them. *Did you get home safe?* Seemed a little late to ask that question. He'd thought about texting the night before, but a midnight text felt weirdly intimate when she knew he was alone in the hotel room she'd just vacated. *Did you have a good day?* Lame. And unnecessary. They didn't need to know about each other's days. They only needed to know where their next meeting was. But Delia had just asked if he got home safely . . .

> When will you be home?

The tips of Jack's fingers tingled. Why did she want to know that? *Why did he want her to know that?*

> Packing up. I'll be home in thirty. Everything good?

The idea that Delia might need something from him or have a problem he could help with sent his pulse racing. He lowered his phone and reached for his shirt hanging on the hook in his locker. Delia had texted back by the time he pulled it over his head.

> I'm in a green room. They don't have tea, so basically dying

Jack grinned and knew exactly what to text next.

> Do they have toothbrushes, though? Then you can at least dig into the squirrel food

> No squirrel food either. Only candy and gross protein bars

> For the squirrels on a bulk

He sent it too fast to question whether that was actually funny, then stared at the messages. Delia was in a green room? She hadn't mentioned anything about a show tonight, though they hadn't talked about anything beyond Bond girls and pizza toppings. It had been nice. Simple. *Not real though.*

OMG of course that would be your first thought

Jack laughed.

"God's gift to women" doesn't happen on accident. Also, why are you in a green room?

The three dots appeared below his message, then disappeared. Jack was already imagining her biting on her lower lip. He needed to stop. He had a thousand other things he should be thinking about right now, including but not limited to how he had three pending distribution agreements that needed finessing before they were going to be accepted, as well as his current conditioning predicament. This was a relationship he didn't need to spend any time on.

But maybe that was the problem. After Ange he didn't want to put time in . . . but that was all he knew. He knew what real was. He knew what he was capable of, and he wasn't used to half-assing anything in his life.

I'm the musical guest for "Late Night with Ken Massey". Airs tonight at midnight MST

Jack audibly gasped, then cleared his throat to cover it up in case any of his teammates heard. She was doing a Late Night show? How had that not come up yesterday?

It was last minute. Tony phoned me after I got home. Otherwise, I would've told you

Something warmed in his chest. *No. It didn't matter.* He didn't need to know what was going on in her life. Though, it was probably good that he did. Kind of awkward if someone asked about it and he had no idea what his girlfriend had on her schedule.

I'll watch. Good luck

Break legs. We don't say good luck because it's actually bad luck

Who's we?

Performers. Actors. All the people you didn't know growing up because you were too cool

I wasn't too cool for the drama nerds. I mean drama kids

I KNEW IT

Why would you make the one phrase used universally to give blessings of luck to mean the opposite?

We had nothing to do with the decisions of our predecessors

Feels like you could have a town hall meeting or something

I'll put that on my list. K, they just knocked on my door

Break legs?

Exactly

Don't ever say that to me before a game

What should I say?

I don't know. Beat the shit out of them?

That sounds mean

I play hockey, Delia

That's why I don't watch

> Your stance on luck statements is why I don't listen to lyrics. It's a picket line I won't cross

Leaving now

> It's a good thing you aren't a Bond girl. You'd be dead before you left the hallway

At least I wouldn't be bound by a no-sex contract

Jack laughed out loud. When he looked up, he discovered that half the dressing room was empty. Only Lindholm and Monahan were still getting dressed behind him, and by the few creaks and slams the next aisle over, he assumed it looked much the same over there.

"Night, Jack." Monahan picked up his coat and waved as he headed to the door.

Jack hung his skates and left his dirty jersey and pads on the bench for cleaning. Again, it felt wrong not to be packing all his gear out to his truck. He closed his locker and walked down the aisle, nearly running into Liam as he stormed out of the washroom looking green around the gills. "Easy bud."

Liam muttered something under his breath and shoved past him. Jack didn't push back, though he wanted to. In the old days, something like that would've been enough for him to go to the coaches. Suggest mentorship or training to get a player straight. But that's what had gotten him in trouble in the first place. *You think you know my players better than I do?*

Hell, yes, he had. But the more he pushed, the less playing time he got.

Lace his skates. Zip his trap. Show up at the media spots and dance monkey, dance.

Jack exhaled and pushed through the dressing room door into the hall.

———

"You're going to fall asleep." Jack dropped onto the chair in the living room next to Clara and Oscar. Oscar laid on the couch with his head propped up on the pillows, and Clara was draped over him, snuggled into his chest.

Clara grunted. "No I'm not. My shower was just too hot."

Oscar played with her hair, and Clara's eyes flickered every time his knuckles brushed against her temple. "Do you have a shift at eight?"

Clara nodded. "I only have two like that this week. Thursday's off so I can recover then."

"We can DVR this. You don't have to watch it live." Jack lifted the remote, but Clara put out an arm in protest.

"Stop it! I want to see your fake girlfriend on live TV!"

Jack gave her a look. "It's not even live. She was taping hours ago."

Clara put her finger in her ear and started humming. "Stop ruining this for me. I can pretend it's live if I want to."

Jack picked up his bag of chips and shook his head. "You're ridiculous."

"Shhh!" Clara pointed at the TV as the theme music started.

"Does the musical guest come on closer to the end?" Oscar asked.

Clara nodded. "Like after the first interview, and then they all sit together on the couch."

Jack threw out a hand. "What is this, you don't shush him?"

Clara waved him off as Ken Massey appeared through the midnight-blue velvet curtains to his band's version of Shiny People. Jack didn't know all of Delia's songs, but he had been listening to them as he drove to practice. For research purposes.

They listened to the opening monologue, and Jack realized he'd forgotten how funny Ken was. He'd gotten his start in stand-up—he'd even done a stint at the Stampede. Jack had seen him live accidentally his first summer in the city. Then he'd taken over the late night slot on CBC before Christmas.

Ken announced the guests in order of appearance, Katie Mackey, an actress in a sitcom up for multiple Emmy awards, then Delia, then Zack Prior.

Clara coughed. "Zack Prior? Holy hell. He's . . ."

"He's what?" Oscar shifted on the couch under her.

"Uh, I think some women find him attractive."

Jack snorted. "Some women?" Clara's cheeks were pink.

Oscar looked unimpressed, and Clara cuddled closer. "I didn't mean it, baby. You're the only one hot enough to handle—"

"Yeah, thank you." Oscar tickled her ribs as punishment.

Jack's heart twinged, and he turned back to the TV. He loved spending time with Clara and Oscar. Loved that they were happy. But sometimes it hurt.

He thought of Delia texting him in the green room. *She'd said she was alone, hadn't she?* Had there been time where she would've interacted with the other guests? With Zack Prior? Clara was massively understating his sex appeal based on the number of times he'd seen women go catatonic the second he showed up on screen or on a billboard at the mall for a cologne ad. He'd had to wipe Clara's drool more than once while they were Christmas shopping, and there had been a fan club blocking the entrance to the Apple store.

That was Delia's life. She saw guys like Zack on a regular basis.

Jack tensed as they watched the interview with Katie. She seemed vapid and boring, but he didn't say anything since Clara seemed to be enjoying her lame-ass responses. After the commercial break, Jack's insides started to shiver. He was cold and hot and couldn't get comfortable on the chair.

"You okay, there?" Clara smirked. Jack ignored her and turned so he could rest his feet on the coffee table.

"Our next guest, I'm so excited about this you guys, she has been

absolutely dominating the charts with her new releases." Ken slapped a CD cover up on his desk, showing off the artwork to the camera. *"If you haven't heard of this woman, you've been living under a rock. She has some of the most poetic lyrics and her voice— well, I'll let that speak for itself. Everyone, welcome the beautiful and talented, Delia Melise!"*

The camera view flipped to Delia standing with her guitar in front of a mic stand. She wore Mary Janes. Jack didn't know why that was the first thing he noticed, but it was. His eyes eventually lifted past the little black straps over her feet, and he took in her cropped pants. They shimmered like satin. Her Victorian style blouse tied at the neck, and there were her perfect auburn waves that framed her face. Her eyeliner was thick, giving her eyes a smoky ring that made the blue edging of her irises pop.

She started singing, and Jack recognized the song immediately. It was the one she'd recorded in the studio. He was surprised, considering that song hadn't been released yet, but maybe that was the point? If she was doing a media spot, she wouldn't want to play something everyone knew. Or maybe it was better to do something people knew. Jack couldn't help over-thinking it to give his brain something to fixate on outside of her voice. At least on TV it was removed. He couldn't feel it reverberating through him like the live show or in the studio. That helped.

A thrill went through him as the studio audience cheered, and he thought of all the people watching the show around the country. All the clips that would be reposted on social media. He'd seen firsthand how hard she'd worked on that song. She deserved it. All of it. *He wanted them to love her.*

"She's incredible." Clara sighed into Oscar's chest. "How does she do that? Look so at ease in front of all those cameras?"

Jack grinned to himself. She probably thought she was going to throw up at any moment. At least that was how it was for him. For the first shift anyway. Then he could usually drop into the game and forget everything else, but sometimes it wasn't that simple. If he wasn't playing well, it was easy to look up and see the angry faces. Let them get in his head.

At least on a late night show, nobody was her enemy. Those would come later online. He thought of all the YouTube comments he'd read over the years, and they all carried more weight now that he knew there was a real person on the other end of it.

Delia finished her song to more cheers and applause, and then Ken was standing on the platform with her.

"Delia Melise, everyone! Wow, that was incredible!" He put his arm on her shoulder and presented her to the audience like she was something he created, then motioned for her to come to the desk. Delia handed her guitar to a man dressed in black and followed Ken to the couch where Katie Mackey was already seated. Katie stood and gave her a hug. Delia's smile slipped just a little, and Jack grinned to himself. *Not a real hug.*

He was probably a prick. Shouldn't he want her to make friends? Especially after her conversation about loneliness? It was late and his life was a runaway train. He was grappling for control over something, but it needed to not be Delia.

Ken settled behind his desk. *"Delia, congratulations on your latest single hitting number one. It must be wild to have had so many massive hits in less than a year."*

"Thank you, yeah. It's surreal, honestly. Every artist dreams of reaching people with their music, and seeing this kind of response is just . . . it's beyond words."

Katie Mackey leaned in. *"It's not surprising, though. I saw clips of your pop-up show in Calgary. You were incredible."*

"That is so nice of you to say, thank you."

Ken leaned back in his chair. *"Speaking of that pop-up, that was the first time you were spotted publicly with a certain special some-one."* He grinned as Delia blushed. *"Are we allowed to talk about it?"* Ken looked behind him as if checking with his producers. *"That's not an off-limits topic is it?"*

Delia shook her head. *"No, it's fine. That was the first night we had a chance to sit down and talk."*

Ken leaned in with a goofy smile on his face. *"I think everyone's dying to know how this all happened. Did you message each other, or . . .?"*

Delia looked down at her hands in her lap. *"We had a mutual friend. That night was kind of a blind date."*

"How do I get a friend like that?" Katie adjusted her skirt as the audience laughed. *"No, I'm serious, my friends refuse to set me up."*

Ken threw out his hands. *"Well, I knew you were both supposed to be here. Everything on this couch happens for a reason. So when Katie is dating a hockey player next week—"*

"Oh, please. If that happens, I'll be back here thanking you in person." Katie and Delia laughed.

"Delia, you need to give us something, though. Jack Harrison is on fire with the Blizzard, and you two are all over the news. I've never seen anything like it. People are dying for even a morsel of this story, so maybe you can drop a crumb here?"

"A crumb?" Delia was trying not to smile and failing. It was compelling. If Jack didn't know that they weren't actually dating, he would've been convinced she had stars in her eyes.

"Just a tiny morsel." Ken sat there grinning, and Delia finally relented.

She waited for the audience to quiet down, and Jack didn't realize he'd pulled his feet off the table. *"I wasn't planning on saying anything about this tonight, but since you asked . . ."* Delia spun a ring on her finger, and Jack could hear the gasps in the audience. Holy hell she was good at milking the moment. *"I just found out I'm going to be collaborating with an incredible songwriter who happens to live in Calgary, Ethan Hayes."* The crowd erupted, and Delia waited for them to quiet down before continuing. *"And that means I'm going to be relocating there for the next month or so."*

A second explosion of applause. Ken stood up and put out

his hands, trying to calm them down. *"Does this mean you'll be in town for the end of the NHL season and the playoffs?"*

Delia smiled. *"That's convenient, I guess."*

"You guess?" Ken clapped his hands together. *"Sounds like Jack Harrison is one lucky guy. And speaking of guys that everyone wishes they could get lucky with, we'll be right back with Zack Prior!"*

Clara pushed up, and Oscar grunted. "Jack, what is wrong with you? Why didn't you tell us Delia was moving to Calgary?"

"Umm, probably because I didn't know." *Delia was moving to Calgary.* The phrase ran on repeat as he stared at a commercial for a diabetes pump. Had she known that when she texted earlier? Was that why she wanted him to watch? Jack pulled out his phone and froze when he saw he already had a text from her.

Did you see it yet?

Blood rushed in his ears. Clara was saying something, but he couldn't focus.

I did. You're moving here?

Sorry I didn't tell you earlier. Tony made me promise to wait and announce it on the show

He would

I was a little worried. I told him we should've asked you first

"Jack? Is everything okay?" Clara leaned toward him.
He nodded. "Fine."

Why would you need to ask me?

Because I'll be there in the city. It doesn't mean we have to hang out more. We can still stick to the contract

Jack's thumbs hovered over the keyboard. He didn't know how he wanted to respond to that. Just as he was about to change the topic completely and compliment her on the show, another message popped up.

Unless there are Bond movies and pizza

THREE DAYS LATER, Delia stepped off the plane to a sleepy airport. Mary was right that flying in the morning made for less ruckus, but she abhorred dragging herself out of bed at four thirty in the morning. Even with a hat and glasses, their off-time strategy hadn't saved her from being recognized—proof that her online presence was exponentially growing. At least she had her new security detail.

Their chaperone in Toronto had been Bryce—basically a member of the King's Guard. No smiles. All efficiency. He didn't say much in the airport and didn't accompany them on the flight. The company Mary had hired said another security guard would meet them on this end, and they'd kept their promise. A young Vin Diesel look-alike had been waiting for them at the gate and was trailing the two of them to baggage claim.

Delia pulled out her phone and kept her head down with her hat lowered over her eyes. Her hair was pulled back into a bun at the base of her neck to make her even less recognizable.

Did you land safely?

Any bumps? I know bumps make you nervous.

Did security show?

Delia grinned at the messages from her mom. She answered them, then turned to Mary. "Where are we staying?"

Mary grinned. "You'll see."

Delia rolled her eyes. "Why are you and Tony being so cryptic? It's not like I'm going to tell people where we're holing up for the month."

"It's just more fun to make it a surprise."

"For it to be a surprise, I'd need to know something about this city." Delia stopped at their assigned luggage carousel, her mind spinning. Had they booked an apartment? That Airbnb? Mary wouldn't be pretending this was going to be a good surprise if it was a nasty extended-stay hotel.

Or would she? Delia imagined dirty shag carpet, cigarette burns on the sheets, and bars over the windows. They'd had to stay in one of those rooms once when she was first starting out. Vancouver had not been kind to them that trip. It would be like Mary to bring something like that back for nostalgia's sake. Delia shuddered.

"I'm sorry to bother you, but my daughter is positive you're a famous singer." A woman with a blonde bob tucked behind her ears stood next to them, gripping the hand of a little girl who looked to be about ten.

Delia smiled down at her daughter. "What kind of songs do you think I sing?" The little girl pulled her hand free and started listing them off, beginning with her first album and moving on to the songs on her most recent one, then jumping into the singles she'd played live but hadn't officially released yet. Delia laughed. "That's impressive. What's your name?"

The little girl bounced on her heels. "Norah. Can I get a

picture?" Her smile was contagious, and Delia nodded without hesitation. She crouched down and put an arm around Norah as her mom stepped back and held up her phone.

"Thank you so much. I love your music. I love your shows." Norah stepped back and snatched the phone from her mom, swiping to see the photos.

Her mom stepped forward. "Thank you so much. She has ADHD, and music is the only thing that helps her get her homework done."

Delia's heart squeezed. "You have ADHD, Norah? So do I!"

Norah's eyes lit up. "You do?"

Delia nodded. "Yep. I take medication for it sometimes, except when I'm writing or performing. Then I have to use my superpower."

Norah's little brow creased. "I don't know what medication would feel like."

Her mom sighed. "She doesn't want to feel like there's something wrong with her."

"Oh I get that. At least you have the option. When I was growing up, everyone told me my head was in the clouds, and I should figure out how to pay better attention."

Norah's jaw dropped. "My teachers tell me that all the time."

Delia crouched back down to look at Norah eye to eye. "Our brains are special. I used to wish I was like everyone else, but now I'm grateful I'm not."

There was so much she wanted to tell Norah. That school was probably going to suck for a while longer. That even when she got out of school, she was still going to have to do things that felt like pulling teeth, and she'd mess it up plenty of times before she got it right. That the world was never going to be perfectly built for people who wanted to stay up until two in the morning and sleep until noon, but that it got easier to adjust as you got older. That her creativity was so much more expansive than she knew, and as she scratched away those layers of expectation shellacked onto her through her teenage years, she'd continued to discover new ways she didn't fit and new ways she did.

Since her bags were already dumping onto the carousel, she settled on, "Find what your brain loves, and do it as much as you can. Don't worry if you get sick of it and move on to something else. It's not quitting, it's just opening a new chapter."

Norah nodded, absorbing every word like an acoustic panel. Delia didn't know if any of that advice would've been helpful for her at that age when she was struggling to make sense of the world around her. At least it could've given her hope that there was something to look forward to. The mother-daughter pair thanked her again and walked away. Delia scanned for Norah's father, but they looked to be alone. *Maybe he was at home waiting for them.* Delia chose that narrative as she waved and walked back to help Mary with the bags.

Mary grabbed a luggage cart, and they worked together to load their eight bags onto the metal rails, then walked with their guard, Alvin—Mary had gotten his name while she'd been talking to her young fan—to the parking garage. The cold air snapped against Delia's lungs. It had been frigid in Toronto, but that was next-level arctic.

"When is it spring here?" Delia zipped up her coat.

Alvin chuckled. "On and off between now and July."

Mary laughed at the expression on Delia's face. "It's next to the mountains, which means bipolar weather. It's fun."

"I have enough uncertainty in my life, thank you very much."

Alvin led them to a black SUV and opened the back hatch. He loaded their bags in, and Delia took the cart back. She jogged, hoping that would get her blood pumping.

"You can just leave it on the curb!" Mary called out, but Delia would do no such thing. She'd worked at a grocery store where people left their carts strewn across the parking lot and it had been the worst part of her shift to gather them up. Even the sound of the luggage cart knocking into the others made her wince.

She turned back to the car, and something shiny caught her eye. Delia bent down and picked up a scuffed toonie. She jogged to Mary's window and held it up like she'd just won the lottery.

Mary gave her a look as she opened the door. "Seriously? It's disgusting."

Delia rubbed it on her jeans. "That's a coffee, my friend."

Mary slid over in the back seat for Delia to squish in. "At some point, you're going to be less cheap, right?"

"Like when I'm finally getting royalty checks?" Delia fastened her seatbelt. "Yeah, I doubt it." Mary snorted, and she held out her hands in defence. "I hate wasting things. There were years when we barely had enough for two meals a day. If I didn't eat every scrap of food at school lunch, I was going to be hungry until six o'clock. Unless I wanted to eat a plain baguette for an after-school snack. Which I did on multiple occasions."

Mary took off her coat and straightened her hair. "You're as bad as your mom. I don't think she's going to quit her jobs, even if you are bringing in money."

Delia scoffed. "She will. Once she sees we have enough savings."

"She won't know what to do with herself."

"I'll force her to take a spa day. She'll get addicted and never look back." Delia doubted her mother's body would let her work much longer, even if she wanted to. She hoped it wouldn't have to get to that point.

Mary chortled. "I'll believe that when I see it."

They wound through the airport streets and into the city. Though she'd been to Calgary plenty of times, it was still shocking how much it *didn't* feel like a big city. There was one small plot of high rises off in the distance, and the rest of the buildings were suburbs popping up out of prairie grass—brown, dead prairie grass. She doubted they'd be there long enough for her to see it turn green.

"Where are we staying?" Delia asked, and Mary shot her a look.

"I'm never going to tell you now. You know that, right?"

Delia slumped back, recognizing a lost cause when she saw one. She pulled out her phone, and her heart started to thump. She hadn't texted Jack since the other night after the show. Tony said he knew when she was coming in and that he was on hold for a planning meeting. Since she would be local, Tony wanted to get every one of their outings and public appearances on the books so he and the Blizzard's head of marketing could properly amplify them.

It felt clinical, but that was a good thing. The night before, her mom had caught her daydreaming twice over dinner. She'd picked up Mediterranean food and they'd sat together in the living room and talked for an hour or so. Twice during dinner Delia had let her mind wander off, and both times it landed on the same subject: Jack. The hotel room. Bond movies. Pizza.

It had to be because anytime she went online, she saw pictures of him or pictures of herself next to him. Her brain was being inundated. Plus, the woman in those pictures seemed like a figment of the media's imagination, and her brain fixated on dissonance. Like obsessing over it would force it to make sense, which it hadn't. She existed here in joggers, and a hat pulled low while that girl was living a fairytale romance.

That girl was far more exciting, but the story was already scripted. She knew the ending, and it wasn't a happily ever after. It was a very strategic, very public break up. It was moving back to Toronto and releasing her new album. It was never talking to Jack Harrison again after the playoffs.

"Holy shit." Mary shoved her face up to the window, and Delia dropped from her thoughts, landing back on the seat next to her.

"What?" She shoved closer to try and glimpse whatever had caught Mary's attention.

"I was not expecting . . . that." Mary sat back, giving Delia a clear view, and her jaw dropped.

"Is that—?" She couldn't finish the sentence. How could she

describe what was waiting for them on the sidewalk as Alvin pulled their SUV up to the curb?

If she had a way with words that weren't song lyrics, she would've described it as overwhelming masculinity. The hockey player calendar every Canadian woman didn't know they needed. Jack stood on the sidewalk with at least ten other men with broad shoulders and all the athletic hotness. Every single one of them, whether they wore joggers and long-sleeve T-shirts or baggy jeans slung low on their hips with toques and puffy vests, looked like they belonged in a Zack Prior cologne ad.

"Was this the surprise? That we're moving in with Jack and all his friends, because I don't think I'll be able to think straight with all of this happening. If they're walking around in boxers every morning . . ."

Mary laughed out loud. "Reign it in, Melise. I had no idea these guys were going to be here."

"Did I manifest this? All of my complaining about no decent guys in Toronto, and then we move to Calgary where it's dripping with testosterone-riddled hot hockey players?" Delia scanned the line, but her eyes kept slipping back to Jack. This was worse than shag carpet.

She sighed and dramatically fanned herself.

Mary laughed out loud. "This was the thing that broke you? You talked with effing Zack Prior last week, and *now* you've devolved into a cat in heat?"

"Zack Prior was kind of a douchebag." Delia's hand slipped as the car pulled to a stop, and she scrambled back to her middle seat, hoping Jack hadn't seen her cheek pressed against the glass. "I don't even know what to do with this."

"This wasn't my surprise, I—"

"*My face is on fire, Mary.* Jack's arm around my shoulders on the way into the studio is the most action I've gotten in—I don't even know! I can't feel my toes. Jack is going to see my splotchy skin!"

Mary grinned like the Grinch. "Are you going to tell him that you're imagining tripping and falling into a pile of sweaty hockey players?"

"I'm serious!" Delia smacked her shoulder just as Alvin opened the back hatch. The guys on the sidewalk moved to the back of the car, and Delia snapped her mouth shut. *Holy shit was right.* In less than a minute, all their bags were out of the trunk, the backseat was clicked back up, and Delia and Mary were standing on the sidewalk watching a line of men walk their bags into an adorable brick house.

"I think I've landed in someone else's erotic fantasy," Delia whispered.

"Not yours?"

"My imagination is *not* this good."

Mary linked arms with her and pulled her up the walkway. "*This* is the surprise, by the way." She gestured at the house. "Tony reached out to Jack to see if he had any recommendations for places to stay. Turns out his teammate Tyler and his fiancee Emma restore historic properties in the city. This is one of the first ones they completed, and they offered to rent the whole thing to us."

"How many rooms?"

"There are only four, so Alvin will have one, you and I will have ours, and then . . . well, it's totally up to you, but the other one could be for Jack. If you two thought it would be convenient to be in the same place."

Convenient. Delia blinked. "But Jack has a place."

Mary nodded. "Right, so probably unnecessary. But it's available for whatever. Maybe your mom could come out and visit. More importantly, there won't be random people staying here and realizing they're next door to Delia Melise."

Delia and Mary walked into the building, and she wondered if she had secretly been submitted for an episode of Property Virgins. She half expected someone to jump out with confetti. That or all the players to start stripping. Instead, Jack walked toward her with a man who had a perfectly straight nose and a smile too pretty to belong to a hockey player.

"Hey." Jack shoved his hands in his pockets, and Delia's throat swelled like she'd just gulped down boiling hot tea. "This is Tyler. He owns the place."

Delia nodded, her hands clamped around the straps of her backpack. Her voice came out like she was in the middle of being strangled. "Hey. Thank you so much for letting us stay here."

Tyler nodded. "Emma will be here later, she had a shoot she couldn't get out of."

Delia wondered what kind of shoot but couldn't find her way to words with the thousand other questions bouncing around her head like ping-pong balls.

Jack motioned to the other players, holding their bags. "Want to tell us where to take these?"

"Oh, right. Yes. The ones with the ribbons are mine, all the others are Mary's."

Jack nodded and passed along the instructions. The guys hoisted their bags up the stairs like they were white-gloved servants from the Swan Princess. Delia watched in awe until she realized Jack was still standing next to her. And suddenly, the words coalesced. "What just happened?"

Jack grinned. "You got Snowballed." Delia pursed her lips, and Jack ran a hand over his face. "That didn't come out right."

Delia breathed a laugh. "I mean, depends on your definition of 'right.'"

Jack chuckled. "These are all my teammates from the Snowballs."

"I got that much. But don't they have better things to do on a Friday?"

He shrugged. "They do, but I told them you were coming in, and after Mary signed the contract with Tyler, they were all magically available." He leaned in. "I think they just wanted to see you in person."

She blushed. "They don't know . . ."

He shook his head. "My sister Clara and her husband are the only people who know about the contract. I signed the nondisclosure, remember?"

"Sure. Of course." Delia glanced around at the cozy living room. The window that let streams of light into a white-washed kitchen with a chrome hood over a gas stove. One by one, players made their way back down the stairs. They smiled at her. Raised eyebrows at Jack.

"You bring things to move in, too?" a clean-cut guy wearing a puffy vest asked, clapping his hands on Jack's shoulders.

Jack shook his head. "No, I—"

The player held up his hands. "Sorry, no pressure. You've only been dating for what, a couple of weeks? I didn't mean to make it weird."

Jack turned to Delia. "This is Curtis. He's been married for fifteen years and has four kids. He's always trying to shove us to the altar."

Curtis scoffed. "It's not my fault you all have an aversion to healthy relationships."

"Leave me out of that!" Tyler called from behind the stairs. He pulled a box from the storage closet, then grabbed a space heater from the back and shoved the box back in.

A player with wavy blond hair and a tattoo peeking out from the underside of his shirt sleeve strode toward them. *More stories.* Delia glanced at Jack's arm, but it was covered.

Jack pointed. "This is Brett."

"Hi, Brett." Delia put out a hand, and he shook it. "What do you do?"

"Construction."

"He's a general contractor and project manager for a bunch of corporate and residential stuff around the city," Jack clarified.

Delia grinned. "Impressive."

Brett shook his head. "Not as impressive as this guy. He's living the dream."

Jack's eyes darkened, and Delia slingshotted back to their conversation that night over tacos. The guilt over his success. The loneliness he'd gotten so practised at hiding.

Every teammate there was proud of him—clearly, they were invested in his life outside of hockey. But Delia knew from personal experience that it didn't matter how much people wanted to be involved in your life if you were intent on shutting them out.

"He definitely is. We both are." Delia smiled at Jack, hoping he caught what she was throwing. They might only be connected by digital signatures, but he didn't have to be alone in this. They could be friends, couldn't they? Maybe they already were. The idea made her insides fizz. "Why don't you introduce me to the rest of the team, and then I'll go unpack."

Jack gave a silent smile of thanks, and the understanding in his eyes gave her more pleasure than it should have. He led her around the room and introduced her to the other men coming down the stairs. Ryan, with the man bun and a daughter who was definitely going to kill him when she got home from school and found out he'd met Delia Melise without her—Delia assured him she'd be happy to take a picture another time. Mike, with the long braid down his back. André, who waved with a cigarette in his hand from the front porch. Country, who she might've grinned a bit too widely at when she was introduced, and Jack might've noticed. She met Sean, their captain, Steve, Suraj, and Darcy. Not Rob because he was a social studies teacher and had a student competition he couldn't get out of, and not Fly because he'd aged out of the team last year, and Jack had taken his place.

She loved that they mentioned their teammates who were missing. Like they were still a part of the team. Delia, on the other hand, forgot almost all of their names within ten minutes of walking up the stairs and then decided she was a terrible person. She'd need to study up online in her downtime so she didn't seem like Katie Mackey the next time she was with the team.

Delia slumped onto her bed and stared at her suitcases neatly stacked against the wall. The room was beautiful. A long window stretched across the far wall, bathing what looked to be original, restored hardwood in golden afternoon light. The smell of aged wood and the subtle scent of lavender from a bag of potpourri on the dresser was dreamy, just like the four-poster bed crafted from dark, polished walnut. The quilt was soft under her fingertips.

Delia stood and perused the rest of her new living space. There was a cozy reading nook featuring a vintage armchair upholstered in soft, emerald velvet. A simple glass table held a stack of books and a brass lamp. She already knew her guitar would sit there. That thought gave her a momentary panic attack before she remembered that she'd seen the case downstairs next to her backpack. She'd go down and drag it upstairs later.

The frames on the walls held pressed flowers and mountain watercolours. Delia trailed her fingers along the thick door trim as she walked into her private bath and gasped. There was an actual clawfoot tub. The fixtures were brass, and there was a full oval curtain rod to turn the tub into a shower, though Delia doubted she'd use that. Her mother had the only tub in their house, and while she knew she was welcome to use it, she'd never actually soaked there.

This was incredible. She hadn't been thrilled about moving away from Toronto for a month, even though it did mean a much-anticipated collaboration and plenty of media coverage. She liked her life at home, and she hadn't ever spent more than ten days away from her mother, which, at twenty-five, sounded a bit pathetic.

It wasn't, though. They'd only had each other since she was seven years old, and it wasn't stupid to love someone, especially when she had so few someones in her life to love.

But this. She stared again at the tub. This would be an actual vacation. Something that wouldn't feel like much of a sacrifice, especially if she could convince her mom to come out for a bit. *A fat royalty check would do half the convincing.*

Delia couldn't keep the smile off her face as she waltzed back into the bedroom and tipped her largest suitcase onto the floorboards. She flipped open the top and piled her clothes onto the bed. Underwear. Bras. And not just the practical ones. She'd debated when she'd been packing at home but had ultimately decided to bring most of what she owned in that regard. Sports bras. Lace numbers.

Her mind landed back at Jack without permission. How she'd stayed in his hotel room instead of going with Mary. How she was still a little turned on after seeing him standing in front of the house . . .

Delia's head snapped up when a floorboard creaked. A black lace bra was looped over her fingers. And Jack was leaning against the doorframe.

CHAPTER

Fifteen

JACK COULDN'T KEEP his eyes from dropping to the bit of fabric strung between Delia's hands. *Black. Lace.* Delia dropped it onto the bed where Jack saw *there were more of them.* He forced his face to stay neutral, pretending it was completely normal to see women's lingerie, and opened his mouth to say something like, *"Do you need help unpacking?"* Instead, he said, "That's nice."

Delia's lips parted, and her skin grew splotchy, which he knew she hated. He, on the other hand, quite enjoyed seeing her reactions in real-time. A little too much.

Heat flushed to his middle when he realized the main floor was quiet. The guys had gone home, and he shouldn't have stayed. He shouldn't have invited her to his hotel in Toronto, and he definitely should've taken Tyler up on the offer to drive him over instead of driving separately.

Staring at Delia again after the week of separation, he knew exactly why he'd done both things. An ache grew low in his belly. *He'd missed her.* He liked spending time with her. He liked looking at Delia, and he liked talking with Delia.

He didn't like that he liked any of it, but he couldn't get himself to stop.

"Thanks." Delia shoved the pile back on the quilt and sat

down in front of it. She crossed, then uncrossed her legs. Then crossed them again. "Thanks for bringing in the cavalry to get us moved in. That was quite the welcome."

Jack ran his thumb over a nick in the door frame. "I couldn't keep them away." He talked himself down. *They had a meeting scheduled, that was why he'd driven separately. They needed to talk logistics.* Which he could've done by waiting down in the living room, but instead he'd listened when that little string tugged on his chest and led him up the stairs.

Delia tried to cover the pile of bras that were already seared to his retinas. "I can't believe Mary and Tony reached out to you about a location. That was brilliant."

Jack stared hard at the lamp on her dresser. "I was glad they did. This is way better than some of the other options in this part of town."

"Are we close to where you play?"

He nodded. "And close to the studio you're going to be working at. I think. Mary told me it was kind of a triangle between the Saddledome and here."

Delia's eyes narrowed. "How often do you talk to Mary?"

The question caught him off guard. "Not often. Probably once a week or so? Is that—sorry, should I not be?"

She laughed. "No, it's fine, I was just surprised. Mary didn't tell me about your clandestine communication."

"I can tell you when she reaches out in the future."

"No, please. I'm not your babysitter."

Jack shifted on his feet. "I'm sorry you had to disrupt your life to come out here. I tried to figure out how I could make more trips work, but—"

Delia waved him off. "It makes a lot more sense for me to be here. I can work at any studio."

"But Finn's not here." It was bait, and he knew it.

"Finn can work on digital files. I finished all my recording with him. Now it's just mastering."

It sounded all-business, and the buzzing in his head settled a bit. "Did he work on your other albums with you?" Delia nodded. *They had a long history.* Jack simply didn't like the dude. He was too smiley. His hair was a little too perfect. *And who wore V-necks?*

"You don't like him, do you?"

Jack coughed. "What? No. I don't have enough experience with him to like or not like him." He answered too fast, and Delia raised an eyebrow.

Jack turned back to the hall and picked up her backpack and guitar case. "I brought these up if . . ."

"Oh, thank you. You can set them wherever." Delia searched for something on her phone as Jack set them down next to the suitcases. He backed up and looked awkwardly around the room. "Here. You can—" She shifted to the side, making room for him on the bed. Jack's heart hockey stopped.

It was a place to sit, and he was an idiot. Losing his ever-loving shit over a black lace bra or sitting next to a girl on a floral quilt like he was in grade nine trying to tone down his voice cracks. They were grown-ass adults. *He was a grown-ass adult.*

Jack sat, and the bed creaked. "You hear from Tony?"

Delia shook her head. The movement sent a breath of air that held a hint of cinnamon his direction. It reminded him of his piano teacher's mints, and Jack's jaw tightened.

"I just sent him a text. I'm sure we can meet over Zoom or Google Meet or something if you have to get going."

"No," Jack grunted. He scrubbed his hands on his thighs. "I don't have practice until later tonight."

"What about your day job?"

Jack could've answered that he'd stayed up until past one in the morning to get all of his proposals submitted and emails responded to so he could be at the bed and breakfast when she arrived. He hadn't worked into the night on purpose, he simply hadn't been able to wind down. That was becoming more common as of late.

Understandable, though. When Ange died, his therapist reiterated how brains tried to deal with change. After something traumatic, his human lizard-instincts screamed warning messages to every cell in his body. *We aren't safe.* Landing a spot in the NHL, having people recognize him in the street, and sitting next to a national superstar who had a pile of dangerously sexy bras behind her sent his subconscious into an equally confusing frenzy. Add in the guilt that dragged him down like an anchor every time he thought about Delia and not Ange, and his body was a chemical soup eating him from the inside out. Strange that he couldn't relax and get some shut-eye.

Jack looked up to find Delia watching him, a half smile on her lips. He froze. "What?"

She shrugged. "Nothing, I've just never seen it happen to someone else like that."

His brow furrowed. "You've never seen what happen?"

She twirled her finger in the air and whistled. "You spiralled."

"No, I didn't."

Delia stood, her eyes locking onto him in challenge. "How long do you think it's been since I asked about your day job?"

Jack blinked. He'd forgotten entirely about the question. "A few seconds."

Her smile widened until creases formed at the corners of her eyes. "Yeah. It feels like that." She opened the top drawer of the dresser, then began folding the tiny, delicate articles of clothing on top of the quilt and dropping them in.

Jack didn't even pretend not to watch that time. *Grown. Ass. Adult.*

"Has it been a while?" Delia's eyes flicked to his.

Jack's blood felt like it was pumping through a crazy straw. "Hmm?"

"Since you've played hooky?"

Jack licked his lips. *His day job.* Right. "Yeah. No." He ran a hand through his hair and turned so she couldn't see the shape of his jeans rapidly changing. "My schedule's been strange since I started with the Blizzard. My boss is a good guy. He's fine with me holding irregular hours as long as I get the work done."

"Which company do you work for again?"

"Big Rick."

She paused, her hands halfway to the drawer. "Did you tell me that before? I don't think you did because I would've remembered that. I always wanted a Big Rick coat when I was a kid."

"Did you get one?"

She shook her head. "Well, that's not totally true. One time, this guy in high school—he was two years older than me, only by grade, we were really a year and a half apart but his birthday was in the summer and mine was in the fall, so it wasn't that weird that he was into me. Not weird because of age, but totally weird because he was on the curling team and everyone knows they only date incestuously. Did you know people on the curling team?"

Jack shook his head, trying to keep up.

"They're basically the same as jazz band kids, though they at least open up their dating pool to ROTC and theatre kids. But this guy, Antoine, heard me talking about how I wanted a Big Rick coat and said he would sell me his because his dad was buying him a new one for Christmas, and he liked the idea of seeing me in his coat every day at school."

"Okay. Creepy."

"No—yes, totally creepy in hindsight—but at the time, it was completely hot because he was a year and a half older than me, and when I tried on the coat, it smelled like Axe body spray and was way too big for me."

"That's a good thing?"

She paused with a pair of white satin panties in her hand. "Yeah. It made me feel tiny."

He swallowed. "You didn't buy it, did you?"

"I definitely bought it. It made me feel petite and wanted.

Which, it turned out, were the exact two things I was struggling with in grade nine."

"Feeling small?"

"No, *wanting* to feel small. I took up too much space."

Jack frowned. "But you are small."

She laughed and dropped another three pairs of underwear in the drawer. He knew there were three because he was watching the colours and counting. "I'm small compared to you, but I'm not small compared to other women."

"Why does that matter?"

"It matters."

"I would hate feeling small."

"Well, la-dee-da mister *beat the shit out of them.*"

Jack laughed. "That might be the worst story I've ever heard." *Lies.* It was the best story he'd ever heard. He felt like he'd jumped on a merry-go-round and was still clinging to the bars because it wasn't slowing down.

She sighed. "I know. I ramble when I tell stories. That's why I stick to poetry."

Jack regretted his statement. He wanted all the rambling.

"I was kidding, by the way." Delia arranged something in the drawer.

"About which part?"

"You're not one of those asshole hockey players I knew growing up." She glanced down and realized the clothes were all gone from the bed, then leaned over and picked up another pile from her suitcase. Socks this time. Jack didn't try to hide his disappointment. "I guess I don't know for sure, for sure, but you've always been nice when I'm around."

"Guys are usually nice when women are around."

"That. Is false." She dropped the socks into the right side of the drawer. "I was once on a date with a guy who called our waitress a 'paper bagger.'"

Jack's eyes widened. "People still say that?"

"Apparently. Yes." She put her hands on her hips and

scanned the half-empty suitcase, then stepped over it to slide open the closet doors. "Perfect." She grabbed a handful of hangers from the bar.

"Here, let me help." Jack reached out and she handed him a few, then stacked a few blouses on the bed next to him.

"See? You're nice."

"I'm bored."

"Right." Delia hesitated, and Jack grabbed a shirt.

"You better not be thinking about how your room isn't clean or whether you should find a way to entertain me."

Delia's eyes shot to his. "I wasn't."

Jack grinned and slipped the sleeves of a pale-blue blouse onto the hangers, allowing his thumb and forefinger to linger on the fabric. "Why are women's clothes always softer than men's?"

"I don't think they are."

"Feel this." Jack held out his arm and Delia slipped her fingers on either side of the sleeve of his shirt without hesitation. *Bad idea.* Her thumb grazed his arm, right over his owl feathers. His skin tingled like he'd licked his finger and jammed it in a live outlet.

Delia pulled back with a jerk. "It's soft."

"But compared to this?" His voice was unsteady as he held out her now-hanging blouse.

She assessed, careful to avoid his outstretched hand. "I think those are in two totally different genres."

"Genres?"

"Yeah. Like categories." She turned back to her pile.

"You think of everything in musical terms?"

Delia nodded and took the shirt, then leaned over to hang it in the closet. "I think you could find soft men's clothing if you looked for it."

"If I paid more than twenty bucks for a T-shirt."

She smiled. "You're in the NHL now. Don't you need game day fits or whatever?"

He chuckled. "That's not a thing."

"I think it's a thing. Ooh!" She lit up. "Maybe that could be something we do together? I could take you shopping?"

Jack slipped a button-up shirt onto a hanger. "I'd rather go curling."

Delia shot him a look. "But then you'd have to sleep with other curlers."

"You said there were options. Plus, if I would've known that was all I had to do to get laid, I would've bought a push broom years ago."

Delia put a hand on her hip. "You keep saying BS like that, and it's completely unbelievable, you know that, right?"

"How so?"

She grabbed more hangers and traded them for the full ones he had in his hands. "There is no way in hell you couldn't walk out that door and bring home any girl you happened to run into out there. I see the way women look at you."

"Oh yeah?"

"Stop answering with questions, Jack Harrison." She drew out his name, and it sent a shiver down his spine. "It's like you're playing this part. Like you should be this cocky athlete, but you can't quite bring yourself to do that, so you pretend you're just unlucky in love, but that doesn't work either." Delia slowed her hands and lifted her chin. "I'm sorry, I didn't mean that to sound—"

"No, it's fine." His brows knitted together as he put the last shirt on the hanger. "It's probably true." It was true. Exactly true. Something swirled inside him, and he felt unsteady on his feet.

She took the hanger from him and smoothed out the collar of the cream shirt that zipped up the back. It looked like it would drape over her hips and cut low down her chest. Maybe he did like V-necks after all.

"It's her, isn't it?" Delia didn't meet his eyes.

The air sucked out of the room. Jack's hand started to shake. Not because he was upset by her question. He wasn't. He couldn't think of the word for what he was until the lyrics from

Delia's song ran through his head like he'd flicked on the faucet. She'd sung them in French, but he'd looked them up multiple times in English since. He'd listened to her sing it on TikTok, along with all the other songs she'd posted there before IndieLake.

With relief and regret. Nobody ever talked about Angie with him besides Clara. She was the only one who was willing to bring her up, and even though his ribs cinched, it was a relief. To have someone else validate that she was real—that his pain was real. The regret came second. Without exception.

Now this girl he barely knew, who he'd told once about what happened, had just read him like a damn book. Twice. And had the balls to call the shot.

Jack struggled to draw in a breath. "What happened to the coat?"

Delia looked at him, assessing. "Big Rick? I wore it every day until I heard some guys joking that I was Antoine's property. Then I gave it away in a coat drive."

Jack's heart beat like a kick drum. "You never bought a new one?"

She shook her head, then set her jaw. "Have you slept with anyone since Angie died?"

Jack shook his head. He didn't even try to sugar coat it. *Three years.* "It's been a long time since I played hooky." He hadn't told anyone that. Not his teammates. Definitely not Clara.

Delia didn't blink. She didn't look away, and the intensity of her focus made him feel like a moth with its wings pinned to a corkboard. That invisible string tugged with such force, Jack nearly leaped up from the bed and reached for her.

Instead, it was Delia who jumped when her phone ringer punctured the silence. She nearly tripped over her suitcase, and Jack reached out a hand to keep her from falling into his lap. As she righted herself, her hand left a trail of heat across his forearm.

"Hey! Tony!" Delia's tone was too bright, and she was out of breath even though she'd been standing perfectly still in front of him. "Mmhmm, we're both here. A link? I haven't checked my email, but I'm sure it's there."

The skin on her neck had turned two different colours. Jack had zero memory of anything she said to Tony after he noticed that.

CHAPTER
Sixteen

DELIA SAT in the chair Jack pulled over next to its counterpart on the opposite side of the fireplace. She propped up her phone against a vase that looked like it had been shattered and glued back together.

"Aren't you two adorable?" Tony leaned back from the camera. "Having fun playing house?"

Delia smiled, pretending his comments didn't pull tight on the tangle in her stomach. "This place is amazing. You and Mary outdid yourselves."

Tony pointed through the screen at Jack. "You have him to thank. It was the perfect option."

Delia tamped down her instinct to ask how much it was costing the label to book the place. Mary had kept her stream and rank numbers top of mind for the past few days, so she understood their strategy was working. She still hated not having access to the raw numbers and what money was coming in. "Well, thank you, Jack."

"Are you going to be staying there, too?" Tony asked.

Jack exhaled through his nose. "Uh, no, I'll be at my place. It's only about ten minutes up the road."

Delia kept smiling even though something dropped through her middle like she'd just slid over the lip of a waterslide. It was fine—good even—that he wasn't going to be staying there. Based on how her skin had heated in her bedroom after their conversation, she worried she wouldn't be able to focus with him sleeping next door.

She knew next to nothing about him still, so was it just the fact that he was a good-looking guy with a pulse? Was she really that desperate? He didn't even like her music, for crying out loud.

Putting her lyrics out into the world was the equivalent of flipping herself inside out and allowing everyone and their dog to inspect the inner workings of her heart. If someone didn't like that, they didn't like her. Though to be fair, none of her hit songs were written by her.

But Jack had heard her poetry. At the concert. "Oubliet." *In relief and regret.* Hadn't he talked about his disinterest in lyrics *after* he'd heard that?

No. Her heart revolted just like it had in Toronto. The way he'd looked at her. The way he'd mentioned the song the second she told him about her dad. He'd listened.

"Of course, that makes sense that you wouldn't want to disrupt your life completely, it's just . . ." Tony cleared his throat.

Delia forced herself to focus. She knew that look on his face. The one that said *I'm about to say something you're not going to like, so I'm going to pretend it isn't a big deal by shrugging my shoulders and hedging a little until you make me spit it out.* He used it all the time when he was about to tell her IndieLake had made a decision about one of her songs. "Tony—"

"What do you two think about your public persona as a couple?"

Delia frowned. "Public persona?"

Tony scrubbed a hand over his pixelated face. "Right, your Jelia personality, or Deliack if you prefer that."

"Gross, one sounds like a gelatinous dessert and the other like he's allergic to me." Delia grimaced. "Don't tell me that's what people are calling us."

Tony laughed. "No, those were just examples I made up."

"Delia, he's your publicist. You should trust his instincts."

She shot Jack a look. "Hard pass."

"Okay, those names weren't the point. I was asking about your mutual branding."

Jack exhaled. "No idea what you're talking about."

Delia shifted in her seat. "Tony, don't you think it's a little early to think about that? We've barely been fake together for two weeks."

"Never too early! I'll tell you, my concern is that you two aren't coming off as smitten."

Delia's frown deepened. "Smitten?" She didn't like where this was headed. Smitten meant close proximity. Smitten meant hands. Smitten meant eye contact.

"Right. Head over heels. He shits rainbows and smells like the air that puffs out of a freshly opened bag of maple cookies, and she makes your blood race south so fast you have to wear compression shorts."

Delia blinked. So. Not business only.

Jack stared hard at the screen. "You're not getting those vibes from us?"

"Ha. Ha." Tony adjusted his camera and reclined on whatever chair or couch he was sitting on.

Delia ran a hand through her hair. "That's not real love, Tony, that's infatuation. If I saw people acting like that, I'd be ninety percent sure they were going to break up within the month."

"That's because you're a cynic."

Jack raised an eyebrow. "You are?"

"No, I'm a realist. I've been there, done that, and relationships that start with heart eyes and panting only lead to disappointment and awkward text conversations."

"I think I need those transcripts." Jack smirked.

Delia rolled her eyes, but Tony was already talking. "Nobody cares about reality, Delia, you know this. They want a story, and unfortunately, a healthy relationship where both parties gradually jump through rational intimacy hoops is boring."

She huffed. "So you want me to perpetuate this idea that you should meet a guy and have his tongue down your throat by the second date? Lust at first sight?"

Tony nodded. "That would be perfect. If we could get a picture of Jack's tongue—"

"Tony!"

He held up his hands. "I'm not here to debate the morality of what makes headlines, I'm here to sell you more records and put more bums in seats."

She exhaled. Fair. She could hate the entertainment industry and the distractibility of the general public all she wanted, but arguing with Tony wasn't going to change the world.

Jack leaned forward, resting his elbows on his knees. "What are you getting at, Tony?"

Tony pursed his lips. "Your contract states that public displays of affection are expected. It doesn't have to be anything huge, and you both need to agree on what you feel comfortable with, but right now, we're not getting a whole lot."

"But you're getting something, right? Jack had his arm around me when we walked into the studio."

Tony nodded. "That was sweet, but he could've been helping an old lady cross the street. It didn't look . . . you know."

"Like I needed compression shorts," Jack finished.

Tony grinned. "Exactly."

Jack stared at the screen, and Delia swallowed hard. "Smitten." She pronounced every syllable

"Yep, and now that we've gotten that out of the way, I was hoping we could talk dates . . ." Tony kept talking, and Delia zoned out. Tony had access to her calendar, as did Mary, so she didn't need to double-check anything.

Jack pulled out his phone and the two of them started negotiations for public appearances. Jack was a willing participant, but Delia was surprised at how full his schedule was. Not that she didn't also have a busy life, but he hadn't been kidding when he talked about the juggling act of a day job, his practice schedule, building relationships with his team, and showing up prepared for game day.

"Nope, I've got a podcast recording that morning," Jack said, and Delia tuned back in.

"You're recording for a podcast?" Delia asked.

He nodded. "Two guys who discuss the ins and outs of Canadian hockey. Lisa, our head of marketing, set it up."

Tony grunted. "Right, I knew about that. It was on the schedule she sent over."

Jack glanced up from his screen. "What if we go to a Snowballs game that night? They're in the playoffs."

Tony clapped his hands together. "Yes, fantastic. That'll hit everything: community support, nostalgia, loyalty, a folding in of Delia into your regular life—"

Again, Delia zoned out. *What was she going to say to Jack after this call ended?* She'd told him they didn't have to do anything physical—she knew it was a pain point for him—and now Tony was talking about tongues and throats and . . . blood rushing. Delia's eyes landed on Jack's crotch and she turned away from him so fast, her neck cracked.

She settled enough to look back and found Jack teasing his teeth over his lower lip. *He was just a good-looking guy with a pulse.* Not emotionally available. Ignoring the hockey-boob situation, he'd straight up told her his hands and his heart were off-limits. Also, they lived across the country from each other, were both focused on their careers—or they wouldn't be in this situation in the first place—oh, and they already had a scheduled, permanent breakup date.

"Alright, I think that's all for me." Tony turned his attention to Delia. "Where's Mary, by the way?"

Delia pondered this. *Where was Mary?* And Alvin, for that matter. She hadn't seen either of them since they'd brought in the luggage. "Probably unpacking. I don't know, I haven't seen her."

"Well, tell her I've added these to the calendar, and I'll make sure we get plenty of press. How's the security detail working out?"

Delia pressed her hands into her knees. "So far, so good. We got here safely from the airport with minimal fuss."

Tony nodded. "Perfect. Okay, you kids have fun." He ended the call while Delia was mid-goodbye.

She plucked her phone from the table. "Well. I'm sorry about—"

"He's right."

Delia froze and looked up. Jack looked like he was coiled tight enough to pounce. "Right about what?"

"That we're not selling it."

She set her phone down. "Jack, I meant what I said at breakfast."

"I know." He was staring at the table like her mom did when she spotted a fingerprint.

Delia's pulse fluttered. "So . . ."

He locked eyes with her. "I don't do things halfway. My whole life, anytime I committed to something, I was all in. That's why I went so far in hockey. I was never the most talented guy out there, but I was willing to put in the work."

"This isn't your livelihood, though."

"It kind of is. I've had two meetings with my management team since those pictures went public, and they've scheduled me on a morning show and two different podcasts for the next week. I don't hate my job at Big Rick, but the idea of having a career in the NHL?" He leaned back in his chair. "If I think about it differently, like a job, maybe it won't—maybe it will be fine."

Delia nodded, ignoring the speeding of her heart and her

splintering thoughts. *This was a job to him.* Of course it was. And his job was to touch her. More frequently. But what was he willing to touch? *What did she want to touch?* Touch. Touch. *Touch.*

Heat exploded in her middle. *Everything.* She wanted to touch everything. If Jack wanted to sell it, she had some ideas that she was absolutely *not* willing to make outside thoughts. "We could keep it simple. Hold hands or something?" she squeaked.

Jack shook his head. "I don't know if I'm ready for that."

Delia couldn't keep her jaw from dropping. "What? You just said you wanted to sell it. What's smaller than holding hands? A pat on the arm? I saw you do *that* with your team captain earlier."

The skin on Jack's neck reddened. "I didn't mean—" He drew a deep breath and held it. "I was thinking we should kiss."

Delia gaped at him. "Explain to me how that makes any sense." She could barely hear herself think. Kiss. Kiss. *Kiss.*

"I've kissed plenty of people. I've only held hands with two."

Delia's eyes narrowed. "Wait, hold on. In your book, holding hands is more intimate than swapping spit?"

He nodded, and the expression on his face sobered her. That line of reasoning seemed batty, but she wasn't the one who had lost her fiancée. Hell, she hadn't even gained a fiancée to lose. "Okay. I'm fine with kissing." She straightened her shirt. "But what kind of kiss are we talking about?" Her insides began to squirm.

Jack started to say something, then stopped. "Are you okay?"

Delia tried to smile, but even without seeing it, she could tell her face wasn't doing what she wanted it to. "Yes?"

Jack's lips twitched. "So, no."

She blew out a breath. "I'm sorry, this just feels like—" She lifted her hands and shook them out. "When I said that, it sounded like I was one of those guys on the apps. The ones that send messages like, where do you want my lips? Ugh, it's so disgusting. Like I can feel their hot breath coming through the screen." She held out her phone for emphasis. "And now *I* said that, and I feel skeezy like I'm sitting in a dark room with my hand down my pants or something."

Jack's eyes crinkled at the corners.

Delia scowled. "Are you laughing at me?"

His expression tightened. "No."

"You're laughing at me."

He put a hand over his face and pretended to cough.

"That was a pathetic cover-up."

A goofy grin stretched across his face. "What? I'm sorry! That was entertaining."

She folded her arms over her chest. "Well, I'm glad my pain is amusing to you."

He laughed again. "I'm sorry. I can see both of your hands, and you're nothing like those guys on the apps."

"Do you know the guys on the apps?" She crossed her arms in front of her.

"I know plenty of guys who would be guys on the apps."

Delia didn't know where to go from there. Jack was leaning toward her, his dark hair mussed, his forearms flexed, making the swirls of ink over his left forearm pop with colour. *His hands were nice.* She'd noticed them the first time they'd sat across from each other. His knuckles were broad, and his nails short and clean. They looked rugged. Capable.

Shit. This was a spiral. Delia tapped her elbow.

Jack lifted his hands, and Delia couldn't stop staring. He took a step past the couch, walking toward the kitchen. *Good.* That was good. She needed more space.

"Do you want a drink?" he asked.

Delia nodded. "Just water." She drew a breath through her nose and exhaled after he disappeared around the corner. Maybe she was the one who needed to think about this differently. This was work for her, too, and she could figure out how to view kissing Jack as a business transaction, couldn't she? Felt a little whorey, but not impossible.

In all her therapy appointments over the years and through all the reading she'd done on productivity and basically how to seem like an average person, she'd picked up plenty of strategies. She was religious about setting alarms and then second alarms on her phone. She surrounded herself with people who were more organizationally functional than she was so they could pick up the slack when she was in full-blown creative mode. She still carried fidget toys with her in her purse and—

Yes. That was it. She just needed something physical to link her thoughts to the reality of the situation and bypass her emotions. She'd done that plenty of times before. In grade twelve, she'd carried around a smooth rock she'd found in a river on vacation. She'd created a friction groove in it by the time her finals were over. That, combined with deep breathing techniques, progressive muscle relaxation, and tapping, had gotten her through.

But this had to be something inconspicuous.

Simple.

Something she could employ in seconds without drawing attention to herself.

Delia brought her hands together and pinched the tip of her left forefinger between her right thumb and pointer. She pressed for three seconds. *That would do.* Every time they touched, she could press and allow it to remind her that this thing with Jack wasn't real. It was a job. Touching him had nothing to do with real feelings, which definitely did *not* make her like those creepy guys on the apps. According to Jack. *Her business partner.*

Jack returned and handed her a glass of water.

"Thank you." Delia took a sip.

He sat back in his chair. "So. What kind of kiss?"

Delia nearly choked on the water in her mouth. She quickly swallowed and blinked to clear her watering eyes.

"Sorry." Jack set his glass on the table.

She shook her head. "Wrong tube."

Jack exhaled. "It can't look unnatural."

"The kiss?"

He nodded. "It has to look like we've been doing it regularly because what couple would kiss for the first time in public?"

"Mmhmm."

"That's it, then. We just have to do it regularly."

She was blacking out. *Was she blacking out?* The world shimmered like she was having an ocular migraine. "I'm sorry, what?"

Jack shrugged. "Maybe that would make it less weird. If we just . . . kiss. A lot."

His words and her understanding were like oil and water. They danced around each other but didn't mix. "Like, just start kissing." *Had Jack taken something while he'd been in the kitchen?*

He rubbed his chin. "I don't know, it seems like that would make it more believable."

I don't do things halfway. Delia's mouth went dry. He seemed sober. And dead serious. "How often is 'regularly?'"

"Probably anytime we see each other."

Delia couldn't think about what was happening to the nerves under her skin. They sizzled like a thousand wildfires were sparking to life, about to spread across her landscape with the faintest breeze.

She'd kissed people before, plenty of them. Grayson Pike was her first at grade eight graduation. Then it had been Merrill McKay in grade nine. They'd kissed more than *regularly* in the three weeks they dated, and she wasn't sure she'd enjoyed a single one of their encounters. He'd swept her mouth with his tongue like he was dusting his bookshelves.

Then there was Emile. *Oh, Emile.* That boy could kiss. He'd been her boyfriend for nearly eighteen months and his hands were always on her neck, her cheek, in her hair, or down the back pocket of her jeans. She'd loved his constant touch. *Like she was petite and wanted.* So predictable. That break up started her Degrassi and dry cereal era, which lasted for half of June and all of July 2016.

But how did Jack kiss? Once the question entered her head, she snatched it by the scruff. "Okay." Delia nodded.

It would be fine. Like he said, this would make their appearances more believable. Or, maybe she'd get lucky and he'd kiss like Merrill. It would permanently cool the slow simmer in her midsection when she thought about Jack touching her with those *capable hands.* That's all she needed. A thorough, repellant tongue dusting. Delia almost snorted and grabbed her glass of water to take a drink.

"Okay. Good." Jack yawned. "I should probably get going." He stood and took one step before noticing her expression. "What?"

Delia bit the inside of her cheek. "Nothing."

"You look annoyed."

"I'm not annoyed." She dropped her gaze and tried to rearrange her features. Why couldn't she keep her thoughts from writing themselves all over her face in permanent ink? She was absolutely annoyed. More annoyed than she'd been probably ever. He'd brought up kissing and worked her up to the point that she was hoping for his tongue to make her want to throw up a little in her mouth, and then, what? He just stretches his hands over his head and *goes home?*

Jack jammed his hands in his pockets. "You're annoyed."

"Fine, maybe I'm annoyed." How could he not recognize what he was doing to her? Yanking her this way and that and then waltzing out?

"Why?" He looked honestly confused, and that only pissed her off more.

"Because, Jack, you said we needed to kiss and now I've been thinking about how that's logistically going to happen and now you're going to leave and I'm still going to be obsessing about when we're actually going to start the *regularly* part. What if it's weird? What if you hate it, or what if I hate it, and we never make it look normal and then people are going to post it everywhere and they won't believe us when we say we're dating, and—"

She sucked in a breath. Jack was standing in front of her. *When had he gotten there?* Delia looked up, surprised at how much she had to crane her neck to look him in the eyes at that distance. "What are you doing?"

He lifted a hand and brushed her hair back from her face. He didn't say anything, just let his eyes wander over her face. Her heart did something akin to the flute solo in Peter and the Wolf.

"What are you doing, Jack?"

"What does it look like I'm doing?"

"A skin check."

Jack smirked. "Glad to know I've still got it. I thought women liked it when men took their time."

Jack's palm was rough and warm against her cheek. Delia couldn't feel her toes, but that was more normal than she would've liked to admit. The more pressing concern was the way her vision was still blurring at the edges. "I don't know what women like."

"No?"

"I've never been in the majority." She swallowed, and the sound of her throat closing may as well have been broadcast over an amp. Jack didn't seem to notice. His hand settled between her neck and shoulder, and as he ran his thumb slowly over her collarbone, Delia couldn't help her shuddering breath.

"Still terrible?"

"Mmm. I've had worse."

He nodded like he wished he had a pen and paper to take notes. "I think it might help if you were touching me."

Delia blinked. *Right.* She was standing like she was ready to do a pencil off the diving board. She forced her arms up and placed her hands on his hips.

Something happened in that moment. She didn't know if it was the soft cotton of his shirt or the feel of his obliques edged by the waistband of his jeans, but Delia turned from butter straight out of the freezer to butter that had been sitting on the counter for a week and was then spread over warm toast.

Her exhale was like every dying breath she'd ever heard in the movies. Rest. Release. *Finally.* Her skin fizzed like champagne, and she *was* that neon sign humming over the Jukebox as Jack's fingers tightened around the back of her neck.

As he lowered his head—as he pressed his lips to hers—expletives strung together in her mind in one unending word that would've made Mary Poppins proud because Jack *did not kiss like Merrill.* He didn't even kiss like Emile. His kiss was something wholly its own. Deep. Intense. Like he needed that moment, the feel of her, more than he needed air in his lungs. He raged like a hurricane, washing over her and pounding through her boarded-up windows until she was soaked through.

Jack took his damn time, and if other women liked that, then she *was* other women. Her heart couldn't decide whether to start or stop as he pressed against her and held, then pulled back just enough to let her catch a breath before he was coming back for more.

She didn't realize she'd gripped onto his belt loop and twisted his shirt through her fingers until his lips slowed. Until his breath against her lips sent those fires under her skin blazing. Until he pulled back.

The fabric of his shirt stretched, and Delia slammed back into herself so hard her teeth rattled. Her eyes flew open. Her lips were swollen. Her tongue tasted like his peppermint toothpaste.

"How was that?" Jack rasped.

Delia dropped her hands. Where was she? *What the hell day was it?* She nodded and stepped back, bumping into the chair she'd forgotten was sitting behind her.

Jack cleared his throat. "Okay. Hopefully that looked believable. We could ask Mary for a third-party opinion." He rubbed the back of his neck, and Delia couldn't look up from the rug. "I'll see you in a couple of days then? For the Snowballs game?"

"Right. Yes." She stumbled back, abandoning her glass of water on the table. "Have a good night."

Jack scanned the room and found his coat draped over the half wall near the entrance. "You, too. Goodnight." He walked out the front door, and Delia followed on unsteady legs, locking the deadbolt.

She turned and pressed her back up against the door, then grabbed onto her pointer finger and squeezed for much longer than three seconds.

ON TUESDAY, Jack stepped out of his truck and locked the doors, then strode into the farm-to-table place where his team-mates always went for lunch. From the time he signed his contract, he knew how this was supposed to go. If you joined a team, you were committing to making that group your new personality. You couldn't show up and expect to have a good outcome if you weren't close with the guys you were going to battle with.

The only problem was, he was being torn in too many direc-tions. He thought back to his time at World Juniors, how it had been immersive, all consuming. How all the guys had slept, eaten, and breathed alongside each other 24-7. When his team stepped on the ice, they didn't feel like individual players. They became a Megazord or whatever the hell that was called when all the Power Rangers connected into one giant beast. They sensed each other's motivations—understood each other's strengths and weaknesses.

That's what he was supposed to create here with the Blizzard, or at least be a willing participant in. At twenty-nine, he was one of the oldest guys there, and that niggled at him. He should be joining in with the other veterans and finding ways to support the new guys. Instead, he was juggling meetings and workflows, and now adding media appearances and time out with Delia.

He pulled open the door of the restaurant and looked for the guys. They were at a table in the back. Even though the place was packed, it wasn't hard to spot them. A pang of envy sliced through him at their smiling, laughing faces. Their full-time jobs *were* becoming a team and honing their hockey skills. His full-time job was Big Rick, and he didn't know how to put that on the back burner and jump all-in to this pipe dream.

Why would he give up a solid career for something that might not evolve past that season? On the other hand, if he didn't jump in, he was pounding the nails into his own coffin. Hammering nails made him think of Delia and her off-the-wall metaphors. His pulse quickened.

It wasn't just that his attention was split between work and, well, work. A much larger piece of the pie was being occupied by one person. Delia. Their faux relationship had been presented as something he could put on autopilot. Set a few meetings, show up, and call it good. The only problem was, she had become a puzzle his mind was obsessed with. Especially after that kiss.

"Jack!" Monahan motioned for the rookie to move over so Jack could take a seat at the end of the crowded table. Monahan wore a Mickey Mouse T-shirt that stretched across his broad shoulders, looking almost comical against his hardened features and missing tooth. "I didn't know you were coming out."

Jack smiled and sat down. "You know I wish I could be here every day."

Nathan reached for a fry. "I know. I can't imagine running the schedule you are, bud."

Jack wondered how many of the other players knew what that schedule was or whether they cared. It was comforting to think that someone at least understood why he wasn't acting like a full member of the team.

"Here you go." Monahan passed him a menu.

Jack thanked him, then stared at the loopy title font and lines of text. He'd thought about that kiss with Delia all morning. Had he suggested the kiss because it was a good strategy? Or had he simply wanted it? Or, third option, had he been curious about whether he'd feel the way he always did when he kissed a woman post-Angie?

If he was being honest, it was all of the above. Strategy was the only justification he'd spoken out loud, but since he'd sat on her bed, the blood flow to his brain had been limited. Part of him wished she wasn't so attractive. If she could be less interesting— less funny. Stop squinching her nose when she laughed or pulling her sleeves over her wrists.

His body was full to bursting when he'd walked out her front door. He'd wanted more. For the first time since Angie's death, he hadn't felt instantly sick after touching a woman, and sheer relief had poured through him at that realization. Maybe he could have that again. Touch. Connection. Sex. But then came the grief. The soul-crushing wave of regret and hopelessness. *Relief. Regret.*

One side of his head screamed that he couldn't keep clinging to Angie's memory. To feel beholden to a woman who was a metre under. But the other side shouted with equal ferocity that he owed her. That he'd lived and she'd died, and who knew whether she was up there in the ether watching him? What would she think if she saw him touching Delia? Even *wanting* to touch another woman? That thought made his stomach twist until it was snarled like an old extension cord.

He had things. He'd told Delia that the first time they'd met. It didn't have to be that deep. He could do his job. Play hockey. Sell tickets. Everything else would fade in a few weeks anyway.

"You ordered a salad?" Lindholm stared at Johannsen. "Bud, are you on a cut? Got someone to impress?"

Johannsen gesticulated. "It looked good! Maricona almonds and mulberries!"

Jack looked up from the menu. The rookie sat two seats to the right across from him and already had a beer in front of him. His eyes seemed less bloodshot today, but he still had that look about him. The one Jack had seen in so many players over the years who burned themselves out embracing the high life they thought they were entitled to since they'd "made it."

That spike of guilt wedged itself further into his gut. *He should be helping him.* He should be a leader. He'd always wanted that opportunity, and now he was stretching himself too thin. What had he said to Delia the night before? That he never half-assed things?

He was a hypocrite. The problem was he couldn't quite figure out *what* he needed to do with his *whole ass.* Was he going to focus on the hockey? Focus on the team? What did that even mean anymore? *It's good for the team, and what's good for the team is good for all of us, right?* Lisa's words came back to him. She was convinced shoving him and his relationship with Delia into the limelight was a valuable contribution. *But was that what he needed? What the team needed of him?*

Maybe that's how pro hockey was. More business than sport. Here he was whining when he probably wasn't such an anomaly. Jack scanned the table, taking mental note of the guys that had been playing in the NHL for more than a handful of years. Nathan Pelletier. Nils Johannsen. Noah Gaudreau. Not to mention Owen Monahan. Maybe this wasn't about him coming in and trying to help the younger guys. Despite his age, maybe he was still a kid who needed some guidance too.

"I'm telling you, I've had it happen before. It fell out like your mother's third child." Nils mimed in the air in front of him. "Straight out of my pants onto the ice."

Gaudreau laughed. "You left it there?"

"Hell, no! I stickhandled that cup back to my bench, flicked it over the boards, and kept playing. Nobody said a word!"

Liam chomped on a fry. "Probably because it was so small, it wasn't noticeable."

Nathan's face contorted with laughter as Nils leaned back in his seat. "Your sister says I've grown substantially since U13."

Liam flipped up his middle finger and reached for the ketchup. Jack grinned like a kid finding a dollar under his pillow after losing his first tooth. As strange as it was, that BS was what finally pulled Jack out of his head. *This was what he'd been missing.*

Jack pushed aside his menu, already decided on the western burger. "No way that happens in adult leagues. A cup can't escape past those logs." He pointed at Tkachuk's upper thighs.

Tkachuk wrapped both hands around the circumference of his right leg and had at least twenty centimeters between his thumbs. "Still hold the squat record."

Nathan scoffed. "Only because you didn't go up against me three years ago when I was your age."

"Deterioration, old man. You're already shrinking." Tkachuk stole one of Liam's fries.

Jack put in his order when the waitress came by their table, the wheels in his head finally gaining traction. *Something had to give.* This thing with Delia wasn't going to last forever, and *this* was what he wanted.

The thought sent his heart racing. He could do it. Quit his job. Give his two weeks' notice and play hockey until May full-time. *And then be jobless living in his sister's basement when he didn't get re-signed for next season.* Or get that contract.

"Jack, what does this look like to you?" Monahan held up Nils' arm and pointed at one of his tattoos.

He went with the first thing that came to his head. "A cat with no teeth."

Monahan burst out laughing, and Nils yanked his arm away. "Those aren't eyes!"

Jack's sides ached by the time they finished their meal and it was time for him to go back to work. He reluctantly pushed his chair back and stood as his teammates began gathering their things.

"Jack, you joining us for movie night?" Monahan asked.

It was the first he'd heard of it. "When is it?"

"Sunday afternoon. My place. I'll text you the details."

Nils leaned in. "You don't want to miss it."

His mischievous smile made Jack suspicious. "It's not porn, right?"

Nathan guffawed. "So much better."

Monahan clapped a hand on his shoulder. "Just show up, eh?"

Jack nodded, noticing that the rookie had already left the table. *What would Delia be doing Sunday?* If it wasn't on his calendar from Tony, it didn't matter, did it? "I'll see what I can do. Thanks for the invite."

————

Delia slid into the back seat of the car next to Mary with lipstick on and her hair pulled up into a messy bun. She may have also been wearing the bra that Jack had seen her folding a few nights prior which, she told herself, had nothing to do with anything. It was just a *bra*.

Mary passed her a bottle of water as their driver pulled away from the curb with Delia's security guard, Alvin, in the passenger seat. "You haven't stopped smiling since we left that meeting this morning."

Delia couldn't even pretend she was wrong. That morning, they'd met at a studio downtown with Ethan Hayes about the song they were collaborating on. All night she'd been a ball of nerves. After so many instances where she'd hoped to be a creative partner on one of her songs and walked away disappointed, she put in a lot of effort to keep her hopes well tethered to the ground.

This one had gotten away from her. She loved Ethan's work, and because she hadn't had a good outlet for the past few months, her creativity was shaking the bars of its cage. Inside that studio, she'd been set free. For an hour they'd sat and played —*just played*—like she had when she was sixteen lounging in her friend's basement messing around on their guitars and recording songs with janky equipment and duct taped microphones.

Delia sipped her water and dabbed her lips with the back of her hand. "My lyrics are going to be in that song."

Mary sighed. "Well it's about damn time."

"He genuinely liked my ideas, right? He wasn't just putting on a show?"

Mary shook her head. "He was not just putting on a show." She shifted on the leather seat. "Delia, you are an incredible songwriter."

The words soothed like a balm. "Sometimes it's hard to remember when everyone continues to tell you that your songs aren't 'leaning the direction they were considering for the album.'"

"Okay, 'everyone' in that sentence is IndieLake, and that's, like, three people total in the entire world."

"Well, maybe that's why I can't stop smiling. Because my world just opened up a little bit." Delia realized she hadn't put on her seatbelt and sat back, pulling it over her shoulder.

"Are you nervous?" Mary asked

"For Christian to hear it? Not really. I didn't go too far out of the box, and with Ethan's stamp of approval, he shouldn't have any issues."

"No, I meant to get together with Jack."

Delia shrugged. She'd been so amped up about the studio meeting after arriving back home, she'd phoned her mom between shifts and told her every minute detail of the session, then spent most of the afternoon on her guitar with her notebook and pencil on the bed next to her. She hadn't had much time to think about meeting Jack at the game tonight. Now that they were on their way, his face and the way it had felt next to hers two nights ago was at the forefront of her mind.

She started to get the jitters. Delia hadn't talked to Jack much over the past two days, which she hoped meant that he'd been just as busy as she had and not that he was ghosting her because of what had happened. It was embarrassing how much she'd thought about that kiss. It was like commercials on the radio, constantly interrupting her regularly scheduled programming.

That was normal though, right? Her body didn't know the difference between a real boyfriend and a fake boyfriend. She was having a normal biological response to a potential . . . *Potential what?*

She took another sip of water and looked out the window, hoping Mary didn't notice her cheeks flush.

"We're meeting him there, right?" Mary asked.

Delia nodded. "Yeah, he wanted to get together with the team beforehand."

"How long did he play with them before joining the Blizzard?"

"I don't know." Delia frowned. Even though she'd scoured the internet for Jack Harrison related content, there wasn't anything about his time with the Snowballs. She only had what Jack had said or what she'd seen from the guys when they'd unloaded their bags at the house. It was like the beginning of a puzzle on Wheel of Fortune.

Why did he care so much about a team he'd only played with since October? Especially now that he had an NHL contract? Curiosity tugged at her. *Again, normal?*

They parked at the rink, and Delia made the cameras out before they spotted her.

"Ready for this?" Mary asked.

Delia nodded. "Looks like Tony did his job well."

"He always does." Mary pushed open her door. As soon as Alvin was out standing next to Delia's, he opened it for her. And that's when the mayhem started.

"Delia, are you in love?"

"Why is Jack still going to his Elite League team when he's playing for the Blizzard?"

"Did you move to Calgary to be with Jack?"

Questions slammed one after another into her, not giving her enough mental space to answer any of them. She'd been trailed by paparazzi before and had done plenty of media events, but it had never been like this. There were at least twenty reporters and then a crowd of fans beyond that.

She and Mary had arrived early to get settled before the stands started filling up. The Ice Arena wasn't like a stadium where they could hide themselves in a suite.

"A little too well, maybe?" Mary shouted over the chaos.

Delia kept a smile plastered on her face. These pictures would be all over the internet, and she hated the candids that caught her resting bitch face. That she even had one had been a September discovery, and try as she might, she hadn't found a solution. Maybe that was why her online dates kept crashing and burning?

She waved as they entered the arena, and Alvin kept the press from bottlenecking her and Mary. They made it inside, strode through the open entryway, and beelined for the stairs. Jack said the Snowballs were playing on rink number three. They were supposed to go down the stairs, turn right, and walk past the first rink and enter the second one that direction.

As soon as they made it down to the bottom level, it was obvious by the numbers painted above the doors which rink was which.

"Jack said he had friends saving seats for us at centre ice."

Mary feigned delight. "Well good, because I refuse to watch a hockey game in the nosebleeds."

Delia snorted. First of all, there weren't any nosebleeds in this place, and second, Mary had never watched a hockey game in her life. Neither had she, at least not in person, but she'd studied up. Not to impress Jack, though there was a small part of her that wondered how he'd react if she knew the basic rules and a few slang words she'd looked up online, but more to make a good first impression with his friends. She hated the feeling of being the odd man out at a party. These days, she seemed to be on the other side of a window in most social situations.

While she'd never been around celebrities before she signed with IndieLake, she'd sat in rooms with plenty of big names since. Every time, she tried to avoid doing all the things people did to her now. Lowering their eyes. Sneaking glances when they thought she wasn't paying attention. Trying to take pictures while pretending to scroll their Instagram feed. It made her feel like a piece of meat.

Alvin walked with them through the doors of rink number three, and Delia immediately started scanning the benches. Jack had told her to look for Clara, possibly her husband Oscar who "looked like a swimmer," then a half-Korean woman and a girl with dirty-blonde hair standing next to his captain Sean's parents. Who were old white people she was assuming?

With such vague descriptions, it was a miracle she spotted them at centre ice a few rows up from the floor. Clara's eyes lit up as she stood, waving their direction. There were others sitting in the stands, and their conversations hushed as Delia strode past along the boards. She was still getting used to that, too.

"Do you know any of these people?" Mary asked in a hushed voice.

Delia shook her head. "We know Clara, at least."

They climbed the stairs to the fourth row, and Clara threw out her arms for a hug. "I'm so glad you could make it!"

Delia squeezed. "Thanks for saving us seats."

Clara pulled back and motioned to two fold-out cushioned seats set up in the middle of the row. "Those are for you and Jack. Our goal was to keep you both in the centre and surround you with the rest of us so everyone else don't get cheeky. Kind of like bison encircling their young."

Delia grinned. "Where are your horns, then?"

An older man next to them crouched and pulled a red stadium horn from the floor. "I've got you covered."

Delia laughed, then motioned to Mary standing next to her. "This is my friend and manager Mary, and this is Alvin, our security guard."

The group in front of them smiled and nodded, then the man with the horn reached out a hand. "I'm Gary Thompson, Sean and Emma's dad."

"Sharla." The woman next to him waved, not quite able to reach them if she stretched. "I'm Sean and Emma's mom, and I'm so glad to finally meet you. At Sunday Supper, everyone was telling me all about—"

"Mom." A woman with dirty-blonde hair flowing out of the bottom of her toque bumped Sharla with her hip.

"What? I was just saying—"

"I'm Emma." She gave Delia and Mary a small wave. "I apologize for the people on this bench that might get a little excited despite multiple conversations about etiquette." Sharla shot her daughter a look.

Delia started to piece things together based on what Jack had texted that morning. Emma was with Tyler, another newer addition to the Snowballs. Emma was also Sean's sister, and Delia was already writing song lyrics in her head about secretly dating your brother's teammate. She mentally rolled her eyes at her nightmare brain that immediately latched on to the most dramatic backstories possible for anyone she saw out in public. *Sharla and Gary were giving off high school sweetheart vibes...*

There wasn't anyone else down the line. Emma noted her scanning the bench and said, "Everyone else should be here soon. Kelty's running late, she's Sean's girlfriend." She pointed at the coats and mittens they'd strewn over the benches to save seats. "Hopefully we've got enough."

Delia looked to Mary and Alvin. "You two can have those comfy seats if you want. Jack and I can—"

Mary adamantly shook her head. "No, there's no reason for us to be cocooned. We'll sit behind you."

Alvin nodded brusquely. "I already did a walk-through this morning. If you need to go to the washroom or you want concessions, let me know. There's a private staff area we can use. They won't let the press in until twenty minutes to puck drop."

Delia thanked him, and he followed Mary down the row just above where they were standing. Delia stepped past the others to sit in the furthest stadium seat so Jack wouldn't have to step over her. She pulled her gloves from the pocket of her coat and slipped them on. The rink wasn't that cold, but the chilled air nipped at her fingertips.

"They'll turn those on, right?" Mary pointed up at the long heaters full of grey coils hanging above them.

Gary nodded. "Should be any minute now."

Delia took in the glistening ice and all the coloured lines and dots that she now at least had a basic understanding of. The red line that marked centre ice, and was mostly important for icing violations, which she didn't fully understand. The blue lines, which divided the rink into three zones. Defencive, near their own goal, neutral, between the blue and red lines, and offencive, by the other team's net. The face-off circles, which only made her think of Nicolas Cage pulling off his skin, and the goal crease, which was meant to protect the goalie.

She had no idea when any of that knowledge would come in handy during a conversation, but she was damn proud of herself for memorizing it when it wasn't one of her lyrics.

Clara shuffled past the Thompsons and plunked down next to her. "So, how are you enjoying Calgary?"

Delia smiled. "Honestly, I haven't had much time to explore. I was moving in, then working." She thought back to unpacking her things in her bedroom and shivered.

"You'll have to get Jack to take you up the Calgary Tower. There's a nice restaurant up at the top. It's mud season right now, so that means there won't be as many tourists in Banff if you want to take a weekend away."

"Mud season?"

Clara nodded. "When all the snow is beginning to melt. Slushy or icy ski slopes and muddy hiking trails."

"Got it. Do you ski?"

"Yep. You?"

Delia shook her head. "I took a school trip to Blue Mountain, which I'm sure is nothing compared to what you have here. I thoroughly embarrassed myself by not even being able to master the bunny hill." She turned and saw a few smartphones pointed their direction. People were trickling into the arena and had noticed them.

Clara grinned. "How old were you?"

"Old enough to know better than to sign up." Delia had never been the athletic type. Not that she couldn't kill a good interval ride on an exercise bike or pilates or yoga class, but playing team sports? Her personal coordination hell.

Clara sighed. "I didn't say I was good at skiing, by the way. Just that my family forced me to go out at least three times a season, even though it was a long drive. Now Oscar and I choose it."

"You're glad your parents pushed you?"

Clara nodded. "It was like piano lessons. I complained every second, but that only seemed to make my parents dig in deeper. Glad for that skill, too."

"So that's all there is to good parenting? Just force your kids to do everything they try to avoid?"

"Exactly." Clara laughed. When she smiled, she reminded her of Jack. Their lips didn't rise much above the tops of their teeth, and they both had the same smile lines with the faintest dimple on their right cheeks. She wondered whether Jack's nose had looked like his sister's before his hockey career, and lost what she was about to say.

Thankfully, before the silence stretched, they both caught

movement on the opposite side of the rink. Players with light-blue jerseys tromped out of a long hallway with their hockey sticks in hand and poured onto the ice through the gate in the boards.

"Time for warm-up!" Clara rubbed her palms together.

Delia barely heard her. A tall, dark, and handsome man with his hands shoved into a black puffy coat, wearing jeans that looked tailored to his frame with dark hair feathering out from under a slate-grey toque, rounded the west end of the boards. He looked up, and the corner of his mouth lifted. *Jack.*

Eighteen

HER WHOLE BODY sang like the quick slide of breath through a harmonica from bottom to top. *We should kiss regularly.*

Delia's senses flooded. She'd hoped by building space between them the past two days she'd be more centered around him, but it was the opposite. Like only having a fuzzy tongue after trying peanut butter the first time and then needing a full-on epi pen the second.

She could almost feel his hand cupped around her neck. Smell the subtle, clean scent of his soap. Her body remembered everything she'd tried to push out of her head, and the hairs on her neck stood at attention as Jack strode down the walkway next to their side of the boards.

He grinned up at her again. *Was that smile for her or the cameras?* The Snowballs were the ones scheduled for ice time, but she and Jack had an equally important game to play. *I want you to look smitten.* Kiss. Kiss. *Kiss.* The idea of his lips on hers grew like Morning Glory, choking out everything else in her head.

"There he is." Clara waved at her little brother, and Delia gave her best *Oh, I hadn't noticed* expression. Clara lowered her voice as Jack ascended the stairs. "Is it weird? This whole thing?"

Delia exhaled, focusing hard on the players circling the ice.

"Yep." Her lips snapped a little too hard on the end of the word, and she gave an apologetic smile. "Not because of Jack. He's great. You know what I mean."

Clara nodded, but her brows creased. "I've been worried about him. He's not—I don't know if you've talked about it, but dating hasn't been one of his top priorities the past couple of years."

Delia nodded. "I know about Angie. I'm so sorry for your loss." She'd done it. Said the thing that made no sense because what else was there to say? She wanted to apologize again, but bit her tongue.

Clara's shoulders relaxed. "I thought this whole thing might . . . I don't know. I keep trying to get him to move on." She looked as if she wanted to say more, but Jack was closing in, shuffling down the aisle.

"I think you're in my seat." Jack grinned at his sister.

Clara rolled her eyes, then forced a bright smile. "I was keeping it warm for you." She stood and gave him a hug, then shifted so he could get past.

Jack's eyes locked on Delia, and his lips twitched. He didn't sit. "Hey."

He towered above her, and her face was directly in front of the worn button of his jeans. Delia swallowed hard, forcing her head straight up. Jack's eyebrow raised, a silent message that she understood instantly. *They're watching.*

Delia stood, her heart punching against her ribs. Jack reached for her, and as his hands circled her waist, it felt as if someone trailed a feather down every bone in her spine. She inhaled sharply and forced her knees not to buckle.

Jack pulled her against him and lowered his head, his cheek brushing hers. He'd shaved. "I hope Clara wasn't fangirling too hard." His breath tickled the baby hairs next to her ear.

"She wasn't." Delia's heart was in her throat, and she couldn't tell if the overhead lighting was blinding her or if she was seeing spots. *Breathe.* She slipped her hands under the bottom of Jack's coat so she could link her hands behind his back to squeeze her pointer finger. *This wasn't real. This was only a show.* "How have you been?"

Jack reached up and tucked her hair behind her ear, and Delia shivered. "Are you cold?"

She shook her head. *Thank the hockey gods he couldn't see her face.* She was starting to sweat. "No, I'm good," she squeaked.

"You're trembling."

"I'm nervous," she whispered. *Name the feeling.* That always helped, didn't it? His smile spread against her cheek. That sure as hell *wasn't* helping. Why wouldn't her body listen to her damn thoughts? *This isn't real.* She repeated it over and over, but the more she pushed, the more her body bucked against her.

"Why are you nervous?" His voice was a low hum.

An ache spread through her middle, and Delia squeezed her eyes shut, wrapping her arms tighter around him without meaning to. It was sheer comfort to be pressed up against him, which immediately activated her inner therapist. *Maybe if you spent more time cultivating personal relationships and had more physical touch in your life, you wouldn't be hyperventilating when a man put his arms around you.*

Pressure built in her head until she couldn't keep the words from spilling out. "Umm, let's see. I'm meeting a bunch of people I don't know, who all understand this sport that you love and I know nothing about. I actually searched up the rules last night on the internet, and I wasn't going to tell you that because I wanted to look like I *did* grow up in this country paying attention to something other than chord progressions and poetry. Especially because I always tease my mom about not being officially Canadian, and then here I am knowing nothing about hockey. There are hundreds of people here with cameras, and I've been thinking a lot about how I have resting bitch face, which isn't something I can really fix, but it does make sense of a thousand other life experiences, and then I see you walking over here and—" Delia pressed her lips shut, cutting off the word vomit. "I'm sorry. I talk when I'm over-whelmed."

"And when it's late after a show." His lips brushed her skin.

Delia nodded. "Also after I laugh really hard, but not when I'm mad. I shut up when I'm mad. I think I should've given a better disclaimer that night at Malley's."

He huffed a breath through his nose. "Sometimes it's more fun to figure it out."

"Maybe with some people. I'm pretty sure my hidden trea-sures are cursed." She imagined Jack lifting a hand to the moon-light and only seeing his bones.

Jack chuckled, and the sound sent a thrill of pleasure through her. She pressed her finger. *Not real. Not real.* "I'll teach you about hockey. I won't even ask for your Social Insurance card."

"What about my birth certificate?"

"Nope."

Delia's shoulders relaxed an inch. "I'm not sure I believe you." She could hear his grin widen.

His hand moved an inch up her back. "Why?"

"You still haven't taught me that song."

"What song?"

"The Tony Knows one. From breakfast."

Jack shifted on his feet, his chest moving the lace under her shirt. "I never said I'd teach you that. This, I'm offering."

"Maybe I want to know the song more than I want to know hockey."

"That'll cost more than proof of Canadian citizenship."

Delia laughed. "I have nothing more valuable." She was soft butter again. Her hands were no longer clasped. *When had her fingers splayed over his lower back?* And when had she stopped shivering? She glanced up and saw the grey coils hanging in the heaters now glowing orange. Delia pulled back and looked up into Jack's eyes. They were dark behind his lashes.

"I'll be the judge of that."

Her heart skipped. "I could just search the song up online."

"Then why haven't you?" He raised an eyebrow in challenge. Delia pressed her lips together, redistributing the lip balm she'd applied in the car. He glanced over her shoulder and pressed his lips to her forehead, whispering, "Lots of cameras."

When he pulled back and his gaze lowered to hers, it held another silent question. It was stupidly simple to read him. She'd sat across from how many first dates over the past year trying to figure out what to say, and then here she was with Jack where she either couldn't keep her mouth shut or didn't need to say a word.

Delia answered with a nod, her blood already rushing in her ears. Jack's eyes flicked to her lips, and her whole body vibrated like a plucked string of her guitar. She tipped her chin, hyper-aware of the lull in the chatter around them. People were watching. That's what they wanted. Still, the thought that she, Delia Melise, hadn't been photographed kissing someone ever blared like that red horn in her head.

Her mind grasped for a hundred different threads, then snapped back into one solid string the instant Jack's lips met hers. Everything inside her went still. The sound of blades and sticks on ice, footsteps on stairs, shuffling on benches, laughter, and conversation faded to a low, gentle buzz. She instinctively flexed, pressing her fingertips against his shirt.

And then he was gone.

Jack stepped back. He paused a moment, then drew a breath and grabbed her hand, tugging on her arm to join him. Delia stared at their entwined fingers as she sat on her cushion. *I'm not ready for that.* Jack Harrison was holding her hand, and Delia was still reeling from how torturously short that kiss was when she'd wanted it to be like it was the other night. When he'd been all hunger and angst, not whatever that was, all gentle and practical without a storm raging behind it, like—

Like they'd done it a thousand times before.

Because it was for the cameras.

Delia sucked in a breath and held it, then slowly exhaled as she replayed their conversation in the living room on Friday. Yes. He said he was going to think about it differently. He was going to focus on the business side, on what he wanted with the Blizzard.

That was all this was. *Perfect.* Delia stared at the players swirling around the rink and swallowed hard.

"You okay?" Jack asked.

Delia nodded, her throat thick. "Mmhmm."

Jack didn't let go of her hand, instead pulling it close and lacing his fingers with hers. Bile rose in her throat. "So what did you look up?"

"Hmm?"

"You said you looked up hockey rules."

Right. *Hockey.* They could've been sitting inside a Chuck E. Cheese for all their setting mattered to her at the moment. Delia's world had shrunk to the warmth of Jack's palm and the feel of his hip brushing hers. She scooted her cushion an inch to the right so they weren't touching.

Jack's eyes flinched, and then someone's hands landed on his shoulders. He swivelled, dropping Delia's hand, and his face split into a smile of recognition. "Fly, you made it, bud." He stood and pulled the man behind them into a hug.

Alvin was perched on high alert on the next bench up, and Mary signaled for Delia's attention. *"What was that?"* She mouthed. Her eyes were wide. Delia waved it off, realizing she'd forgotten to mention their new public-displays-of-affection strategy.

Jack was already turning back. "Fly, this is Delia."

Fly put out a hand and Delia stood to shake it. His smile was wide. "I've heard a lot about you."

Delia wrapped her arms around herself. "Whatever you read online, it's not true."

Fly chuckled. "I don't read gossip online, I get it straight from the source." He winked at Jack.

Delia looked between the two of them. "You told him about me?"

Fly grinned. "I don't think dating you is something any guy would want to keep quiet."

Delia's cheeks warmed in spite of herself. *Maybe not if they were actually dating.* Jack had said the only people that knew the truth about their relationship were Clara and Oscar, so what was he telling his teammates? His friends? Delia hadn't talked to anyone about Jack outside of her close circle. But, truthfully, she didn't have anyone outside her close circle that she talked to under normal circumstances.

When had that all died out? What had been the final blow to her weekend jam sessions or the indie concerts she used to attend with her friends she'd waitressed with at Earls? It had definitely been her doing. She'd been the one to start turning down their invitations. She'd been the one to prioritize her own projects, new people and artists that she hoped would open up her opportunities.

"Fly was on the Snowballs before I finished with the AHL. He's the reason I found them in the first place," Jack explained.

Fly shook his head. "You would've found an Elite League team without me, I just wanted it to be mine."

Delia frowned. "So how do you know each other if you didn't play on the same team?"

"Fly was helping out on the coaching staff for World Juniors the first year I was there."

"World Juniors?"

Fly leaned in so he didn't have to yell over the noise from the crowd. "A tourney for national teams with players under age twenty."

Delia turned to Jack. "National teams? As in, you played for Team Canada?"

Jack nodded. "So did this guy. Just back when you and I were in diapers."

Fly scoffed. "You were at least swinging on the monkey bars by then, bud." He pointed at the other side of their bench. "That's my girlfriend. She didn't want to walk over everybody, but I'm sure she'd love to say hi to both of you at some point."

"Between first and second." Jack said.

Delia got the reference and felt embarrassingly pleased with herself. *There are three periods in hockey.* At least she had that much straight.

The stands were filling up fast, and their own section had multiplied exponentially since they'd sat down. Delia nudged Jack as Fly shuffled back toward the steps. "Tell me who everyone is."

Jack started at the top with an older woman wearing a navy blue quilted coat over a sweater that looked like it had come straight off the rack at Northern Reflections. She was showing something on her phone to a little girl with strawberry blonde hair. "That's Ryan's mom and his daughter Amaya."

"He's on the team?"

Jack nodded. "Yeah, I'll point him out to you during the game. That's Jenna—"

"I know her from the livestream."

Jack shot her a look. "If you fake cheat on me with Country, we're going to have words."

Delia laughed. "Imagine the press on that, though. You'd be the poor sap who got blindsided by a fame-hungry pop star. Women would flock to you." Joking was good. Even if she was still circling her attraction to him like a coyote. How was it so bad? *How was it So. Good?*

"True. Though, I doubt Jenna will see the benefits." He pointed at a group of women sitting next to her. "Those are some of Jenna's friends. I honestly don't remember all their names, but I know that one sitting next to her is Rhonda."

Delia raised an eyebrow, noting Rhonda's bronze skin, her high cheekbones and tight sweater. Interesting that he remembered her name and nobody else's. Guilt sank in her stomach at the thought after everything Jack had told her back at the bed and breakfast. Jack hadn't been with someone in three years. On paper, they both sounded crazy.

But hookup culture was stressful. Awkward. She'd faked an orgasm just to make one of her trial experiences end, then pretended she had a dog that needed to be let out so she could escape before nine o'clock. Not that he would've wanted her to stay since they hardly knew anything about each other. She'd never felt so empty as when she'd walked down that sidewalk to her car.

Sex felt incredible, yes, but with someone she didn't feel a real connection with? There were a lot of things that were pleasurable for longer than two minutes and didn't chase with existential dread and self-loathing. Sitting on the beach. Eating a dark chocolate brownie, for example. If anything, Jack's avoidance of physical relationships after being with someone he'd wanted to spend forever with made her jealous, not judgmental. He'd had something real. *What was her excuse?*

"That's Mike's family, Curtis's wife and kids." Jack finished off the row, then pointed to the end of their bench. "You already know the Thompson's, but that's Penny on the end there. Brett's girlfriend. And right below her are two of Emma's friends, Lindsay and Vaughn. She works with them doing design and photography. They come to the pub and Sunday Supper every once in a while. They're the ones that helped with the renovation of the bed and breakfast you're at."

Hands shot up, waving at Jack when they noticed him looking their direction. Delia took them all in. Talking and laughing, handing out beers from a cooler, hugging, smiling.

They sat back down on their fold-out foam seats. "You've only known these guys since October?"

"Yeah."

She shook her head. "It's impressive. How close everyone seems. Like you're one big happy family."

Jack exhaled. "That's what a team is supposed to be."

Delia thought about the only teams she'd ever been on, most recently IndieLake. Some of them had felt like this. Debate team. Definitely a strange, close-knit little family in grade ten. Her weekend team at the restaurant. Some of them had been better team players than others, specifically the cook who always left her a thick slice of mocha mud pie on the edge of the counter around eleven o'clock when the lounge was still full but the dining room was slowing down.

But IndieLake didn't feel like a team. Not like the Snowballs, at least.

Delia perked up when all the players started back toward their benches. "Are we starting?"

Jack nodded, and it was only then that Delia noticed his brows were knitted together. *So easy to read.* "Are you nervous?" He shot her a confused look. "For the Snowballs. You said this game will determine who they play first in the playoffs, right?"

"Right, sorry. I was in my head. Yeah, if they beat Zambone It tonight—"

Delia held up a hand. "What did you just say?"

"If they beat Zambone It—"

"*That's* their name?" Delia pointed at the white jerseys with grey and mustard-yellow arm stripes crowded around the boards of the visiting bench. Jack nodded. "What are the other names in the league?"

Jack's mouth quirked. "Uh, let's see . . . they're all very serious. Stiff Sticks and Dangle, Mill Hoodies, Puck Me, Don's Cherry Pickers—"

Delia laughed. "I thought this was a competitive league?"

"Damn straight."

"But you name your teams like sixteen-year-old boys."

He scoffed. "Those puns are way too sophisticated for your average teenager."

Delia shook her head as an announcer pointed their attention to the north side of the rink. A woman who looked like she was ready to open for Donny Osmond at Caesar's Palace stood with a mic in her hand. The audience rose and faced the flag as she sang the national anthem a cappella. As the final phrase, *we stand on guard for thee*, rang out, the crowd erupted.

Delia's heart swelled. She might not understand the game, but the rush of energy from sitting and cheering in a crowd was palpable.

The starting players from both teams circled the ice as music pumped through the speakers and the referee skated out from a box in the middle of the boards.

Delia nudged Jack's arm. "If you aren't nervous, then what had you in your head?" She was a glutton for punishment. The more she knew what was in Jack's head, the more she wanted, but she couldn't force herself to stop.

Jack drew a breath and leaned over his knees. "You were talking about this team being family." He ran his thumb over his chin. "I guess it made me think about what the differences were. Here compared to the Blizzard."

"I imagine the level of competitiveness is higher."

Jack shook his head. "No, I meant the difference with me—"

"What'd we miss?" Clara appeared next to Jack holding a bucket of popcorn with Oscar standing behind her, and the moment was gone. Jack sat up straight as they took their seats next to him. "No face off yet?"

"Just in time." Jack stole a handful of her popcorn, and Clara smacked his hand.

Delia grinned. "I can have Alvin or Mary go get us popcorn if you want some."

Jack shook his head and shoved the handful in his mouth. When he finished chewing, he said, "No, I don't want any. I just wanted some of Clara's."

"Are you *that* brother?"

"Hell, yes." Jack stole a napkin and wiped his fingers, then reached out and took her hand again, pulling it over to rest on his thigh. And just like that, Delia's head was louder than the fans packed into the stands.

The game started with a puck drop. Delia tried to make sense of it. Jack leaned in and whispered explanations for whistles and calls, but Delia didn't want to be a chore. She stopped asking questions mid-first period and just took everything in. The fast pace of the game, the crowd, trash talking or cheering depending on who had the puck.

She winced every time a player got slammed into the boards, regardless of whether their jersey was blue or white. When two players dropped mitts and started hammering each other with their fists, Delia tensed and turned her head as the fans went wild. "How? How is this something people want to see?"

Jack's voice was barely audible over the roar. "It's imperative to the game."

She scowled. "It makes no sense! We pride ourselves on being kind and considerate, *not* violent, and this is our national sport?"

"We pride ourselves on not putting up with shit." Jack ran his free hand through his hair. "Maybe it's not even pride, just gratitude, and we won't let some dickhead high stick and ruin what we've got going."

Delia's attention was drawn back to the ice where the ref led both players to the penalty box. "Wait, so fighting isn't even allowed?"

Jack shrugged. "You have to weigh the benefit and risk."

Delia's eyes narrowed. "*You* fight in games?"

"Not always. I've never been an enforcer."

"Which is?"

"Someone protecting their players. In charge of keeping the other team honest."

Delia turned back to the ice. "Was that the Snowballs' enforcer?"

Jack nodded. "Sean. He's the captain."

"Emma's brother." Delia glanced down the row, and her eyes

widened. Emma was cheering louder than anyone as her brother took a seat and wiped the blood from his nose. "This is insane."

"Welcome to my world." Jack grinned as he stood and cheered. It made less than zero sense to her how grown men could be excited about getting their noses bashed in, but watching Jack get riled up was enough to make her curious. There was something about the intensity in his eyes. The vein pulsing in his neck.

He stripped off his coat and dropped it over the back of their fold-out seats, and as he raised his arms, he exposed a strip of his stomach. It wasn't much, but the flash of muscle and dark hair was enough to send her belly swooping.

She needed to get laid. But that was the problem wasn't it? She didn't want to *just get laid*. She glanced down the bench at Clara and Oscar. Gary and Sharla. Then she focused hard on the blue jerseys as the game started up again at one of the painted-on circles to the side of the net.

Jack lowered back to his seat. His skin was flushed as he rolled up his sleeves, exposing the ink swirling on his left fore-arm. *Not all bad at all.*

The first period ended with the score still 0-0, and Delia turned to Alvin behind them. "I'd love to take you up on that washroom break." Jack gave her a questioning look. "He has a private staff washroom we can use so we don't get accosted."

Jack looked impressed. "I'll come with."

It was slow going. Everyone wanted to say hi to Jack on the way to the stairs, and once they got there, strangers reached out of their rows to catch both of their attention. Asking for a quick selfie or autograph, which both of them gave without complaint. Finally they reached the cement floor next to the boards, and Alvin pointed to the south bend, following them closely. They passed a security guard protecting the player dressing rooms, and Alvin took them through an empty hall to a washroom next to the lower-level offices.

Jack motioned for Delia to go first, and she breathed a sigh of relief as she entered the room. Silence. Her ears buzzed like she'd just gotten out of a concert, and her whole body sighed with relief from the intense stimulation of sitting in the stands. The game was fun, but she was quickly reminded of why she didn't normally do things like this. Why she'd stopped going out to clubs or crowded restaurants with her friends. It was too much.

She took care of business and washed her hands, then used a paper towel to grip the door handle and pull, using her hip to prop the door and dropping the soggy paper in the trash. "Your turn," she started to say then realized Jack was frowning, staring at his phone screen. "Is everything okay?" She stepped out to stand next to him.

He exhaled. "That podcast I recorded went live this morning."

Delia wanted to congratulate him, but held her tongue. His expression was bleak. "Not good?"

"It seems I said something that is creating a bit of a stir."

Delia sighed. "Yeah, I've been there. In October I said something about ADHD that people didn't like. Never mind the fact that I have it."

Jack looked up. "I was joking about puck bunnies."

She made a face. "Eesh."

"It was a joke."

"Probably came off as slut shaming."

He balked. "I would never—"

"I know!" Delia put a hand on his chest. "I said it might've come off that way, not that you meant it."

Jack's nostrils flared. He drew a breath and dropped his eyes. "Yeah. Lisa, our head of marketing, says I have to go to media training."

Delia pursed her lips. Gone were the proverbial Tarzan yells and fists beating his chest. Now he was like a puppy walking away with his tail between his legs. "I'm sure you're thrilled about having to sit in front of a computer screen alone for two hours answering multiple choice questions."

Jack shook his head. "She wants me to do it in-person." He turned his phone screen, and Delia read the name on the suggested appointment. *Jenna McAllister.* Her eyes widened. "Wait, does this mean if I came with you, I could talk to Country?"

CHAPTER
Nineteen

ON THURSDAY MORNING, Jack walked up the porch steps of Country's ranch house. He'd only been here once before. They'd played shinny on the pond and had a bonfire back when Country lived here alone. From what he'd heard, Jenna had moved in three weeks ago and they'd set up a studio there in the house where they filmed all their livestreams.

Jack raised his hand to knock, but the door swung open before his knuckles hit the wood.

Country pulled him into a hug. "What the hell, bud, I haven't seen you in ages."

"I was at the game Tuesday."

"You didn't come to the pub." Country pulled back and motioned for him to come into the house. Jack stepped in and took off his shoes.

"Yeah, we had to scoot."

"Press has been a bit much, eh?"

Jack sat on the couch in the living room and scanned Country's bookshelves. "That's why I'm here. So I don't piss anyone else off."

Country laughed and dropped into the chair across from

him. "Good luck with that. If you ever want to feel good about yourself, read some of my YouTube comments."

"Never read the comments." Jack lifted his hands behind his head and stretched over the back of the couch. He'd made that mistake when his name and player profile first exploded in articles and posts all over Canada.

"So." Country leaned over his knees. "How are things?"

"Good. How are things with you and Jenna?"

"Good."

"Good."

Jack's chest tightened. The guys on the Snowballs were his best friends in the city, and it seemed wrong to keep such a big secret from them. He couldn't tell Tyler and Brett, but Country understood living in the spotlight. He had to deal with the same kind of celebrity. He got away with saying whatever the hell he wanted on his livestreams, but Jack had never once heard him throw one of their teammates under the bus.

Jack cleared his throat. "I signed a contract."

"For next season?"

Jack shook his head. "I wish. No. A contract with Delia."

Country's brows pulled together, the wheels turning in his head. "You're going to have to give me a little more than that, bud."

Jack dropped his hands and rubbed his palms on his jeans. "She and I are together for publicity purposes." He let that sink in a moment. "I contracted for appearances and social media—"

"No. Shit." Country laughed out loud. "What day is it?" He pulled out his phone and opened the calendar.

"It's past April Fools if that's what you're wondering."

Country looked at him in disbelief, then launched into twenty questions. Jack gave him the best answers he could. Saying it out loud made him hyperaware of how much extra time he'd spent with Delia. He'd done more than the minimum, and ever since he'd started asking himself why, he couldn't stop. *Why did he think to text her at night before going to bed? Why did he think of her when planning anything with work or the team?*

He'd had to force himself to touch her. To kiss her. But not because he didn't want to. It was exactly the opposite. He wanted it too much.

So, he'd dropped into playing a game with himself. Wanting things he shouldn't and justifying why it was reasonable to have them given their business arrangement. It had worked up until Tuesday night at the game. When he'd seen her sitting in the stands. Then every rationalization sagged and broke apart like a toothpick and marshmallow bridge.

"I don't know, bud. I saw the pictures. You two don't look like you're pretending." Country raised an eyebrow.

Jack had avoided going online since Tuesday. He'd answered his chats and checked his email, but he wouldn't allow himself to open up his apps. He'd long since deleted his old profiles since previously, every time he logged on, there would be some memory popping up of him and Angie. Now it was him and Delia. He didn't want to see that other Jack. The one who could hold Delia's hand without guilt and kiss her in the stands.

When Jack didn't say anything, Country sobered and let out a long exhale. "If I can give you some advice?" He rapped his knuckles on the coffee table between them. "It's okay to want to be happy."

Country's words cut through all the chaff and sank deep, brushing the surface of the inky well gaping inside him since Angie died. He'd tried to bury it. Tried to ignore it. When that hadn't worked, he'd gotten damn good at closing it off most of the time, even if it meant turning his back on everything connected to it. He lived comfortably in the top half of himself, floating on the surface and never allowing himself to dive deep.

It's okay to want to be happy. Like hell, it was. How could he be happy when she was gone? When she didn't get to feel that jolt of electricity in her chest at a touch or the rush of adrenaline from a kiss?

"I lost my fiancée, Country." The words scraped out of him. Rubbing his throat raw. "She died three years ago."

Country watched him. "I won't pretend my experience is equal, but I know what it feels like to lose someone." He told Jack about his time in Toronto. How he had a ring and was planning to propose to Jenna, and then she'd slipped through his fingers.

Jack thought in some ways that would've been worse. To know the person you wanted still existed but you couldn't have them. To wonder why and get no answers.

"By some miracle, I got a second chance." Country rubbed his palms across his jeans and leaned forward. "That's probably a dick thing to say."

Jack shook his head. "I'm happy for you, bud." He sniffed and stretched out his back, then drew a deep breath. "Would you have moved on? Eventually?"

Country stood, catching sight of something out the window. "For twelve years, I tried. I think with me and Jenna . . . I don't know. There was something here that told me it wasn't finished." Country put a hand over his heart, then dropped his head. "Sounds hippy dippy, I know." He walked to the door and opened it as a sleek, black car turned off the county road and parked next to Jack's truck. *Delia.*

Jack quickly swiped at his eyes and cleared his throat. "Thanks, bud."

Country looked back. "My advice still stands, eh?" Jack nodded, and Country motioned to the hall. "Will you yell out back and tell Jenna she's here?"

———

When Jack meandered back into the living room, his head felt clear from the fresh air. That lasted all of two seconds once he saw Delia standing in the entry.

". . . I assumed you'd already had plenty of media training," Country finished. Jack hadn't heard the beginning of that sentence, but he saw the effect of it on Delia's cheeks.

She flushed as she stood upright after pulling off her boots and plastered a smile on her face. "I have. I just wanted to be supportive. Plus, I've been writing all morning and wanted to see Jack." When neither of them responded to that, her eyes narrowed. She looked between Country and Jack. "You told him, didn't you?"

Jack opened his mouth, then closed it again. How had she caught on to that in the ten seconds she'd been standing there?

Country grinned. "He did, but I promise your secret is safe with me. Jenna and I—"

"Jenna and I, what?" a voice called from the kitchen. A petite woman with long, blonde hair stepped past Jack and strode toward Country. She planted a kiss on his lips, then took off her coat and hung it on the hooks mounted to the wall next to the door.

"Jenna and I know what it's like to play games at work." Country raised an eyebrow, and Jenna shot him a look.

"I don't want to know why that's coming out of your mouth right now, and—" she held up a hand. "Don't comment on that, please."

Country smirked. "I'll save my thoughts for later."

Jenna rolled her eyes, then looked between Jack still standing in the entrance to the hall and Delia next to the door. "I'm sorry that was your introduction to what I'm hoping will be a much more professional—"

"They're not dating. It's fake," Country interrupted. He reached out and pulled Jenna against his side, sliding his fingers into the front pocket of her jeans. Jack watched Delia notice that detail and his blood hummed.

Jenna blinked, but the announcement didn't throw her for more than a second. "Well. No wonder you need some training."

Delia looked at Jack, with an, *Are you sure we can trust them?* look in her eyes. Jack nodded once.

"Let's get going, then." Jenna led them past the kitchen into a bedroom at the other end of the hall that contained no furniture other than a desk and chairs. Though the room was bathed in natural light from a tall window along the side wall, a ring light stood on a telescoping stand, pointing from the opposite direction. A webcam was mounted between dual monitors on a tripod, and there were two microphones suspended from scissor-arm stands on either side of the desk.

A squeak escaped Delia's lips, and Jack turned. "You going to be okay?" he teased.

She fanned her face. "Sorry. I'm not even into hockey, but I watch your highlight reels. They're hilarious."

Country looked a little too pleased with himself as he pulled two chairs off the back wall and set them in front of the desk.

Jenna sat in her swivel chair and rested her elbows on the polished wood. "We're playing it cool, but both of us were dancing in the kitchen to 'Shiny People' an hour ago."

A smile stretched across Delia's face, and Jack's heart stumbled. He'd looked up the lyrics to that one yesterday. *Shiny people, in the neon glow, Dancing fast, and living slow.* He hated them.

"Did you write it?" Country asked.

Delia fiddled with the hem of her sweater. She shook her head. "Nope. IndieLake isn't a fan of my lyrics."

Jenna frowned. "You had lyrics for it?"

Delia sighed. "I have alternate lyrics for all my songs, but I think it's going to be a while before I get to use them."

Jack cocked his head. "Do you know them?"

"Know what?"

"Your lyrics." Curiosity itched at his throat. He could hear the melody in his head and wanted to know what words she would've chosen to come out of her mouth.

"Yeah." Delia pursed her lips.

"Ooh, what are they?" Jenna leaned forward on the desk. Jack silently thanked her for jumping in so he didn't have to ask.

Delia shifted in her seat. "I'm not going to bore you by reciting the whole thing."

Jack grinned. "Just a stanza?"

"How do you know what a stanza is?" Delia's eyes narrowed, and Jack's skin heated. He might have been searching up more than just her lyrics.

He threw an arm over the back of his chair. "I was doing research."

"On what?"

"On music. You researched hockey rules, so I thought I should probably know something about what you do."

Delia's expression was unreadable. He liked that he could surprise her. Put her off balance. *Again, a little too much.*

Country leaned over the desk. "You two are doing homework on each other? Adorable." Jenna smacked his arm.

Jack's heart sped as Delia's shoulders curved inward. Was he embarrassing her? "Delia, you don't have to—"

She cleared her throat and started to recite. "Shiny people, gleam so hollow, Draped in smiles they barely swallow, Mirrored hearts, so thinly veiled, In their glow, the truth impaled." Delia drew a breath. "There. One stanza." She gave him a pointed look.

Jack's stomach flipped as her words built images in his head. It was his laughing face staring back at him with cold eyes, his chest with a hole plunged through the center, and his heart on a spike. *Shiny people.* Those lyrics were ten thousand times better than the ones he'd found online.

Jenna's expression hardened. "They wouldn't let you use those?" Delia shook her head. "Let me guess, 'you've got so much to offer and you just need to put in your time until you're more experienced?' Or, my personal favorite, 'what you have to offer isn't right for our target audience.'"

Delia's eyes widened. She didn't have to answer for Jack to know Jenna hit it right on the head. Thinking of Delia hearing those things from her record company made his throat burn like he'd struck a match and swallowed it. *It was wrong.* Delia's songs were popular, but if even he, an emotionally castrated, testosterone fueled, mitt dropping player, could see it, how could a music producer be so blind?

Jenna put a hand on Country's arm and clicked her tongue. "She's like I was ten years ago. Just so sweet and naive."

"When were you ever sweet and naive?" Country raised an eyebrow.

Jenna smiled with knives. "Delia, just remember they don't own you. Even if you think they do." She shook her head. "I know how easy it is to forget."

Delia's smile slipped a bit. The urge to reach out for her hand rose like a tidal wave, but then Jack remembered they didn't have to keep up any ruse here. Good. *That was good.* He drew a breath, and the moment passed.

"What am I thinking? We should've saved all of this for the livestream. You two, get over here." Jenna moved her chair.

Since they were all there, Country had suggested they do a fifteen minute rapid fire session before the training, and Jack knew Lisa would love the idea. Delia and Jack pulled their chairs over and squished in behind the web cams, and when they wouldn't fit, Jenna got them a small bench. They sat down and both almost fell off the ends.

Jenna pointed. "Put your arm around her, Jack. Create more space."

Delia's eyes flicked to his, then she sat and leaned in. As Jack's arm settled around her, something flipped in his chest. He thought about what Country had said. *There was something here that told me it wasn't finished.* Jack's heart had laid dormant for so long, he didn't know if it had anything left to say.

Delia clapped her hands over her mouth. "I can't believe we're doing this. I'm going to be on your channel!"

Jenna adjusted the camera. "Trust me, this is a symbiotic relationship."

The feed went live and, thankfully, Jack didn't have to do much work. Jenna and Country were permanently riffing off each other, and any questions they sent his way had to do with hockey which was so second nature, he didn't have to think. Especially because he trusted them not to ask him anything controversial.

When they were about to end the stream, Country turned to the two of them. "I have one more question, and it has nothing to do with music or hockey."

Delia pursed her lips. "You're making me nervous."

"No, it's a good one. We've had Brangelina, Bennifer, and now Tayvis, so what's your couple name?"

Delia and Jack looked at each other. "Deliack," Jack said just as Delia blurted, "Marrison." They both burst out laughing.

It took a minute for Jenna and Country to finalize the stream and post it on their various social channels. Delia and Jack replaced the bench along the side of the wall and took their previous seats on the other side of the desk.

Jack turned to Delia. "Marrison?"

"Don't even! You went with the digestive disorder!"

"Alright, Jack. Let's get on with it." Jenna opened her tablet, and Jack sat straight.

"I'll be a model student."

"Jenna won't know what to do with that." Country grinned, and Jenna rolled her eyes.

She moved through rules, some obvious and some not so obvious. Jack listened as best he could with Delia next to him, running her finger over the arm of the chair and wetting her lips. He'd never thought so hard about *not* touching someone in his life. It definitely impacted his retention.

Then they moved into role-playing, and Country was disappointed there weren't costumes. Jenna put his comments up as the example of what not to do while Jack did his best to answer with her rules in mind. Not easy or motivating with Delia grinning from ear to ear every time Country pulled out a juicy innuendo. After listening to her laugh at his jokes during the livestream and then seeing her hanging on his every word during the training, Jack had to work hard not to shoot daggers at his friend.

"That's all I've got." Jenna closed her tablet.

Country looked at his watch, then grinned at Jack. "Pond's still frozen. Want to dangle?"

Jack ground his teeth. "I didn't bring my gear." He wanted nothing more than to take Country out on the ice. And he wanted Delia to watch.

"It's not in your truck?"

Jack shook his head. "Nope. Stays in the dressing room."

Country grinned. "That's right, you're big time. I've got extra skates and a stick."

Delia turned. "I've never seen you play in person."

"But you've seen me play *not* in person?" Jack asked.

Delia flushed. "I—yes, online. Your highlights are everywhere." She looked down at her hands a little too quickly.

Adrenaline rushed through his veins. "I'll play. As long as the two of you lace up." Jack pointed at Delia and Jenna.

Delia's head whipped to Jenna. "Do you know how to skate?"

Jenna tried to play it off, but Jack had heard stories. Jenna played hockey in college. She'd handed Country his ass more than a few times. "I'm alright. You?"

Delia balked. "The last time I skated was in high school gym class."

"That wasn't that long ago." Jack grinned.

"Let me add: I almost failed gym class. I had to do extra credit by organizing equipment and cleaning the floors."

Jack's smile widened. "Sounds like you could use a refresher."

DELIA STEELED herself as Jack glided smoothly across the ice toward her. So far, she'd been able to avoid notice. Jack had been intent on starting a game with Country, and they'd been battling it out for at least a half hour. When Jack sent Country sprawling after stealing the puck, Delia wondered if there would've been a better way for him to burn off the tension rolling off him during the training.

Once Jack was up three to one, Jenna joined Country's team, then switched to play with whoever was down a goal. Even though her toes were cold, it was worth it. Watching Jack skate up close, especially without pads, was like going backstage to a concert. Every movement, every muscle flex, created new shapes —beautiful shapes—and for the first time since high school, Delia thought about picking up a sketchbook.

Jack turned his skates parallel and stopped in front of her. "You going to come out?"

She shook her head and pointed between the three of them. "Not with all that going on." The air was crisp, and despite wearing Country's extra gloves, she had her arms wrapped around herself to keep warm. Jenna had vastly underplayed her skillset in the studio. The moment Delia watched her push onto the ice and do a crossover, she'd committed to standing with her blades safely planted in the snow-covered grass.

"Jenna says we have to get back to work." Country stopped with a scrape next to Jack, sending a snow cone over his skates.

Jenna threw up her hands behind him. "You have a playoff game in four hours. How am I the bad guy?"

Delia breathed a sigh of relief, then shuffled to the log bench next to her and leaned down to unlace her skates.

"Not so fast." Jack laughed and reached for her arm.

Delia groaned as Country and Jenna slid off the ice and took her place, tugging on their laces. *Was Jack really going to make her do this?* She turned to the bench. "Neither of you are allowed to watch." Really, she didn't want Jack to be the one watching, but since he was holding on to her, it wasn't a safe option to blindfold him.

Jenna gave her a thumbs-up as Jack led Delia onto the ice. She felt like a toddler, her legs shaking like a newborn foal. She gripped Jack's arm. "Country wasn't lying about the pond being frozen through, right?"

He turned them to the middle. "Should we find out?"

"Jack!"

He laughed. "I'm kidding. You saw us skating all over this thing. Yes, it's frozen."

It was different when she was the one on the ice. She'd watched them stealing the puck from each other and sprinting down the pond. But since her mind had latched on to the idea of cracking ice and drowning in freezing cold muddy water, she wasn't thinking straight.

"Okay, let's start with something simple." Jack flipped backward and positioned himself in front of her. "Just try to march in place."

Delia attempted to mimic him. At first, her stiff movements were more akin to stomping than marching, but after a minute she started to feel more steady.

"Is it coming back?" Jack asked.

"Is what coming back? The shame and humiliation of holding onto the boards the whole way around the rink?"

Jack nodded soberly. "Unresolved trauma. Got it."

Delia rolled her eyes, then gasped as Jack let go of one of her hands.

"You're okay, I'm just moving back a bit to give you space to push off."

"Push off where, exactly?" Her voice was tight. Panicked. She wanted to be the cool, easy going girl. The athletic girl who could jump in and try something new and not look like they needed training wheels. But that had never been her lot in life.

Jack grinned like he was enjoying her consternation, his eyes glued to her skates. "Push off with one foot and just let yourself glide. I've got you."

"I can't."

"That four-letter word isn't allowed on my ice."

"Your ice?"

Jack nodded as he met her eyes. Delia was about to say it wasn't technically a four-letter word since there was an apostrophe, but the argument died on her lips. Jack's eyes darkened. That hunger she'd seen the other night in the living room shifted beneath the surface.

She teased her teeth over her lower lip, stuffing down her complaints. "I'll try."

"That's better."

If her heart hadn't been in her throat already, it was then. She didn't want to fall, but with that one phrase of approval, she craved Jack's praise more than she feared the crash. Delia pushed off into a shaky glide. It lasted barely a second.

"Good." Jack's voice was warm as he backed up again. "Bend your knees a bit. Lower center of gravity equals more stability."

Delia pushed off again.

"You look great."

Heat erupted in her gut like she'd just flicked the switch on a gas fireplace. Jack said something about using her edges, but she couldn't process it. She followed the sound of his voice as her muscles tensed. When she pulled up next to him and he started to move back, she pulled on his arm.

He straightened. "You need a break?"

Delia nodded, reaching for the zipper of her coat. She needed air. Minutes ago, her teeth had been chattering, and now she was going to self-combust.

"Here." Jack pulled her in and put her hand on his hip, then yanked off his gloves and opened her coat. "It's more work than you think, right?"

"Mmhm." *Skating.* That was definitely what was making her body pound like a bass drum. "Thank you."

Jack didn't step back. His fingers still held her zipper as he nodded, his head bowed to look at her. His brow twitched, and all the air in Delia's lungs whooshed out like she'd opened the neck of a balloon.

"Should we keep going?"

Delia didn't want to keep going. She wanted to stand right there and feel the warmth radiating from his body. She wanted him to keep watching her and say *you look good* and *we should kiss regularly.* "Sure."

Jack slid back and took her hand again. She reminded herself what Jack had taught her already and pushed off with one foot, then the other. The blades of her skates were still unsteady, but the grass seemed to be passing faster on their right.

She was about to try pushing harder into the ice when she spotted dots of grey. Shadows. There was an uneven patch less than a metre ahead. She tensed, clenching Jack's hand, and that small movement—the tiniest shift—sent her skate blades slipping. She gasped and tried to grab onto Jack, but her gloves slipped off the fabric of his coat and then she was flat on her back, staring up at wispy clouds and blue sky.

Her chest seized, her lungs burning. Pain radiated up her spine as cold seeped into her skin.

"Shit, Delia. Are you okay?" Jack crouched down on the ice

next to her, lifting her head and placing his gloved hand between it and the ice.

Delia stared up at his face, backlit by the fading sun. She'd known a crash would come, and she pushed off anyway. Because Jack asked her to. *No, she wasn't okay.* Self-pity and embarrassment washed over her in equal portions as she finally sucked in a breath. Tears stung her eyes, and she tried to blink them away. "Who in their right mind decided they would strap blades to their feet and try to walk on ice?"

She wasn't sure which hurt more, her tailbone, her pride, or her heart, which felt like gelatin in her chest. These feelings she had for Jack weren't going away, and she wasn't going to pretend she wanted them to. Even though that was going to play out exactly like the last thirty seconds.

Why was she wearing gloves? She needed to press her finger.

Jack held back a smile. He wanted to laugh, and she couldn't blame him. She wanted to give him permission, but she couldn't quite force her lips to curve.

He shifted to his knees and pulled her up to sitting. "Did you hit your head?"

"I don't think so." Delia wiggled her fingers. Pressed them against the hard ice beneath her. Forced herself to be in her body instead of in those thoughts that made her eyes glassy. "Just bruised, I think." She rubbed her backside.

Jack's eyes dropped to her hips, and his hand twitched. He cleared his throat. "You were doing great before—"

"Before I fell flat on my ass?" She stared up at him, her jaw set.

The corner of Jack's mouth curled. "You were doing great before you stopped trusting yourself."

Delia frowned. "What do you mean?"

"Your knees locked up. You tensed."

Delia pointed behind them. "Because I saw those bumps in the ice and—"

"You would've glided over them just fine."

Delia bit her lower lip, staring at the uneven surface of the pond. Trusting herself hadn't worked out the way she wanted. *Why would she trust herself now?*

Jack sat on the ice next to her. "I think I'm going to quit my job."

Delia gaped at him, wondering if she'd heard him right. *Where had that come from?* "What?"

He let out a slow exhale. "At the game, you asked about the difference between the teams."

Right. The conversation they never got to finish. *But why was he bringing it up now?* Delia ignored the fact that water from the melting ice was soaking through her jeans. "You said there was a difference in you."

Something behind Jack's eyes flickered, and she raised an eyebrow as if to say, *Yes, I was listening.* He drew a breath. "I don't know if I'm going to be signed on for another season. I doubt I will, honestly. I've been playing well, but there's talk about other free agents management is interested in, and it doesn't make sense that they'd use their budget on me when they could get some young buck with fresh legs."

Jack's legs looked plenty fresh to her. "But?"

He looked out over the pond. "It doesn't feel right. I have to go all in. If I don't, I'm always going to wonder if . . . I don't know. If it would've made a difference." He blew out a breath and turned to stare at the brown prairie grass. "It might not make a difference, though. Then I'll be out of a job."

He clenched his jaw, and Delia's heart tried to cram through her ribs and out of her chest. She knew that feeling. Even if she couldn't rescue herself from it, she felt compelled to try and save him. "Hey, you could always just date me for longer and have a steady source of minimal income."

He turned to face her, a slow smile spreading across his lips. "I don't think Tony would be on board. He's banking on the messy break up."

Delia laughed. "So am I, honestly."

They sat there, smiles on their wind-chapped faces, neither of them speaking. Finally, Jack pressed up off the ice and reached for her hands. She slipped as she stood, but he held her steady.

Delia broke the silence first. "I think you were doing great before you stopped trusting yourself."

Jack chuckled. "That's not fair."

"What?" Delia steadied herself, still gripping onto him.

"To use my own words against me." Jack held tight to her left hand and skated backward a few strokes, then flipped to line up with her. Delia threw out her right hand for balance, resembling a land-locked starfish. "Relax." Jack's voice hummed next to her.

"Easy for you to say," she muttered. They skated around the pond twice, which was enough to at least partially redeem herself from her cartoon flailing earlier. If nothing else, she'd proven she wasn't a quitter.

The sun dipped lower in the sky, and by the time they sat on the log bench, the pond was bathed in gold. Muscles that Delia didn't realize she had ached in her thighs and calves. "Are these my hip flexers?" She pressed a gloved thumb into the crease between her upper thigh and hip bone.

Jack chuckled. "Yep. Sore?"

"I need a hot yoga class."

He pulled off his skate. "Do you have to apply for that?"

Delia yanked at her laces. "What are you talking about? Like, sign up?"

"No, prove your attractiveness."

Delia blinked, then laughed out loud as realization dawned. "No, 'hot' as in high temperature. It's a sweat session. It loosens up your muscles." Jack grinned, and that's when she realized he was joking. "Ha. Ha."

Delia pulled off her skates and shoved her feet into her now freezing boots. "Where should I put these?" Country had lent them to her. He had at least ten pairs of hockey and figure skates hanging in his garage and unfortunately, one of them had fit her perfectly.

Jack motioned for her to set them on the bench next to him. She pulled out her phone and checked her missed messages while he put his shoes on. Nothing too imperative. Mary letting her know she'd scheduled their next studio session with Ethan, which made her heart leap.

She flipped over to her socials, and browsed her notifications. She always had plenty of tags and mentions, and she liked going in and commenting when she could.

Delia tapped on the first one as Jack tied the skate laces together and looped them over his shoulder. "We can leave these on the . . ." He kept talking, but Delia wasn't listening. She stared at the post from Ellie May in front of her. From the first ironic quotation marks, she knew she shouldn't keep reading, but her masochistic curiosity won out.

♪♫♪ᵤzᶻ In the latest news, pop 'sensation' Delia seems to be making waves again, though not through her music—unless we're talking about the kind that's perfect for putting you to sleep. It's baffling how her tracks, as forgettable as last season's fashion, keep popping up. Is it music or just background noise for more interesting conversations?

Enter Jack Harrison, a man who knows a thing or two about real talent and hard work. Unlike Delia's tunes, which vanish from your memory faster than her lyrics from a teleprompter, Jack's achievements stay with you, the mark of true dedication and skill. It's a shame to see such a star dimmed by association with music that's as bland as diet water.

And that supposed kiss? My dog uses more tongue. I, for one, am not convinced Jack feels anything more for Delia than he does for his sister.

While Jack scores goals, Delia seems content scoring tabloid head- lines. Perhaps it's time for her to take a page out of Jack's playbook and actually put some effort into her craft. Until then, she remains the weak link in this pairing, her forgettable songs a mere footnote in the shadow of Jack's masterclass of raw skill and perseverance.

To Delia, a word of advice: next time you hit the studio, aim for something that won't be lost to the annals of one-hit-wonders and 'Who's that again?' trivia questions. And to Jack—your fans hope you find someone who matches your commitment, both on and off the ice.

♪ ♫   *#JackDeservesBetter #PopMusicPurgatory #Remember-TheMusic*

Jack put a hand on her arm. "Hey, is everything okay?" With his touch, his voice finally broke through the roar in her head. Delia couldn't force a smile or a response. It was a mirror of her experience moments ago when her fall had knocked the wind out of her, but this time constriction in her chest was only the beginning.

Anger flooded her system, holding a magnifying glass over every frustration she'd tried to sweep away since September. *Those lyrics weren't hers. The song choices weren't hers.* Even the idea to date Jack hadn't come from her.

Her life was destined to crash. Over and over again. It was never good enough, so *why the hell did she keep getting back up off the ice?*

"Hey, Delia, can you look at me, please?" Jack hunched in front of her. He put a hand on her cheek. She tried to focus, but her thoughts exploded like fireworks, blinding her and then vanishing, leaving clouds of smoke trailing across her vision.

Jack took the phone out of her hand. She didn't try to stop him. She needed to move. Delia turned and stormed down the packed snow path toward Country's house. She wanted to smash something. Shove her face into a pillow and scream. Quit her job like Jack and never look back.

To IndieLake she was useful. A tool. To her listeners, she was entertainment. To Mary . . . she hoped she was a friend, but what kind of twisted friendship was it if Mary did everything for her and got a paycheck?

And to her Mom? Delia skidded to a stop, spraying almost as much snow as Country had on the ice. It was like someone had dumped a bucket of ice water over her. *When was the last time she'd heard from her mom?*

"Hey, Delia!" Jack called out behind her. She turned, and he was running toward her with his arm outstretched, his breath pluming in the twilight.

He stopped in front of her and handed her the phone. "You need to take this."

Twenty~One

JACK TRIED to catch his breath as Delia pressed her phone to her ear. "Tony?"

She listened, then exhaled through her nose. "I already saw it." A head nod. "Ellie's post. It was scathing."

Not the post. He'd been reading it, trying to figure out what had upset her, when Tony phoned. He'd answered by accident trying to decline the call, and Tony hadn't waited to make sure it was Delia on the other end.

"Delia, I promise, we're taking care of this. I'm working with IndieLake's lawyer right now to send cease and desist letters to all the platforms—"

"Hey, Tony? This is Jack."

"Oh!" Deep exhale. "Hey, Jack. Sorry, I thought—"

"What's going on?"

"Are you with Delia?"

"Yes." Kind of.

"Has she seen the video?"

Jack's stomach dropped to his knees. "What video?"

"If she hasn't seen it, you need to make sure she doesn't. I'm working with IndieLake's lawyers right now."

"Tony, what the f—"

"It's porn, Jack. Someone posted AI porn of Delia and it's pretty damn believable."

Jack reached out. "Delia, it's not the—"

Her face went white. "What?" The phone pulled from her ear, and Jack could hear Tony's voice through the speaker.

"We're on it, Delia. I've got the whole team submitting cease and desist requests on every platform. I'm working with IndieLake's lawyer, and we'll do everything we can to get it taken down."

Delia's hand started to shake. "Did you watch it?"

"I—yes, I saw what it was, but—"

"Did you watch it, Tony?" Delia hissed.

"Just enough to know what it was."

"And what is it?" Her fingers were like claws around the phone case.

"I told you, it's—"

"No, Tony, what's *in* the video? How long is it? What specifically does it show?"

Jack's stomach roiled. By the way Tony was acting, he doubted it was vanilla.

Tony coughed. *"Delia, I'm not—"*

"I can just search it up!" Her whole body was trembling.

Tony cursed under his breath. *"Don't search it up. Seriously."* He let out a long sigh. *"It's twenty-two minutes. Like I said, I didn't watch much, but there's . . . bondage."*

Jack clenched the wheel as they drove back into Calgary. He hadn't let Delia request her car and insisted on taking her home since he was going that direction anyway.

She still hadn't stopped crying. After she'd hung up with Tony, she got into the passenger seat of his truck and curled into herself, turning her face away from him. He could still see the tears streaming down her cheeks and hear her trying to hide her sniffles.

If he'd felt helpless sitting on the Blizzard bench for the first time, this was a hundred times worse.

Jack reached over the console and put a hand on her shoulder. Her face pinched. The only sign that she noticed his touch, and not the one he was hoping for. "I'm so sorry, Delia." He pulled the truck up parallel to the curb in front of the bed and breakfast.

Delia nodded once, then unfurled her legs and pulled on the handle. Since the truck wasn't in park, it didn't open. She fumbled for the unlock button, then swung the door wide and stepped out. "Thanks, Jack."

Her voice was so soft, he wasn't positive she'd said anything. As she shoved her hands in her coat and walked up the sidewalk, adrenaline surged through him. He couldn't let her leave like this. Was Mary even home? Was she going to walk into the house and sit in her room alone?

Maybe that was what she wanted, but Jack thought of those shadows on the ice.

He officially parked and turned off the truck, then launched himself onto the street and jogged around the hood.

Delia looked back. "Jack—"

"No." He took the steps two at a time until he was standing on the front landing next to her. Her key was already in the lock. "No." He pulled her against his chest and wrapped his arms around her so tight, he could feel her shoulder blades touch.

Delia's breathing quickened. Her arms stiffened against his chest. And then, as if reaching the top of a hill on a rollercoaster and accelerating down the other side, she collapsed. Jack held her up as she shook, no longer crying silent tears, but letting out deep, wracking sobs.

He ran his hands up and down her back, wishing he could push all the anger and embarrassment out of her like a tube of toothpaste. She didn't need to be ashamed. Whatever it showed had nothing to do with her, and whoever had made that smut— whoever had posted it and reposted—needed more than a full throttle punch to the balls. Jack clenched his teeth so hard, he smelled iron.

Tony told him to keep her from watching it, but Jack knew that if something like that had been posted about him, he'd absolutely be searching it up as soon as the lights were out. Not because he'd want to see it, but because he couldn't not. It was impossible to know that thousands, possibly millions of people were watching a fake video with your face on it and not have the curiosity rip you to shreds.

The problem was, it didn't sound like this was a video Delia, or anyone else for that matter, would be able to get out of her head.

Jack thought he might be sick. Porn was soul-deadening enough on its own, but to have your image, your body, used like that?

He had to find a way to get the video down.

Tony said he was working with his lawyers, but he didn't put a lick of faith in that process. They needed the big guns. And Jack knew exactly where to find them.

———

Delia tried not to think about what the front of Jack's coat would look like when she pulled away. Her face felt like it had been stung by a hive of bees. The last hour blurred together. The pond, the phone call with Tony, the drive home. All of it lay under a thick, black, oppressive cloud.

She exhaled a shuddering breath. Her eyes were so puffy, she could barely see through her lashes, and she'd stopped trying to keep her nose under control since escaping Jack's truck. Delia didn't want him to see her like this—she didn't want anyone to see her like this—but the second he'd pulled her into his arms, she'd given in.

Click.

The sound of a camera shutter sounded behind Jack. He muttered a string of curses and reached out, turning her key in the lock.

She gripped onto his coat. "Don't—"

"I'm not leaving. I promise." His voice rumbled in his throat. "Where the hell is Alvin?"

Delia had no idea. She hadn't phoned in the car, and hadn't even thought to text him while they were driving back into town. Alvin knew she was with Jack, and he was entitled to a day off. His replacement had driven with her to Country's ranch, but she'd told him to go home. It was her fault for not communicating her return time.

"Don't you have practice?" she squeaked as Jack covered her body with his, shielding her as they entered the foyer. He slammed the door behind them.

"Nope. " Jack knelt and unzipped her boots. Delia had zero concept of time, but she was almost positive he'd told her he did. Before she could kick her boots off, Jack was next to her, his arm around her shoulders. He turned the deadbolt and kept them clear of the two narrow windows on either side of the door. "Are you hungry?"

Delia shook her head. She didn't think she'd ever eat again, not after hearing Tony describe what was moving like wildfire across the web. *Damn it.* How ironic that she'd been upset about a petulant blog post by Ellie May? Her head started to pound.

"Upstairs, then." He stripped off his coat and held it out like they were sheltering from the rain. They climbed to the second floor, not even bothering to turn on a light until they reached Delia's bedroom.

He helped her out of her coat. "Where's your cell? I can phone Alvin and fill him in. Let him know we have company."

Delia nodded, no longer hyperventilating. She dropped her purse on the bed and pulled her phone from her pocket. Without hesitation, she unlocked it and handed it to Jack, then stumbled into the washroom and splashed cold water on her face.

How could someone do this? Delia thought back to all the times she'd heard about leaked sex tapes or deep fake pictures or videos. If she was honest, she'd never quite believed the celebrities when they went on talk shows insisting it wasn't them or swearing it was filmed without their permission.

Probably a publicity stunt. She almost gagged. What a self-righteous, judgmental asshole she'd been. What had given her the right to sit back and assume she knew anything about someone else's life? Who was she to read the gossip or look at the stolen photos?

It was madness. That anyone felt entitled to exclusive access to the most intimate parts of someone's life. She wanted to set her social apps on fire and never get on the internet again.

Jack's voice hummed behind the door, and a thought sent a bucket of ice down the back of her shirt. *Would he watch it? Would Mary or Alvin? Had his teammates seen it?* Every man she'd ever known or dated in her life flashed through her mind's eye, and she threw herself to her knees in front of the toilet.

She clenched her hands into fists as her stomach emptied, then coughed and sucked in a breath before she heaved a second time.

When her heart rate came down and her stomach wasn't trying to flip itself inside out, Delia forced herself up and rinsed the sour out of her mouth. She brushed her teeth, then washed her face properly and applied moisturizer.

Looking at herself in the mirror only made her want to cry again, so she dropped her eyes and braved the bedroom where she knew Jack was waiting. Something inside her shifted like wet sand at the realization that she'd asked him not to go.

Her heart stuttered as she stepped past the threshold. Jack looked up from his phone. Hers sat next to him on the comforter. He didn't ask if she was okay. Her pale skin and puffy eyes answered that question.

She wanted to say something. To make a joke like she had on the ice or use another tool from her toolbox to process the last hour, but her thoughts and emotions were a snarled ball of yarn that she didn't have the energy to start unraveling.

Instead, all of her worst habits floated to the surface. She should drink. A lot. And watch a terrible rom com with chips and queso and a box of doughnuts.

She knew from personal experience that none of it would work. She was going to crash. Again, and again, and again.

Delia glanced at her guitar propped against the chair. For the first time in a long time, the idea of playing it made her stomach lurch. If she had to avoid her feelings, that was not the way to do it. Something about her fingers against the smooth wood and strings wouldn't allow her to lie to herself.

It was the same reason she couldn't phone her mother. Not yet. She would just sob, and the last thing her mom needed was more stress in her life. Lying was what she needed right now. Delia closed her eyes and drew a deep breath. *Sleep.* She just needed to crawl into the bed and close her eyes and tell herself the last hour had been a terrible dream.

When she opened her eyes, Jack was still watching her. He jammed his hands into the pockets of his jeans. "Alvin and Mary are a few minutes away. He's going to make sure nobody tries to approach the house." Delia nodded, rolling and unrolling the hem of her sweater. "I know I'm not your boyfriend, and I'm not trying to—" He flinched and lowered his eyes. "I don't have to be here in your room if you don't want me to be, but I can't go,

Delia. I'm not going to leave you alone. So I can be here with you or I can go sit—"

"Be here with me." Delia's voice was a whisper, raw from throwing up and swollen from crying. She didn't know what it meant for him to be there, but the idea of him walking out the door made her insides yank from her middle.

Jack let out a relieved breath. "Okay. Yeah." He glanced around the room like a dog hunting for the perfect place to curl up and nap. Jack being close normally sent her heart into rhythmic gymnastics, but not then.

The idea of him wound around her suddenly felt like the end of a good book. Like placing the final piece of a jigsaw puzzle. The chord resolution at the end of the bridge.

Delia took the few steps to her dresser and reached under her shirt to take off her bra. Jack faced the door while she changed, only turning back when he heard her pulling the sheets and comforter back on the bed.

He reached out and handed her her phone so she could plug it in on the bedside table. Delia took a moment to send a text to her mom just for peace of mind.

Hey! Thinking of you! Are you feeling okay? How was work? Love you!

It was too many exclamation points, but she sent it anyway. When she was settled under the covers, Jack turned off the light. It took a moment for her eyes to adjust to the inky dark.

"Please." It was the only word she could get out, and she hoped he understood. She wanted him there, right next to her. Holding her together so she didn't shatter into a thousand pieces.

A streetlamp sent pale light through the thin strip between

her curtains and the wall. It was just enough to catch Jack's silhouette as he approached the bed. He climbed onto it, staying on top of the covers as the mattress compressed. Delia's skin prickled at the sound of his jeans rubbing on fabric. At the way she rolled back into him.

His breathing shifted from shallow to deep. "Is this okay?"

Delia nodded, then reached back and grabbed his wrist, pulling his arm over her waist. Jack moved closer, pressing his chest against her back, unintentionally pulling the covers tight over her shoulders and hip. The pressure was soothing, like a weighted blanket, and Delia exhaled, sinking into the mattress.

"Do you need anything? Water?" he whispered.

Delia shook her head, then reached up and smoothed her hair so it wouldn't be in Jack's face. When she dropped her hand, she gripped onto Jack, pulling his hand to her chest. Her thoughts depressed, slowing for the first time all afternoon, but the questions from the washroom still rolled through her head like marbles. "Do you think people believe it?"

Jack drew a breath and exhaled. "I'm sure some people do. But anyone who knows you—"

"People don't know me, Jack." That was the honest-to-God truth. She hadn't known how to get close to people at the same time as she was working to build her dream career, so she hadn't. She was hopefully likable in her interviews, but she hadn't always been herself. Mostly because *herself* hadn't always been especially successful at winning friends and influencing people. She was only truly herself with a few people. Mary. Her mom. Tony, most of the time. And . . . now Jack. The realization sent a soft glow buzzing under her skin.

"Maybe you're not giving people enough credit."

"Well, *people* just posted my fake sex tape, so . . ."

Jack chuckled, and her shoulder moved with his chest. "Fair point." He shifted his legs and completed their partial spoon. "I think I know you, though."

"Yeah?"

"Enough to know you wouldn't like any of the shit Tony mentioned in that video."

Delia breathed a laugh. "Right. I'm so easy to read in real life, you've figured out my sexual preferences."

Jack brushed his nose against the back of her head. "You're not as cryptic and mysterious as you think."

The crushing weight on Delia's chest slipped an inch. "Some people don't even listen to my lyrics."

"Maybe those people would listen if they were actually yours."

Delia's heart thudded loud enough, she was sure Jack could hear it. She gripped his hand tighter. "You should teach me that rhyme." Jack didn't answer right away, and Delia realized her mind had skipped well outside normal trains of thought. "The Tony one," she clarified, and sensed Jack grin behind her.

"That's unfair," he whispered.

"How so?"

"Because you know I can't say no when you just had a leaked sex tape."

She laughed. "I know, it was brilliant. I said to myself, 'Delia, just be patient until the sex tape leaks, and then you can finally get your answers.'"

"Diabolical." Jack pulled his hand from hers. "Okay, it's really difficult, so I need you to pay attention." Delia nodded, her heart fluttering like a butterfly trapped in a jar. "It starts with toes, which I can't reach right now, but just pretend."

Delia stretched her arm downward, barely reaching past her knee. "Okay, got it. I'm as far as I can go."

"Right, so 'Toe, knee,'" Jack tapped her knee and waited for her to follow. "'Chest.'" He didn't touch there, instead keeping his hand over the back of hers. "Then 'nut,' that's your head."

"Of course it is." Delia tapped her forehead.

Jack tugged on her wrist. "'Nose.'"

Delia cackled. "Ow! That's my eyeball!"

"Well pull in your fingers, geez, Delia. You don't need a claw for this exercise."

She balled her hand into a fist and used just her pointer finger. When it was resting on the tip of her nose, Jack pulled her hand back. "Now you actually do need to touch your eye."

Delia closed her eyes and let Jack drop her hand until her fingertip tapped her eyelid.

"So, 'nose, eye' . . ." Jack hesitated, then dropped her hand back to her chest, his fingers wrapped around hers. "Love you."

They sat there a moment with only the sound of their breathing breaking the silence.

"Is that it?" Delia asked.

Jack swallowed. "That's the first part. Then you just repeat 'Toe, knee, nose.'"

Delia yawned. "I'll have to practice."

"Like I said. High level of difficulty."

She grinned, lacing her fingers through his. They lay there in the still and quiet for what could've been ten minutes or thirty.

After her thoughts had worn themselves out, Delia yawned. "You know what I'm most upset about?"

Jack's reply was slow like molasses. "What?"

"That I can't make sex-tape jokes anymore."

Jack breathed a laugh and kissed the crown of her head.

CHAPTER

Twenty-Two

JACK WOKE in the same position as when he'd fallen asleep. Curled around Delia, his hand still in her grip. He held still, listening to make sure he hadn't jolted and woken her, then slowly retracted his arm. She didn't stir.

From the lack of light outside the window, he guessed it was probably around five, which was perfect. Jack slowly rolled to his opposite side, sliding an extra pillow behind him to make sure Delia didn't notice his absence, then grabbed his phone off the nightstand where he'd left it. *Five twenty-two.* He gave himself a mental pat on the back, then turned off the alarm he'd set for five forty-five.

When he'd texted Tyler the night before, he hadn't expected a reply. They had a playoff game, and he knew the whole team would be celebrating. Tyler had written back within a couple of minutes. News of the video had spread, and the Snowballs had already been talking about a plan of action. He didn't know how many guys were going to show up at the bed and breakfast at six, but he'd told Alvin ten just to be sure.

Jack dropped his legs over the side of the bed and stretched, then tiptoed over the old floorboards to the door. He let himself out into the hall, grateful the door hinges had been WD-40'd recently. His stomach grumbled, sending him down the stairs and straight into the kitchen. After flicking on the light, he opened the fridge and took inventory.

His eyes widened at the shelves stacked with eggs, bacon, yogurt, and fruit. *Yes, please.* When he spotted the English muffins on the counter, his mind was instantly made up. Jack reached in and grabbed a package of bacon and carton of eggs. He had over thirty minutes. Plenty of time to make a hell of a breakfast.

———

At six on the dot, Jack's phone buzzed. He set the mustard and mayonnaise next to the bowl of eggs and plate of cooked bacon, then wiped his hands on a towel. He pulled his phone from his pocket.

Hey, bud. Didn't want to ring the doorbell

Coming

Jack exited the kitchen and strode to the front door. He flicked on the porchlight and unlocked the deadbolt. As the door swung wide, he found Tyler, Brett, Sean, Country, Ryan, André, Mike, and Curtis on the doorstep. *Eight.* Not bad.

He stepped out of the way to let them in. "Morning."

They whispered greetings as they removed their shoes and followed the smell of bacon.

"Hell, yes, Harrison." Mike was the first to grab a plate and dish up, but it only took seconds for the rest to follow.

"Wasn't expecting breakfast." Tyler snagged a toasted English muffin from the cookie tray.

"Maybe you should offer up your services more often." Sean winked.

Jack waited till the rest of the guys moved through the line, then made his own sandwich. They sat around the table in the dining area in the next room where he'd already put out cups and a jug of orange juice. Hopefully Delia and Mary wouldn't mind that he'd dug into their supplies.

"So. What did you find out?" Jack asked as he took a bite.

Tyler held his hands over the plate, mustard dripping down his pinky. "Whatever dickwad uploaded it used a slew of anonymizing techniques. Multiple VPNs, bouncing through servers across different countries. It's like chasing a ghost through a maze."

Country chewed and swallowed. "Not an amateur."

Tyler nodded. "Not their first rodeo."

Jack's chest tightened. Tyler worked in cyber security. There was dressing room lore about how he'd broken into federal security systems and locked down corporate bank accounts. This had to be within reach. "You found them, though, right?"

The corner of Tyler's mouth curled. "Hell yeah, I found them."

Curtis and Brett leaned over and fist bumped him. Jack breathed a sigh of relief. "Can we give that info to Tony? Maybe—"

"I doubt Tony's going to have much luck with his lawyer," Tyler said. "For sure they'll be able to get it taken down on third-party sites, but the host site's buried in layers of legal protections designed to shield asshole users."

"Perfect," Jack grunted. He wasn't surprised. He hadn't said anything to Delia, but he wasn't holding his breath to hear good news from Tony. How was a lawyer supposed to get a video down fast enough? After he submitted his paperwork and jumped through whatever hoops he had to, the damage would already be done. "So what do we do?"

Tyler grabbed a napkin and wiped his fingers. "There's only one option that kills this thing, and it's not legal."

"I like it already." Mike grabbed the jug of orange juice and unscrewed the lid.

"Probably not a big deal for us, but you, Jack. If you were connected to it—"

"Whatever, he'd have the Blizzard legal team behind him. We're the ones who would end up paying a shit-ton of fines for whatever you're proposing." Brett took the last bite of his sandwich.

"What are you proposing?" Jack asked. He had zero understanding of what it took for Tyler to figure out anything about the video let alone get it pulled down.

"Launch a cyber-attack against the twat. Digital retribution. Flood their network until we either force them to take the video down or render their system inoperable." He leaned back in his chair. "The good news is, if the user decided to nark, they'd have to admit to posting the video. *That* we could turn over to Tony and his lawyers. Wouldn't necessarily get it taken down immediately, but it would be good fodder for headlines if we had a name."

"Damn, Bowen." Brett gaped at him. "Remind me never to get on your bad side."

They cleared their plates, half of them eating a second sandwich while standing over the counter in the kitchen, then filtered into the living area where Tyler was already setting up. Now the bags and boxes they were carrying made sense. There was a mass of cords snaking across the floor and multiple monitors winking to life on the desk.

"You need this?" Curtis picked up a sleek, black box. Tyler took it from him and plugged it in. "This is a VPN concentrator. It allows us to mask our location. Hopefully better than they did.

I've got a burner computer and nobody try to be smart and get on the WiFi here."

Curtis nodded. "So we don't go to prison."

"Exactly." Tyler stood as light flickered on the box. He picked up a device no larger than a smartphone. "This is a hardware firewall. If they try to trace us or hit us back, this will keep our network secure." He worked to get everything hooked up and running and, after typing in his passwords, he brought up a complex-looking interface on one of the screens.

Curtis grunted. "I think I just had a stroke."

Tyler chuckled. "This is the software that will orchestrate the attack. It's designed to flood their server with more requests than it can handle. Clogging a pipe until the pressure becomes too much."

Country clapped his hands on André's shoulders. "Like this guy when he takes a shit at the rink."

André smirked. "I can't help it if everything about me is too big to handle."

Curtis shook his head. "Too early for dong jokes, André."

Jack leaned in toward the monitor. "I'm a little scared of you right now."

Tyler's fingers danced over the keys. "This little pissant isn't going to know what hit him."

"If anyone asks, I wasn't here. I have a family to think about," Curtis said as he dropped into a wingback armchair.

Sean scoffed. "And we don't?"

Jack laughed, trying and failing to figure out what the hell Tyler was doing on the screen. Numbers. Codes. All of it moved too fast for him to follow. It was like he was in the middle of a Bond movie watching Q work his magic.

Bond made him think of Delia. He glanced up the stairs and checked that her bedroom door was still closed. He hoped that when she did eventually wake, he'd have good news.

Watching Tyler work made him antsy, so he retreated to the kitchen and started washing dishes and putting things away.

Doubts circled in his mind like crows. *What if it didn't work? What if they got caught and the video still didn't come down? What if the original video came down, but versions of it perpetuated anyway?*

He glanced up to find Country walking toward the sink. He grabbed the bacon grease covered baking sheet and the frying pan Jack had used to scramble the eggs. "How are you holding up?"

Jack put a half sheet of foil over the leftover bacon. "Holding."

Country blew out a breath as he squeezed the bottle of dish soap. "Yeah. No kidding. You stay here last night?"

Jack nodded. "I didn't even ask how the game went."

"Because it's not important." He turned his head. "But we kicked their asses. Five to one."

"Hell yeah, bud."

Country scrubbed the pan. "You have a game tonight?"

"Yep."

"You going to be able to focus?"

"Doubtful."

Country grinned. "Still think this relationship is fake?"

Jack's arm jerked, and he nearly dropped the eggs before setting them back on the shelf in the fridge. Country gave him a smug smile when he turned, and Jack reached for the bottle of mustard.

He shoved it into the fridge and closed the door. "This is wrecking her. Even if Tyler gets it down, I don't know how we can combat the viral shares." Jack still hadn't opened his social apps, but after talking to the guys last night, it sounded like the video had been reposted on every platform. When it was reported for explicit content and taken down, it was just put up again. A never-ending cycle.

"I do." Country propped the pan in the drying rack. Jack frowned. "Fight fire with fire, bud. You know those photographers camped out on the street? Guess what they want to see more of?"

"Delia."

Country shook his head. "Nope. You. Delia. Both of you. The *myth* of you." He leaned into the counter. "Plus, in my experience, the internet loves nothing more than a pissed-off hockey player."

CHAPTER
Twenty-Three

DELIA WOKE to the smell of bacon. It was almost enough to
stave off the dread that slugged her in the stomach seconds after
she registered where she was. In her room. In her bed. Where
she'd curled up after crying her eyes out. With—

She rolled and found it was a pillow against her back, not
Jack. Her dread turned to worry. Had he stayed the whole night?
Had she kept him from his hockey commitments? Delia groaned
and reached for her phone on the nightstand. Seven thirty.
Surprising she'd slept so late considering she'd gotten into bed
just after eight.

Another waft of bacon fat hit her nostrils. *Was Mary cooking?*
Mary never cooked, but considering the circumstances, she
wouldn't be surprised if her friend had decided to go emergency
domestic. Delia took off her knitted sweater from the night
before and pulled on a cotton crewneck. No bra. *No bra for the
rest of forever.*

Delia picked up her phone. Two new messages from her
mom and a hundred others she wasn't able to deal with at the
moment. She tapped on her mother's name.

> Thinking of you always
>
> Work was good. Breathing well, so no more
> articles, love 😊

Delia blew out a slow breath and pressed on her mother's number. She couldn't put it off any longer.

Each time the phone rang, Delia's pulse kicked up a notch. She wanted her mom to pick up so she could share the awful news and get it over with, but when it went to voicemail, she breathed a sigh of relief. Now she could spit it out without answering any questions. Or crying again because she was already halfway there just hearing her mother's voice telling her to leave a message.

"Maman. I don't know if you've heard anything in the news, but someone posted a video online. It's fake. It's a sex tape of me that they made with AI tools. Tony said he and the lawyer at IndieLake are working on it, and I'm so sorry something like this happened, and I love you—" Her voice broke. "Anyway, I needed to tell you. It'll be fine. I'm doing fine, and I hope you have a great day, and I miss you." Delia ended the call before her voice lifted into a supersonic register.

She dropped her phone, padded into the washroom and brushed her teeth, scouring her mouth of the moments spent above the toilet the night before. *Ugh.* Jack had heard that. He'd seen her completely melt down. No wonder he'd left before he had to face her in the light of day.

She splashed cold water on her face, peed, then washed her hands, shut off the washroom light, and fell back on the bed, grabbing her phone. Her heart slammed against her ribs the second she swiped up on the screen. *It was out there.* That video. If it had already started to go viral when Tony put out an SOS, what had it done overnight?

Delia knew she shouldn't look at it. She knew it would

destroy her mental health. If she struggled to see low-res pictures of her walking down the street or couldn't handle holding Jack's hand, what would it feel like to see a rendition of herself nude? In compromising positions?

Still. Curiosity ate at her insides like battery acid. Maybe she didn't have to search up the video. She could go on her socials and feel things out through her followers? She tapped on the screen because *not* looking wasn't an option.

Had she been standing, her knees would've buckled at the number of notifications blaring at the top of her feed. Panic and desperation burbled up her esophagus, but she couldn't stop herself from clicking.

@oldminer: And this is all women are good for, amiright?

The caption sat under a black square with the message, "This video has been removed for explicit content." At least there was that. Delia scrolled to the next post.

@helikeshats: I didn't like her voice until I heard her beg

Bile rose in her throat. She moved to the next. And the next. Tears stung her eyes, but she couldn't stop. One after another, the captions were like paper cuts. Like candle snuffers, burying her in darkness.

When she thought she might need to run to the washroom again, something appeared on her screen and she froze. Delia blinked, the face in front of her not making any sense.

Jack.

Had someone posted a fake video of him now? Jack didn't have social media accounts, or if he did, he never posted. But there he was. His face—his dark eyes and morning stubble—taking up the entire frame. It didn't register for another fifteen seconds that his mouth was moving but there was no sound.

Delia restarted the video and turned up the volume.

"Hey, this is the first time I've ever posted something on this app, and I'm going to be honest, I'm not thrilled to be here. I'm a private person, but something happened yesterday that I felt compelled to speak up about."

Delia's heart jumped into her throat. *Was this real?* Jack was wearing the same grey cotton shirt he'd been wearing the night before. Had he recorded this last night? Was that why he left?

"By now, many of you have seen or heard about a video circulating online showing my girlfriend, Delia Melise. I'm not here to give it more airtime than it's already stolen, but here's the thing—it's fake. Completely and utterly bogus, but the damage it's doing is real. Not just to Delia."

Jack ran a hand through his hair and exhaled. *"I've been thinking a lot about this since I watched the woman I care about shrink because of a bullshit video. She's not the first to have something like this happen to her, and I know she won't be the last. I'm going to censor myself here because I don't want this video to come down, but trust me when I say there is no word strong enough in the English language to describe how pissed off I am that men think they have a right to consume a woman's body. They don't."* Jack's eyes glared directly into the camera. *"You don't."*

He took a moment to compose himself, drawing a deep breath. *"I don't care whether the videos are real, leaked, or in this case*

AI curated, everyone here on this app and others like it?" He made a circle with his hands. *"We're the problem. That shit wouldn't get shared if people here refused to watch it, so I'm asking you to put on your big boy pants and shut it down. Vote with your clicks and attention. I refuse to participate in a system that uses people. My dad always said, 'Use things, love people, and worship God.'"* Jack clasped and unclasped his hands, then growled, *"Delia is not a damn thing."*

He let that hang in the air a moment, then cleared his throat. *"I ask that you join me in reporting this absolute embarrassing filth now and in the future. And if you're in Calgary, I'll see you on the ice tonight."*

Delia pressed pause as the video looped. She reached up, shocked to find her cheeks were wet. That light inside her that had been reduced to smoke and ash seconds before was now blazing. *Delia is not a damn thing.*

She closed the app and flipped over to her contacts and found Jack's number. Texting wasn't fast enough, she needed to talk to him—to hear his voice. She pressed his number and waited for the call to connect. Her shoulders drooped when it went straight to voicemail.

"Damn it," she muttered, then realized he was probably on his way to work. Her stomach gurgled—she hadn't eaten anything since late afternoon the day before. She pulled her hair up into a claw clip and walked into the hall, then made it halfway down the stairs before she heard the voices.

Delia stopped and looked up, then stilled with the toes of her right foot barely touching the next step.

Men. So many men in the living room. Her brain finally started processing faces, though many of them didn't look familiar. She saw Country and her heart kicked into high gear. If he was here, then—

"Good morning." Jack's eyes were shadowed. Wary and hopeful. "I made breakfast, there's—"

Delia bolted down the rest of the stairs and ran to him, not caring that she had purple bags under her eyes or that she hadn't thought to put on deodorant. She threw herself into his arms.

He grunted, then absorbed her into his safe harbour. But she wasn't satisfied with resting her head against his chest. With letting her heart match his rhythm. With saying a whispered "thank you."

That flame that had roared to life inside her bedroom was raging like a damn forest fire, and she had to do something to quell the heat. It was pure, unadulterated instinct. Desire. *Need* that shot Delia's hand up to wrap around Jack's neck and pull his face to hers.

He was strong. He was safe. *He was funny and charming as hell.*

She kissed him, kneading her fingers against his skin, pressing her mouth so fully against Jack's, she could taste him. She pulled his lower lip into her mouth and released, ran her tongue over his, breathed his air, and none of it was enough. What Jack had done—what he'd said—was the hottest thing she'd ever heard in her life.

It was only when she remembered she and Jack weren't alone in the room, not by a long shot, that she reigned herself in. Delia pulled back, panting. "Sorry."

"For what?" Jack murmured.

"That was impulsive."

"Uh-huh." His breath came in quick bursts, and as he searched her face, he looked like he might lift her up and carry her back up the stairs.

She wanted him to. Her inner thighs ached. Her ribs expanded like they might rip her in half. Delia clenched her hands against his skin, then dropped them from his neck and stepped back, letting Jack's hands fall from her waist.

"So . . . I'm assuming you told her?" Tyler leaned on the desk next to what looked like the Matrix's back office.

Delia looked between Tyler and Jack. "Told me what?"

A shy smile crept onto Jack's face, and she wanted to kiss him all over again.

Then reality hissed against the blaze inside her. What was everyone doing there? Why did it look like there was a whale's umbilical cord stretching across the floor? How long had the Snowballs been there, and *why did she still smell bacon?*

Jack shifted on his feet. "Did I ever mention to you that Tyler works in cyber security?"

———

Jack sat across from Delia in the kitchen, barely able to sit still.

"So, let me get this straight." Delia took a bite of her sandwich, her words slightly muffled by a mouthful of egg and cheese. "Tyler turned into a cyber ninja overnight."

"I think he was already a cyber ninja."

"Which was why you brought him in?"

Jack nodded. "I didn't know if he'd have any ideas, but I figured it was worth a shot."

"He did it?"

"If by 'did it' you mean got the original video down, yes. There are still plenty of clips circulating, and we're working on that." He looked behind him through the window into the living area where his teammates were dismantling the equipment. Jack glanced at his phone. *Eight fifteen.* He had just enough time to get home and shower before he needed to start working for the day, but no part of him wanted to leave that kitchen.

Delia shook her head, her eyes glassy as she chewed. "I don't even know what to say."

Jack wanted to explain how much he'd enjoyed the way she'd thanked him earlier, then thought better of it. *That was impulsive.* Delia was grateful. Delia had big feelings. Those things had come through loud and clear. Jack was dying to know if there was anything else behind that kiss, and that slicked any excitement with an oily film.

He wanted this. For the first time in years, he woke up in the morning excited to see someone. Elated to see her name pop up on his phone. As cliché as it sounded, that kiss had made him feel superhuman. Like it didn't matter he was quitting his job because, of course, he'd get a contract next season with the Blizzard.

You're allowed to want to be happy. That thought slid like a skewer into his gut. He could want happiness, but could he have it? They lived in a temporary bubble now, but Delia would go back to Toronto. He'd be there in Calgary.

Nevermind the logistical issues, was it possible for him to open up again? He'd never tried—never wanted to try. Until right then.

"What can I do for you?" Delia wiped a bit of mustard from her lips.

Jack frowned. "What?"

"Do you have data entry you need done? Your washroom cleaned? Dinner tonight? Please, let me do something to thank you for this."

"Delia—"

"I'm serious, Jack. I'm going to go insane if I have to sit here all day in your debt."

He laughed. "You're not in my debt."

"You missed practice last night! Don't even try to deny it, and you're probably going to be late for work—yes, I know you're quitting Big Rick, but you don't strike me as the kind of guy who slacks off in his last two weeks. Plus, I know you want to spend more time with your teammates, and—"

"Okay, okay." Jack held up his hands in defeat. He thought about Clara's texts that morning.

Shorthanded at the hospital

Picked up an extra shift

Not coming home this morning, but I'll be back around four

She was working a double, and Oscar was in Vancouver for another day and a half. Jack exhaled. "Dinner. Clara's working a double shift, and I have a game tonight. Dinner for her would be great."

Delia beamed at him. "Dinner it is."

She wouldn't let him clean up the rest of breakfast, so Jack reluctantly walked back out into the living room and helped carry the last of the equipment out to Tyler's truck. The morning was surprisingly warm without a hint of wind. "Thanks again, bud. You're a miracle worker."

Tyler slammed the back door shut. "Still a lot of work to do. I'll keep reporting the clips, and hopefully it'll start to lose traction."

Jack nodded. "Me, too. With all of us on offence, I'm sure it won't take long."

"Speaking of offence, tonight determines your seed for the playoffs, right?"

Jack nodded. "I think we'll win. Should be up in Edmonton by Monday."

"You feeling connected with those guys?"

Jack shrugged. All of his momentum where that was concerned had been killed by the last forty-eight hours. "Working on it."

Tyler clapped a hand on his shoulder. "You're a hell of a player. Ignore the circus, eh?"

Jack nodded, then turned back to the house. He walked

inside, but the only thing he found in the kitchen was the hum of the dishwasher and drying baking sheets.

He could look for her. He could walk up the stairs like he had last night and slip onto her bed—

Jack stopped at the bottom of the staircase. She was talking to someone. *Mary.* He heard a shriek of laughter, patted the bannister, and walked out the front door to his truck. He turned the key in the ignition, the low rumble of his engine breaking the morning stillness in the neighborhood. Either nobody commuted or they'd all left already. He went on autopilot, enjoying the blue skies and the hint of buds on the tree branches.

He arrived home in twelve minutes flat and parked the truck in the driveway. It seemed like a week, and he took a moment to let the sun warm his face before walking inside. Since he'd been there last, his life had flipped upside down.

On the outside, not much had changed. He'd put in his two weeks notice, but that was the furthest thing from his mind at the moment.

You're allowed to want to be happy.

He wanted the NHL. He was working to accept that he sure as hell wanted Delia.

But who was he to have a happily ever after? He didn't deserve that more than anyone else. He certainly didn't deserve it more than Angie.

Jack's shoulders bunched as he walked to his room and stripped off his clothes, tossing them in his dirty bin in the closet. He checked his phone before plugging it in. It was at ten percent after sitting out all night next to Delia's bed.

Heat pooled in his middle thinking about holding her. Sleeping next to her. Then feeling her desperate, hungry kiss that morning and wishing he could've picked her up and carried her right back up the stairs to that bed.

Jack opened a text from Country.

> You're already at 300k views, bud. Might want
> to read the comments this time

Jack's jaw flexed. *Good.* He wasn't ready to check it, but he made a mental note to open his brand-new socials that afternoon. He tapped on a text from Ben, his product manager at Big Rick.

> Just got the news. Sucks that you're leaving,
> but good on you

> Wanted you to know that coat's ready
> whenever you want to pick it up

Jack plugged in his phone and stalked into the attached washroom and turned on the shower.

Hot.

CHAPTER

Twenty-Four

WITH ALL THE EXCITEMENT, Delia had completely forgotten about her second studio session. Thankfully, Mary had come into her room and reminded her. By the time she'd thrown on a better outfit—and reluctantly, a bra—Jack had already left.

She hadn't texted him on the way to the studio, figuring she'd already taken him away from work and the Blizzard enough for twenty-four hours.

But as her hands trembled getting out of the car, she regretted it. She had to face real people. Cameras.

She ignored the shouted questions from the paparazzi as she pushed through the entrance to the studio behind Mary, then tried to keep a smile on her face as she sat down next to Ethan Hayes. They were supposed to record vocals, and while Delia had run through things over the past week, all of it had evaporated like dew.

Ethan dragged a stool over and gave a small wave. "You ready for this?"

Delia nodded with as much conviction as she could muster, but she could tell by the look on Ethan's face it was lackluster.

He studied her. "It's been a shit day."

Delia blew out a breath. *He knew.* Of course he knew. The whole world knew, and—

"Your boyfriend's a menace," Ethan said, and Delia frowned. He chuckled. "It's a compliment. Means he has balls of steel."

"I can't comment on that, but if you're talking about his post, yeah. He's badass." Delia's chest warmed just thinking about Jack's face on the screen. The words that had come out of his mouth.

She glanced down at her tablet, scrolling through the lyrics they'd written down the last time they'd met. "You know . . . Ethan, do you mind if I change a few things?"

When Ethan gave her the go ahead, Delia started scribbling. She worked at the lyrics until they felt right. She wasn't the same person she'd been when she initially wrote the song, and there was something cathartic about giving that fact space. Speaking from a new heart. One that had both been broken and opened up.

It was probably the fastest recording session she'd ever done. After a few re-records and adjustments with the backing track, she and Mary left the studio at two o'clock. Alvin accompanied them to the grocery store, and the timing was perfect. The only people there were old ladies who had no idea who she was or moms with kids who gave her a second glance, but were too busy trying to keep little hands from throwing Shreddies in the grocery cart to stop her in the aisle. She did take a picture with a couple as they waited for their groceries to be rung up.

They didn't mention the video. She wouldn't have expected them to, but it put her off kilter to stand in front of people who may have seen her fake-naked.

Had her mother gotten her voicemail yet? What was she going to think about all this?

Delia breathed.

She imagined Jack's arms around her.

She envisioned herself a year in the future, not even giving that video a second thought.

They drove home and faced the cameras waiting on the sidewalk, and after Alvin brought in the groceries, Mary followed Delia into the sunlit kitchen. It still smelled like the bacon Jack had cooked that morning, and her heart stuttered.

Delia unpacked, leaving out the ingredients she needed for dinner and putting the rest in the fridge while Mary tackled the pantry items. For a moment, all she heard was the rustle of paper bags, the clink of jars being set on shelves, and the soft thud of produce being placed in drawers in the fridge.

"So. Jack." Mary folded the paper bag in front of her. "His truck was here last night."

Delia's cheeks warmed. "Yeah. We were at media training when I got the call from Tony. He didn't want to leave me alone." Mary raised an eyebrow, but Delia didn't let her respond. "Which begs the question, where were you last night?"

Mary's eyes flitted to the living room. Delia frowned. Alvin was the only one in there sitting on the loveseat near the fireplace and typing something on his phone. "I went out for dinner."

"At seven thirty?" Delia hadn't fallen asleep until at least eight, and she hadn't heard the door open.

"There might've been some dancing."

Delia narrowed her eyes. "Have you been swiping right without telling me?"

Mary snorted. "No. Just out with friends."

"And then Alvin drove you home?"

Mary turned and pulled a glass from the cabinet. Delia got the hint. She didn't want to talk about it, and Delia didn't have the energy to dig, so she put a pin in it.

"Want to help me dice veggies?" she asked.

"I've never wanted anything more." Mary filled her glass with water and took a drink. "Where are the cutting boards at?"

Delia laughed. "How long have we been here, and neither of us knows where the cutting boards are?" She turned and started opening cupboards. Once they'd found all the supplies, they stripped the produce bags off zucchini, eggplant, bell peppers, and yellow squash. Delia washed the veggies and revelled in the cool water running over her fingers. She'd debated what to make for Clara, but eventually settled on a traditional French ratatouille, a recipe she'd always made with her mother. Clara might not need comfort food, but she sure as hell did.

Delia passed the zucchini to Mary and started peeling the eggplant.

"You deflected." Mary dropped the knife.

"Deflected what?"

"My question."

Delia ignored the impulse to snap that she'd done the exact same thing when she'd asked about Alvin. "About Jack? I told you, he—"

"He stayed the night."

Delia couldn't keep the words out of her mouth any longer. "Alvin drove you home."

Mary's eyes flicked up. She either had to give something up about the *friends* she was avoiding or let the whole thing go. Mary cleared her throat. "What did you two do all evening?"

Delia rotated the eggplant and slid the peeler from base to tip. "Had mind-blowing sex." Mary rolled her eyes, and Delia scoffed. "What did you think we were doing? I'd just found out there was a porno of me going viral. It didn't exactly put me in the mood for anything besides pathetic weeping and curling up in the fetal position."

Mary exhaled. "Fair. I'm so sorry, Dels. I can't even imagine. The second I heard, I came back, but your door was already closed."

Delia sighed. "It's fine." *Jack was there.* She dropped the eggplant on the cutting board and started slicing. "I mean, it's not fine, but I didn't expect you to be sitting here at my beck and call. I'm glad you went out and had fun."

Mary scooted past yet another opportunity to give her insider information. "It's incredible Tyler got it taken down."

"I know. I'm so grateful, it physically hurts. I feel guilty for every time I made fun of the computer nerds in high school."

Mary laughed. "You think Tyler was a computer nerd?"

Delia had to smile at that. If they searched the antonym for "nerd," Tyler's beautiful face would probably be the Google generated response. Delia put the eggplant slices in a strainer, then sprinkled salt over the pale coins and set the strainer in the sink.

"You have a game to go to tonight?" Mary asked.

"Yep. Didn't have a chance to talk about it with Jack in all the hubbub, but he told me last week I have a spot in their suite if I want it."

"It's not one of your contracted public appearances?"

Delia licked her lips. "No."

"What about the media training?"

Delia reached out for the peppers. She shook her head.

Mary raised an eyebrow. Her knife went still. "So. Jack."

Blood rushed in her head, making her dizzy. "Mmhmm." Mary pursed her lips, fighting a smile. Delia's brows pinched. "What?"

Mary shook her head, focusing hard on the zucchini in front of her. "Nothing."

———

Two hours later, Delia stood on Clara's porch dressed in khaki trousers and a white tank top layered under a patchwork sweater with baggy sleeves that hung mid-hip. *It was Jack's house, too.* Something fizzed inside her at the thought of walking into his living space. She wondered if she could find an excuse to peek into his bedroom, then realized she was being creepy and banished the thought from her head. As best she could.

Clara opened the door, still in her scrubs. Her eyes widened, then she looked down and saw the casserole dish in Delia's hands. "What's this?" Clara pushed the storm door open.

"Jack didn't tell you?"

Clara shook her head and moved to the side so Delia could step inside.

Delia handed her the dish. "This is for you. Dinner."

Clara's jaw hung slack. "Seriously?" She took the dish and looked up. "You brought me dinner?"

"Technically, Jack brought you dinner. I owed him one and he asked me to drop it by."

Clara motioned for her to come inside, and Delia slipped off her shoes. "Are you going to his game tonight?"

"Yep. I'll head over early. Get in the box before it gets crazy."

Clara set the dish on the counter. "Good. I'm glad he got you a private spot."

"Are you coming?"

Clara shook her head. "No, I'm exhausted. I'll probably be in bed by the time it starts."

Delia noted the shadows under her eyes. She slipped her hands in her back pockets and looked around the kitchen. It was clean and modern. "I love your place."

"Me too." She paused and pursed her lips. "Maybe a little too small, though."

"Well, you do have Jack taking up a room."

Clara conceded that point, then lifted the foil and lowered her head, taking a long whiff. "This smells amazing."

"You can dig in, I already ate with Mary at home. I made an extra pan for the two of us."

Clara didn't take much convincing. She turned and pulled a low bowl from the shelf, then plucked a spatula from a ceramic holder and a fork from the drawer in front of her.

Delia didn't mean to notice, but when she lifted her arms, her stomach showed. Clara was thin, but her belly pushed well past the waistband of her scrubs. She blinked, then forced her eyes anywhere but on Clara's midsection as she approached.

Clara scooped a serving of the steaming ratatouille into her dish and blew on it. "This is so kind. I haven't slept in thirty-six hours."

Delia scoffed. "That's insane." *Especially if she was in the condition she now suspected.*

"That's nursing. And I guess it's not totally true. I did take a couple of power naps." Clara took a bite and closed her eyes, humming in her throat. "So good. Thank you."

"You're welcome."

Clara set down the bowl. "Do you want water or tea or something? I'm so sorry, I'm being a terrible host."

Delia shook her head, then jumped when her phone buzzed in her purse. She pulled it out and saw Tony's name on the display. "Do you mind?" Clara waved her on, and Delia turned to answer the call. "Please don't tell me you have more bad news."

Tony barked a laugh. "Nope. Amazing news. Where are you?"

"Just visiting a friend before the game. Mary and Alvin are in the car."

"Perfect. You need to go to the Saddledome now."

Delia frowned. "Why? We still have forty-five minutes—"

"Not anymore. The children's choir that was scheduled to sing the national anthem had a breakout of strep. Kels just texted and said you're in."

Delia blinked. "What?"

"They want you to sing the national anthem for the game tonight. Both of them, actually. You know the Star Spangled Banner, right?"

Her hands started to buzz. "Yeah, I haven't sung it in a while, but I'm sure—"

"Great. Good luck, kid."

Good luck. Delia groaned. "We don't say 'good luck' Tony!" she hissed at the phone before putting it back in her purse. She turned to find Clara looking at her. "Sorry. I didn't mean to say that out loud."

Clara swallowed the bite in her mouth. "I didn't mean to eavesdrop."

"You heard?"

"He talks pretty loud."

Delia snorted. "Yeah. He does."

"You're singing?"

Delia nodded. "Looks like it. I'm so sorry to drop food and run." Her heart fluttered in her throat, but surprisingly, her thoughts were still. If she could get through the past day and a half, she could get through two national anthems.

Clara set her bowl down and followed her to the door. "Do you need anything? Lemon water? Lip gloss?"

Delia exhaled. "Unless you can download the lyrics of The Star Spangled Banner into my head, I think I'm good."

Clara winced as Delia bent to slip on her shoes. "Yeah, can't help with that one." When Delia stood, Clara stepped forward and pulled her into a hug. "You'll be amazing." She pushed back and held onto her shoulders, stifling a yawn. "I'm really glad you're fake dating my brother."

"I'm really glad you're my fake sister-in . . . not-in-law. Now get some sleep." She wanted to force that woman into bed. After she had another two helpings of dinner.

Clara grinned and pulled her into another hug. "Break a leg."

———

Delia adjusted the mic in her hand and looked up at the empty stands. The doors were set to open within the next fifteen minutes, which meant she didn't have long to rehearse. Mary had drilled her on the anthems on the way over. She didn't have time to make it fancy, and she would've preferred to bring her guitar.

As she waited for the accompaniment, it occurred to her that she was living her literal nightmare. Standing in a stadium naked. Not actually naked, but with thousands of people *imagining* her naked.

That video wasn't you. Her mom had said that at least three times when they'd finally connected in the car on the way over. Delia told her about what Jack had posted, how she'd kissed him, and how she was singing at the game.

Why she'd worried what her mother would think, she had no idea. Her mom had barely paid attention to the news about the deep fake and had skipped right to the kiss. After skirting the line between embarrassing herself with Alvin in the front seat and satiating her mother's curiosity, Delia had ended the call.

The relief was as palpable as setting down a twenty kilogram backpack. She'd wanted to curl up in the back seat and weep. Instead, she'd clenched and released the muscles in her hands and feet, somehow managing to keep her tears from smearing mascara down her cheeks.

That video wasn't you. Delia squeezed her eyes closed and lifted the mic to her lips as the music burst through the speakers. Singing felt like lifting the lid off a pot of boiling water. All her stress and tension faded behind the resonance of her voice in that vast open space.

When she was a kid, she'd made noise purely because she loved the physical sensation. The warmth in her throat. The gentle buzz in her jaw. It was comforting and fascinating. That she could expel air from her lungs and make different sounds? It was pure magic.

In her mid-twenties, it still hadn't lost its lustre even though she was constantly trying to complicate it. Delia relaxed and absorbed the waves of sound bouncing off the boards and plastic seats, hitting her from all angles. *Listen to yourself, not the echoes.*

She'd learned that early when singing in baseball and football stadiums. On stage she had an earpiece, but not here, and she didn't want to get lost in the overlapping sound.

She finished with a lilting *land of the free and the home of the brave*, then moved on to the Canadian anthem. She almost blanked in the middle, but caught the words and added a stylistic pause to catch her breath. When she finished, she turned back to the marketing manager, Lisa, and the sound guy who'd handed her the mic.

"Perfect." Lisa clapped her hands. "Thank you so much for filling in at the last minute."

Delia walked back over the mat they'd laid out on the ice for her and returned the mic. "You're welcome. Thanks for the invitation."

Lisa winked. "So glad to have you. We put your pop-up appearance in all our socials, and we've already seen a last-minute ticket surge."

Hopefully they knew she'd be fully clothed. "Glad to hear it." Delia settled nicely into her performance persona. The one who didn't twitch her fingers or ask inappropriate questions. She'd played the part for so long, she hadn't realized how much her act compressed like restraints until she had something to compare it to. The last day with Jack was like crisp oxygen in her lungs. Even when she'd been breaking. Even when she'd wanted to crumple. She'd been herself, one hundred percent. The good and the ugly.

And he'd stayed when she asked.

Delia clenched and unclenched her hands as Lisa motioned to an area just off the main player tunnel. "You're welcome to wait here if you want to be in the middle of things, or we've got a room—"

"I'll wait here." Delia smiled. "Could be fun to watch the stadium fill up." *Not the whole truth.* She wanted to see Jack the second he came out of the dressing room. The idea of him walking out in his hockey gear made her internal organs flip places.

Lisa nodded and held up her phone. "If you change your mind."

Mary and Alvin joined her once she was alone and they waited together. Music played over the loudspeaker as fans poured in through the entrances and found their seats. The energy in the air built like static, growing in intensity like a swipe of socks over carpet every ten minutes. When her ribs felt like they were cinched into a corset, Delia finally heard them. Stomps down the tunnel. Deep voices.

"Don't get worked up if people sing during the Star Spangled Banner."

Delia did a double take. *Was Alvin talking to her?* "Okay."

He drew a deep breath. "They always shout out 'sea' and 'glare.' It's tradition. Because you can't see in a Blizzard."

"Right. Thanks." She turned to Mary to share a look, but the stomps grew louder, breaking the dam on the thoughts she didn't know were waiting patiently in her subconscious. *What if she choked? Should she have posted on her socials? Should she have—* Delia gasped and grabbed Mary's arm. "Jack doesn't know I'm here."

"He didn't know you were coming?"

"No, he knew I was coming to the game, but he doesn't know I'm on the floor. Singing the anthems."

Mary shrugged. "So? It'll be a good surprise."

"But what if I can't—" She grappled for the confidence she'd felt at Clara's. *Why was she suddenly freaking out?* It wasn't the music. It wasn't the thousands of people in the Saddledome. It was only one.

Mary's eyes lifted past her. "I don't think you need to worry about that." She grabbed Delia's shoulders and turned her. There, stopped in front of her while all the other white jerseys continued on to the ice, was Jack. He held his stick in one hand

and his helmet in the other. With his pads on, he looked like Thor.

"Hey." Delia stepped forward with a little help from Mary.

Jack looked between the three of them. "What are you doing here? Is something wrong? I wasn't checking my phone—"

"No, nothing's wrong. They had a cancellation for the anthems." She twisted her hair around her finger.

Jack blinked. "You're singing?"

She nodded. "I'm going to double-oh-do it." Delia winced. "Sorry. That was . . . I shouldn't be allowed to talk to people when I'm nervous." *Or just you. You make me nervous.*

Jack stepped toward her, towering above her head with the added height of his skates. "I was thinking we were overdue for a Bond night."

Delia grinned. "We could watch something tonight, or . . . " She stopped as Jack's smile slipped. "Or in a long time. A scheduled time." She smoothed her hair from her face, her lungs screaming for a normal breath.

"No, I'd love to, it's just that the team is going out after the game. Then tomorrow we have a thing. Before playoffs."

He was saying no. She wanted him to say no. She wanted him to do what he needed to. "Right. Of course."

Jack shifted on his skates. "Maybe in Edmonton?"

Delia's brows knit. "When are you going to Edmonton?"

"Monday. For the first round of playoffs."

Her eyes narrowed. "You know your placement already?" She was slowly absorbing pieces of his hockey talk, filling in those letters of the puzzle.

He gave a smug smile. "We will in about two hours."

She raised an eyebrow. "Ah. Arrogance. It looks good on you."

He leaned in, the cage of his helmet hovering over them like an umbrella. "C'mon. You know the Sharks don't stand a chance."

Delia's breath quickened. *She knew someone that didn't stand a chance.* She wet her lips. "Sharks sound deadly."

"And 'Blizzard' doesn't?"

She looked up into his eyes. They were quickly becoming her favourite colour. Like smooth melted chocolate. "Edmonton isn't in our contract."

"Neither is sleeping over. Seems like we've already been breaking the rules."

Delia's insides liquified. They were instant soup plunged into boiling water. She swallowed hard and tugged on the fingers of her gloves. "I'll-I think I can watch Bond with you in Edmonton."

He grinned, his lashes brushing his cheeks when he blinked. "Okay, then. Monday."

Delia nodded, then watched as he retreated through the now empty tunnel. She turned and walked back to Mary on Bambi legs. "So. Jack."

Mary smirked, and as they cheated closer to the boards to watch the players warm up, Delia could've sworn she saw Alvin brush a hand over Mary's backside.

JACK PULLED up to Monahan's house fifteen minutes late. He had no excuse. It was Sunday, and he had nothing to do all morning, but it'd taken him an hour to drag himself out of bed and into the shower.

The past three days had been a whirlwind. After his goal and assist on Thursday night against the Sharks, the press 'opportunities' were relentless. It had only been doable to meet Lisa's expectations in that regard because of the team at Big Rick. After the game, they'd insisted Jack take his remaining PTO as part of his two weeks notice. He'd gotten a little choked up when Ben's text came through.

This is bigger than Big Rick.

Remember I didn't chap your ass about your lost receipts for that Vancouver trip when you're a regular on the roster

He was done. Paid for the time off. And jobless after the playoffs if he didn't get an addendum to his contract. Adrenaline poured into his veins every time he remembered that fact.

Since Delia was slammed finishing her recording with that TikToker so she could come to Edmonton, Jack had leaned in to everything Blizzard. He'd done the media appearances, eaten at the rink and hit the gym with the team. He was finally starting to feel like he belonged, and it couldn't have come at a better time.

Still, he couldn't stop thinking about her. About her voice before the game. About the way she'd run down the stairs and kissed him. Ever since that night in her bedroom, the energy between them had shifted. He knew they had a contract, but it didn't seem relevant in the least. He wanted to see her. Based on the fact that she'd accepted his non-contractually obligated invitation to Edmonton, he thought maybe she felt the same.

Jack stepped out onto the sidewalk. The sun peeked over the Rockies, painting the sky in shades of pink and orange behind the brick facade of Monahan's house. He couldn't help but compare his own guest bedroom situation as he walked up the wide concrete steps.

His heart beat with anticipation. Not for the movie night, but for Monday night. After the game. When Delia would be waiting for him, and—

"Hey," a voice called out behind him. Jack turned to see Liam loping up the walkway. He was a mess. His shirt askew, boxers hanging out of the top of his jeans, his hair wild beneath a beat up Maple Leafs cap and the same dark circles under his eyes.

The coaches were pushing Liam hard, trying to "draw out his potential," but so far his performance was on a decline. Monahan reamed him out between second and third, and he hadn't gotten a single shift the rest of the night.

Nobody talked about it. Mostly because Liam had changed and pitter-pattered before Jack had even dried off from his shower.

"Hey." Jack grabbed his hand and clapped him on the shoulder. "Didn't think I'd see you here."

Liam stepped back and looked at his feet. "Yeah."

"Wait, did they tell you it was porn?"

Liam chuckled, but the joke tasted bitter on Jack's tongue, considering. Just that morning he'd found and reported ten more clips of Delia that had popped up overnight. *I can't make sex tape jokes anymore.* Jack almost grinned. He turned toward the door, then thought twice.

He turned back to find Liam was staring at his hands, tapping his foot on the concrete. "Are we going to talk about it?" Jack asked.

Liam's right hand shook as he slid it into his pocket. "Talk about what?"

"You know what."

Liam's eyes flashed. "I don't have anything to—"

"Don't give me that, MacDonald. I'd love to tell you this is the last time I'm going to ask you what the hell you're taking before and after games, but that's not the truth. You're shitting all over this opportunity, and I doubt it's on purpose. I'm trying to help you."

Liam clenched his jaw. He seemed like he was about to boil over. Then his face twisted as he drew a sharp breath.

Jack took a step closer. "Pills?" Liam nodded. "Fent?"

"No. I get the real stuff. I was too scared to fail testing."

Jack exhaled. If he was getting it from a pharmacy, he was definitely stealing from someone. Probably someone close to him. He wished he'd paid more attention to Liam's situation. "Well at least you're not a dummy." Jack ran a hand through his hair. "Have you told the coaches?"

Liam swore under his breath. "No, and if you—"

"I'm not going to nark, but the NHL has resources."

Liam shook his head. "I don't want them to know. It'll brand me."

Jack didn't argue with him. Not because he thought it was

true, but because he didn't think he could convince him it wasn't. "I've got a friend you can reach out to. He's in recovery. Good guy, plays Elite League."

Liam nodded, blinking like he had a piece of dust in his eye.

"If you're ready, he'll help you get healthy."

Liam looked up with red-rimmed eyes. His throat worked, but he didn't say anything. They stood there on the step, the Sunday afternoon sunshine warming their faces. Jack thought about Kreviasuk getting in Liam's face. Coach Novak pointedly leaving his name out of the praise he'd given after the game. Monahan laying into him. His lack of shifts.

His stomach twisted. Liam using prescription meds was shooting himself in the foot, but nobody latched themselves to a sinking ship when they thought they could swim. "I'm going to talk to the coaches."

"Shit, Jack—"

"Not about the pills. About their coaching strategy. The way they're handling this isn't helping. You need more opportunities, not less. I'm telling you now so you can get your head out of your rear and take this seriously."

Liam sucked in a breath. "You'll send me your friend's number."

"Right. You better be in contact with him in an hour or less."

He nodded. "I will."

Jack pulled out his phone and searched up Brett's number. "Nobody can make this happen for you, but you better believe I'll be crawling up your ass if Brett tells me you're ghosting him."

Liam breathed a laugh. "Got it."

Jack sent the text with Brett's number, but before he could say anything else, the front door flew open behind him. "Hey! Look who the cat dragged in!" Monahan greeted Jack and Liam, then ushered them into an airy foyer with gleaming wood floors and walls the colour of Caribbean sand.

They walked through a spacious living area to a kitchen three times the size of Clara's with an island filled with platters of gourmet sandwiches and charcuterie. And a sushi station. Jack was suddenly twelve years old tagging along with his parents to a cocktail party.

Nils pushed his blond hair out of his eyes as he reached for a cornichon. "Mr. Popular has arrived. Now the party starts, eh?"

Jack shrugged. "I can't help it if everyone wants a piece of me." Two weeks ago that comment would've cut, but he'd been on the scoresheet Thursday and spent the last two days with these guys. They'd already gotten the digs about him and Delia out of their system. Nobody had heard anything about Beefus. The rumours about free agents had gone underground. Jack didn't know if that was because the team valued him or if the other shoe was about to drop.

They knew he was a publicity hire. Had his goal not gone viral, he wouldn't have even been on Alex's radar. Jack never pretended to be anything he wasn't, and that was enough for the boys to let him in. Nathan never pretended his knees didn't hurt. Gaudreau didn't pretend he wasn't an asshole. Nils never pretended to enjoy brie more than larb.

Jack glanced at Liam grabbing a beer from the fridge. Now they had one more player that was willing to show his face. He hoped to hell he hadn't taken anything that morning, but knew the odds weren't in his favour. He needed to text Brett ASAP.

"I saw a stat this morning I thought you might like." Tkachuk put two pieces of sushi in his mouth and chewed.

Jack reached for a plate. "If this goes back to you being pissed Iginla didn't make the top one hundred—"

"No. Better." He swallowed, the lump visible as it travelled down his throat. "Thursday you took seven more shots, made an assist, and spent five more minutes of penalty time than usual."

"And?" Jack selected a roast beef sandwich and a handful of All Dressed chips.

"Better stats than your other appearances. More hotheaded. Some people say it's because Delia was in the stands."

"Well, no shit." Jack grinned, and Tkachuk laughed, showing off his missing incisor. He added more food to his plate. Had her appearance at the game really impacted his play that much? A little disconcerting. His pulse sped as he took a bite of a sandwich.

Tomorrow. The word slammed on repeat in his head. He would see Delia after the game, and then . . . what? He reminded himself of all the clues that led to him believing she was on the same page as him. She reached out when she didn't have to. She kissed him when no cameras were looking. She'd said yes to Edmonton. This had to be more than the contract for her now, too.

Shame and confusion washed over him as he made his way down the buffet line. What would Angie think of this? Him standing with his teammates parsing out signals from a girl he'd agreed to have a fake relationship with. He'd signed a contract. Touched her, kissed her in public to advance his career. To solidify a spot on an NHL team that may not even be interested in him come June. And now he'd gone and wanted more.

"Grab a second plate if you need to! Show starts in five," Monahan called out from the stairs.

Jack reached for a beer sitting in a tub of ice at the end of the counter. "Is anyone going to fess up and name the movie we're watching?" he asked Nathan and Chris Lindholm, who were both leaning against the double fridge.

Chris grinned. "They didn't fill you in?" Jack shook his head. "We're making our way through the best worst movies of all time."

Jack shook his head. "Of course you are. If this is Return to Blue Lagoon, I'm out."

"Tonight's Wagon's East." Nathan pushed off the fridge and reached for another plate. The crowd in the kitchen started to thin as the guys followed Monahan down the stairs at the other end of the room.

"I haven't seen it." Jack knew what it was. A western that was undeniably terrible, but Canadians were forced to love it because it was John Candy's last appearance on film.

"Don't expect a quiet viewing experience." Chris laughed.

Jack took his food and drink and followed the others down to the basement. There was a pool table, air hockey, foosball, and an indoor lap pool behind a wall of glass windows. At the end of the massive room, they walked through a doorway into a home theater with tiered seating.

Not bad. He couldn't help himself imagining a world where he had a house like that, and the thought made his stomach churn. He was starting to want too much. To hope for too much.

Jack chose a leather recliner next to Nils. He pulled out his phone and sent off a quick email with a meeting request to Coach Novak and Kreviasuk. *Keep your skates laced and your mouth zipped.* That had been his strategy. It turned out, he was only good at one of those things.

"Just a warning, I'm not Canadian, so my commentary might be brutal." Nils crunched on a handful of chips next to him.

Brutal was just what he was in the mood for.

———

JACK

Hey. Just checked in

DELIA

Is the hotel nice?

> It's a Marriott. I had chocolate strawberries waiting for me on the dresser

> Well aren't you fancy. Did you pour champagne and eat them in the tub?

> All alone

> I bet Monahan would've joined you

> No, I have a no sex contract with him, too

Delia stared at the last text message she'd received from Jack the night before, her heart pumping faster than it should at eight o'clock in the morning. He'd sent it after the team's flight up to Edmonton, and she had yet to respond.

Sex. That was the only word in his sentence her brain had cared about for the past ten hours. *Sex, sex, sex.*

She'd pretended she was asleep so she couldn't respond with something she'd regret. The morning brought back her filter, but hadn't done anything to dull her fixation.

> So sorry, I was exhausted last night. Mary and I are almost on our way. Don't break legs today!

There. Informational. Practical. Not obviously linked to the fact that all night she'd been thinking of sex or no sex with Jack in a soaking tub with champagne and strawberries. She groaned and tossed her phone on the bed, then threw another pair of pants into her suitcase. It would've been helpful to know exactly how long they were going to be in Edmonton, but she and Mary hadn't gotten that far. Did she want to stay for both of the games or just one? Could she afford to stay most of the week?

She'd gotten the rest of her recording done with Ethan, but who knew what would come up during mastering. She wanted this song to release on schedule. With all the press and her streaming numbers shooting through the roof, a new release plus a collab would hopefully cast her net even wider. Especially since Ethan was fishing in a completely different pond.

She needed to start posting more consistently. Posting with Jack had more than doubled her following, but she didn't want people to watch purely because of her relationship. She wanted them there because they loved her music. But . . . that would require her doing what she'd done in the first place. Share pieces of songs in progress. Her own music. Her own lyrics. All of which, IndieLake wasn't a fan of.

Becoming "IndieLake Delia" online after she'd built an authentic account was proving difficult. It felt forced to plug the songs from her new album since she hadn't written any of them. Getting in front of her phone with her guitar had never given her anxiety before she signed, but now, she'd do dishes or scrub toilets to avoid it. It was strange that she didn't feel the same level of dread for a live show. None of it made sense. How could being in person feel less intimate than posting a stupid video?

"Hey, you ready?" Mary leaned into her room, suitcase handle in hand.

Delia chewed on her lower lip. "Almost. Do you think we'll do anything fancy? Should I bring a dress?"

"There will be after-parties, right?"

"I know, I'm just not sure about the dress code." Delia stared at the pile of clothes still splayed out on her comforter.

"I don't think it matters."

Pressure built in Delia's chest. She knew it didn't matter. Logically. But her mind couldn't let go of the idea that she'd end up going out with Jack in a socially unacceptable outfit. *Why did it matter so much?* There had already been pictures of her sporting no makeup and joggers splashed across every media outlet in the country.

But something had changed since that video was posted. She needed to prove that she was fine. *Better than fine.* She wanted the whole country to know that she wasn't mildly obsessed with hunting down every last clip and reporting it. That she was living her normal life with her hot, hockey player boyfriend, and *things had never been better.*

"I can't decide, Mare!" Delia stomped into the washroom and brushed her teeth, then dried the bristles on her brush and tossed it and her toothpaste into the top of her toiletry bag. When she stalked back out, her suitcase was closed.

"I finished it for you."

"What did you—"

"You'll like it, c'mon." Mary wheeled both their bags out the door. Delia grabbed her coat and purse and ran after her, making sure her friend didn't have to carry both suitcases down the stairs.

Mary was first out the door, and she nearly tripped over a box that sat smack dab in the middle of the door mat. "What the hell? Did you order something?"

Delia shook her head. She rolled her bag next to the shoe rack and grabbed the box, searching for sender information. Nothing. No address, no stamps. Just her name. *For Delia.* "It looks like it was just left here."

"Don't open it." Mary dragged her bag to the car waiting at the curb. It didn't look like there were cameras that morning, thank the heavens. Mary returned with Alvin a moment later.

He pulled out a box cutter on his key ring. "Step back."

Delia moved back into the house. Alvin waited until Mary was next to her, then took the box down to the sidewalk. He sliced the tape and opened it, then frowned as he reached in and pulled out—

"Oh my—" Delia ran forward as Alvin held up a gorgeous, oyster coloured snowboarding coat with gun-metal zipper pulls.

Before she could put her hands on it, she spotted a piece of folded paper on the cement by Alvin's feet and picked it up.

Thought you could use a new memory with Big Rick. Hope it's not too big.

— Jack

DELIA

> Jack. How in the hell? This coat is incredible

> It fits perfectly btw

> Thank you

Delia stared at her phone as the car pulled up to the Marriott ICE District at noon. No response. She hadn't expected Jack to text back, he was probably with his team and unable to even see her messages. It didn't relieve the excitement.

That same feeling overtook her, when she'd bolted down the stairs and kissed him in front of his teammates. Like a tea kettle at a full boil about to whistle. *How did he keep doing that?* Surprising her so thoroughly that she felt like an overfilled balloon.

"You coming?" Mary was already halfway out the door.

Delia nodded. She donned a toque and sunglasses, zipped up her Big Rick coat, and walked in with Mary and Alvin while their driver grabbed their bags and delivered them to the bell-hops. Tony had arranged things with the hotel, so all they had to do was show up at the check-in desk and show Mary's ID. With keys in hand, they walked back to the car and got in.

"What time are we meeting everyone?" Mary asked.

Delia pulled out her phone. "Clara said they were all checking in around the same time as us. We can just head over and find something to do until they're ready?"

Mary nodded and gave their driver the go ahead once Alvin was in the front seat. They had all afternoon to kill before heading to Roger's Place for the game, and West Edmonton Mall was the place to be. All the Snowballs players were staying there since it was cheaper and more fun for Curtis's kids and Ryan's daughter, Amaya. Delia was honoured that she and Mary had been included in the invitation to hang out with the rest of the team.

"It's incredible, right? That Jack's old team would drive all the way up here–bring their families–when they have their own playoff game on Thursday?" Delia watched out the windows, looking for anything familiar. She'd played multiple shows there, but didn't remember much since she'd stayed next to the venues.

"Honestly, I never thought hockey players cared about anything more than scoring and beer."

Delia snorted. "I see what you did there."

"Seriously, though. It's been an education." Mary swept her perfectly straight hair behind her ear. "I think Jack's great, Dels."

Delia stared harder through the glass. "Mmhmm."

"Mmhmm? That's all you have to say?"

"Yep." Her head started to spin. It was true. There wasn't a cohesive thought in her head that she could string into some-thing intelligible. She ran her fingers over the smooth fabric of the coat Jack gave her. Her thoughts about Jack were more images than words.

He was a bobbing throat and a lazy blink. A hand half

shoved in a pocket. A beautifully uneven nose. A smile with all teeth. Dark chocolate fondue eyes.

Not to mention the feelings that tagged along. Warmth that sank into her skin like she was sitting below the rink heaters. Laughter that bubbled through her chest. A comfort blanket. *Home.*

Guilt coated that last word with a slick sheen, and Delia pulled out her phone and clicked on the text chain with her mom. She needed to get her out for a visit ASAP.

Delia

> Morning! I know you're probably at work, but I want you to know I love you! I'm in Edmonton for the next two days. I'll phone in a bit? 🩶

"Are you going to tell me about the coat?" Mary asked.

Delia set the phone in her lap. "I did. Jack worked for Big Rick, and—"

"I saw your face, Delia. I know there's more to it than that." Mary huffed a breath. "You're not talking to me like you normally do."

Delia shifted in her seat. "We haven't exactly had a lot of alone time."

"But even when we do, you're just . . . I don't know. You hate superficial conversations, and now it feels like that's all we have."

Delia's cheeks warmed. "It hasn't only been one-sided." She sent a meaningful look to Alvin in the front passenger seat, and Mary's eyes widened. Her mouth opened and closed like a fish, then she turned to face the opposite window.

Delia winced. She searched for something to say to lessen the impact of her last sentence when her phone buzzed in her purse. She pulled it out while she searched for the right apology.

JACK

> Wow. Didn't think a coat would warrant an I love you

Delia blinked. She re-read Jack's text, then scrolled up and groaned. The last message she'd sent. It had been meant for her mom but ended up going to Jack instead. Just screwing up with everyone it seemed.

DELIA

> I've said it for a lot less

She regretted it the instant she sent it. It wasn't true. She'd never said "I love you" to someone. And Jack had.

He'd never stopped loving the person he'd said it to.

Delia's mouth dried out like it had been swabbed by strips of gauze as she typed.

DELIA

> Kidding! That text was meant for my mom. Sorry, I'm not detail oriented in the least

> Now I want to intercept more texts. Preferably juicier

> That would require me to have relationships outside of you, Mary, and my mom

Mary. Delia exhaled. "Mary, I didn't mean—"

"It's fine." Mary cut her off. What was happening between them lately? Mary had been distant, but had she spent two seconds thinking about it? She hadn't made time for two seconds of thinking about it.

Delia looked back at her phone.

JACK

> Top three. I'll take it

Her blood hummed under her skin. That was flirting, right? It was hard to read tone over text, but that *had* to be flirting.

> I'm excited to watch the game tonight!

At least she could say something right to someone.

> I think I might throw up. So same

Delia snorted, then remembered she was still in a car with three other humans. And one of them was annoyed with her.

> Chug a litre of water. Always used to work for me before a big show

> Thanks. I'd brush my teeth between periods but I don't have anyone stocking extra toothbrushes in the dressing room

> I'll let Mary know you're in need of her services

Jack sent a laugh emoji but didn't write back.

She and Mary sat in silence the rest of the way to the mall. When the car pulled to a stop, Delia pushed her door open and drew a deep breath of the crisp spring air, then pulled her new coat tighter around her.

"It doesn't look like much," Mary said as they walked through the doors to entrance twenty-four. She wasn't wrong. The outer walls looked like any regular mall they had back home in Toronto.

"How high do these numbers go up?" Delia's voice echoed as they pushed through the airlock with Alvin a few steps behind. Sears was on their right, so they turned left and started down the hall. It was the middle of the week and at that time of day, there weren't many people wandering through the shops. Delia still pulled her toque a little lower over her head to hide her waves.

"Do you know where we're supposed to meet them?" Mary asked.

"Probably by the hotel, I would think." Delia pulled out her phone to see if anyone had texted.

. . .

Eᴍᴍᴀ

Almost ready. Meet at the pirate ship?

"Let's find a map." Delia scanned until she found one, grateful they were on a mission so they didn't have to deal with whatever had happened in the car. Mary's words ran through her head. *Now it feels like that's all we have.*

The words stung because they were true. When was the last time Delia had opened up to Mary? Talked about something real? When was the last time she talked to anyone about something real? Moments ticked one by one in her head, and they all had one person in common. Jack.

Delia swallowed the lump in her throat as she scanned the map, trying to orient herself. "I think . . . maybe I have feelings for Jack. And I know that's stupid because he's only with me because he's being paid, which, ugh. That sounds so pathetic saying it out loud and ridiculous that I'm even entertaining the idea that there could be something more, but Mares. He makes me feel things, and I think about him all the time, and he's been there for me even when he didn't have to be, and I'm nervous and confused, and I think excited because I haven't met someone like this in so stupid long, and—"

Mary pulled her into a hug, and Delia's eyes filled with tears. "Thank you for finally admitting it. I can see it all over your face every time you talk about him or look at him."

"I didn't want to say it because what if—" Delia sucked in a breath. *What if it was all in her head?* What if Jack was just bucking athlete stereotypes left and right and happened to be the most thoughtful, sensitive guy who—

Delia pulled back in a panic. "*Damn it, Mary!* What if he's gay?" That would be exactly her luck. Find the guy of her dreams through Tony, of all people, and he wasn't even remotely attracted to her.

Mary laughed out loud. "Oh. He's not gay." She shook her head resolutely.

"But that would make sense, wouldn't it? Why he was willing to do this in the first place?"

"He didn't want to *do this* in the first place. You had to bully him into it."

Delia scoffed. "I didn't bully him!"

"And wasn't he engaged?"

Delia's heart rate immediately dropped. Right. Jack had been engaged. *To a woman who died.*

She exhaled, and her shoulders slumped. So why hadn't he tried anything? He'd obviously pushed past his initial physical hesitancy. They'd had plenty of opportunities, but it was always *her* pushing past the boundaries of their contract.

What if there was something else? What if it was her? Or . . . what if it wasn't her, but he wasn't ready to move on with anyone? She couldn't decide which option was worse.

He'd told her as much, hadn't he? In the café over breakfast? *I have things,* he'd said and she'd been more than happy to accept that. She was broken. He was broken. Perfect. *But now?* The idea of his things making it so he didn't want to touch her—didn't want to be with her—made her stomach ache.

Mary pointed at the map. "There's the hotel."

They continued on down the hall and made their way past the ice rink. Delia gaped at the tall ceilings and massive sunroof. "I'm sorry I haven't been opening up."

Mary exhaled. "You were right. I haven't exactly been forthcoming either."

Delia glanced behind them, making sure Alvin was out of earshot. "Is there something going on between you two?"

Mary pursed her lips, linking her arm with Delia. "There can't be because that would be problematic with his job."

"To protect us?"

"Technically, he's just hired to protect *you*."

Delia turned to look in a tattoo parlor. She'd never seen one of those in a mall before. "Well, if he's interested in you, wouldn't that increase the chances that he'd do everything possible to protect your best friend?"

Mary gave her a sidelong glance. "Theoretically."

Delia laughed. They walked past the aquarium and finally spotted the Snowballs group in front of the pirate ship. Clara ran forward and gave them both hugs, then introduced them to the people they hadn't officially met, even though Jack had given her the rundown in the stands.

Their first stop was Bourbon Street. They perused the long line of restaurants and settled on an Italian place for lunch, then the rest of the afternoon was taken up with mini golf, laser tag, skating—which Delia was more than happy to watch from the sidelines—and a lengthy discussion with Amaya about how they didn't have time to go to the water park before the game, but they'd absolutely go in the morning before they drove back to Calgary. It was a team effort, and Penny was finally able to convince her that Galaxyland, the indoor amusement park, was more fun in the afternoon anyway.

By the time they parted ways to get back to their hotel in time to change for the game, Delia felt like she'd known the whole group for far longer than four hours. Better yet, she felt closer to Mary than she had in weeks. Which was a good thing since she started to spiral the second they walked into their hotel room.

"Where's my bag?" Delia moved Mary's to make sure she wasn't crazy. She checked the closet, the washroom, the opposite side of the second queen bed. Nothing.

"I can run down to the front desk?"

Delia shook her head. "We can tell them it's missing on the way out, but we don't have time for them to search for it. We need to be at the rink in fifteen minutes."

Mary nodded and flopped her bag on its side, then unzipped

the suitcase and opened it like a clamshell. She pulled out her toiletry bag. "You can use anything in there."

Delia took her up on it. She reapplied blush and powder on her forehead, then used a flosser, and lastly slathered Aquaphor on her lips. She'd had an outfit picked out for the game, but it wasn't like what she was wearing was terrible. A little more casual, maybe, but at least her sweater was blue.

"Ready?" Mary stood at the door. Delia set her makeup back in the case and grabbed her coat and toque. Her hair was already flat from wearing it at the mall, so she wasn't going without it.

Alvin found them in the lobby and they all hopped in the car for the short drive to the arena where full chaos ensued. Reporters and paparazzi swarmed them as they exited the car, making it almost comical that nobody had approached them in the mall earlier.

She signed a few autographs for kids and teens who were lined up at the barriers, her favourite being a glossy picture of Jack with his signature already on the top right corner. Warmth spread through her at the sight of their names scrawled in Sharpie next to each other.

They walked down the mostly empty corridors to their booth and got settled. Delia was about to grab the spoon for the queso dip when the door to the suite opened. She looked up and was fairly certain her spirit left her body.

Standing in front of her was a slight woman with dark hair that swooped over her forehead and a man that looked exactly like Jack.

Twenty years older Jack.

CHAPTER
Twenty~Seven

DELIA

> Is there a reason you didn't mention YOUR PARENTS were going to be in the suite tonight?

She didn't expect a response since Jack was most likely warming up with his team or changing in the dressing room, so she jumped when her phone buzzed against her thigh.

JACK

> Was that meant for your mom again?

> Ha. Ha. Seriously! Why didn't you say something?

About what?

YOUR PARENTS!!!

Okay I thought you were joking

Not a joke. Your parents are here. Sitting next to me. And the hotel didn't deliver my bag, so I haven't reapplied deodorant

You're screwed then. My parents have noses like bloodhounds

NOT FUNNY JACK

I laughed

I can't believe they're there. They didn't tell me they could make it

You invited them?

What kind of person doesn't invite their parents when they're in the NHL playoffs?

Fair. You still could've mentioned it

Have to run. Talk about coin collections and you'll have my dad eating out of the palm of your hand

I know nothing about coins

Jack

JACK

Delia shifted in her seat as Marc and Leslie Harrison took the two seats to her right. She searched the stands for the rest of the Snowballs players just to have something to keep her occupied.

What did they know? Had Jack told them the truth about their relationship like she'd told her mother?

Clara and Oscar were supposed to join them at some point, but there wasn't enough space in the suite to fit everyone from the Snowballs. Alvin stood at the back next to the door, and Mary was still dishing up food.

"Jack doesn't know we're here. We can't wait to surprise him," Leslie said as she sat, then took her plate of food from Marc's lap.

Delia groaned internally. Hopefully Jack was a good actor because she'd already blown that cover. "I can't believe you drove here all the way from Moose Jaw. How long of a drive was that?"

"About seven and a half hours if you drive straight through. We did over half of it yesterday, stayed the night in Battleford."

That meant nothing to her. As far as Delia was concerned, Saskatchewan was one large swathe of blue sky and prairie grass between Alberta and Manitoba. "Glad you got here safely."

"We really wish we would've been able to attend the last game in Calgary. Jack didn't tell us you'd be singing the national anthems!" Leslie dipped her chip in the puddle of salsa on the edge of her plate.

"It was a last minute thing. Jack didn't even know until he came out of the dressing room." Delia's insides warmed thinking of the way he'd looked at her as he walked through the tunnel. *That was when he'd invited her here.*

Marc popped the tab on his can of Molson. "Well, we're thrilled you decided to make the trek up. Especially considering the effect you have on Jack's game play."

Delia frowned. "What effect?"

Marc took a drink, then set the can on the small shelf on the rail in front of their seats. "All his stats were elevated significantly in the game you attended. People think having you in the stands makes him play better."

Hadn't someone told her that was a thing? She thought back to their first conversation with Jack in the dressing room. Kels.

He'd given a stat and Jack had asked what the numbers said about fake girlfriends.

Leslie shrugged. "It makes sense. You always wanted to show off for me when we were dating."

Marc shook his head. "I wasn't showing off . . ."

They continued to banter, but Delia's mind had taken off in another direction. Would a fake girlfriend have the same effect? Did Jack hope it did? Was that why he'd wanted her to come? *No, it couldn't be.* She hadn't even attended a game before he'd invited her to the playoffs.

But maybe there was some other motivating factor? She thought back to her rehearsal. To Lisa's words right as she finished. *We put your pop-up appearance in all our socials, and we've already seen a last-minute ticket surge.*

No. Delia pressed her feet into the floor and drew a breath deep. She was not going to do this again. She wasn't going to tense up and crash because of shadows. Jack had invited her here. He was flirtatious in his texts. He'd stayed the night with her when she needed him to and had called in friends to help in a crisis. None of that was in her contract.

He hadn't done anything wrong. So why was she flinching at every tiny thing?

A thought scrawled across her consciousness like her signature on the posters outside. *You're terrified of making this real.* What the? Delia turned the phrase over in her head, inspecting it from all angles.

She wasn't afraid of being in a relationship, was she? She'd been trying to make one happen for years. Sure, she was hesitant to jump in, but that was just smart. Guys always pretended to be something they weren't. She'd learned that the hard way enough times to look at everyone with a skeptical eye.

But Jack wasn't pretending. At least she didn't think so. Yet she was tearing the house apart for a reason to back away.

"Oh! There they are!" Leslie leaned forward in her seat as players began appearing behind the boards. They glided out onto the ice in a steady stream, like water being poured from a pitcher. "There's Jack!" She pointed, and Delia found him without even having to rely on the name on the back of his jersey. After watching his clips online and seeing him play in person, she knew his gait. Was that what it was called on the ice? His . . . canter? Delia almost laughed out loud at the mental image of a horse on skates.

Delia turned to see where the hell Mary was and found her standing next to the counter talking to Alvin. She smirked. *Of course she was.* As she scoured the far recesses of her mind for some tidbit about historical Canadian currency, the door to the suite opened and Clara and Oscar walked in. Saved by the sister-not-in-law. "Oh hey, Clara's here."

Leslie and Marc shot up, nearly spilling their food all over their laps. They set their plates down on the rail and walked up the stairs to Clara.

"What?" Clara clapped her hands over her mouth. "I didn't know you were coming!" She hugged her parents one at a time, the giddy smile never slipping from her face. There was a definite bump there. With her coat undone, it was obvious. But not obvious enough for her to ask about it. Not directly. She made a mental note to grill Jack about his sister's fertility later.

Delia pulled out her phone. She scrolled an embarrassingly long way down until she found her mom's contact and pressed. It only rang three times before her mother picked up.

"Allo? Delia?"

"Allo Maman." Delia grinned, but it didn't last. Her mother exhaled with a wheeze. "Mom, are you okay?"

"I'm fine." She cleared her throat.

"You don't sound fine."

She scoffed. "I had a little cold."

Delia's chest tightened. "A little cold—"

"Don't do that, mon chou. You don't need to worry about me."

"Well, I do worry about you."

"I should be the anxious one. Are you with Jack? Is he treating you well?" her mother asked.

Delia breathed a laugh. "I'm at his hockey game. You can watch on TV if you want. It's their first playoff game."

"I'm heading to work, but I'll turn it on for a moment." There was a clattering of pans and she muttered something under her breath in French. "Tell me what you've been doing while I eat."

Delia trained her eyes on the white jersey with Harrison stretched across the shoulders. He gracefully circled the ice, taking shots on an open net. "I've been busy. I finished recording that collaboration with Ethan Hayes. I love it."

"When does it release?"

"It's with IndieLake now, so whenever they decide to publish it. Shouldn't be more than a few days. They like to rapid-release normally, so I bet they'll push even harder with this. Since the press is having a field day with me and Jack."

Her mother clicked her tongue. "Your face is everywhere. It's like you aren't even gone."

Delia groaned. "I'm sorry. That must be annoying." She tensed, waiting for her mom to mention something *else* that was appearing everywhere online. Then she remembered her mother barely looked at more than newspapers and magazines. "I saw the picture of your kiss with Jack Harrison."

Delia barked a laugh. "Where did you see that?"

"Toronto Sun! Page three!"

"Wow, they must be hurting for content." She ran a hand through her hair, then waved as Clara and Oscar appeared in the aisle. They took seats on the other side of the stairs.

"Was it—"

"Yes." Delia whispered the word against the speaker. "Very good."

Her mother sighed. "Ah, and . . . the rest?"

Delia frowned. "What do you—"

"Is he a *good lover*, Delia? Does he take you out of your head and—"

"Mom!" Delia turned so she was facing Mary's empty seat and crossed her legs. As if that would put out the heat that was suddenly shooting across her inner thighs. "*I don't know.*"

"You don't know if he's a good lover, or—?"

Delia shrunk further in her seat. "I don't know because we *haven't.*" She stopped herself at the sound of Leslie and Marc behind her. "You know *what this is*, Mom. I told you—"

"I know, I know, but I've seen the pictures, Delia. You don't look like you're faking *anything.*"

"Okay, I think the game is about to start—"

"I have it on TV, Delia. The players are still warming up. You can just tell me you're not in tune with your body and it makes you uncomfortable to talk about natural desires and needs."

Delia groaned. "I'm *so* glad I phoned."

"What kind of mother would I be if I didn't tell you to experience life, mon chou? All it has to offer. None of us know how long we have on God's beautiful earth, and you worry too much. Just be there. Enjoy the moment. If you love, you love. If you get hurt, you get hurt. There is no ending you can't write a new story from."

Delia breathed as those words sank in. It sounded lovely. And completely impractical. "Love you, Mom. I wish I was there to eat with you."

"We'll eat together soon enough." Her mother made a kissing sound. Delia sent one back to her.

"I'll be back in Calgary at the end of the week."

"Good. Don't talk to me until then. Find out if Jack's a good lov—"

"Okay! Love you, Mom!" Delia laughed and hung up the call. Weren't most mothers telling their children not to sleep with athletes?

"Everything alright?" Marc asked as she turned back to face the ice.

Delia nodded, her cheeks hot. "Yep. Just talking to my mom."

Leslie smiled. "I love that you have a good relationship. I didn't ever have one with my mom."

"No?" Delia picked up her Coke.

Leslie shook her head. "My parents didn't have a happy relationship. Which was why I waited a little longer to settle down." She patted Marc's leg and left her hand on his thigh. "We were so thrilled when Clara met Oscar, and then Jack—" She stopped and looked between Delia and Marc.

"He told her." Marc patted her hand. "We talked about it right at the beginning."

Right at the beginning? She processed that statement. Jack must've talked to his parents about her and mentioned their conversation about Angie. Her hands tingled at the image of Jack sitting in his room with his phone pressed against his ear, reliving the words they'd said to each other.

Leslie looked up with a shimmer in her eye. "Okay, then. Well. You might not know, but Jack hasn't dated anyone since Angie, and both of us have been heartsick about it. Of course we miss her, but we don't want him to be lonely, and . . ." She put her right hand over her heart. "Anyway. We were over the moon when Jack said he wanted to start dating you. Not only because you're *you*. But because he sounded so happy."

You're scared of making this real. Delia's ribs shrunk like a wool blouse that had been accidentally put through the dryer. In an instant, it was like she was a gecko on the ceiling staring down at the relationship timelines of her life. Her mom working three jobs to make sure she could pay for music lessons. Mary and Tony making her reservations and dinner arrangements and dropping everything to accompany her to Edmonton or wherever the hell else she wanted to go for a show. And now Jack. Staying the night with her. Getting the video taken down. Putting a coat on her doorstep.

Delia dropped back into herself and pressed hard against the armrests. Maybe she was scared. Because everyone around her *had* to love her. She was an only child, and after losing her father, she was all her mother had. She'd gotten used to being doted on. To being the apple of someone's eye. *She liked it that way.* Because she knew all too well that even the people who were supposed to be there for her could leave at any moment. It simply wasn't worth the risk to leave anything up to something as volatile as choice.

Leslie leaned forward. "I'm sorry, I didn't mean to presume—"

"No, it's okay." Delia shook her head and folded her napkin in her lap. "Jack is wonderful. I'm so glad we met."

The idea of stepping into a relationship without collateral sent her reeling. What if she couldn't be like her mom? Like Mary? What if she was incapable of giving like they did? She hadn't even been able to bring in enough money to keep her mother at home tending her herb garden instead of putting on a uniform and leaving the house at nine o'clock at night. *What if she'd always have to pay the people around her to make sure they stayed?*

The lights in the arena dimmed and the announcer's voice came over the speaker. A spotlight landed on a children's choir and the Canadian flag. They all rose for the national anthem, and Delia scanned the arena in awe.

Had there ever been a time that she'd stood in an audience as massive? Probably only at a few concerts when she was a teenager, but this was different. Then they'd been united for the love of music. Never had she felt united for a love of country.

She sang the words to their anthem in barely more than a whisper and her throat grew thick. Her emotions were wild and unleashed, and she couldn't get a grasp on the reins.

She wanted Jack.

She needed Jack.

She loved making music.

She needed her music.

And as the children's angelic voices sang *God save our land,* that tangled fear and need and love swelled into gratitude so big, it couldn't be contained inside her.

She loved and needed the hell out of this place she lived. This country that had embraced her mother with open arms, even if she was barely making her citizenship official. Canadians weren't people who hung flags in the beds of their trucks or who looked for opportunities to blow things up to prove they were beyond the reach of the old world. Well, except for maybe on Guy Fawkes Day . . . or Victoria Day and Canada Day in Toronto. But that was beside the point.

Canadians were generally more subtle. They tattooed the maple leaf on their wrists and hips to keep a reminder close. They put small flags on their coats and backpacks to humbly announce exactly what they stood for.

It wasn't so much a symbol of who they weren't as Canadians, but who they *were*.

Kind.

Tolerant.

Eternally apologetic.

Hard working, nature loving, muscle-it-out people whose national hero wasn't someone with power, influence, or money but a teenager who lost his leg and then ran halfway across Canada on a prosthetic for cancer research. Sleeping in a camping van.

Holy. Crap. Tears sprang to Delia's eyes, and she almost laughed out loud.

That was why people loved hockey.

She finally understood.

Everything Jack was trying to tell her clicked into place like her ears had finally popped after a long flight. For the first time, she *got* the camaraderie and physical intensity. Even the fights made sense, and that was ironically what tipped her tears over the edge. They would go to battle for their team.

Jack had gone to battle for her.

Delia's heart swelled like one of those foam animals that

grew ten times their size when soaked in water. As the cheers died down and the lights came up, Delia pulled out her phone to text Jack, even though she could see him standing in his jersey with the rest of his team on the ice and knew he didn't have his phone.

"I always get emotional during the national anthem," Leslie said, noticing Delia swiping at her cheeks. Delia didn't feel the need to explain herself. She nodded and clapped as the arena erupted with cheers and the pump-up music started back up.

She slipped her phone back in her purse and hid her face as she sat. It felt wrong to have two borderline spiritual epiphanies sitting in a suite at a hockey game. Without beer and before the whistle even blew.

Yet there it was.

Her camera lens that had pointed straight at herself shifted, and suddenly it was pointing . . . everywhere else. She wanted to be like a hockey player. The skating wasn't going to happen, but she could gear up.

She would be a better friend. She'd spend more time worrying about what she could do with her platform instead of complaining about how it wasn't big enough yet. *Who gave a rat's ass if someone made a fake porno of her?* It had happened to so many women before her, and she needed to say something instead of shrinking back and hoping it faded into the ether of the internet.

She needed to stop being afraid and trust herself.

If you love, you love. If you hurt, you hurt.

Delia stood and cheered with the rest of Jack's family as the Blizzard won the face-off. She still didn't understand half the rules of the sport, but it was easy to take her cues from Jack's parents. As she went to sit down, Clara motioned for her to come over and join them, so she did.

They chatted through the first period. Clara filled her in on how Oscar had been insistent they drive to the south side for donairs at a place called High Voltage. After his dramatic retelling of their culinary experience, Oscar refused to let Delia get up for water until she agreed to try one on the way back to Calgary.

Midway through the period, the Blizzard had a power play. Thanks to Jack, Delia knew what that was and cheered as loud as anyone when Gaudreau snagged a pass from Tkachuk and slipped it in the left side of the net.

Jack saw his first ice directly after the goal, and Delia's whole body buzzed like it was connected to a power outlet. She silently pleaded for him to play well and *not* get injured, but also to not be disappointed if nothing amazing happened because he still played a solid shift, and her thoughts and pleas became so jumbled she was sure that if there was a higher power listening, he'd turned off her channel entire paragraphs before she actually got to the point.

She needn't have been worried. Jack was the glue between the offence and defence. Always breaking up the charges from the Oilers and there to receive the puck anytime the defence sent it past the blue line.

Delia screamed her voice raw when he got slammed into the boards, then cheered until she couldn't breathe when he assisted the Blizzards' second goal at the beginning of the second period.

It was two to one heading into the third. Delia thought it was probably a good time to take up a nail-biting habit, but thankfully her gels prevented her from taking the plunge. Instead, she gripped the chair arms like a cat hanging from a tree branch. When the Oilers scored in the first minute and a half, she might have left fingertip bruises on Clara's arm.

"They have to shut down Merc and Holden in the middle," Oscar muttered as he got up for another beer.

Clara kept her hands clasped and her fingers steepled as Jack skated back to the bench. "C'mon, c'mon."

Someone tapped Delia's shoulder, and she turned with the ferocity of a she-bear. "What?"

Alvin nearly stumbled as he jumped back on the stair. "Sorry.

I wanted to let you know if you'd like to meet Jack after the game—"

"Yes." Delia shot up, searching for her purse and the coat he'd given her. Jack's dad reached onto her previous seat and handed her the bundle. "Thank you. It was wonderful to meet you both." She turned, then froze midstep. "Wait . . . do you want to come, too?"

Leslie looked up. "To meet Jack?"

Delia nodded. "You said you wanted to surprise him, right?"

Clara stood and clapped her hands together. "Yes! That would be so perfect!"

Leslie and Marc grabbed their things and made sure to put their plates and cups in the garbage can before following Delia, Alvin, and Mary out the door to the private elevator.

"Are we going to miss the rest of the game?" Marc muttered to his wife behind her, and Delia smirked.

Alvin took them to an area similar to where she'd waited when she sang the national anthem in the Saddledome. They could see the ice and the player benches. Marc was as wide-eyed as a bush baby when he realized he'd get to hear the coaches and watch the shift subs.

Delia clung to Mary's hand as the minutes ticked down. The Oilers scored with less than three minutes left, and Delia's heart sank to her knees. "No! They have to win this! They can't be done just like that!" She snapped her fingers, and Alvin gave her a curious look.

"They won't be done. They'll still play again on Wednesday night."

Delia blinked. *Right.* Playoffs. It wasn't like her high school battle of the bands where you had one shot and then you were out. "Mmhmm. I know that. I just thought . . . it would be a lot better if they won the first game."

Mary snorted, and Delia elbowed her. The Blizzards battled to the end and even pulled their goalie in the last minute, but when the horn blasted, the score was three to two, Edmonton.

"Alright, come with me. We'll wait right outside the dressing room." Alvin and two other security guards led them to an area that would've made an excellent tornado shelter. Delia had to work to keep out thoughts of the whole arena crumbling and crushing her with concrete pillars.

Luckily, she didn't have to distract herself for long. Jack was one of the first players out of the dressing room. His hair was damp from the shower. He wore a flannel jacket over a grey T-shirt and those jeans she loved. His eyes locked onto her and his step faltered, then his chest lifted with a deep inhale. He strode toward her like he was under the impression her plane had crashed or her ship had gone down in the Atlantic.

Delia barely had time to blink before she was in his arms. She breathed him in. Freshly shampooed hair, the clean scent of his clothes and deodorant or cologne. She couldn't tell which, only that it was different than usual.

"I'm so sorry," she breathed into his neck.

"Yeah."

She pressed her cheek into his chest, wishing she could change the last five minutes of the game. "You were incredible." A deep exhale was his only response, so Delia continued. "I wanted to text you at the beginning of the game, but I knew you wouldn't get it."

"About how pissed you were that I didn't tell you about my parents?"

Delia clenched her fingers against his back. "Umm no, actually about how I think I get why you love hockey so much, but now that you mention it." She pulled him close. *"They don't know you know they're here, so please don't out me."*

Jack pulled back and looked up, feigning academy-award-worthy surprise when he saw Leslie and Marc standing a few paces away. He stepped away from her to embrace his parents, and Delia immediately felt the loss of him.

She wanted to find some way to ease the hurt he had to be feeling after such a tough loss. He was probably starving. She wanted to take care of him like he'd taken care of her. Delia pulled out her phone and started searching for restaurants. They could go for food, or hadn't Mary said something about an after-party? Though, maybe they wouldn't be celebrating without a win. They could—

"Hey." Jack trailed a hand up her arm, and she shivered. "You still up for watching something?"

She inspected his face, trying to get a read. Did he actually want to watch Bond movies and eat pizza or was he doing that for her?

She flicked her tongue over her lower lip. "We don't have to. If you're tired, we could grab food and then—"

"I've been looking forward to it all day."

Delia swallowed hard and nodded. "Then I'd love to. But do you want to get food?"

"Hell yes."

She laughed and glanced past his shoulder, then lowered her voice. "What about your parents?"

He leaned in. "I told them I was exhausted and we'd spend the day together tomorrow. My mom's setting up brunch because she knows I don't like to get up before ten after a game."

Delia grinned. "Are you a mama's boy?"

"Hell. Yes."

CHAPTER
Twenty-Eight

JACK'S HAND shook as he pulled out the card to his room. He glanced down the hall to make sure the security guards posted at the stairwells had successfully kept the hoards of people contained in the lobby and parking area, then swiped it over the mechanism. When the light turned green, he pressed down on the handle and pushed.

He hadn't even been tempted to meet with the rest of the guys in the suite they'd booked for meals. He'd spent the last three days with his team, and they couldn't blame him if he wanted some time with his girlfriend. He and Delia had put in their food requests, and one of the staff was going to bring it straight to his room.

Girlfriend. Was that what she was? Regardless of what they'd spelled out on paper, he was having trouble seeing any of this as a publicity stunt anymore.

Delia grabbed his elbow before he could step in. "Jack, I just remembered. I don't know where my bag is."

"It's not in your room?" His pulse spiked. *Was she second guessing this?* The first time they'd sat in a hotel room together it had been a logistical necessity, and his pulse hadn't been rushing like the Humber River after a downpour.

She shook her head. "They took it when we checked in, and —" Delia stopped as Jack pushed the door open wider. "Oh."

Jack turned his head and found a rose gold suitcase sitting next to the closet door. "Well. That wasn't there when I left for Roger's Place." He walked into the room and held the door for Delia to follow.

"Why would my bag be here?"

Jack peeled off his jacket. "Probably because most couples like to stay in the same room together."

Delia's eyes flicked to his, then back to her bag. She looked like she was about to say something, but bit her tongue. His heart was pounding out of his chest, and he turned, hoping she couldn't see his flushed cheeks in the dim light of the lamp.

"Do you mind if I change? I've been wearing this since we left the house this morning." Delia pushed her suitcase into the room and unzipped it.

"Go ahead. You can take a shower if you want."

Delia's eyes widened. "Do I smell? I probably do. I was in a car for three hours and—"

"No, you don't smell." Jack laughed and sat on the end of the bed. "I was offering in case you wanted it."

Delia grabbed cotton pants and a shirt from her bag and stood. "Okay."

Jack reached for the remote, working hard to ignore the rush of blood in the opposite direction of his head. He cleared his throat. "I'll see what's on."

He concentrated on the red, half-moon power button harder than anything else in his life as Delia nodded and turned to the washroom. As soon as the door clasped shut, Jack flopped back on the bed and drew a much-needed full breath.

He couldn't think. His stomach swirled like he was about to jump off a ten-metre diving board, and his tongue moved like he had peanut butter stuck to the roof of his mouth.

What did he want out of tonight? It was the stupidest question he'd ever asked himself. His muscles were gassed. His legs trembled even sitting still on the bed. And yet all he could think about was movement. Exertion. What Delia's skin would feel like under her shirt. Under her—

A knock at the door made him jump. He dropped the remote, realizing he hadn't done anything other than turn the TV on, and stalked to the door. He peered through the peephole and saw the second best thing to Delia's bare skin. *Food.*

Jack ripped open the door and took the first tray from the staff member. The man didn't look surprised to see him, so someone must've prepped him for the room he'd be stopping at. Jack returned for the second tray at the same time that Delia opened the washroom door. She stepped out, and the man's eyes bugged out of his head. Jack took the tray before he could drop it.

"Holy hell. D-delia Melise?" the man stammered.

She smiled and nodded.

"Oh, and you're—sorry, I didn't put the name together. Jack Harrison. Duh. Makes perfect sense now." He took a step back from the door. "Edmonton's my team. Obviously. But sorry about the loss, and—you two have a good night."

Jack gave him a wave and shut the door, then took the second tray to the desk. When had it become so ordinary to have someone fall all over themselves because he and Delia existed? It was ludicrous, and yet it had become so common-place, it was almost stranger when someone *didn't* know who they were.

He loved that the employee hadn't known him until he spotted Delia. Maybe most men would've wanted it the other way around, but he didn't. The idea of being known as Delia Melise's boyfriend sent heat flashing under his skin. It was stupid, but seeing that other people saw them belonging to each other made him more sure he wasn't crazy for wanting it to be true.

Jack took the lids off the plates and the aroma of steak, pota-toes, and roasted vegetables filled the room. He audibly exhaled.

Delia laughed. "Wow. I've never seen a person food-gasm before."

Jack turned and raised an eyebrow, and Delia blushed, her skin getting all splotchy on her neck. It was an impossible situation. Whether to put the steak or Delia into his mouth first. But since he hadn't quite grown the balls to tell Delia about the thoughts in his head, the steak won out for the moment.

His stomach gurgled as he grabbed his napkin-wrapped cutlery and the packet of HP sauce, then took his plate to the bed. He propped himself up with the extra pillows and started to dig in.

"Ooh, the TV guide. Riveting." Delia set her plate down on the comforter and tossed him the remote, then went back for a bottle of water. "You want one?"

Jack nodded, his mouth already full of steak and potatoes. Delia brought one over and set it on his nightstand, then retrieved her plate, set her water on her side, and shuffled onto the bed next to him.

Jack set his fork on his plate and scrolled through the channels. "Hey, there's the original 'Iron Man.'"

"That fits our theme. Men who fly solo and eventually lose everything they love."

"He doesn't lose Pepper."

"Not in *this* movie."

Jack frowned. "Wait, doesn't he eventually die? He sacrifices everything for the Avengers?"

Delia pondered. "Yeah. I guess he does break the mold. He builds real friendships."

"Does that mean I have to find something else?"

She grinned and took a bite of roasted broccoli. "No, let's do it."

Jack didn't care what they watched. He just wanted the decision made so he could eat and figure out what to do next. Time with the team had been a good distraction right up until he'd gotten those texts from Delia before warmups. Then all he'd wanted to do was bust out of the dressing room and climb however many flights of stairs he needed to to get to her suite. He was elated that his parents had driven from Moose Jaw, but he couldn't help but put them in the backseat.

"I love the coat."

Jack cut another bite of steak. "You mentioned that."

She turned, considering him. "Why did you do that?"

"Because you said you wanted one."

"I know, but people say they want a lot of things. They don't usually have someone around who makes their dreams come true."

Jack dipped his steak in HP. "I believe in over-delivering. It's one of my best features."

Delia quieted next to him, staring intently at Tony Stark standing in front of a group of military personnel. He hoped she was thinking about all of his other best features.

"Ooh, the coat!" Delia turned, almost spilling her food onto the comforter. "Is Clara pregnant?"

Jack blinked. "What does your coat have to do with Clara being pregnant?"

Delia laughed. "No, *her* coat. She came in the suite today and her coat was open, and there was definitely a bump there. I didn't say anything because who knows, right? But that would be strange for her to gain weight just there and nowhere else."

Jack processed this, then thought back to that night in the Jukebox. How he couldn't remember the last time he'd seen her drink. Had it been New Year's? "I think she might be pregnant."

"Right? Wouldn't that be so exciting?"

Jack's head felt like a dust storm. Exciting, yes, but it also turned up the heat. If Clara was pregnant, they'd need that extra room.

He was doing everything he could to be considered for the next season, but even if he was impressive, they had to have a slot open for him. The ground still shifted like quicksand under his feet.

They ate in silence, though Jack couldn't focus on one iota of the action on screen. Delia, on the other hand, seemed riveted. It knocked his confidence down a notch.

"I forgot this movie started with his Hummer getting blown up," she murmured.

"Brutal." Jack scooped up the last of his potatoes and set his plate on the nightstand.

Delia finished her meal a few minutes after him. She stood and rounded the bed to collect his dishes.

"You don't have to do that."

She met his eyes for the first time in fifteen minutes. "I know. I want to." Delia stacked his plate with hers and took everything back to the desk. "Do you want your cookie?"

"Maybe later." There was something different about her, but he couldn't put his finger on it. Like some push and pull inside her had been resolved. A question answered. It made him nervous.

Delia walked back to her suitcase and pulled out a toiletry bag. "I'm just going to brush my teeth." Jack grinned, and Delia pursed her lips. "Don't you dare laugh."

His smile grew wider. She was so hot when she put a hand on her hip and told him what to do. "I'm not laughing."

She rolled her eyes and padded into the washroom. It was then that Jack realized if he wanted anything besides watching a movie together to happen, he'd better make sure his mouth was clean, too. He turned down the volume on the TV and walked to the door. "Mind if I join you?"

There were two sinks, and Delia shifted to the far one so Jack could use his supplies that were already placed by the first. As he put toothpaste on his brush and watched Delia in the mirror, nostalgia and grief crashed over him like a tidal wave. *They'd done this every night.* He clamped his eyes shut and gripped the edge of the counter.

"Jack?" Delia dropped her flosser and stepped closer to him, pressing her hand into his lower back. "Are you okay?"

He nodded and forced himself to breathe. "Yeah. Sorry, just —" He pushed back to standing, but Delia didn't step back.

"Just what?"

Jack set down his toothbrush and found her eyes in the mirror. "It's been a long time since I brushed my teeth next to someone."

Delia exhaled. "I can go out."

Jack shook his head. "No, it's good. It's been a long time, that's all."

Delia's placid expression cracked. "Jack—"

He twisted and pulled her between him and the counter, finally giving himself permission to touch her. *Really* touch her. As his hands settled on the curve of her waist, feeling the edge of her hip bone under the thin cotton shirt, he realized his mistake. He'd opened up a floodgate that he had no energy left to close back up.

He let his eyes travel slowly up her body until he met her gaze. "Have I earned this?"

Delia frowned for a moment, then her focus sharpened. She knew exactly what he was referring to. That morning in the café. When she'd said the word he hadn't been able to stop thinking about since. *Sacred.*

He'd toyed with that concept every night as he lay alone in bed, analyzing the years since Angie left. It explained everything. Why he couldn't bring himself to touch other women, why he couldn't push past the first awkward moments to begin building an actual relationship.

He knew connection, body and soul, and nothing else was good enough. But growing that with Angie had taken time. Pain. Effort. It had all been so much work, and he'd convinced himself he didn't have the energy to do it again. He didn't *want* to have the energy to do it again, because for years he'd been looking back. Wanting only her. Living in a past he couldn't tap into, and ignoring half the life he was forced to stand in.

Then came Tony's call. Dinner with Delia. His signature on

that contract. It had forced him to step into a world he refused to enter on his own, and now here they were. Standing in a hotel washroom. His hands on her hips. Looking into her eyes of ice and fire.

No place had ever felt so hallowed.

Without meaning to, he'd dipped his toes into the water, then stumbled in up to his knees, and he'd been toying with the idea of plunging his head under the surface since he'd seen Delia at the Saddledome.

He was ready.

Was he ready?

Delia swallowed, then nodded her head. "You've earned a lot more than this."

Jack's knees went weak. He blamed his shredded hamstrings and widened his stance. An ache built in his middle as Delia pulled him closer. When he spoke, he sounded as if he'd just skated a double shift.

"I don't want to be your fake boyfriend anymore." Jack lowered his forehead to hers. "I don't want to kiss because we're trying to make it look real, and I don't want to stick to a damn schedule." He paused, trying to figure out how to make his words honest. "I don't know what I'm doing. You know it's been years since I've wanted to be with someone, and I don't know—I can't promise you I won't be a mess, but I want to try. With you." He stood there breathless, his hips against hers, giving away every last thought in his head.

Delia pulled her hands off the counter and placed them on his stomach, then moved them over his chest, sending shivers down his spine. "What about the contract?"

Jack lifted his head and tucked her hair behind her ears. "To hell with the contract."

"What about the money?"

"I don't need it." He didn't know if that was true, but he sure as hell wasn't going to take another dollar out of Delia's pocket.

"Do you know if they're bringing you back for next season?" she asked. He shook his head. "Then—"

Jack put a finger to her lips. He didn't want Delia to ask any other questions—he was all too aware that his life was in shambles. That they didn't even live in the same province, and that Delia would have to go back to Toronto eventually. It was terrifying that a growing part of himself hoped he didn't get signed to the Blizzard so he wouldn't be stuck on the other side of the country.

Delia snorted. "I didn't know you lived in a fantasy world, too."

He knew she meant it as a joke, but the words hit home. *Was he kidding himself?* "You of all people should love that."

Delia's voice dropped to a whisper. "I do love that." She slipped her hands into his back pockets. "We're supposed to have a public break up in a couple of weeks."

Jack worked to catch his breath as he pressed his lips to the soft skin just under Delia's jaw. "I'll happily sign an addendum."

Delia sighed and tipped her head back. The sound sent another rush of blood to his middle, and after waiting three years, the thought of waiting another thirty seconds to tear her damn loungewear off sent him out of his mind. He fumbled for the hem of her shirt, but Delia stopped him.

"Jack." She lifted a hand and ran it through his hair. "I know it's the least sexy thing in the world, but I do need to brush my teeth."

———

Delia sucked in a breath as Jack grinned against her skin and kissed the underside of her jaw, then stepped back, wincing at what she could only imagine was the tight fit of his jeans. She forced herself not to look down as she reached for her toothpaste and toothbrush.

Jack hastily spread toothpaste on his brush, wet it, and shoved it in his mouth. He didn't come close to the recommended brush time since he was standing there leaning against the sink before Delia was even half done.

"That's not helping," she said around the whir of her electric toothbrush.

"What?"

"You. Watching me." She lifted a finger to swipe away a drip of white foam, and Jack laughed. He turned his back, and Delia exhaled. She looked ridiculous, and the last thing she wanted to do was kill whatever energy they'd had a few moments before.

When her toothbrush beeped for the final time, she spit and rinsed, then set it on the counter and found a washcloth to dry her lips.

Blood rushed in her ears as she stared at Jack's backside. She was done, but she had no idea how to reenter the situation. Jack must've noticed the lack of movement or sound behind him because he turned. "Done?"

She nodded.

"Then why are you still standing over there?"

Delia's hands shook as she stepped forward. Jack had a good reason for taking a dating hiatus, but she didn't. Her relationship desert had come purely because of her inability to match well with someone. So even though she could feel the electricity pulsing between them, her thoughts started to get away from her.

What if you can't get there? What if he thinks that means you're not into it? What if he just lost a game and then has to walk away disappointed from this, too?

Jack reached out and tilted her chin up. He turned her head side to side. "Just checking."

"For what?"

"Pupil size."

Delia couldn't help her confused look. "What?"

"You looked like you were about to have a stroke or something—"

Delia smacked her hand against his chest and, just like it always did around Jack, the truth came tumbling out. "I'm nervous, okay? Haven't you ever been nervous?"

Jack laughed and grabbed onto her wrist, pulling her out of the washroom. "All the time. I threw up before the game."

"And you kissed me with that mouth?"

"I brushed in the dressing room! They actually had supplies in there this time."

Delia squealed as Jack pulled her onto the bed and caged her beneath him. "I chose the wrong profession."

She sank into the mattress as Jack pressed his leg between hers and lowered himself against her body. He held his weight on his forearm as he lifted a hand to her cheek. "Based on your pond skating, I think it's wise you didn't choose hockey."

Delia groaned. "My tailbone is still bruised, by the way."

Jack reached his hand under her hip. "Yeah? Where does it hurt?"

"Stop." She laughed.

"Here?" He ran his hand along the waistband of her joggers.

Delia shook her head, suddenly sober and breathless. She looked up at him through her lashes. "A little lower, I think."

Jack's jaw tightened as his eyes snapped into focus. He slipped his fingers under the cotton fabric, feeling along the top of the lace thong she might have worn purely because it matched a very specific bra she'd put on in Jack's washroom.

Jack's breathing changed, sending a thrill from the crown of her head to her toes. "There?" His fingers played with the scalloped edges.

"Getting closer."

Jack dropped his mouth to hers, his hand growing more frantic as he explored her skin, pulling the waistband of her pants tight. She reached down and tugged her joggers over her hips, then let Jack do the rest. His fingers brushed against her legs as he pulled them off, and she'd never been more grateful she'd shaved the night before.

Jack wrapped his hand over her calf, pressed his finger into the back of her knee, then slid his palm up the sensitive skin on the inside of her thigh.

Delia sucked in a breath, arching against him as she reached for his waist and pulled him closer. She yanked at the hem of his shirt, suddenly desperate to get her hands on bare skin. Jack ripped his shirt off and tossed it onto the floor.

"Yes." The word slipped out of her as she pushed him onto his side and ran her fingers over his pecs, taking in the dark hair there that she'd only gotten glimpses of when he'd lifted his arms.

Is Jack a good lover? Does he get you out of your head?

Delia's stomach fluttered as she traced the swirls of ink on his skin. The pinecones. The owl. The mantis.

Jack stilled as he watched her finger follow the lines. "It was a joke."

"What was?"

"The praying mantis."

Delia's breath quickened. She leaned in and kissed a flower bud on his bicep.

"She was fascinated by them, and I told her it was because they ate their mates. When we got engaged, we got matching mantises and promised not to eat each other alive."

Delia kissed his shoulder. His collarbone. "I'm so sorry, Jack."

Jack rolled onto his back and Delia dropped next to him, throwing her leg over his hips. "I'm sorry. I shouldn't have brought that up."

She nestled against his chest. "I'm glad you did." It was the truth. She loved that he knew how to love. She only hoped he had room in his heart for one more. She wanted to tell him they didn't have to do this, but instead she waited, listening to his breath.

Eventually Jack's hands brushed up her thighs and found their way to her backside. "Are you wearing it?"

She tilted her head to look at him. "Wearing what?"

The corner of his mouth twitched. "You know what. That bra. The one you were holding in your bedroom."

She shrugged. "Hard to remember."

"You are such a *tease*." Jack pulled her shirt up and Delia helped it over her head. He pushed her back on the pillows, raking his eyes over her as his hand dragged across the curve of her hip. "Yeah. That's it."

Delia grinned. "It wasn't hard to tell you liked it."

"I'm glad I'm so transparent." Jack tucked his fingers under the strap, then kissed her with the same hunger she'd sensed that first night in the bed and breakfast. Her body lit up like the sky on Canada Day.

"I love that," she sighed.

"What?"

"When it feels like you want me."

Jack breathed a laugh. "I do want you."

Delia reached for the button of his jeans. She clumsily pushed until it came free of the buttonhole, then pulled on the zipper.

Jack grunted. "I need to get a condom."

Delia held onto his arm and pressed her hand against his boxer briefs. "I have an IUD."

Jack's heart raced next to hers, making her pulse squirrely. "I don't want—"

"Jack, I trust you."

He kissed her cheek. "You're aware what sport I play, right?"

She grinned and dragged her teeth gently over the stubble on his jaw. "Oh, I know. I waited until your mom corroborated your abstinence story."

Jack tensed. "She what?"

Delia laughed and strategically moved her hand until Jack dragged in a breath and held it. "She may have mentioned you hadn't dated anyone in a long time." *Since Angie.* She avoided saying her name just like he had. "You said you haven't been with someone in three years. I haven't been with someone in at least a year and a half, and I always get tested at my annual physical."

Jack's grip tightened on her hip. "You're sure?"

Delia wasn't sure about anything, but she knew she wanted this. She wanted him. Possibly more than anything she'd wanted in the known universe. She was drunk on the sound of his ragged breath, of the clench and release of his fingers against her skin.

"If you keep doing that, there won't be any need for this discussion." Jack's voice was raw as he placed his hand over hers and interlaced their fingers, then drew her arm up over her head. He brushed his cheek against hers and pulled the lobe of her ear into his mouth. His tongue was hot against her skin, and Delia writhed against him.

Jack kept her tethered as his other hand found its way back to lace. "I think it's your turn to teach me something."

Delia whimpered. "I don't . . . know any nursery rhymes."

"Mmm. Good thing, what I'm hoping to learn would never be appropriate for a classroom."

She breathed a laugh as Jack sank against her. She'd been exactly right. His hands were gentle and extremely capable. He was slow, tantalizing, and full of that storm she'd been desperate for.

Yes. Jack Harrison was an excellent lover, and for the first time since she could remember, Delia's head was so full it was silent.

CHAPTER
Twenty-Nine

THE ROOM WAS dim when Jack awoke, with only a snatch of light sneaking in around the edges of the drawn curtains. His body ached, but at the same time was more settled than he could remember. He'd slept like a rock.

Delia breathed next to him. The sheets were crisp against his skin as he rolled to his side as quietly as possible. She laid sprawled on her stomach next to him, and even though he'd never asked her how she slept, this was exactly how he'd imagined her. Arms and legs splayed, hair mussed. Uninhibited and free.

Jack watched her for a moment as emotions swirled like a wind tunnel, each taking turns gripping his full attention. Love. Warmth. Gratitude. Pleasure. Disbelief. *Guilt.* He exhaled. Ah, his ever faithful companion. At least it had lessened. The hole inside his chest had started to stitch together—he could physically feel it shrinking even though he could still punch a fist through it.

He was allowed to want happiness. *He was allowed to want this.* He knew it, and yet the questions still came. Did this mean he didn't love Angie? Did she hate him for sleeping with someone else? Could he ever love someone the way he'd loved her?

Normally, the fact that he didn't have answers would have sent his stomach cramping, but this time they sat there, not sinking deep like usual. Jack moved closer and threw an arm over Delia's bare waist under the sheets, pressing against her like he had in her room the other night.

She drew her limbs in like a disturbed hermit crab. Her skin smelled like herbal hotel soap, not her regular floral, and he missed it.

Delia grabbed onto his arm, wrapping it more tightly around her. "Morning."

Jack kissed the back of her shoulder, and she hummed in her throat. Almost all the sounds she made sounded like singing, even the ones he'd drawn out of her the night before. His heart rate quickened remembering those.

"Someone's happy this morning," Delia teased, reaching behind her and slapping his hip.

"How could I not be?" He grinned and nuzzled into the hollow between her shoulder and neck.

Delia squeezed him out, laughing and rolling to meet his eyes. She cupped a hand over his cheek, and Jack wished he'd taken the time to pull back the curtains so he could see the colour of her eyes. She dragged her nails through his scruff. "What time is it?"

"I don't especially care."

Her grin widened. "Don't you have to meet your parents?"

Jack groaned and reached for his phone on the nightstand. He tapped the screen. "Nine fifteen."

"Hmm. And you have brunch at ten?" Delia trailed her hand over his stomach.

"Ten thirty." He sucked in a breath.

"Interesting."

"Very interesting." He rolled back to face her, pulling her flush against his front. "Am I allowed to kiss you?"

Delia scrunched her nose. "I haven't—"

"I know. Just your lips."

She raised an eyebrow, and Jack laughed. "Please?" When she nodded, he lowered his head and kissed her. Slow and gentle. It was already the best morning he'd had in years, and he hadn't even had bacon yet.

Delia pulled back and ran her hands over him, giving special attention to any places that made him shiver. "Washroom. Then I'll be back."

"Mmhmm." Jack fell back on the pillows and waited. When she exited the washroom, he took his turn, making sure he counted to twenty while he brushed so Delia wouldn't accuse him of skipping teeth.

His pulse was already jumping by the time he returned to the room, pulled open the curtains, and slid back under the covers.

Jack moved on top of her and disbelief clawed its way past pleasure and warmth to the top of the pile. "How am I this lucky?" He brushed away her soft waves and kissed her forehead.

"Tony's just damn good at his job."

Jack chuckled. "He told me that, you know. Right after he asked if I was an asshole."

Delia laughed. "He asked? That's a big deal. Normally he just assumes."

"He cares about you."

"As much as a publicist can care for their merchandise."

Jack worked his way down her neck to the warm, freckled skin of her chest. "You're not merchandise." He knew that feeling all too well. Being a number on a printout sheet of paper. Managers and coaches passing him around from one team to another. The coaches always seemed to care until he stepped outside the lines.

He pushed away the flash of worry about the meeting he scheduled with his current coaches in Calgary at the end of the week. It had been too much to schedule something between travel games, but he couldn't wait much longer. According to Brett, Liam had fulfilled his end of the bargain. That was something.

Jack closed his eyes and breathed in the clean scent of Delia's skin. Right then there were no meetings or futures he needed to worry about. He only wanted to be there in that bed. His lips on her neck. His legs laced with hers.

Delia sighed. "But I am a paycheck."

He conceded that point with a kiss. "You can be a paycheck and still have people care about you."

She ran her fingers through his hair as his kisses travelled lower. "Maybe, but—"

The talking stopped right around when he reached her belly button.

———

Delia sat across from Jack in the booth, her body humming. She hadn't meant to steal an invite to brunch, but she wasn't complaining about the sweet potato, spinach, and sausage hash in front of her. Clara buttered a biscuit, and Leslie was telling Jack something about his high school hockey coach when Mary showed up next to her. She and Alvin had insisted on sitting at their own table even though Leslie had invited them to join their group.

"Change your mind?" Delia asked.

Mary shook her head and crouched. "Have you checked your email?"

Delia frowned and shook her head. She'd barely glanced at her phone since about nine thirty the night before.

Mary held out her screen, and Delia gasped. "It's live."

Delia held back the curse words bubbling to her lips and

turned back to Jack and his parents. "I'm so sorry, just a second. My new song just came out." Jack moved to stand, but Delia waved him off. "It's okay, stay with your parents. I'll be right back, I promise."

She jumped out of the booth and went to Mary's table, ignoring the cell phones pointed her direction from across the restaurant. She could just see those headlines. *Delia leaves Jack holding the bill. A lover's spat?*

Mary held up her speaker between them and pressed play. The song started off exactly as they'd planned, and it felt like she'd downed two Red Bulls. She bounced her knees to keep from jumping up and down. The guitar dropped, then the bass, and then Ethan's signature keyboard riffs. It was gorgeous, exactly what—

Delia froze on the bench as it moved into her verse. Those weren't her updated lyrics. She'd recorded new versions when she went to the studio but these were the original versions they'd put together weeks ago.

"That's not right?" Mary gave her a look, and she nodded. Delia reached into her purse for her own phone and impulse-dialed Christian. To her surprise, he answered on the second ring.

"Delia! My girl! I'm assuming you got the memo about the drop."

She forced a shallow breath. "Yeah, I did. I was just listening to it with Mary. I think there's been a mistake though. My vocals are off."

He grunted. "They sound perfect to me."

"No, sorry, the lyrics. We rewrote them, and—"

"Ah, right. Ethan submitted that, but I asked for the originals we'd initially approved."

Delia's pulse thudded against her temples. "Did you listen to the new ones?"

"I did, and while they were excellent, we didn't feel they were on-brand."

She clutched the phone so tightly, she thought the case might crack. She wanted to scream. To quit. To do anything but sit there in the booth and pretend she wasn't shrivelling up and dying on the inside.

Christian shuffled something on his desk. "Streaming numbers are through the roof. It's out-performing the first hour of any of your recent singles, so give yourself a huge pat on the back. We're thrilled with all the work you and Tony have done on this. I know there's only more to come."

More to come. Meaning more songs she didn't care about. A breakup she had zero desire to follow through with. *More to come.* It sounded like a death sentence.

"Listen, Delia, I've got to run, but let's get together once you're back in Toronto. I've got some ideas for your next single."

Delia thanked him—*thanked him*—and ended the call. *What the hell was wrong with her?* She had a contract with IndieLake. She'd just gotten off the phone with one of the country's most celebrated music producers, her first ever positive royalty statement was probably going to land in her inbox within a month, and she was a household name across Canada. She'd even seen her account tagged on radio stations and news outlets in California and Colorado. She had everything she wanted. And here she was about to cry in a booth because of some damn lyrics.

"What did he say?" Mary searched her face.

"Just that they thought the original lyrics were more on-brand." Delia bit the inside of her cheek. She would not make this about her. Mary had tromped around Alberta with her for weeks and she was finally sitting here having a nice breakfast with Alvin. On the other side of the booth, Jack was less than a day out from an NHL playoff loss and he hadn't complained once. Granted, they'd been doing plenty to keep his mind off it, but still.

She had to figure out how to be a better friend, and that started now.

"Delia, I'm so sorry, I know how—"

Delia held up a hand, cutting Mary off. "Nope. Totally fine. The song is doing great, so I'm not even going to worry about it." Mary blinked, and Delia didn't give her time to comment on how this was disturbingly out of character. "How was your night?"

Mary raised an eyebrow. "I could ask you the same thing."

"But you won't because we're in a public place." Delia kissed her cheek and stood.

"You found your bag, I assume? Since you're wearing one of the outfits I packed for you?"

She nodded. "Yep, and it's perfect. You're amazing, Mary. Thank you." Delia left Mary with a befuddled look on her face and scooted back into the booth next to Leslie and across from Jack.

"You good?" Jack asked, concern etched in his expression.

Delia took a forkful of hash and nodded. "Mmhmm. Good!" It was too chipper, and Jack was immediately skeptical.

"Sounded like you were talking to someone."

She nodded. "Yep, just my producer. But I want to hear the rest of your mom's story."

Leslie looked pleased and dove back in where she'd left off. Jack wasn't fooled. He reached under the table and put a hand on her knee, swirling his thumb over her skin. She reached down and held it, giving him a squeeze. They sat like that while she finished her food and the waitress brought their check. Marc insisted on paying, which both warmed her heart and made her wildly uncomfortable. Less so since she knew she wasn't fully lying to them about her intentions with their son.

They exited the restaurant, stopping at a few tables to greet fans on the way out. Jack was more popular with the brunch-goers, but Delia winced every time they mentioned how thrilled they were that Edmonton won while complimenting him on his game play. They were about to duck into the car with Mary and Alvin when Jack stopped her.

"I have to get to the arena for a team meeting. I'm going to catch a ride with my parents."

"You're not practising are you?"

Jack shook his head. "No, just game strategy. Then I'll be back at the hotel." He handed her a key. "If you want to meet me?"

Delia smiled up at him. "I guess all my stuff is there already."

"The room is half yours now."

She took the card, and a jolt of electricity shot up her spine.

Jack pulled her to his chest and dropped his mouth to her ear. "Don't for one second think we're not talking about what happened in there."

"It was nothing. It—" Her voice caught in her throat as he kissed that tender spot on her neck, then turned her head so he could press his lips against hers.

"Be back soon."

Delia nodded, her knees wobbly as she watched him turn and retreat to the parking lot.

———

Jack forced himself to focus fully as Assistant Coach Kreviasuk debriefed from the game the night before. They were all aware of their screw ups, and Jack already had opinions on what they could do to fix them. Thankfully, he didn't have to be a loud mouth. Monahan and Coach Novak covered the essentials, then moved on to their typical spiel on hydration and rest.

That was going to be a tough sell, considering he had Delia waiting for him in his hotel room. If being in bed counted as rest, then he was going to be resting. Hard. If they'd ever wrap the meeting up.

Ten agonizing minutes later they finished, and Jack made the rounds with his teammates who weren't heading back for treatment with the physical therapist.

"Don't tire out those legs, eh?" Lindholm winked as he walked past him.

"Team comes first!" Jack barked.

To which Lindholm replied, "Oh, someone comes first, alright." He laughed and disappeared through the door.

Jack looked around and caught Liam rubbing Tiger Balm on his calf. "You need to get that looked at?"

He shook his head. "No. Just sore." He finished and screwed the lid back on the tube. "Talked with Brett."

"Yep, he told me."

Liam lowered his voice. "I'm going to a meeting with him on Friday."

Jack's eyebrows lifted in surprise. "Fantastic. Good on you, bud. Are you okay at the hotel?"

Liam nodded. "Yeah, I'm going to head back and rest. You want to share an Uber?" Liam shoved the Tiger Balm back into the training bag.

"Yeah. That'd be great."

They were halfway to the door when his phone buzzed in his pocket. He took it out and saw the picture he'd added to Delia's contact on the screen.

"Hey, Harrison. Can we borrow you for a moment?" Coach Novak motioned for him to follow him into the office past the lockers.

Jack nodded and declined the call, then shot her a quick text.

Meeting. Phone you right back

He turned to Liam. "Sorry, you don't have to wait."

"All good. See you back there."

Jack waved, then followed Coach Novak through the office door. Kreviasuk motioned for him to close the door, and Jack's palms started to sweat as he sat in the chair across from the desk.

"Nice that you've taken MacDonald under your wing." Coach Novak exhaled as he sat in the rolling chair and scooted in.

"He's a good kid."

"He's struggling."

Jack nodded. "That's what I wanted to talk to you about on Friday, actually."

Novak's eyes widened. "Oh really? Well, perfect. Coach and I realized you were still out there and thought we'd snag you for a quick chat anyway."

Jack shifted in his seat, wondering whether that was a good idea or not. "Do you want to give me what you've got first?"

Kreviasuk turned the computer monitor his direction. "Sure, let's get at it." He started the reel, and Jack immediately understood what he was after. The fact that they hadn't scored on their second power play. They'd barely pulled it out on their first.

"They're shutting down our single swing, so we want to pull out centre lane tomorrow night." He paused with his finger on top of Vic Hussen. "He wants to bite. It's like he's begging for it, so we're going to send Gaudreau out as bait, then you'll be our first wing option."

"Not Monahan?"

"He'll be there, but he's the obvious choice."

Jack nodded. "Got it. Anything else?"

"More forechecks. We need you there on the boards."

"Right." Jack wondered what Delia would think of that. *Why would people pay to watch people hit each other?* He stifled a smile, remembering he was supposed to phone her back.

"Let's hear it, then. What do you have for us on the rookie?" Novak leaned back in his chair.

Jack drew a deep breath. He hadn't had time to organize his thoughts, and he scrambled for any advice he'd heard on how to give criticism kindly. Praise first? Sandwich method? "Uh, I've been concerned. He's got a lot of potential, and I don't think we're seeing it."

"Damn straight. He needs to lock in."

Jack clasped his hands together. "I don't know if he does, actually." Novak frowned, and Jack's insides twisted. This was where it happened. Where he pissed everyone off and killed his chances for ice time. "I think there are a lot of players who thrive under pressure, who battle harder under a firm hand, but I don't think Liam's one of them."

"We can't be soft on him if that's what you're asking, Jack—"

"It's not being soft. It's a different strategy." He looked pointedly at the screen. "Liam's got some things he's working through, and he already feels like shit. He needs to feel wanted. Like you're not going to give up on him, even if he gets his ass handed to him."

Kreviasuk scoffed. "That's our job, Harrison. We have to weed out the bad eggs."

Jack's jaw tensed. "Sometimes an egg can be deceiving." He pushed up from his chair. "I know what it's like to be thrown in the compost. I had plenty more to give, but my coaches had made up their minds. It's up to you. I'm not a coach, and I'm not trying to overstep, but MacDonald was drafted for a reason. Might be worth a little upfront effort to get him there." He nodded and walked to the door, not waiting for a response, and dialed Delia as soon as he exited into the hall.

"Jack?"

His heart stopped in his chest at the panic in her voice. "Delia, what's—"

"I'm on my way to the airport. I'm so sorry. I had to leave as soon as I heard."

DELIA STRETCHED her seatbelt until she could shove her head between her knees. She wasn't made for moments like that. Put her on a stage and she'd stare down a thousand people no problem, but tell her that her mom was running a fever of a hundred and four? Nope. Her brain turned into Cream of Wheat.

"Okay, slow down and try one more time." Jack was still on the other end of the line even though she wasn't making any sense. This wasn't the plan. She was going to be there for him. She was going to be sitting in the hotel room waiting when he got back. They were going to have a naked nap and she'd massage his shoulders or something and force him to drink enough water and eat protein or whatever he needed to get ready for game two.

"I can't, Jack. I can't think. I wanted to be there–I'm so mad I'm not there for you–but I had to—"

"Delia, take a breath. Please."

People always told her to take a breath, and it never helped. It only made her lungs forget they'd ever known how to breathe in the first place. But it wasn't his fault. Jack didn't know that. He didn't know that what she was supposed to do was start naming facts about her surroundings and—*oh, damn*. Had she just therapized herself?

Delia looked up. The seat was leather. It was black. Her brain scrambled to hold onto the chaos, but Delia turned her head and kept noticing. There was a piece of lint on the floor. Her suitcase was on the seat next to her because she'd dragged it in before her driver or Alvin could put it in the back. It was rose gold. Alvin had stripes of grey in his beard. He was coming with her because Mary was going to drive back to Calgary and close things down at the bed and breakfast since they only had it for another week and a half—

Nope, that thought wanted to send her down another spiral of leaving Calgary and missing Jack, which was the opposite of helpful.

The driver had on a black sport coat. She was wearing her favourite jeans. Better. Delia drew a deep breath. That was better.

"Okay. I think I can talk now."

Jack exhaled, his breath turning into static in the microphone. "I was about to phone my dad and get in his truck."

Delia sniffed. "I'm sorry. This is the last thing I wanted."

"Just tell me what's going on."

"Okay. Okay." She leaned back in the seat, readjusting her seatbelt as she closed her eyes. "We have a friend who lived next door my whole life. Her name's Tenille and she's in her seventies now . . ."

Delia recounted how she'd just arrived back at Jack's hotel room when Tenille's number popped up on her cell phone. She hadn't remembered saving her as a contact, it had been so long since they'd been in contact. Moving away from their apartment had been bittersweet, *with relief and regret*. Delia and her mom still stopped by every week or so to check on her and drop off cookies or help her chip the ice off the edge of the walkway since management still hadn't fixed the leaking eaves.

She had no idea how Tenille had even gotten over to their new house. She couldn't remember ever telling her where they lived. But somehow she'd made it past the gate and showed up on their doorstep. She'd knocked and waited for almost a half an hour before her mom had been able to make her way to the door and open it.

"She must have pneumonia or something, I don't know. Her cough sounded terrible. That's where her Lupus attacks hardest, and she's already taking Ibuprofen for her pleuritis, but she won't take the steroids they keep trying to get her to take—"

"Alright. Wow. Well I'm really glad someone found her. Did they go to the hospital?"

Delia groaned. "No, my mom is so stubborn. She hates doctors and is convinced that if she waits it out and drinks her herbal concoctions, she'll be fine." Delia was sure as hell going to have a conversation with the service they'd hired to help her mom in her absence. *Why hadn't someone contacted her?*

"Can't blame her. She has a one hundred percent track record."

Delia laughed, and the sound surprised her. "How do you do that?"

"What?"

"Make me laugh when I feel like the world is caving in?"

"It's not hard to make you laugh, Dels."

Her chest warmed. Only Mary and Tony called her Dels, but she was immediately in love with the way it rolled off his lips. "It's hard for most people."

"Well, I'm not most people."

"I'm becoming acutely aware of that." Delia wanted to be back in that hotel room. She wanted to press herself against him and forget about that phone call. She glanced out the window as they hit the exit for the airport. "I'm so sorry, Jack. Last night was . . ." She caught herself, remembering that Alvin sat directly in front of her.

"Yeah. It was."

She heard the slam of a car door. "Are you back at the hotel?"

"Yep."

"I left you something. It's not nearly as cool as a coat."

He chuckled. "Yeah, you're not going to beat that anytime soon."

She grinned. "I'll phone you when I land?"

"Text. I'll probably go to bed early so I'm rested for tomorrow."

"I'll watch the game. Every second. Even though I'm not there, you'll know I'm seeing it, so your stats should still go up, right?"

Jack laughed out loud. "Wait, you know about that?"

She'd seen it on two different memes when she braved the internet before Tenille had reached out. "I like being your good luck charm."

There was the ding of an elevator. "I'm a big fan."

Delia's car pulled to a stop in front of the WestJet sign. "I have to go check in for my flight."

"Yep. Travel safe."

It felt wrong to say *sleep well* or *rest up* like she'd say to any random acquaintance. The words she felt in her soul bobbed to the surface like a cork, and she wasn't fast enough to shove them back under. "I love you, Jack."

Her throat closed like she'd just swallowed poison ivy. She shouldn't have said it—it was too soon, and then he was going to feel pressure to say it back, which she absolutely did not want, so she did what she did best and panicked. Which might've involved her finger pounding against the screen until she hung up on him.

"Nice." Alvin gave her a thumbs up, then opened his door and got out of the car.

———

DELIA
10:01 PM

Landed. Heading home. Hope you're sleeping

JACK
6:34 AM

I was out by 8:30. I feel superhuman. But maybe that's because of the bra

DELIA
8:56 A.M.

Lol. You found it

JACK
8:57 A.M.

I slept with it

DELIA
8:57 A.M.

Jealous

JACK
8:58 A.M.

How's your mom?

DELIA
8:59 A.M.

JACK
9 A.M.

Delia settled into the armchair she'd pulled across the room to be directly next to the couch. Her mother was asleep, and Delia was fairly certain no matter how high she turned up the volume, she wouldn't wake her.

She'd successfully gotten her in the door to their family doctor, who had tried to check her into the hospital, but when her mother started cursing in French, he relented and gave Delia all the instructions to care for her at home. She had pneumonitis and needed antibiotics and corticosteroids, which Dr. Kemp had been sure to keep just between him and Delia. *Vitamins. For the love of God, just tell her they're vitamins.*

Delia had followed his advice and successfully gotten the first doses down her mom's throat. Dr. Kemp had also threatened her mother with bad luck if she didn't drink a glass of water every hour. It didn't seem that Delia was going to have to force the issue on that, though she would have to wake her if she slept too long.

For the moment, things seemed to be looking up. Tonight, she would watch Jack play. Tomorrow, she'd clean the house and take flowers to Tenille. She wanted to be back in Edmonton cheering in the suite, but sitting there in her living room with her mom curled up on the couch felt equivalent to drinking a cup of tea next to a roaring fire. Her mother needed *her* for once, and she'd dropped everything and jumped on a plane. It made Delia inspect herself through a new lens, and she liked what she saw.

The puck dropped, and Delia glued her eyes to the screen, hunting for Jack at every moment, whether he was on the bench or the ice. While she was no hockey expert, she knew he was having a killer game. He stayed out longer than usual and rarely lost the puck to a defender. He was graceful and strong. *Superhuman was right.*

Her favourite plays were the ones where he skated in loops like he was carving a name in cursive on the ice. Not his name, a name with lots of s's and o's. It was beautiful. She cheered when he attacked the net, cringed when he slammed someone against the boards or got crunched himself, and sat on her hands as they entered the third period tied at ones.

"C'mon, Jack." She closed her eyes and tried to keep her silent prayer simple that time. *Help him show what he's capable of.* The crowd erupted, and Delia's eyes shot open. There was a huddle of blue jerseys with mitts slapping on helmets and she jumped from her seat. "Did they score?" she yelled at the glass. As if in response, the image cut to a replay of what she'd missed.

Gaudreau. He had the puck. Streaking down the ice. A defender barreled toward him, and he reared his stick back for a slapshot. The defender dodged right, and Gaudreau slowed his shot, tipping the puck left.

Where Jack was waiting.

Delia stood on her tiptoes. Jack arced toward the net, faked left, then flicked the puck toward the opposite side of the goal. It flipped end over end past the goalie's glove and landed in the back corner of the net.

Delia screamed. She jumped up and down. Then clapped her hands over her mouth and dropped to her knees to make sure she hadn't given her mother a heart attack.

———

. . .

On Thursday, Jack waited for Mary to roll another bag into the hall. He'd already taken two down and had no idea how many still awaited him. "I'm sure Tyler and Emma could've extended your rental."

Mary shook her head. "We didn't want to do that to them. They were already losing money by only charging us for the two rooms. It's not a big deal to get a hotel if we come back out."

If. That word landed like a sucker punch to his gut. *If?* Did Mary think they wouldn't be coming back out to Calgary? Jack's resolve to beat the Oilers compressed into granite. Two more games. Then it was a foregone conclusion they'd play the Maple Leafs. The first two games would be at home, but then he'd be in Toronto. The thought made the ache in his chest turn torturous.

Mary rolled out another suitcase, and Jack hoisted it up and carried it down the stairs. This was only temporary. Delia's mom would get better. The playoffs would eventually be over, one way or the other. He'd have the whole summer to spend however he wanted, unless he got signed for another season.

His goal in Edmonton had poured kerosene on that torch of hope. Had he done enough to prove himself? Doubtful. He'd sold tickets, but he'd been less than a team player for a majority of his time there. Last he'd heard, Beefus was healthy as a horse, but his doctor and physical therapist were requiring him to take another three weeks before hitting the ice.

Three weeks and his position on the Blizzard would be officially filled.

Alvin pulled up in a black SUV and parked in front of the steps to the house. Jack grabbed two of the suitcases and hauled them down to the sidewalk.

"Today's the day." Alvin popped the back hatch. His voice held a note of sadness, and it was only then that Jack wondered why Alvin was there in the first place.

"You're not—are you going out to Toronto to work for Delia?" Jack handed him a bag.

Alvin loaded it in the back and reached for the next one. "No, I'll be moving on to a new client. Starting next week."

"Another singer?"

"A politician."

Jack put his hands on his hips. "Anyone I'd know?"

"It's not something I can talk about."

"Right." A clatter sounded behind them, and they both looked up to the porch where Mary was attempting to bring two more suitcases out onto the step. Jack jogged back to help.

It didn't take long to get everything in the back, and after Mary ran back into the house twice for things she'd forgotten in the shower and the fridge, they were strapped in and ready to go.

Mary rolled down her window. "Good luck with the games. I know Delia wishes she could be here."

Jack's lungs compressed like a luggage strap was cinched tight around his ribs. "I wish she was, too."

"Her mom will get better." Mary started to raise the glass, then paused. "Hey, Jack? I know you're not on socials regularly, but you should probably check out Delia's channel. You might see something you like."

She winked as Alvin drove away from the curb, and Jack pulled out his phone. He clicked on the app, but it had to re-download since he hadn't used it once after spending a few hours answering comments on his video the week before.

He stared at his screen, watching the download pie slice get bigger over the square icon. Jack hoped Delia's mom would recover, of course he did, but that wasn't what was giving him heart palpitations. Delia living in Toronto and him in Calgary was now the permanent state of things. Unless he got fired from the Blizzard. Or Delia dropped her contract with IndieLake, if that was even possible.

What was their plan? To keep flying out and seeing each

other between games and shows? He dropped his fist against his chest. He'd spent three years on his own, but now he couldn't imagine spending a week without Delia there with him.

The download stalled, so he climbed the steps and locked up with the keys Tyler had given him, then strode to his truck. Just as the app opened, a message came through on his phone from the Blizzard's GM, Alex Renard. As if the Universe had heard his thoughts and wanted to pile on.

Jack. Meet me in my office at 4:30

CHAPTER

Thirty-One

JACK WALKED into the same office he'd stood in at the end of February when the Blizzard had offered him a spot on the team. When Alex told him about Beefus being injured. Then again when he'd been summoned by Alex and Lisa about the publicity surrounding Delia. Both of those meetings had left him feeling like he'd just eaten a Pizza Pop. Sweaty and conflicted.

"Jack, have a seat." Alex motioned to a leather chair in front of his desk, and when Jack walked in, he realized they weren't alone. Coach Novak and Kreviasuk were both already seated. Jack's stomach dropped like a lead brick. He'd gone too far. He'd overstepped again, and this time they didn't have to keep him on the roster for pretense.

He did as he was told and sat, his palms already cold and clammy. *It was fine.* He'd gotten to play in the NHL, something he never thought would happen. He'd scored two goals on the biggest ice in the world, and unlike the other night in the hotel with Delia, he didn't need it to last longer. He could go back to Big Rick or find a new job if they wouldn't have him. He'd work his way up, and . . .

His thoughts petered out. He didn't want to sit at home on his computer. He didn't want a desk job. He wanted to play hockey, and his attempts to find silver linings couldn't distract him from that fact.

"How have you liked playing on the team?" Alex sat behind the desk and pulled back a ball on his Newton's Cradle to send it ticking.

Jack swallowed. "It's been a dream come true." That wasn't an understatement. Even though he hadn't meshed immediately with the guys, he'd lived for practice and games the past two months. Now that he had a good thing growing with the other players, the energy between them on the ice was even more addictive.

"Well, you've certainly exceeded our expectations on and off the ice. It's not a typical occurrence to have a player going viral online for something we can applaud."

Jack chuckled. That was the truth. The last two massive hockey stories he'd heard were a sexual assault accusation and a racist statement given during a press conference. "It's been an honour representing this team. You've got a good group of guys. Good coaches, and I'm just grateful—"

Alex held up a hand and stopped him. "That sounds a hell of a lot like an exit speech." He looked to Novak, then back to Jack. "Do you think we're firing you?"

Jack's breath caught in his throat. "I assumed. Given that Beefus is back soon, and—" *And the recent conversation where I told my coaches their strategy wasn't working.* "My age."

Alex laughed. "Jack, your age has nothing to do with anything. I saw your physical results. You're healthy. Probably healthier than most players I've seen who are five years younger. You haven't even had a blown-out knee yet."

At least he had one thing to be grateful for after sitting on the bench with the Admirals. Less wear and tear. "I feel good."

"Glad to hear it because we'd like to offer you a spot. Not right winger because as you mentioned, Beefus is back. But . . ." He tapped his fingers on the desk. "We recently had a spot open up on the left."

Left winger. That was Gaudreau's position. And Liam MacDonald's.

Which meant they hadn't listened to him. He'd told Novak and Kreviasuk that Liam needed to feel a part of something, to feel wanted, and here they were kicking him to the curb right when he was finally taking steps to get better. It was short-sighted, and Jack couldn't in good conscience take his place. But was this the hill he was going to die on? Would he give up a permanent spot on the roster to prove his point?

Jack's heart started to sprint as he turned to his coaches. "I know you might not think I know what I'm talking about, but the kid just needs more time."

Coach Novak frowned. "Who needs more time?"

Jack threw out his hands. "MacDonald. If you cut him out now, he—"

"Harrison, we're not cutting MacDonald." Novak opened his mouth to say more but stopped and looked at Alex.

Alex nodded. "It's fine, you can tell him. But this doesn't leave the room."

Jack gripped the arms of his chair as Coach Novak started to talk. "Gaudreau's played with us for almost six years. He's the glue on this team, as you know. He and his wife just found out their four-year-old daughter has leukemia."

Air rushed out of Jack's lungs like he'd pulled the plug on an air mattress.

Novak continued, "The good news is that the treatment is good. Recovery rates at that age are higher than adults who are diagnosed, so they have all the hope in the world she'll come through treatment and enter remission, but he can't focus on anything else. He won't be able to focus on hockey, and he's built a good life for himself. He's going to announce his retirement after the series with Edmonton, win or lose."

Jack struggled to process. The idea of losing a child, or worse having to watch a child suffer, made him want to throw up. The idea of losing Gaudreau on the team because of it added another layer of injustice. Lastly, the thought that they would want him to replace such a giant . . . . "I don't know if I'm the right guy. Those are massive skates to fill."

Coach Novak leaned forward, resting his forearms on his knees. "Harrison, I'm not looking to build a team of heroes. I'm looking for guys that will get their ass out on the ice and work hard. Not make excuses. Lift their teammates up. I'm looking for loyalty and love for the game. You've shown us all of those things under a set of shit circumstances. Alex asked us who we wanted, and it's you. Alex agrees you're a solid choice. If you're up for it."

Jack's eyes stung at the corners, and he coughed to cover up his emotion. "Alex only agrees because he knows he doesn't have to pay me Gaudreau's salary."

Alex barked a laugh. "That's a plus." He grabbed a slip of paper from a stainless steel holder and scrawled something on it. "Here's the number we're prepared to offer you." He pushed it across the desk. "Obviously other details we need to work out, and if you want to get an agent . . ."

Jack stopped listening as soon as he saw the nine and the five were followed by five zeroes. "Yes. I'm up for it." He didn't even have to think about it. Should he have gotten an agent? Probably. But what leverage would they have? This was currently his only opportunity, and the only way he was going to increase his value was by playing in the big show.

Alex dropped his hands to the desk. "You know that's in Canadian dollars, right? Don't get too excited." Jack chuckled. "I'll have everything else drawn up and you can look it over. When Gaudreau officially announces we'll do the signing. Lisa will give you the date, and of course, Delia is invited to attend." He winked.

A sliver of ice wedged itself between Jack's ribs as he stood and shook Alex's hand, then thanked both of his coaches for the opportunity. It slid deeper as he strode to the door and pulled out his phone.

Everything he'd been working for had just come to fruition and the first person he wanted to talk to about it was the person this change of events would affect most. Jack wouldn't have the summer off. It wouldn't be practical for him to fly out to Toronto regularly, and was he that guy who would ask his girlfriend to make all the sacrifices? *Hell, no.*

As he rode the elevator to the ground floor, he pressed on the app he'd meant to open back at the bed and breakfast. It took him a moment to remember how to search, but he knew Delia's handle by heart since it had been tagged thousands of times on his one and only social media post.

When her channel populated, he clicked on the latest video and turned up the volume. There was Delia with her guitar. Her freckled nose and wavy hair that he'd give anything to run his hands through.

"I've been doing a little writing lately, and I wanted to share this verse with you today. Hope you like it." Delia grinned, and her nose wrinkled like a baby rabbit. When she started singing, Jack's heart flipped in his chest.

I met an older you and liked him,
    But I guess that's not a surprise,
    Since you've become something familiar,
    Like those school yard nursery rhymes

The elevator doors opened and closed, but Jack didn't notice. He stood transfixed by the plucked strings of her guitar. The curve of her shoulder. And her lips moving around words she'd written just for him.

———

. . .

Delia flopped down on the couch. "I miss you."

"I miss you, too."

She and Jack had talked nonstop since he'd phoned her Friday with the news of his contract. They talked about what it meant for his schedule. They talked about how sore he was after that last game in Edmonton and how he planned to up his protein for the next round. They talked about her mom. They talked about how Clara had officially announced her pregnancy over the weekend and how Jack was already looking for a new place.

They talked about the song she'd posted on TikTok that was already over a million views. Delia loved how Jack tried to dig deeper into the lyrics, fishing for her to admit the song was about him, but she couldn't quite do it because they talked about everything *except* what she'd blurted out on her way to the airport, and her song came from a deeper place than that.

She wanted to brush over the whole thing. Casually bring it up and say something like, *That was funny, wasn't it?* Blame it on being scared or overwhelmed with the emotion of the night before and make up some artistic explanation for the song lyrics.

It was petty, and in the end, she couldn't bring herself to do it. She *had* been panicking in the car, and she had posted that video after midnight. But what she'd said and sung hadn't been a result of emotional delusion. It had been truth escaping past her carefully constructed blockades.

Delia wasn't going to pretend anymore, at least not with herself. She had fallen for Jack way before that ride to the airport. Way before the hotel room. It had started that first night, if she was being honest. Probably had something to do with the way he fixated on her eyes. Or how he put his butt in the window. One of the two.

Then bit by bit that swell had grown like a chord progression, teasing her along until the final resolution.

And that was what Delia was afraid of.

That their song had peaked and they were slowly dribbling through the denouement. They kept stoking the coals with their phone calls and texts, hoping the fire could keep burning a little longer even though they could both see there were no more logs to add to the blaze.

Delia blew out a breath and kicked her legs up on the back of the sofa. "How do you think you'll stack up against the Leafs?"

"Look at you, using nicknames like you're an actual hockey fan."

She grinned. "And here I thought you'd be thrilled I'd taken an interest. Especially considering you still don't listen to lyrics."

Jack scoffed. "I told you, I listen when they're yours."

"Mmhmm. How did the announcement go?"

"Which one, Gaudreau's?"

"Both." She heard a clatter of dishes and imagined him in the kitchen. Maybe unloading the dishwasher after he'd taken a shower. Probably shirtless . . .

"The city is devastated to see him go. Especially under those circumstances. His DM's have been flooded."

"I can imagine. I'm guessing yours have been inundated, too?"

He hesitated, and Delia could tell he was trying to be modest. "Yeah, I think people are excited."

She scoffed. "Jack."

"What?"

"That's like saying you think people might attend the Eras tour."

He chuckled. "Yeah. The signing was a big deal."

"I know, I watched the livestream. Have you read through those comments? There were *fourteen thousand of them.* That's basically all of Alberta." That time he laughed louder, and tingles shot over her skin. "I'm so happy for you, Jack. I can't say it enough."

"Thanks, Dels."

Delia clutched at her heart as her whole body took a collective breath. She loved when he called her that. "So your first two games are at home?"

"Yep, first game is Friday."

"Two more days to rest up."

Jack laughed. "Try a thigh shredding practice first thing tomorrow morning. Then thirty-six hours to rest up."

"Same, same." Delia yawned. "I think I better get started on this bone broth. It's supposed to simmer overnight."

"I still can't believe you bought organic cow knuckle bones."

"Local organic grass-fed cow knuckle bones, thank you very much." She pulled her legs down from the couch and stood, knocking her ankle on the leg of the coffee table. She grimaced.

"You're a good daughter." There was a series of beeps, then the sound of a door closing. *He'd been loading dishes not unloading.* "I'll see you next week, then."

Delia nodded. No matter whether they won or lost these two games, they'd have to play one game in Toronto. She'd get to see him. The thought both thrilled and terrified her. "Yeah, and we'll talk before then."

"Mmhmm. Don't burn your house down."

Delia felt the big *"L"* land on her tongue, but that time she swallowed it. "Good night."

Jack hesitated. "'Night."

Delia groaned as she set her phone on the counter. Why was it so hard? Why did she have to walk around in the world as if she wasn't one of those pressurized cans that would shoot snakes the second her lid popped off. She couldn't tell Christian what she thought of the music they were supposedly producing together, and she couldn't own up to her feelings with Jack because—because *why?*

She picked her phone back up and swiped to her email, then opened up the statement IndieLake had sent over that morning. Four thousand dollars. She'd earned out, and she was getting four grand deposited into her account.

That number wasn't impressive on its own, even though it felt like a veritable windfall compared to the nothing she'd been depositing for eight months. It was the breakdown above it that sent her heart into palpitations. She'd brought in sixty-three grand in a *month*. Even with all her expenses, had that money not been applied to her balance, she would've taken home forty-seven thousand dollars.

In a month.

Delia set her phone down and grabbed the bag of beef skeleton from the fridge, then used a knife to slice open the packaging. She tried not to inspect the bones too closely as she dropped them into her mother's massive stock pot. Why she owned such a large piece of cookware when there were only two of them in the house was beyond her.

Delia glanced back at the recipe and blew out a breath. *Right.* She was supposed to chop the vegetables first. *Sauté them?* Optional. Definitely opting out on that one. She walked to the fridge and opened the door, then pulled out the celery and carrots. Setting them on the counter, she reached up into the hanging colander her mother kept filled with onions and squealed.

The sensation was wet and smushy, both things that onions were not supposed to be. She tilted the bowl and looked inside to find three onions, all of them shrivelled and weeping. Kind of like her soul at that moment. Delia's face pinched as she grabbed them and threw them in the trash, then used a damp paper towel to wipe out the colander and thoroughly scrubbed her hands with lemon dish soap.

Now what? She couldn't make bone broth without onions. Unless she wanted it to taste only of cow knuckle, which sounded abjectly terrible. Knowing her mother, she'd probably find the lack of flavour more appealing, but Delia couldn't bring herself to make a partial batch. *I don't do things halfway.* Ugh. Did everything have to remind her of Jack?

She stomped into the living room and pulled her coat—*the*

coat—from the closet. She stopped at the door. The grocery store was eight minutes away and open until eleven. She could hop in the car, buy the onions, and be back in just over twenty.

Mary's voice rang in her head as she touched her hand to the doorknob. *"Dels, those days are gone. You can't just get in the car and go somewhere, okay? You need to phone your security guard every single time. I know it's crazy, but you just never know when some weirdo is going to spot you in a parking lot or when a crowd of people is going to amass. Love it or hate it, I'm going to use the C-word. You're a full-on celebrity now, babes."*

She dropped her hand from the door and dialed her new on-call guard service in Toronto. They'd already done their risk assessment of her home and community and it still felt pretentious to ring and ask them to bring a car around. But Mary was paying them for twenty-four seven service, so she might as well use it.

Within fifteen minutes of her call, the car was out front. Delia waited like she was supposed to even though the street seemed sleepier than a bear in the middle of winter. When Bryce, the guard who had taken them to the airport ages ago, was on her step, she opened the door.

"I'm sorry to bug you."

He checked that the door locked behind her. "Not bugging. This is my job."

"What do you do when I don't need you?" she asked as they walked down the steps. She was hoping for something juicy, but all she got was,

"Usually watch the news."

Barf. Delia tried to look pleasant as she slid into the back seat. "Is 'the news' a cover for reality TV? Ooh! Or that channel on TikTok where rabbits eat strawberries that are magically growing on vines so the bunnies have to lift up on their little hind legs to reach them?"

Bryce gave her a look in the rearview mirror. "Seatbelt?" She nodded. "Do you have a purse?" Delia held it up. "How many kilograms?"

She scoffed and pulled her purse to her chest. "We don't ask ladies about their weight."

He rolled his eyes. "Just secure it with the clip there on the console. So it doesn't become a projectile."

Delia did as he asked, disappointed she hadn't at least succeeded in dragging a lip-twitch out of him. *It was fine.* She'd win him over, just like Alvin. Though, that had probably been more Mary's doing.

As Bryce pulled the car away from the curb, Delia pulled out her phone and texted her friend.

> How many more booty calls is it going to take to convince Alvin to move to Toronto?

We're back on this again?

> These guys are stuffy

That's good. It means they're doing their job

> When do you get back from the Etobicoke?

Tomorrow. Meet up for lunch? Then . . . take that meeting with Christian?

Delia frowned. How was it that Christian was so uncommunicative before releases and then wouldn't lay off when she was trying to delay a meeting for the first time since they'd started working together.

She started typing.

Has he been texting you, too? I told him—

Her head whipped up. Their horn blared. Bright lights blinded her from the window on the opposite side of the car.

"Hands over your head!" Bryce barked from the front seat.

Delia somehow managed to do as she was told, and her phone clattered to the rubber mat. It was the last sound she heard before the screeching tires and the crunch of metal.

CHAPTER
Thirty-Two

JACK STARTLED awake to Clara shaking his shoulder. It brought him straight back to his childhood when he'd slept past his alarm for school. He grunted. "What is it?" His barely awake brain went to all kinds of weird places. Fire? Lost kitten? It wouldn't have been the first time.

"Jack, you need to take this." Clara shoved her phone in his face, and he pushed to sitting. He blinked to clear his vision, but couldn't read the name ticking across the top of the screen. Before he'd even raised his hand, Clara pushed the phone against his ear.

"Hello?"

"Jack? Oh, thank God. I've been trying to phone you for an hour and finally found Clara's number in Delia's phone—"

"*Mary?*" Adrenaline surged through him. Why would Mary be phoning him? Why would she be desperate enough to look up his sister's number? He grabbed his phone off the nightstand, yanking the charging cord from the wall. It was only ten o'clock. He'd only been asleep for forty-five minutes. *Fifteen missed calls.*

"Delia was in an accident."

Jack's blood ran cold as everything seemed to drop into slow motion. *There was an accident. She was driving over to drop off the ladder she'd borrowed from the garage.* Jack was sitting at the table across from Tony in darkness, his eyes fixed on Delia under the spotlight as he absorbed her lyrics. *I've never been one to reach for the stars because flying has never felt safe.* He was standing in his apartment in Toronto, listening to Angie's mother weep on the other end of the line. *She's gone, Jack.*

"They took her to Toronto General," Mary continued in a rush. "I tried to phone her, but she's not answering. The only reason I knew is because the security team dinged me—Bryce, her security guard was driving."

"Is she—how bad—" Jack couldn't form words into sentences. Clara sat next to him on the bed wringing her hands.

"I don't know, I'm driving over now. I already phoned her mom and Tony. I'll keep you post—"

"I'm on my way." Jack stood, throwing off his sheets and ripping open his dresser drawer.

"On your—Jack, no, I wasn't trying to tell you to get on a plane right—"

"I'm on my way." He dropped the call and tossed Clara's phone onto the bed next to her.

"You have a game on Friday." Clara's eyes were glassy.

"I'm well aware." Jack yanked a pair of trousers from his drawer and shoved his legs into them, then grabbed a shirt and shoved the drawer closed.

Clara looked as if she was going to protest again, but instead she adjusted her robe and stood. "I'll drive you. Oscar can look for a flight while we're on our way. Just let me throw on some clothes."

———

Jack bolted from security the second his backpack came through the machine. He had twenty minutes to get to his gate. Oscar had reached the airline and convinced them to give Jack a seat on the 11:55 p.m. flight. Clara had sped for probably the first time in her life to get him to the airport in record time. Thankfully, because of the late hour, the place was mostly empty.

He was a sweaty mess when he arrived at the still-open door to the walkway. "Jack. Harrison." They'd called his name over the speakers in the terminal twice. He held out his phone so the attendant could scan his boarding pass.

"Glad you made it." She smiled and motioned for him to go through the door.

The past hour and a half of his life settled against his bones as he made the walk to the plane. Delia was in an accident. *How? When?* He'd been talking to her right before he'd gone to sleep. Why had she left the house?

He found his seat and settled in next to the window, shoving his backpack under the seat. He needed to let his coaches know. He was supposed to be at practice the next morning. Getting permission hadn't even crossed his mind. The second Mary had said Delia was headed to the hospital, his mind had been made up.

What if she's already gone? The thought gnawed at his insides with razor teeth. It wasn't possible. He'd already lost someone he loved in a car accident, and there was no way that could happen twice.

The thought of Delia being taken from him was like being hit by a bucket of scalding water. It washed over him, sweeping away any excuses or rationalizations for why he'd acted the way he had with her. Why he'd pulled back so hard in the beginning. Why he'd harboured so much guilt at the thought of touching her.

Even then he'd known. He'd recognized something in her from the second he'd heard her perform that night at the club. Like chemistry on the ice, he could just feel it. Sense it. As much as he'd tried to push it away, that connection had worn away at him like water through sand.

That night in the hotel room had punched a hole in that dam he'd built three years ago. Then when she said, "I love you" on the way to the airport? Everything had broken loose.

And not just the good things.

He *felt* again, and it sent him reeling. He'd barely held it together long enough to get food in the suite, then holed up in his hotel room and cried like a baby.

He loved her.

He didn't think it was possible to love again like that. He didn't think he was capable of loving. He hated that Angie was gone. Hated that she might exist somewhere and know that he was moving on. But that locked room of his soul had finally burst open and he was *alive* again. Whole.

Sitting on that plane, he kicked himself for not phoning Delia that night and saying those words back to her. For not having a conversation the next morning or the one after that.

As the plane pressurized, he finally understood why he'd hesitated. *That feeling.* The one that came with love, the flip side of that coin. With love came fear. He'd thought it was only fear of them not being able to arrange their lives in a way that allowed them both to fit, but he'd been wrong.

It was how he'd felt on the other end of that phone call.

Sitting on the Blizzard bench for the first time.

Walking back into his empty hotel room.

Watching Mary and Alvin drive away from the bed and breakfast.

"Ladies and gentlemen, this is your captain speaking from the flight deck. Welcome aboard Flight 257 with service from Calgary to Toronto. We're completing our final checks and will be ready to take off in just a few moments. We're expecting a smooth flight ahead of us. Our flight time today will be approximately three hours and fifty-five minutes, arriving just before six in the morning local time . . ."

Jack pulled his bluetooth headphones from the front pocket

of his bag and turned on Delia's single. The one she secretly hated. His stomach pulled tight like a knotted rope as he thought of her smile. The freckles in her eyes.

He had no control over this. He'd had no control over his career, no control over his engagement ending, and damn, if he hadn't worked himself to the bone to try and control everything after that night. Yet here he was again, the rug being ripped out from under him.

Jack stared out the window as the plane rumbled along the runway, then sped until the wings found lift. He kept watching until the Calgary city lights faded into tiny specs, then shut the window shade and closed his eyes to the sound of Delia's voice.

———

The second the plane touched down, Jack turned on his phone. He didn't even wait for his texts to come through, just dialed Mary's number.

"Hey, Jack—"

"Have you seen her? How is she?" He was desperate to quell the chaos in his gut.

"I'm here. She's fine. Just sleeping."

The words didn't process at first. *She's fine. Just sleeping.* "What does that mean?"

Mary exhaled. "It means her driver is a damn genius, that's what it means." She went on to explain the accident in detail. How Bryce had gone forward on a green light and some dumb-ass truck hadn't stopped at the red. He'd reacted with the least intuitive move possible and turned his car toward the incoming vehicle while he gunned the gas. It meant the front right side of the car took most of the impact instead of the back where Delia was. It meant that instead of a straight-on perpendicular collision that would have slammed their car into oncoming traffic, the car spun to the sidewalk. Jack didn't realize he was crying until the A/C cranked up and cooled the moisture on his cheeks.

"He saved her life, Jack. If not that, he at least saved her bones from breaking," Mary finished.

Jack fought to drag air into his lungs. "Nothing's broken?"

"Nope. She had to get stitches for a cut on her elbow. Would've been her head, but she ducked and her arm hit the glass instead. They kept her here overnight because of a potential concussion and shock. She's going to be sore when she wakes up, but she should be able to walk out as soon as they get her paperwork."

Jack swallowed the lump in his throat. "Thank you. For the update." He wiped his nose across the back of his hand. "I'll be there as soon as I can get an Uber."

Mary exhaled. "You're crazy, you know that? I can't believe you even found a flight that late. Oh, here, just a second." She moved the phone away from her mouth and started talking to someone. When she returned, she said, "Visiting hours don't start until nine, so find something to do until then. The nurse told me they'll get a doctor in to assess things as soon as their shift changes."

Jack's skin started to itch. He'd barely slept, he was starving, and the last thing he wanted someone to tell him was that he had to kill a few hours. "How are you there if hours don't start until nine?"

Mary lowered her voice. "Because I told them I'm her sister."

"You look nothing alike."

"I told them I was adopted. My brother said it all the time growing up, and it finally came in handy."

The seatbelt light turned off and Jack grabbed his backpack from under the seat. "Then I'll tell them I'm her husband."

"Uh, too late for that. I already filled out the form saying she was single."

"She's not single." Why would they ask that on a hospital intake form?

"Jack, I'm sorry. It was the middle of the night and the thought didn't cross my mind that you might make it here before visiting hours."

That was fair. He'd caught the last flight out of Calgary by the skin of his teeth. Anything else would've put him in the city around noon. "I'll be there at nine. Thank you for taking care of her."

"The doctors did the hard part. See you soon."

Jack stood with the other passengers and dropped his phone in his pocket. Once they were off the airplane, he headed straight to the rideshare pick-up location and scheduled a trip to Maha's. It was well past the hospital, but it had been one of his favourite haunts when he'd lived in Toronto.

He rode through the city in a daze, grateful his driver wasn't chatty. When he arrived, he tipped the driver, then waited for a table for one. It wasn't until he sat down and ordered that he remembered why he'd found Maha's in the first place.

Pieces clicked into position, shifting and moving like a Rubik's cube until the colours were complete. Of course he'd ended up here. He knew exactly what he had to do next.

Jack ate to the sound of conversation and clinking forks. His body drooped, his head thick. It was bad enough, he briefly considered booking a hotel room for a few hours until he realized the only hotels that would allow that wouldn't have rooms or sheets he'd want to nap in. Instead, he finished his meal and started walking. In the past, he'd driven to this part of town, but since he didn't have a car and the weather was surprisingly warm for seven in the morning in April, he opted to walk.

It was a thirty-minute walk to the cemetery, and the tip of his nose and his cheeks were chilled by the time he made it to the gates. He pulled. They didn't budge. He trudged to the corner and read the sign that listed their posted hours from eight until four, then sat on a bench in full sunlight.

He'd nearly dozed off with his arms wrapped around his backpack when the jangle of chains snapped the world back into focus. He stood and followed the caretaker through the gates, then started down the path he had memorized. He pressed a hand against the trunk of the ancient maple that marked Angie's row, then walked down the aisle of barely green grass.

Jack stopped in front of the headstone he'd visited weekly when he still lived there. The one he hadn't come to in over two years.

Angela Merrick (1995 - 2021)
A spirit too bright for this world, whose love and laughter will forever light our way.

He'd been pissed that her mother had fought for that statement for her headstone. It had seemed too generic. Maybe it still did. But he'd given in when her eyes had shimmered with tears, and he didn't regret that.

Jack dropped to his knees, wishing he'd thought to bring flowers. "Hey, Ange." His voice sounded strange in the stillness. The sounds of the city were far enough away, all he could hear were the birds. "I still miss you."

It sounded like a confession. *I still miss you, even though . . .* Jack ran his hands through his hair. "I came here today because I love you, and I needed to tell you the truth, so here it goes. I've spent the last three years wishing you didn't get in that accident. My life would've been so different—so much richer. Instead I went back to living with hockey teammates, now with Clara, and I couldn't ever make my NHL dream happen, either. So that time we argued, and I told you that you wanted too much from me? That I needed more time on the ice? Yeah. I was dead wrong. More time didn't solve the problem. Especially not away from you."

He paused and pulled a fresh spring shoot out of the dirt. "Then I got a dream job. You would've called it a miracle." He chuckled and shifted to sit on the ground. "That was terrifying and . . . probably the most fun I've had since you left. Which brings me to the last part of my story." Jack's chest tightened, and he clenched his jaw. "I met someone, Ange. At first it was just this game we were playing for the press, but I think I knew right from the get-go that it was going to be more than that if I let it. I didn't want to, at first. I felt like I would be letting you down. But then, it wasn't something I could fight anymore."

Jack looked up and ran his eyes over her name. The dates she'd lived. "Delia got in an accident last night. I know. Dark irony. But that's why I'm here. The second I heard something had happened, I didn't even think. I had to get here to Toronto, and the only other time I've experienced that was—" Jack's voice caught. He took a minute, working against the emotion welling up like water in a bucket. He coughed and cleared his throat. "Was when you phoned and asked me if I wanted to go to the rink. That night we met up with Sammy and Eva. That was the night I knew I wanted to marry you."

He wiped his eyes and drew in a ragged breath. "So. I don't know how things will go from here, but I love her, Ange. I wanted you to be the first to know."

Jack sat on the chilled ground and waited. What for, he didn't know. A pillar of light? A bird to land on her headstone? Something mystical to show he had her approval?

He listened to the waking city and searched for any sense of that feeling Country had described. Something whispering this was unfinished.

His heart laid still.

And he knew.

After a few minutes, Jack exhaled and patted the dirt, then

dragged himself up and slung his backpack over his shoulders. He whispered one last *I love you*, then started back to the gates.

DELIA LAUGHED when the first thought that came to her head was that she ached like she'd been hit by a truck.

"You just woke up, and you're giggling?" Mary stood from her chair and approached the hospital bed. Her hair was a mess, and she had raccoon eyes from smeared mascara.

Delia groaned when she tried to turn her neck, and pain shot up her spine. "I wasn't giggling."

Mary rolled her eyes. "How do you feel?"

"Like shit."

"Excellent. That means you're lucid." Mary pulled up the sleeve of her hospital gown. "Doesn't look like it's bleeding anymore."

Delia tried to see the gauze but couldn't make her head move far enough. She glanced up at the clock. Quarter to nine. Before she could announce her current state of starvation, Mary turned and lifted a bag from the chair next to hers. "Tony couldn't come since he's not *family*, but he had Kels drop off a breakfast bagel." She winked.

Delia sighed and sank back into her pillows. She doubted Tony would've made the effort to come by even if he could've visited, but the thought definitely counted for something. "I've always loved Kels." Mary handed her the bag, and she pulled out the sandwich. She'd almost fully unwrapped it when she paused, her eyes widening.

"Yes, they have toothbrushes here," Mary said dramatically.

Delia grinned and tore off the rest of the paper. Her senses lit up like a Christmas tree as she bit into the just slightly soggy bagel, her teeth sinking into herby cream cheese, crispy bacon, and scrambled egg. She wanted to groan with pleasure, and that immediately made her think of Jack drooling over his steak in his hotel room. She shot up in bed and winced. "Jack?" His name came out a garbled mess, but somehow Mary still understood.

"I phoned him last night. He's—"

Delia's door swung open, revealing her morning nurse with an annoyed expression. "Your boyfriend won't take no for an answer." She moved to the side and Jack stalked into the room with energy like a caged mountain cat. Wild and desperate. "For the record, visiting hours start at nine, not eight fifty." She gave him one last disapproving look, then closed the door and left.

Delia could barely breathe through the frantic beat of her heart. When she tried to say something, she realized she'd stopped chewing and her mouth was still full of bagel. She hurriedly finished her bite and wiped the cream cheese from the side of her mouth. After she swallowed, she met his eyes. He was still standing there at the foot of the bed. Staring at her. "You're here?"

It didn't seem possible. He must've gotten on a plane the second she crashed.

Jack let the backpack slide off his shoulder. He looked over at the chair next to Mary, but Delia held out a hand. "No. Sit here. Please." She patted the side of the bed Mary had just vacated.

He dropped the bag and rounded the bed, then sat so close she could smell his deodorant. His real kind that time, not the Edmonton travel version. The clean scent made her skin buzz.

Jack ran his hands over her, gentle and probing, like he was searching for anything the doctors missed. "That's the cut?" He fingered the edges of the gauze.

Delia nodded as much as she could without inciting another pain spike. "All stitched up."

"Where's Bryce?" he asked.

Mary pointed to the door. "He's down the hall. Just got the X-rays back. He has a broken wrist." Jack blew out a breath.

"I think I owe him an apology." Delia laced her fingers in his, remembering the conversation she and Bryce had on the way to the car.

"Why?"

"I might have been giving him crap about being too uptight."

Mary folded her arms over her chest. "I told you it meant he was good at his job."

Delia had gotten the rundown after the stitches when she was too full of adrenaline and nerves to fall to sleep immediately. From the sounds of it, she owed Bryce more than an apology. Probably a steak. And her firstborn child.

Jack reached out with his free hand and tapped her sandwich. "You should finish eating."

Delia snapped her mouth closed. She'd been talking that whole time with chive breath.

When she didn't move, Jack pushed it closer. "Don't make me chew it for you and feed you like a baby bird." He looked just serious enough, Delia relented. She took another bite and offered it to him. He shook his head. "I already stopped for food. Had to kill some time." He ground his teeth, and Delia fought back a smile.

Mary started asking him about the flight over, and soon they were chatting about how much they hated drink services on overnight flights. By the time they'd agreed that no lights or announcements should be made between the hours of midnight and five, Delia's stomach was full. She handed Jack the trash, then nudged him. "I need to go to the washroom."

Jack moved out of the way and held onto her waist as she

padded in her hospital socks to the toilet. "Do you need me to stay?"

She balked and shooed him out of the room, then regretted it as she swayed a bit trying to pull up her gown. She made it onto the toilet safely, then cleaned up and opened the door. Jack was there waiting to walk her back. As soon as she was settled, he spread out her blankets and sat back at her side. His hand rested over her leg just under her knee, and suddenly she wasn't thinking about Bryce or the accident or the fact that she'd been in such a rush, she'd forgotten to brush her teeth in the washroom.

She was wholly focused on the man sitting next to her. The man who'd flown across the country overnight to make sure she was okay. The man who offered to stand next to her while she peed.

"What happened to the cow knuckles?" he asked, his voice low.

Delia's lips twitched. "My mom probably lost it when she woke up this morning and saw a pot of raw bones on the stove."

"She hasn't seen you yet?"

"No. She's still sick. I told her to hang tight since I was being discharged in a bit." Delia thought back to the conversation she had with Jack before the onion debacle. "You have practice. Right now." She looked too fast at the clock and sucked in a breath at the sharp pain in her shoulders.

"I texted my coaches. They're aware of the situation."

"But you need that practice. You have a game—"

"Delia, it's fine." He squeezed her hand.

But it wasn't fine. From the second she'd been staring into the headlights of that truck, all she'd seen in her head was Jack. When she was in the ambulance and realized her phone was back on the floor of the crushed car, all she'd wanted to do was hear his voice. When she was sitting in triage, the only person she'd wanted sitting next to her was Jack Harrison.

Now, here he was, sharing her hospital bed, and everything he was doing told her he had the same feelings she did. But—

Delia's thoughts vanished like smoke. Jack's hand wasn't on her leg anymore. He was . . . wiggling her toe? She blinked and watched his hand move from her toe to her knee, then back to her foot. "What are—?"

Jack looked up and the question withered on her lips. His eyes were dark. Glassy. He pressed her toe a third time, then tapped her knee and somehow with her crash addled brain, the pieces tumbled into place.

Delia lifted her hand and touched her chest, then her forehead. A smile spread across Jack's face, so slow it was like watching a flower bloom. She watched as Jack touched the corner of his eye, then put a hand over his heart, and finally pointed straight at her.

"Peerrrfect." Mary leaned past Jack with her phone. "Tony made me promise I'd get some good pub shots of the two of you." She straightened and looked at the screen. "Delia, why are you—?" Her head snapped up, confusion written all over her face.

Delia reached up and swiped the tears from her cheeks. "I love you, Jack. I love you so much—"

Jack leaned forward and gingerly pressed her into his chest. Delia barely heard Mary mumble something about ruining their moment. She didn't register the click of the door as it closed.

Jack's voice as he whispered, "*I love you, I love you, I love you,*" filled every nook and cranny of her being. Her world narrowed to the rumble of his throat against her shoulder. The pressure of his broad hands against her back. She kissed his neck, tasting the salt of her tears and the warmth of his skin.

Not once did she think about the faint hint of cream cheese, bacon, and chive.

———

Delia winced as she got out of the car. "You don't have to do this."

Jack gave her a look. "I'm not going to let you unload the groceries."

"But your flight leaves at six—"

"Which is still four hours from now." Jack went straight to the trunk. He and her new security guard took over, so she acquiesced and walked to the front door, slipped in her key, and opened it.

Delia barely took a step inside before her mother was there, wrapping her in her arms. "Oh, mon chou." Her mother stroked her hair, then pulled back and inspected her. She clucked when she saw the gauze poking out from under her T-shirt.

"It's fine, Mom. I'm okay. How are you?"

Her mother dropped her arms. "Better. Those vitamins are working wonders."

Delia bit back a smile and turned as Jack appeared in the doorway, his arms laden with paper grocery sacks.

Her mother looked up and her eyes widened. "Jack Harrison."

Delia exhaled. The sky behind him was grey, bringing out the warmth of his skin "Jack, this is my mom, Camille."

Jack set the bags on the ground, then strode forward and wrapped his arms around her. Her mother let out a small gasp, then her face split into the first real smile Delia had seen since coming home.

Jack pulled back. "It's wonderful to meet you." Delia's ovaries twitched as he turned and bundled the groceries back in his arms, then scanned the living room. "Your house is beautiful."

Her mother's cheeks flushed. "Don't you have a game tomorrow?"

He grinned and took his shoes off. "You follow hockey?"

Her mother nodded, and Delia scoffed. "Since when?"

She shrugged, and Delia knew what that meant. She didn't follow hockey so much as one player in particular.

Delia motioned for Jack to walk with her to the kitchen. There was so much she hadn't told her mom yet. Their phone calls had been sporadic at best while she was in Calgary, and when they had talked, there hadn't been anything new to share.

Now, there was everything.

"Mom, what did you do with the beef bones?" Delia turned in a circle looking for the stock pot.

"When Mary phoned, I couldn't get back to sleep. They were still frozen, so I put them back in the freezer."

Delia reached excitedly into one of the shopping bags and pulled out a sack of onions. "I know what we're doing tonight."

Jack pulled out the apples and cucumbers. "I'm devastated I won't be here for it."

Delia nudged his arm and set down the onions, then transferred the other fruits and veggies to the fridge. When she turned, her mom was watching her with a satisfied expression. *"What?"* she mouthed.

"I didn't sleep well, so I'm off for a nap. Lovely to meet you, Jack Harrison."

He turned, holding a head of romaine. "The pleasure was all mine."

As her mother turned down the hall, Delia exhaled. "You've gone and made her fall in love with you."

"Good." Jack grabbed onto her waist and reeled her in.

Delia grimaced as pain shot across her shoulders. "Sorry. Fast movements."

He curled his hand around her neck, as if he were cradling a Fabergé egg. "No, I'm sorry. I wasn't thinking." Jack smoothed his thumb over her skin and wrapped his other arm around her waist. His eyes dropped to her lips, and he kissed her.

She'd been bone weary after the accident, but breathing him in had the same effect on her as smelling salts. "What is that scent?"

Jack grinned against her lips. "It's called all night on an airplane and—"

"No!" Delia laughed. "*Your* smell. It's your deodorant or cologne or something. I can't figure it out." She'd looked for his toiletries in the hotel room, but none of them had been sitting on the counter.

He kissed her again. "I don't wear cologne." *Kiss.* "I used to in college." *Kiss.* "But then I dated a girl who was allergic to synthetic fragrances." *Kiss.* "I never went back."

Delia grinned. "Thank you for the thorough explanation."

"I knew you'd want the details." *Kiss. Kiss.*

"So deodorant, then."

"Must be." *Kiss.* "I have it in my bag." He pulled back, but Delia gripped his waist.

"I'd rather smell it on you. Products smell different when they aren't on skin."

Kiss. "True."

Delia leaned back as far as she could without her neck complaining and trailed her hands up his arms until her fingers slipped under the soft cotton of his shirt sleeves. "You said four hours till your flight leaves?"

Jack's eyes turned liquid. "Mmhmm."

"So . . . you have an hour before you need to leave for the airport."

"At least." His fingers trembled against her skin. Jack watched her for a long moment, his chest rising and falling like he was fighting for more air. "I was so relieved when I landed. When Mary told me you were okay."

Delia nodded. She reached up and pushed his dark hair off his forehead. *Relief.* She thought of everything Jack had told her over the past month. She remembered the first time she saw him in person. The image of him sitting at the table with his sister, Tony, and Kels at the concert flooded her mind. How the lights turned from glaring to a soft purple haze, making his face visible for a few seconds, and when she'd looked in his eyes, the only song that had filled her head was "Oubliet."

"Dans le soulagement et le regret," she whispered.

Jack lifted her hand and kissed the inside of her wrist. "De toi, je n'ai point oubliet." Delia's eyes widened, and his lips curved into a slow smile. "I know those lyrics. Because they're yours."

Delia's throat grew thick. "So. Relief." She swallowed hard. "What about regret?"

Jack shook his head, pressing his cheek against her palm, and her lips flushed with heat. "No regret. Not anymore."

She pressed up on her tiptoes and kissed Jack's cheek, then ignored the produce still sitting on the kitchen table, laced her fingers with his, and pulled him down the hall to her bedroom.

They say it's a door only I can open, but I don't want to let out the heat. The words of her song poured through her, line after line, and she wondered how she'd write it differently then.

All of it.

All of it would be different.

She was still terrified of flying, but had jumped on a plane without hesitation when it mattered. She was still afraid of letting people see through her doors, but with Jack, no amount of trying had kept them closed anyway.

J'aime, donc je vole. *I love, so I fly.*

J'aime, donc j'ouvre. *I love, so I open.*

Jack's hands were on her waist the second they crossed the threshold. His body close behind her. His breath on her temple, his lips against the shell of her ear.

Delia's hand shot back for the waistband of his jeans.

His voice was gruff. "Careful, Dels. No fast movements."

She sucked in a breath as he pressed the door closed behind them and oh so gently turned her around to face him.

She would write a new song. About feet that left the ground. About doors that opened.

When it was safe.
When it was earned.
Love.
Relief.
But no regret.
Not anymore.

Epilogue

DELIA DREW A DEEP BREATH, held it for seven seconds, then exhaled and strode into Christian's office.

"Hey, there she is." Christian stood and stepped in front of his desk to give her a side hug that quickly turned awkward when she led with her shoulder to protect him from torquing her still sore neck. He cleared his throat and walked back to his desk. "How are you feeling?"

"I'm ok, considering."

He adjusted the sports coat hanging on the back of his chair and sat down. "I still can't believe that happened. When Mary phoned, I thought you were cooked."

Delia sat in one of the modern bucket seats arranged in front of the desk. "Well, thanks for pushing off the meeting."

"Your mom's doing better?"

Delia looked up, surprised. She didn't think he'd listened to a word she'd said after telling him she couldn't meet when he wanted to. "She is. That's actually—"

"I've got some new beats I want you to work with Finn on, and—"

"Christian, before we get into all that, I have some paperwork I'd like you to look at." Delia dropped a manila envelope on his desk.

He frowned and flipped it open. "What is this?"

Delia started to sweat. "I've been working with an entertainment lawyer. I had her look over my contract, and we found a clause that we believe warrants early termination."

Christian's frown deepened. His mouth moved as he scanned the text. ". . . artist development and support? Are you kidding me with this?" His head snapped up, his eyes blazing.

"I haven't had any vocal coaching, songwriting support, or marketing classes, and—"

"Delia, we've taken you from nothing and made you a superstar."

Delia clenched her hands into fists. "And I've made Indie-Lake a hell of a lot of money. If you'd keep reading, you'll see that I'm not asking to terminate. I'm only asking for a few adjustments to my current contract."

Her legs started to shake as Christian returned to the cover page. He read it once, then started again at the top. Finally he exhaled and closed the folder. "You want last say on your lyrics. I understand that. But you have to know that what you want and what your audience wants are two different things."

She nodded. "I get it. But I think I'll be able to find a new audience with—"

"At what cost, Delia? If you're not profitable for the label, then why would we keep you on board?"

She swallowed hard. "I just want an opportunity, Christian." She held out her phone, showing him the video with Jack's song. Two million and counting. "I think I have an audience. But, if it goes south, we can write something in. I'll give it up if it's not gaining traction."

He tapped a finger to his lips. "I'll send a counteroffer through your lawyer. But the Calgary thing . . ." He shook his head. "Why would you want to relocate? There are less than half the resources there, and—"

"It's all done digitally, Christian, and working with Ethan proves there are good studios. I can record there and still work with Finn."

"It's not the same and you know it."

"Then I find someone else." Guilt trickled through her at the thought of writing off Finn when he'd been a huge part of her success, but her loyalty to anyone here in Toronto couldn't hold a candle to the way her heart was being dragged toward the Rockies.

His eyes narrowed. "Is it because of that hockey player? I thought Tony said there was an imminent breakup where he was concerned."

Delia tucked her hair behind her ear. "There's been a change to that contract, as well."

———

Delia swung her arm, taking Jack's with it. It was three weeks out from her accident and she barely noticed the twinge in her neck anymore. "It's so much warmer here."

He grinned. "I know. It's like Calgary plus ten degrees."

"Celsius or Fahrenheit? That makes a difference."

Jack grinned. "I can't believe I have the honour of accompanying you on your first trip outside of Canada."

Delia groaned. "I know, it's pathetic."

Jack pulled her closer as they walked and kissed the top of her head. "Not pathetic. It means we have a whole world to explore."

Delia stopped, and Jack turned back on the sidewalk. He sauntered toward her and dropped his hands on her shoulders. "You okay?"

She nodded, scanning the brick buildings and the strings of

patio bulbs threaded in giant V's over the street. Being in Denver was magical. Not only because the air was warm like actual spring, but because she'd only been recognized *twice*. Jack had been stopped more than that, but there hadn't been any paparazzi. No swarming crowds. Alvin had even let them walk around most of the time without a chaperone, and the entire weekend had been a dream.

Delia looked up at Jack through her lashes. "You probably need some rest, right? For the game tonight?" The Blizzard had soundly beaten the Leafs three to one and now were starting off round three of the playoffs with the Avalanche. It all felt very exotic. Especially since she'd already played her pop-up show the night before and was in full fangirl mode.

The corner of Jack's mouth lifted. "Your idea of rest and Coach Novak's idea of rest are wildly different."

Delia snagged a finger in his belt loop and yanked. "Well, I should hope so."

Jack slid his hand under the hem of her shirt. "I could go back to the room."

Delia's pulse jumped as he gave her backside a gentle squeeze, then retreated down the sidewalk toward the hotel. She hustled to catch up, still gripping his hand.

"I brought the bra." He kept his gaze trained on the sidewalk ahead of them.

Delia's mouth dropped open. "You've had it here for *two days* and didn't tell me?" He smirked, and she playfully smacked his arm. "When am I going to get it back?"

"It was a gift."

"No, it was a loan—"

"It's my emotional support bra."

She barked a laugh. "When I arrive in Calgary with all my stuff, I want it hand delivered to my door."

"What day does that happen again?"

"You know exactly what day it is." May the fourth. She knew

he remembered because every time they talked about it he breathed like Darth Vader. "Ooh, hold on a sec."

Delia stepped to the side of the walkway and pulled out her phone. She grinned and turned the screen to Jack. "I told her to take a picture when she walked out."

Jack peered closer. "She looks so happy."

Delia nodded, barely able to contain her excitement. Five minutes prior, her mother had turned in her badge and walked out of her last job for the last time. After twenty-five years, she'd finally get to do what she'd always wanted. Be a stay-at-home mom.

"You're incredible, you know that?" He cupped her face with his hands and pressed his lips against hers.

She sighed and was about to say something sage like, *No, you're incredible*, when the sound of someone tapping on glass caught her attention. Delia looked to her right and busted up laughing.

"What the hell?" Jack's cheeks turned pink when he caught sight of it–the entire Snowballs team inside the windows of the pub in front of them. Brett was turned with his hands wrapped around his back getting frisky, Tyler was staring dramatically into Emma's eyes as she pretended to swoon, and some guy Delia hadn't met yet was giving Sean a lap dance.

"We have to go in, right?" Delia said through her smile. "Since they drove all the way down to see you play."

"Just for a minute?"

She nodded. "Then straight up to the room for . . . rest."

"*So much rest*." Jack grabbed her arm and spun her into a dip, then kissed her breathless to muted cheers through the glass.

🏒 🏒 🏒

Preorder Now!

Find special edition e-books and paperbacks exclusively at www. CindyGunderson.com

Cindy Gunderson is a voice actress and award-winning author. Since she has commitment issues, she writes both sci-fi and fantasy, as well as contemporary romance and women's fiction under the pen name, Cynthia Gunderson.

When she is not typing away in a quiet corner of her local library, you can find her traveling with her family, narrating audiobooks, or happily digging in her garden. She loves acting and performing, beating her kids in card games, and playing ultimate frisbee with her handsome husband, Scott.

Cindy grew up in Alberta, Canada, but has lived most of her adult life between California and Colorado. She currently resides in the Denver metro area. Cindy holds a B.S. in Psychology from Brigham Young University.

Cindy's first novel Tier 1 was awarded First Place in Science Fiction at the 2021 CIPPA EVVY Awards and her women's fiction novel Yes, And was honored with the Indie Author Award's first place prize for the state of Colorado, 2023.